ELIZABETH LOWELL

MIDNIGHT IN RUBY BAYOU

HarperLargePrint
An Imprint of HarperCollins Publishers

HarperCollins books may be purchased for educational, business, or sales promotional use. For information please write: Special Markets Department, HarperCollins Publishers Inc., 10 East 53rd Street, New York, New York 10022-5299.

Cover art by Boris Zlotsky
Interior design by Kellan Peck
ISBN: 0-06-019740-4 (LARGE PRINT)
www.harpercollins.com

Library of Congress Cataloging in Publication Data:
Lowell, Elizabeth, 1944–
    Midnight in Ruby Bayou / Elizabeth Lowell.—1st ed.
        p.   cm.
        ISBN: 0-06-019740-4
        I. Title
PS3562.O8847   M5   2000   00-29198
813'.54—dc21   CIP

A hardcover edition of this book was published in 2000 by William Morrow

FIRST LARGE PRINT EDITION 2000

Printed in the U.S.A.

RRD   10   9   8   7   6   5   4   3   2   1

**This Large Print Book carries the
Seal of Approval of N.A.V.H.**

For my wonderful daughter

Heather Maxwell

who gave me Faith's music
and told me about the "house wine" of the South.

They brought me rubies from the mine,
And held them to the sun . . .

Tides that should warm each neighbouring life
Are lock'd in sparkling stone.
But fire to thaw that ruddy snow,
To break enchanted ice,
And give love's scarlet tides to flow,—
When shall that sun arise?

RALPH WALDO EMERSON

MIDNIGHT IN RUBY BAYOU

Prologue

St. Petersburg
January

The public areas were above the thieves, buildings three and four stories high that held centuries of art and artifacts collected by rulers whose whim was the very breath of life for their subjects. There was room after room filled with extraordinary sculptures, ancient icons and immense tapestries, paintings to make angels weep and saints envious, quantities of gold and silver and gemstones beyond the ability of even man's deepest avarice to comprehend.

In the darkest hours of the early January night, there was only time and the scrape of guards' worn boots over marble that had once known only the polished arrogance of royalty. The smallest sounds echoed down the long, magnificent

corridors with their gilt and vaulted ceilings supported by columns as tall as ancient gods.

Even the hundreds of public rooms weren't
enough to display all three million items in the
treasure trove. The lesser items, or those out of
fashion at the moment, were stored in basement
warrens where gleaming marble gave way to
crumbling plaster and rat-gnawed wood. Dust lay
like dirty snow on every surface. The bureaucrats
who had once listed and catalogued the imperial
collections were long gone, dismissed by a civilian government that could barely keep its soldiers
in bullets.

Three women and two men moved briskly
down the narrow subterranean hallways. Caught
in the glow of flashlights, human breath came
out in white bursts. In front of the museum, the
river Neva was frozen. So was everything else in
St. Petersburg that couldn't afford or steal electricity. Away from the public areas where foreign
diplomats, dignitaries, and tourists gaped at royal
treasures, the buildings were in disrepair. The
world-class pieces of art—the Rubenses and da
Vincis and Rembrandts—were well maintained.
The rest of the czars' treasures had to be as hardy
as the Russian people themselves to survive.

One of the thieves unlocked a large room and
flipped on the switch by the door. Nothing happened. Someone cursed, but no one was sur-

prised. Everyone in the city stole lightbulbs for their own use.

Using a flashlight held by her partner, the dark-haired woman went to work on a huge, decades-old safe. The tumblers were balky. The door squealed like a dying pig when she opened it.

She was not worried by the metallic scream. Even if the guards above heard it, they would keep on making their rounds through warm, empty halls and imperial rooms. The guards weren't paid well enough to investigate odd sounds. No smart urban citizen poked around in the dark looking for trouble. Enough came in the normal course of life.

Working in whispers, the thieves began pulling open lockers and drawers. Occasionally someone would grunt or draw in a breath at a particularly spectacular piece of jewelry. If their hands lingered, the dark-haired woman spoke curtly. She had her orders: Take only the modest pieces, the forgotten ones, the nameless baubles that were uninspired gifts from long-dead aristocrats or merchants or foreign officials seeking favor with the czars. These were the pieces that were listed on royal inventories as "brooch, pearls with red center stone" or "stomacher, blue stones with diamond surrounds." None of these pieces were valued enough to be documented in the imperial portraits upstairs. None of them appeared in photographs of imperial jewelry. They were blessedly anonymous.

But ah, the temptation to take one of the less modest, more dangerous pieces. The itch to hold an emerald as big as a hen's egg, to feel two hundred carats of sapphires set in a medieval buckle, to slip a handful of diamond bracelets into a pocket, to ease a twenty-carat ruby ring into the hidden compartment behind your belt . . .

It had happened more than once in the past. A swift movement beyond the reach of the flashlight, the sudden weight of wealth tucked against a thigh or belly. Amid all the kilos of glitter, who would miss an ounce or two?

It happened again tonight.

One of the men was methodically stealing every fifth piece of jewelry that lay tangled in a long drawer. When he was finished, he opened another drawer. This one was orderly, with each piece numbered, tagged, and set in its own niche.

"Not that one, shithead," hissed the woman. "Can you not see the value is too much?"

He could see. And he could barely breathe.

The slightest touch of light had set part of the drawer ablaze. A ruby as big as an idol's eye lay inside. There were other rubies in the necklace, magnificent rubies, but next to the centerpiece, they faded into insignificance. Surrounded by

pearls like snow around fire, the huge ruby pendant shimmered and cast its ancient spell of
wealth and danger.

Muttering, he moved to close the drawer. It
stuck, or appeared to. He tucked the flashlight
under his arm, aiming the light away from the
jewelry. Then he jiggled and shoved and yanked
until the drawer was closed and the necklace was
deep in a concealed pocket in his pants.

The first in a long, deadly row of dominoes
began to fall.

1

**Seattle
February**

Owen Walker lived in a bare-bones efficiency apartment overlooking Pioneer Square, one of Seattle's less upscale tourist attractions. The front door was unimpressive, no happy barks or impatient kitty yowls greeted Walker's approaching footsteps. The closest thing he had to a pet was the refrigerator mold that grew while he was overseas on assignment for Donovan International. Lately that had been most of the time.

Other than installing a new, stronger dead bolt when he took over the apartment, Walker had spent little effort making the place into an urban cocoon. The bed was big enough for his six-foot frame. It also served as a couch to stretch out on and watch TV if he was home long enough to get involved in the misfortunes of the Seahawks or the Mariners or the Sonics.

Recently he had been lucky to keep up with his own problems, much less those of the teams whose members were traded around faster than hot gossip. Today hadn't been any different. Even the problems had problems. The latest one was the assignment Archer Donovan had dropped on him this afternoon.

See if the rubies Davis Montegeau sent Faith match any on the international hot list. I don't want my sister's reputation as a designer ruined by using stolen goods. Montegeau sent what she described as fourteen superior rubies, between one and four carats. They're loose now, but could have been part of a single piece of jewelry.

Since Archer didn't want his little sister to know that he was sticking his nose in her business without her invitation, Walker didn't have the actual rubies to work with. All he had was a verbal description.

Walker had spent the past four hours on Donovan International's phones with various global cops. He hadn't accomplished anything but to make his injured leg stiffen up. So far the rubies had come up clean. He had the callused ear to prove it. Tonight he would check them out on the Internet.

But first, food.

Automatically he threw the locks on the door behind him, hung his cane over the doorknob, and limped to the refrigerator to see if anything looked like a late lunch or an early dinner. Whichever.

His body still wasn't certain which continent it was on. Despite the clean black slacks, crisp dark blue shirt that matched his eyes, and close-cut black beard, he felt like something the cat had dragged in and the rat refused to eat. Jet lag—or the beating that some eager Afghani bandits had given him last week—made him feel every one of his thirty-odd years like a separate insult.

Thoughts of the near disastrous Afghanistan trip fled when the smell of garlic sausage from last night's take-out Italian hit him in a wave. After the second breath he decided that the sausage wasn't from last night. More like three nights ago. Or four. Maybe five. He'd had a real craving for Italian when he returned from Afghanistan, but he hadn't wanted to gimp through Pike Place Market looking for fresh ingredients. Instead he had eaten way too much take-out food since he had climbed stiffly down the steps from the company plane into the Pacific Northwest's February gloom.

Cautiously he opened the lid of the nearest leftover box. Nothing looked green, and there probably wasn't enough left to poison him anyway. With a mental shrug he put the sagging box in the microwave and nuked it. While invisible energy tried to breathe new life into old takeout, he decided to call the meal an early supper. For that, he could open one of the long-necked beer bottles that had waited patiently during his absence.

By the time the microwave cheeped, he was on the Internet, requesting a global search for stolen loose rubies bigger than one carat or for stolen jewelry that contained fourteen rubies of more than a carat. While the computer chewed on his request, he walked back to his pocket-sized kitchen, opened the microwave, and grabbed a fork from a nearby drawer.

He took his first bite of lukewarm supper on the way to the computer. The pasta had the texture and taste of rubber bands, but the sausage was still spicy enough to make his mouth tingle. He had eaten much worse food and been glad to get it, both as a boy and more recently, when he had shared campfires and rations with Afghani miners.

Between bites, he scrolled through a list of stolen rubies that had been posted by everyone from maiden aunts to Interpol. Some offered rewards, no questions asked. Others offered a finder's fee, also no questions asked. Law enforcement organizations of various kinds offered telephone numbers and the opportunity to be a good citizen.

Smaller rubies were missing, but most of them were described as having a modern cut. Some were said to be family heirlooms, but in Walker's experience that could mean anything from 1550 to 1950. It was possible that the Montegeau rubies Faith Donovan was designing into a necklace had come from one or more of the long, long list of stolen heirlooms, but he doubted it. The dates on the postings went from last week to thirty years ago, and originated from twenty-three separate countries. None of the lists mentioned fourteen superior rubies—set or loose—that ranged upward from one carat.

So much for work. On to private pleasures.

Walker scraped the last of the pungent sauce from the carton, took a drink of beer, and went to another web site, one he often visited. This one was an international clearinghouse for sales of gems and jewelry of all kinds. As he did every night that he was near a computer, he entered a request for rubies that were carved or inscribed in some way.

Forty-two entries came back. He scrolled through them quickly. Most were only a few steps above what a tourist would find in a squalid Thai alley. The carvings were as lackluster as the stones were dubious. He paused over a good-quality ruby that had a laughing Buddha etched on the long, flat table. After a moment he scrolled on again. He had a similar—and better—gem in his collection.

Walker stopped when he found an exquisite four-carat stone with a heart carved on one side and a cross on the other. It was presumed to be from one of the Crusades. Wistfully he stared at the gem. If it looked half as good under a microscope as it looked on the screen, the ruby would make a splendid addition to his personal collection. He would put in a bid, if the stone didn't cost an arm and a leg.

It did. The price tag had one zero too many. Two, actually.

"Same shit, different day," he muttered.

Three months in Afghanistan hadn't changed much except the way he walked, and that was only temporary. He went back to looking at less costly goods. Nothing he saw interested him.

Grimacing, Walker shut down his computer and looked around for something to do in the hours before he slept and tried not to dream of gun butts smashing his head. Several books beckoned, but his brain was still too fuzzy from adjusting to Seattle's time zone to be much use on his latest project: a kind of do-it-yourself tour through the German language, compliments of a German book on rare gems and gem carving.

Idly he considered scanning the book into his computer, running it through all nine of his translation programs, and comparing the results. The thought brought a grin to his mouth. The last time he had done that, with an article on Thailand's leading gem traders, he and Archer and Kyle Donovan had laughed themselves blind at the results.

That was when Walker had begun teaching himself German, complete with West Texas rhythms on top of his South Carolina boyhood drawl. He had just begun making real progress on reading the language when Donovan International had sent him to Afghanistan to survey the possibilities of buying into the ruby trade there. Walker could speak Afghani, but couldn't read it.

The sound of shouting from the Seattle street below his window barely registered. There was no danger to him in a drunk cussing out pigeons for doing what they did best—crapping all over benches.

He glanced at the battered stainless steel watch on his wrist. Not quite five o'clock. Archer would still be in his office at Donovan International. Walker took the last swallow of beer and punched in the oldest Donovan brother's private number.

"Yeah," came the immediate reply.

"Then you *do* agree to doubling my wages. I could hardly believe it when—"

"Up yours, Walker," Archer said, but there was no real heat in the words. "What did you find?"

"Tell your brother his gut hunch was wrong." Kyle Donovan's gut was famous, or infamous, among the Donovans. As an early warning system for danger, Kyle's lower tract lacked precision, but it was too often right to be disregarded. "If anyone is looking for the rubies Davis Montegeau gave Faith to set in a necklace, they aren't looking in any of the usual places, or even the unusual ones."

Archer pushed back from the desk and absently stretched his big body. "Okay. Thanks. It was the easiest thing to check."

"Easy for you, sure enough. My ear still aches from all those international calls."

Archer snickered. "I'll make it up to you."

"The raise?"

"In your dreams," Archer retorted easily. "Dinner tonight at the condo. I've got another job to run by you. Stateside this time."

"My jet-lagged body thanks you. Who's cooking dinner? You or Kyle?"

"Me. Fresh salmon, compliments of brother-in-law Jake. And my sister Honor, if you believe that the one who nets the fish gets half the credit. She does."

"I'll believe whatever it takes to get fresh salmon on my plate. Anything else?" Walker asked hopefully.

"My wife did mention chocolate chip cookies."

"Hot damn! I'm on my way."

Archer was still laughing when Walker hung up. Although Walker had begun as an employee, he had become a friend.

Within moments of reading his e-mail, Archer's expression settled into its usual hard lines. Donovan International's winning bid on developing a Siberian silver mine had been undercut after the bidding was supposed to be officially closed. The fact that the successful bidder was a local gangster's brother-in-law just might have had something to do with it.

He reached for the intercom. "Mitchell, get me Nicolay. Yeah, I know what time it is there. In a few minutes, so will he."

Faith Donovan set aside the block of tripoli she used to add polishing grit to the buffing wheel. Flexing her aching hands, she bent over and examined the piece of eighteen-karat gold that made up one of the thirteen segments of the Montegeau necklace. Although barely polished, the arc of gold was both elegant and seemingly casual, almost randomly curved.

The curve was neither casual nor random, but the result of a design process that was as exacting as it was rewarding. That was why Faith's fingers and back ached, yet she wanted to smile in spite of the early winter darkness. Even with all the pressure of an impossibly short deadline—barely two weeks for a process that should have taken three months—the necklace was coming together beautifully. Her old friend Mel would have a unique, extraordinary piece of jewelry to wear when she married Jeff Montegeau on Valentine's Day.

And Faith would have a showstopper for the Savannah jewelry exposition the weekend before the wedding. She very much wanted that. Though the expo only lasted a few days, it was one of the most important modern jewelry shows in the nation. She needed to make a stir. The Montegeau necklace would certainly do that.

At least it would if she found a way to insure the necklace between now and four days from now, when she flew to Savannah. Her other pieces were insured, because she had had plenty of time to plan for the expo. There just hadn't been time to leave the rubies with a qualified appraiser and still create a necklace.

Frowning over the insurance problem, she picked up the segment of gold and bent over the buffer again. Beyond the windows of her shop/studio, ice-tipped rain swirled across Pioneer Square on the wind. The streetlights sent out glistening circles that did little to brighten the winter evening.

Eventually the rattle of sleet on the windows

increased until she could hear it above the whir-
ring of the buffing wheel. With a guilty start she
straightened and looked at her watch. Almost
five-thirty. She was supposed to be at the Donovan condo with three of her five siblings, planning a surprise party for their parents' fortieth
anniversary. Or trying to plan one. Archer and
his wife, Hannah, Kyle and his wife, Lianne, and
Honor and her husband, Jake, had been at it for
several days already, but they hadn't even been
able to agree on a site.

Of course, they all enjoyed the noise and
laughter of family dinners at the Donovan condo,
where every Donovan had a full-time or part-time
residence. Keeping track of Donovan International's global enterprises meant that someone in the
family was gone most of the time. At the moment, her twin brothers, Justin and Lawe, were
in Africa, Hannah and Archer had just gotten back
from a pearl auction in Tokyo, and Jake and
Honor lived outside of Seattle.

The fun of having most of the family under
one roof might have had something to do with
the fact that this was the third dinnertime ''summit meeting'' in a row.

And here she was, still wearing old jeans and
covered with fine, mud-brown grit when she
should have been cleaned up and helping to fix
dinner for seven. Ten if you counted the babies.

She would get stuck with the dishes for sure.

With a sigh, she yanked off her dust mask and goggles. Her short blond hair stuck up every which way. Running gritty fingers through it probably didn't help, but the nearest comb was waiting for her in her suite at the condo. The nearest bath, too. Personally, she thought the tripoli streaks on her jeans, forearms, and hands added an interesting, finger-painted effect to her entire lack of ensemble, but she knew Kyle would tease her mercilessly about reviving the Seattle Grunge look.

Well, tonight her siblings would just have to take her as she was, dusted by polishing grit and hollow-eyed from too many late nights at work. If she hadn't gambled and begun casting the thirteen segments of the necklace without final approval of the sketch, she never would have made the deadline. But luckily the patriarch, Davis Montegeau, had approved the sketch without any changes.

Thank God. Davis was an indulgent future father-in-law, but he had left things until the last second. If the future bride hadn't been Faith's best friend in college, she would have refused the commission despite the allure of working with such fine gems—and getting to keep the smallest one as her fee. If Davis hadn't agreed to gold rather than platinum, she wouldn't have been able to meet the deadline at all. Platinum was the most unyielding of all the metals used in jewelry. While she worked with platinum occasionally, because nothing had its icy shine, she much preferred the various colors of gold.

Standing, Faith took off her leather apron. Like the long wooden workbench, it bore the scars of much use. The process of creating jewelry was as grubby as the result was elegant. That was something her ex-fiancé, Tony, had never understood or wanted to understand. He was lazy by nature, so the idea of someone spending her life wearing goggles and hunched over tools that marked her hands as often as the workbench offended him. Especially when her parents were wealthy enough to carry her around on a silk pillow fringed with diamonds.

Faith shoved aside the unhappy memories. Anthony Kerrigan was the worst mistake she had ever made. The important thing to remember was that Tony was right where he should be: in her past.

Sooner or later, he would get the message. Then he would stop calling her and "accidentally" bumping into her. But until then . . .

With a muttered word she reached for the phone and punched in a familiar number. Kyle answered on the second ring.

"Sorry," she said hurriedly. "I know I'm late. Do you want me just to lock up and come home?"

"Alone? Not likely, sis. I'll be there in ten minutes."

"It's not necessary. I could just—"

She was talking to herself. With a disgusted sound she hung up. She had fought having a Donovan International guard assigned to her shop, but she had lost. Part of her understood that it was a sensible precaution, if not for Tony then for the rash of muggings and burglaries that was plaguing Pioneer Square.

But another, less sensible, part of her resented being dictated to by large, overbearing males. Even if they were her brothers instead of her bullying, ham-fisted ex-fiancé.

"No, don't go there," Faith told herself through her teeth. "You already know that you made a mistake. Beating yourself up about it won't teach you anything new."

Sleet spattered and clung to the windows, sliding down in streaks of winter tears. Faith watched the random trails for a few moments and thought about what life would have been like if she had found a good man to love, like her twin sister Honor had. She wondered what it would be like to hold her own child during the day and be held by a man who loved her at night.

"Don't go there, either," Faith said aloud, because the silence was overwhelming.

Maybe she would get lucky someday. Maybe

she wouldn't. Either way, she would still be a good person who had a flair for jewelry design and a family who loved her. She had nothing to whine about and a lot to celebrate.

As Faith locked up the workroom, she played with ideas for a piece of jewelry for her mother's fortieth wedding anniversary. A present for The Donovan, her father, was a much bigger problem. She hoped her brothers had an idea.

She hoped, but she didn't expect much. Her brothers were, after all, men.

Difficult, in a word.

2

St. Petersburg

The river Neva was opaque white, the same color as the wind screaming sideways through the boulevards and narrow alleys. Though the room had a view overlooking a park with the required monument to Russian valor—and the trashed remnants of monuments to Soviet vision—there wasn't much to see, only bundles of black clothes scurrying from shelter to shelter on the street. Vehicles weren't so much parked as stuck for the duration of the storm.

The room was a lush haven from the terrible white winter outside. Richly colored rugs that had once graced an Ottoman sultan's palace covered the walnut floor. Pictures that had once hung in the offices of Jewish financiers brought a glow of grace and serenity to the walls. The desk itself was massive, a masterpiece of baroque carving said to have belonged to a czar's cousin. Six cellular phones lay scattered along its polished surface.

The man whose American passport stated that he was Ivan Ivanovitch lit a Cuban cigar to conceal the anger that was making his hands shake.

Idiots. Shitheads. Dog turds. Do I not pay them twice what they are worth?

But all he said aloud was, "Marat Borisovitch Tarasov is very unhappy with your bumbling."

The black-haired woman was sweating so heavily that her makeup bled down her face like muddy tears. "You know I would never cheat you or him. I took only what was ordered. I never saw this ruby pendant you speak of."

"The Heart of Midnight. As big as a baby's fist. As red as the blood that will gush out of your lying throat when I slit it. Where is the necklace! If you tell me now, I will be merciful." A lie, but perhaps a useful one. In any case, he didn't care about the smaller rubies on the necklace, only the Heart of Midnight. "If you tell me later—and you will tell me—you will suffer."

"Truly, sir." She was shaking, but it wasn't with anger. Raw fear glazed her eyes. Hers would not be the first throat Tarasov's pet assassin had slit, nor would it be the last. And worse, he was famous for torturing his victims first. "We were in the vault, yes, but I gave the same orders as always."

"There was no rummaging? Did no one open those center drawers?" Eyes as pale and opaque as stones noted her every twitch, the jerk of her pulse. "Did you watch each of your miserable thieves closely?"

"Only once did it happen. Yuri opened the wrong drawer and he closed it again very quickly when I told him to. The jewels were tagged and numbered, part of a royal inventory."

"Yes, shithead, I know. So does Marat Borisovitch." And so did Tarasov's worst enemy, Dmitry Sergeyev Solokov, the rival for power who was trying to shove the stupid theft down Tarasov's throat until he choked to death. Stealing was one thing, common enough not to make ripples. Stealing so that your enemies could hang you was quite another.

If the Heart of Midnight wasn't returned before the new wing of the Hermitage opened, Tarasov would hang. But first he would kill the man known as Ivan Ivanovitch Ivanov.

"Send Yuri to me," Ivanovitch demanded.

Yuri didn't have the woman's courage. After two minutes with Ivanovitch, the little thief was crying and begging and regretting the instant when greed had overcome fear.

"I d-did not m-mean to," Yuri stammered. "It—I—"

"Quiet!"

Yuri took a choked breath and waited for Ivanovitch to speak. In all his dreams, Yuri had never imagined standing in such a powerful man's presence.

Now he dreamed only of leaving it.

"You took the necklace."

Yuri whimpered.

"Where is it now? Speak truthfully or you die."

"With the r-rest. I could not k-keep it." *A stone filled with blood and surrounded by pearls. It would bring death. He knew it.* "I w-was afraid of it."

Ivanovitch wished he didn't believe the little worm, but he did. The man hadn't the brains to lie. "Which shipment?"

"To America, s-sir. I h-hid it with the rest."

"When?" Ivanovitch asked sharply.

Yuri swallowed but still couldn't speak. Instead, he looked at his second cousin, who had told him how easy it was to get rich working for Marat Borisovitch Tarasov.

The black-haired woman, who had stood mute and shaking through the entire interview, said in a hoarse voice, "Weeks ago, sir, as you ordered."

Ivanovitch didn't have to look at a calendar to know that his own life span could be measured in weeks unless he recovered the Heart of Midnight. Tarasov wasn't known for his patience.

Neither was Ivanovitch. "Wait in my outer office."

As soon as the sweating thieves left, he picked up one of the many cellular phones on his desk. It took several tries to reach America, but he managed despite hands that wanted to smash things rather than depress dainty buttons.

When the phone was answered by a familiar voice, Ivanovitch spoke without prelude. His English wasn't perfect, but it certainly got his point across. "What did you do with it?"

"With what?"

"The big ruby, shithead. Do not bother to deny. *I know.*"

Silence, then something close to a groan. "It wasn't on the inventory, so I sent it to a different place on consignment. I would have split the money with you like always, you know that."

Ivanovitch smiled at the fear and despair in the other person's voice. He found people to be most cooperative when they were all but pissing with fright. "Where did you send it?"

"Seattle, Washington."

"Where, exactly?"

"A . . ." There was the sound of swallowing, then, "A shop called Timeless Dreams."

"Who has it now?"

Another pause, another swallow. "Faith Donovan."

Dragging deadweight behind them, two men walked out onto the Neva's thick ice. The trail they left looked black until one of the men stumbled and a flashlight jerked. Fresh blood gleamed the color of rubies against the ice. Turning off the flashlights, they hacked out a shallow trough with ice axes, kicked their burdens into it, and started back toward the cold lights of St. Petersburg.

Yuri and his second cousin stayed behind, but they didn't care. They didn't even feel the cold wind or the ice-tipped snow that became their shroud.

In many ways, they had been fortunate. Ivanovitch had been too desperate to get to Seattle to give his bumbling employees the full benefit of his expertise with a knife. They had died quickly and almost painlessly.

Faith Donovan, whoever she was, would not be so fortunate.

3

Seattle

"Can somebody get that? Summer wants to help me chop dill," Archer yelled from the kitchen, above the ringing of the phone. Trying to get ready for yet another dinnertime summit meeting on his parents' anniversary party was driving him nuts. Nobody was here to help cook. Lianne was up to her ears in taking care of her twins, Jake and Honor were napping after the dawn salmon expedition which had supplied tonight's dinner, Kyle and Faith were on their way to the condo, Hannah was still at the Pearl Exchange, and if his niece Summer got any more helpful, he was going to look for some duct tape.

In the condo's living room, a hungry Walker winced at the idea of Summer helping Archer chop fresh dill. She had just recently graduated to semitoddlerhood, and Archer's preferred kitchen knife was nearly as big as she was. In fact, Summer was why Walker had left his cane at the apartment; he just knew she would make a grab for it.

The phone rang again.

"Walker?" Archer yelled. "Pick it up, would you? It's the private number."

"Yeah, I'll get it."

Reluctantly Walker looked away from the living room wall that was hung with the matriarch Susa Donovan's compelling landscapes. Limping slightly, he went in search of the phone. After another ring, he found one of the wireless handsets stuck in a bookcase. He punched in the talk button. "Donovan residence."

"Faith Donovan, please." The voice was a woman's and clipped to the point of being abrupt.

"She isn't here yet. Do you want to leave a message?"

"When do you expect her?"

"Any time," Walker drawled, annoyed by the woman's curt manner.

"I'll call back."

"You do that little thing," he said, but the line was already dead.

With a shrug, he shut off the unit and went to the kitchen. The cheery yellow décor offset the

gloom outside. A thick kind of rain ran and sparkled darkly down the windows that gave a view
of Elliot Bay and part of Seattle's light-shot sky-
line. Leaning against the chopping table in the
center of the kitchen, he watched his boss.

"Who was it?" Archer asked.

"Didn't say."

The big knife hesitated over sprigs of fresh dill
and cilantro. Summer clutched her uncle's knees
and tried to reach the big knife. When she fell
about a yard short, she squealed impatiently. Archer ignored her.

"Man?" he asked Walker. Archer's tone was
the same one he would have used with his
siblings.

"Woman."

Archer grunted and went back to work. The
blade bit through the tender sprigs with speed
and precision. A small mound of feathery minced
greens grew on the long chopping table. "You
sure?"

"Yeah. Why?"

"Tony has been bothering Faith. We had to
change our unlisted number."

"Someone should take that ol' boy out to the
woodshed and teach him some manners."
Though Walker's voice was soft, his eyes were
inky blue stones.

"We'd love to, thanks," Archer said dryly, "but

we promised Honor we would let Faith take care of it."

"You promised *Honor*?" Walker asked. "Am I missing something, boss?"

Summer began squalling in earnest. She wanted that pretty flashing knife.

"Twins," Archer said laconically, ignoring the little storm breaking around his knees. "They watch out for each other. Honor said Faith is really upset that she ever got engaged to a loser like Tony, and having us beat the crap out of him would just make her feel worse."

"Women. Go figure."

Archer gave a crack of laughter. "I don't have to anymore. I found mine."

Summer screamed.

"Lordy," Walker said, raising his voice and looking at the redheaded little girl in disbelief. "She's got a voice like a siren on steroids."

"Just like her aunt."

"Lianne?" Walker asked, startled, thinking of Kyle's small, exquisite wife. "That little darling?"

"No. Faith. She has a scream that would bend sheet metal."

"Do tell." Walker smiled faintly. "Wouldn't have figured it. Slender, delicate lady like her."

"Delicate lady? Faith? My little sister?" Archer was all but shouting to be heard over his niece.

Laying aside the knife, he picked up Summer, lifted her little rugby shirt, and tickled her with his short beard while making rude noises on her stomach. Screaming turned into giggles. Forgetting about the knife, she made a dive for her uncle's black hair.

"Blond, misty blue eyes, slender as a sapling, sad underneath her smile," Walker said calmly. "Your little sister Faith. Delicate."

"Um," was all Archer said as he peeled strong, tiny fingers from his hair. He stared down into his niece's eyes, so like his own, and wondered if he and Hannah would be lucky enough to have their own children. "Hard for me to think of the scourge of the Donovan brothers' childhood as delicate."

"Scourge, huh? Bet y'all were unfailingly kind and gentle to her."

Archer gave him a sideways look from amused green-gray eyes. "You'd lose."

Walker laughed and thought of his own brother. Before Lot died, the two of them had pretty much raised hell around the globe. Or rather, Lot had raised hell and Walker had tried to keep both of them out of trouble. Along the way, Walker had chewed on Lot more than once, hoping to talk—or knock—some sense into him.

Win some. Lose some.

Lot had lost big, thanks to his older brother.

None of Walker's grim thoughts showed on his face. He was sure of it, because Summer reached toward him with the assurance of a child who had never met an adult who didn't love her.

"Here," Archer said, picking up Summer. "Take her before she screams again."

"Uh-uh. Not me. I told you before, I don't know anything about kids." Nor did Walker want to. Kids meant being responsible for another life. No way. Never again. He had barely survived his brother's death. "She's already bored with the fuzzy fake kitty I brought her and wants that damned lethal knife you're using."

"Your point?" Archer handed over his niece, adjusted Walker's grip on her, and went back to preparing dinner.

"I've got a bum leg."

"You're making me cry."

"Uh, Archer, I really don't—" Walker began.

Archer kept talking. Walker's reluctance to handle kids wasn't unusual in a bachelor, but he would have to get over it if he was going to be around the Donovans. Since Walker was becoming a valued friend of Archer's as well as an employee, it followed that Walker was going to spend a lot of time with Donovans of all ages.

"Nobody is born knowing about kids," Archer said matter-of-factly. "It's something you learn along the way, like how to tell a good ruby from a bad one."

Walker looked into Summer's radiant gray-green eyes. Clear yet misty, with luminous shades of green and whispers of blue. "We ever find a gem like her eyes, we'll all be rich."

Smiling, Archer pulled some lemons out of the refrigerator. From the front of the suite came the sounds of a door closing and Kyle and Faith ragging on each other.

". . . about as funny as a freeway accident, bro," Faith retorted. "Guess which one of my grubby fingers is for you?"

"Delicate, huh?" Archer muttered.

Walker smiled.

Summer smiled back at him. Like her eyes, her smile glowed with life and innocence. The sweet curve of her lips shouted that he was the only thing in her universe.

And he was beautiful.

The room seemed to shift around Walker. He forgot the residual ache in his leg. A yearning he wouldn't name and refused to acknowledge went through him like dark lightning. Desperately he looked for a safe place to deposit the little bomb ticking away in his arms.

"She wet?" Archer asked without looking up from squeezing lemons.

"Uh, I don't think so."

"You think she's going to be?"

"Uh . . ." Walker couldn't think of anything to say. Summer was still smiling at him, charming and terrifying him with her innocent certainty of his worth and her own safety with him.

"I just changed her," Archer said, "but sometimes she goes through diapers like fire through a fuse."

Summer pursed her dark pink lips and bounced in Walker's arms.

"She wants a kiss," Archer said.

"Uh . . ."

Gray-green eyes grew big with sudden tears. Summer's little fingers patted against Walker's lips as though to remind him of what they were for.

"Oh, Lordy," he said. "Don't cry, sugar."

"Kiss her and she'll shut up."

Hesitantly Walker bent his head until he could kiss Summer's small, pursed mouth. She bounced and patted him again.

"She wants another one," Archer said, trying not to laugh out loud at the dazed look on Walker's face.

Faith leaned against the kitchen doorway, crossed her grit-stained arms, and watched her redheaded niece wrap another man around her little finger. The smile Walker was giving Summer was unlike any Faith had ever seen on his face—hesitant, delighted, wary, and totally smitten all at once. It made him handsome enough to stop traffic.

It certainly did unwelcome things to her pulse.

"Make a loud smacking sound," Archer advised. "That's how she knows you mean it."

Walker added suitable sound effects. Summer kissed him again with more enthusiasm than precision, then cooed and leaned against him. Between one breath and another she was asleep.

"Uh, Archer?" Walker's voice was barely a whisper.

"Yeah?"

"She went limp."

"It's all in the technique," Archer agreed. "Good going."

Faith snickered. Walker turned his head toward her. The lapis lazuli blaze of his eyes surprised her. Over the last few months while he had been in Afghanistan looking for a source of uncut, untreated rubies, she had forgotten just how gorgeous his eyes were. In fact, she had made a point of forgetting.

"Just in time," Walker said, gesturing with his chin at the sleeping child. "Rescue your niece."

"Why would I rescue her from paradise?" Faith asked.

"Rescue me, then."

"Can't. My hands are dirty." She held out her gritty fingers. "Besides, you look pretty comfortable yourself."

"Kids terrify me."

"Yeah, sure," Faith said, unimpressed. "I could see that right away when you kissed her the third time."

Faith went to the sink and began washing grit from her hands.

"How's the Montegeau necklace going?" Archer asked as he spread marinade over two huge salmon fillets. "Going to be done in time for the show and the wedding?"

"Just barely." She rinsed her hands, shook them, and wiped them on her jeans. Grit dampened on her thighs, making muddy streaks against the faded cloth. They matched the random grit marks on her cheeks.

Archer looked at Walker again. *Delicate, huh?*

Walker just smiled.

"Did you hear from your insurer about covering the necklace from here to Savannah?" Archer asked his sister.

"Not yet." The tone of Faith's voice said that it was none of her brother's business.

Like older brothers since time began, Archer ignored the warning signal. "They'll want a GIA appraisal or its equivalent."

"Tell me something I don't know," she retorted. The Gemological Institute of America was a benchmark of reliability. Unfortunately, GIA-certified appraisers took weeks to get the job done. She didn't have one week, much less several. She simply couldn't let the rubies out of her hands for so long and still get the necklace done by Valentine's Day.

"Is getting an appraisal going to be a problem?" Archer asked.

She didn't answer.

"Faith?" Archer asked. But his steady look told her that he already knew. "You have less than a week before you leave."

"I'll work it out."

Before Archer could ask another question, the phone rang.

"I'll get it," Faith said instantly, relieved. She didn't like being cross-examined by her brother.

Especially when he was right.

"It's by the bookcase near the paintings," Walker said.

"Thanks," Faith called over her shoulder. She found the wandering phone after one more ring. "Hello?"

"Faith Donovan, please."

"Speaking."

"One moment, please."

There was a click as the call was handed off. Then Tony's voice came into her ear, freezing her in place. "Hello, baby. It took me a while to get this number, but—"

"No, thanks, I don't need any tinfoil siding."

"Wait, Faith! Don't hang up! Damn it, you've got to listen to me! I didn't mean to hit you. I'll never do it again. I love you and I want to have kids with you and—"

"I'm sorry," she cut in hoarsely. "You have the wrong number."

Quietly she depressed a button and ended the call. Then she took a deep breath to steady herself. She hated the adrenaline and anxiety that flooded her whenever she heard Tony's voice. Seeing him was even worse. He was a mistake that simply wouldn't go away.

He'll get tired of chasing me, she told herself grimly. *We're not talking the love match of the century. He had a woman on the side while we were engaged. My fault, of course. I wasn't hot enough in bed.*

The phone rang again. Faith jumped as though she had been pinched.

Walker reached past her and took the phone. Summer didn't even stir against his chest. She was used to sleeping in someone's arms.

"Yeah?" Walker said curtly. He didn't like the pallor of Faith's face.

"It's Mitchell," Archer's assistant said. "This Walker?"

"As ever was," he drawled. "You working late again?"

"Just waiting for the wife to pick me up. We're going to the theater. The experimental one, where they're still learning the English language and expect the audience to fill in the blanks."

"Her turn to choose, huh?" Walker said, smiling. Mitchell and his wife traded off picking entertainment.

"What was your first clue?" the assistant retorted.

"You need Archer?"

"Actually, I was looking for you. Remember that contact in Myanmar? The one you said might have a lead on some good ruby rough?"

"I remember."

"There's a package from him."

"Is it ticking?" Walker asked dryly.

"So far so good."

"I'll come by and pick it up. Ten minutes."

He disconnected and looked at Faith. She met his eyes with a stubborn kind of defiance. "Was that Tony?" Walker asked bluntly.

"It was a wrong number."

Walker grunted, not believing a word of it. "Take your niece. I've got to run across to headquarters and get a package."

Archer came into the living room just as Summer was handed off. He looked from Walker to Faith. "Trouble?"

"No," she said coolly. "Summer's wet. I'm going to change her."

Walker didn't believe that, either, but he didn't say anything.

Archer waited until Faith was out of sight and said softly, "Who called?"

"Mitchell was the second call. I'm going to

pick up a package of ruby rough from a new contact in Burma. I'm betting the first call was her ever-lovin' ex."

"Son of a *bitch*."

"On his best days, maybe," Walker said. "Otherwise Tony is pure chicken shit."

Archer raked long fingers through his short hair.

"She's handling it," Walker said.

"I'd rather do it for her."

So would Walker, but as he wasn't even related, it wasn't something he was going to say aloud. His attraction to Faith was at best unfortunate. At worst it could be a disaster.

With a final curse, Archer put Tony out of his mind. "Go to Faith's shop, check out those Montegeau rubies, and get back to me."

Walker's eyebrows lifted, but all he said was, "When?"

"Yesterday. Tomorrow at the latest."

"What about that batch of ruby rough you're expecting from Africa? Still want me to appraise it for you?"

"Damn." Archer raked his hand through his hair again. "Do it first thing tomorrow morning. Then get over to Faith's shop. I want you to stay close to the shop until I arrange for a full-time guard for her." Frowning, he mentally juggled various Donovan projects and their particular needs. Lately it seemed as though he spent most of his time hiring guards, and he still didn't have enough people he trusted. Not with his sister. He wouldn't say the world was going to hell in a handbasket . . . but he wouldn't say it was going to heaven, either. "In fact, plan on going to Savannah with her. I need someone I can trust not to fly off the handle."

"Besides Tony," Walker drawled, "is anything in particular bothering you?"

"Kyle. He's still got a bad feeling about those Montegeau rubies."

"How bad?"

"Really bad. Getting worse."

Walker whistled softly. Kyle had had a really bad feeling about Walker's recent trip to Afghanistan. Walker had gone anyway.

He had nearly died there.

4

"A million bucks for thirteen rubies?" Walker's nearly black eyebrows rose skeptically. He shifted his grip on the cane. He didn't really need it, but the old-fashioned wooden cane reassured people that he was harmless. It also reminded him how close he had come to being totally harmless, as in dead. It would be a long time before he was that stupid again. "I'd have to see the rubies before I'd sign the check."

"You won't be signing anything," Faith said shortly. Then she looked at the workbench in front of her as though to remind Walker that he was interrupting her. "It has nothing to do with you or my brothers."

Walker's glance followed hers. The thick,

rough wood of the U-shaped bench showed the nicks, gouges, and burns common on a jewelry designer's work surface. Pliers of all sizes and shapes, rat-tail files, soldering equipment, goggles, awls, clamps, polishing wheels, a metal block for hammering, a leather-covered mallet, and other less easily identified pieces of equipment were laid out in a pattern that looked random to him, but he had no doubt that Faith could lay her hand on anything she needed without searching. Anyone who used tools to make a living knew how to take care of those tools.

With barely veiled impatience, Faith ignored Walker's scrutiny and turned to the sketches of a jeweled suite she had been working on—necklace, bracelet, earrings, brooch, and ring. The loose papers covered with pencil drawings were held down by an expensive chunk of lapis lazuli. She stared at it—the stone was the exact shade of Walker's eyes.

The thought annoyed Faith. After her disaster with Tony, she had sworn off men, yet Walker kept sneaking into her awareness.

She switched her attention to the large, discreetly wired front window of Timeless Dreams, her combination studio and jewelry store. Her social life might be a disaster area, but she was very proud of what she had achieved professionally.

Beyond the glass, Pioneer Square's mix of

street people, artists, shop owners, and shoppers swirled through the raw early February afternoon. Last fall's leaves had long since been ground to brown paste and licked away by winter rain. Tourists, even the hardy Germans, wouldn't arrive for months. The rain was still at work washing streets, buildings, and pedestrians with the insistence of a mother cat grooming a dirty kitten.

And Walker was still waiting for Faith's attention.

"Damn," she muttered.

Walker just kept waiting. He was good at it. He had learned patience the hard way, as a boy hunting salt marshes and black bayous in order to add protein to the family table. But Seattle was a long way from the torrid Low Country of South Carolina, Walker was a long way from his boyhood, and Faith had fewer survival instincts than the most innocent prey he had ever hunted in the haunting, primeval swamp. Walker knew the high cost of such innocence, even if Faith didn't.

"What do you want?" she asked bluntly.

"Are the Montegeau rubies insured at all?"

"My shop insurance covers them while they're on the premises."

"Then you must have some kind of an appraisal."

"Oh, sure. But it's informal. The man who

owns the rubies gave me a written description of the stones and his estimate of their worth."

"Do tell. What are his qualifications to judge rubies?"

Faith glanced at Walker through narrowed, silver-blue eyes. "The customer's family has been in the jewelry business for two centuries. Satisfied?"

Satisfied.

Now, there was a word Walker tried not to use when thinking about Faith, much less when he was standing close enough to smell her sweet, heady fragrance, like a summer garden at dawn. He wished that Archer Donovan had assigned somebody else to guard his sister's shop. Anybody else. Walker could see he irritated Faith, and she made no attempt to conceal it.

Considering what a loser her ex-fiancé was, Walker was insulted by Faith's dislike. He was also far too aware of her as a woman. A desirable one. Unfortunately she was also the younger sister of his boss. Way off limits for a South Carolina marsh rat.

He rubbed his short, nearly black beard and then the back of his neck. It was his own way of counting to ten or twenty or a hundred. Whatever it took to keep his temper.

"Does Archer know you've started trading in unappraised gems?" Walker asked finally. His voice was an easy drawl. Hiding his own emotions was another thing he was good at. It went right along with the patience of a hunter.

"I'm not trading in these gems. All I'm doing is designing a necklace for them." She rubbed her temples. "It's a rush job for an old college friend. Mel was my first roommate. The university thought it would be a good idea to separate the Donovan twins."

Walker followed the elliptical conversation with surprising ease. "Mel is the one with jewelry in the family for two centuries?"

"No. That's her fiancé, Jeff. The necklace is a wedding present from her future father-in-law. It's a surprise. She's six months pregnant and they just decided to get married. She's truly happy for the first time in her life. I couldn't refuse to design her a necklace. Besides, it's one of the best things I've ever done. I want it to be in the Savannah show."

The twinge in Walker's left leg became an ache. Old friends sometimes turned into new problems. Dangerous ones. "Are you buying the trip insurance and the show insurance?"

Faith looked at the ceiling. "Did you take lessons from my brothers or are you just naturally nosy and bossy?"

"Lessons, huh?" The drawl slowed and deepened. "Now, there's a thought. I'll be sure to take it up with Archer."

"He's too busy with his new wife."

"She's a woman to keep a man busy," Walker agreed, smiling faintly as he thought of last night's dinner with the Donovan family. Hannah's edgy Australian slang was as surprising as her quiet stubbornness. She was every bit as hard-headed as the man she had married. Good thing, too. When the occasion arose, Archer could be a ten on the Mohs' scale, right up there with diamonds.

"Archer isn't complaining about Hannah," Faith pointed out quickly.

"I noticed. It's a burning wonder how quick the Donovan men took to leg shackles."

"Leg shackles! What a way to describe marriage."

"You must have felt the same or you would have married that pile of road apples you were engaged to."

Faith tried not to snicker at Walker's description of Tony Kerrigan. The best she could do was choke laughter off into a strangled cough. She saw the slight upward curve of Walker's mouth and knew that she hadn't fooled him a bit. That was another way he was like her brothers—quick.

"About that insurance," he said. "Who bought it?"

"Does it matter?"

"Only if something happens to the rubies."

"No one would dare. Someone—like you, right

now—has been all over me like a rash every time I leave the shop and a lot of the time I'm here."

"Complain to my boss."

"It wouldn't do any good. Besides," she said with a shrug, "I'm not fighting it. The cops can't be everywhere."

"The muggers can. The last one was two doors down and twenty-one hours ago."

She grimaced. It was the rash of muggings, robberies, and assaults that had made Archer decide to assign a Donovan International security guard to Timeless Dreams, and her. Today he had informed her that Walker was her new shadow. When she had retorted that she couldn't see how much good Walker would do leaning on a cane, Archer had just looked at her and then gone back to trying to sort out Donovan International contracts in a world where national boundaries changed with the six-o'clock news.

"About that insurance," Walker said again.

"I'm checking out the cost of separate insurance for the necklace, just for the Savannah show and the travel out there."

"No one will handle it without an appraisal. A real one, from a GIA-certified lab or one of equal reputation."

Silence.

"Are the stones with an appraiser now?" he asked.

"No." Reluctantly she added, "I haven't found

a qualified appraiser who could guarantee getting them back to me in time to set them in Mel's necklace for the Savannah show.''

"Archer wondered about that." So had Walker, but he wouldn't earn any points mentioning it.

Faith's mouth flattened. Her brother had done more than wonder about it. He had quizzed her almost as thoroughly as Walker and a lot less patiently. "I told Archer I'd take care of it.''

"No problem. I'll appraise the rubies for you.''

"You're a certified appraiser?'' she asked, surprised.

"I know rubies. If I say they're worth a million, Archer will insure them for a million with Donovan money.''

"I didn't know you were a ruby expert.''

"There's a lot about me you don't know,'' Walker said neutrally. *And thank God for it.* "Where are the rubies now?''

"Right here.''

As she spoke, she opened one of the belly drawers in the long workbench and pulled out a small cardboard box. It held a bunch of slim, neat little paper packets stacked on edge. Each jeweler's packet held a single gemstone.

"Judas Priest,'' Walker muttered. "No wonder Archer told me to practice being your skin until you handed the necklace over. You don't even keep the damn rubies in a safe.''

"I have to work with the damn rubies,'' Faith

pointed out with transparent sweetness. Her smile was a double row of hard white teeth. "That's what I do. Design and execute jewelry. Contrary to what my brothers think, I'm a big girl who is quite capable of running her own business. Handling valuable gems is part of that business."

"Most people with a million in loose gems have an armed guard at the door."

"I have a man with a cane."

"Sure enough, you do. Ain't it grand."

This time Faith didn't miss the steel buried in his gentle drawl. "I'm glad it's good for someone," she said under her breath.

Walker heard. "And that someone isn't you?"

"It's not the first time the man had all the fun."

"Are you comparing me to a certain pile of road apples?"

"Road apples don't have lapis lazuli eyes."

Walker opened his mouth, closed it, and shook his head. "Help me out here. I'm pretty sure I just lost the direction of this conversation. What does lapis have to do with horseshit?"

"Exactly. You're not lost at all."

Suddenly he laughed, enjoying her quick, slightly skewed sense of humor.

Despite having promised herself that she would keep Walker at a coolly professional distance, Faith couldn't help smiling at him with warmth as well as teeth. It was nice to know that someone outside of her family could share an off-the-wall joke with her. Tony hadn't liked her "snotty" sense of humor.

"Kyle used to claim that trying to follow my sister's and my conversation was like trying to predict where a butterfly would land next," Faith said.

"Easy. Wherever the nectar is sweetest."

Walker's vivid, dark blue eyes lingered over her mouth. Then his smile faded and he walked the few steps that separated him from the work-bench. The hitch in his gait irritated him more than it hurt. It was a reminder of how stupid he had been. Almost as stupid as he was being now, swapping smiles with Archer's little sister and wondering if her mouth tasted half as hot and sweet as it looked.

Faith's smile wavered. While her unwanted guard wasn't as big as her brothers—much less Tony—there was something very solid about Walker. It made her grateful for his limp. If she had to, she could run rings around him.

"Do you have a loupe in one of those draw-ers?" he asked.

"Shore 'nuf," she said, imitating his soft drawl.

He ignored her, because it was smarter than doing what he wanted to do.

"I'm sorry," she said quickly, rummaging in the drawer. "I didn't mean it that way."

He looked at her bent head and the teeth biting into her lower lip. "What way?"

"Insulting. You know. The male ego thing."

He knew that the Donovan males didn't insult that easily. Neither did any man worthy of the name. "I suppose you're talking about ol' road apples again."

Faith stiffened.

"Well," Walker drawled. "I'm male and I have an ego and teasing me about my accent doesn't insult me or threaten me or any of those man-woman discussion-group things. Your southern accent needs some work, though. Good thing I'm an expert."

She let out a soft breath and gave him the loupe. "I'll keep my childish attempts at humor to myself."

His eyes narrowed at the echoes of old pain in her voice. "Now, that would be right disappointing, sugar. Nothing is as wearisome as a female with no sense of play."

"Sugar!" Faith's head shot up.

Grinning, he opened the loupe. "Gotcha. Nice thing about sisters. Their brothers teach them how to rise to the bait real quick."

"I knew it. You're somebody's brother."

The humor vanished from Walker's eyes, leaving them the deep, empty blue of high-mountain twilight. "Not anymore."

He propped his cane against the bench and

focused his attention on the box of tiny paper parcels.

"I didn't mean—" she began.

"I know," he said, cutting across her words as he selected a fragile little parcel that was barely half the size of his palm. "Forget it."

She sensed that he meant it. Literally. But she couldn't forget the emptiness in his eyes. She hadn't meant to hurt him, yet she knew she had. She just didn't know how.

After a moment's hesitation, Faith let it go. Walker's pain or pleasure was none of her business. She wasn't his girlfriend; the care and feeding of his male ego wasn't her full-time job. It was a good thing, too. She had been as lousy at it as she had been as a lover.

But I'm a hell of a good jewelry designer, she reminded herself fiercely. That was where her future lay—business, not pleasure. She would be the artistic, eccentric aunt who kept cats and brought her nieces and nephews gifts from all over the world at Christmas.

Broodingly she watched Walker unwrap the first ruby with quick, deft motions. His familiarity with the thin paper told her that he had unwrapped a lot of gems.

Curiosity flicked through her, the same curiosity she had felt the first time she had seen the quiet, easy-moving man with the soft voice and slow speech. He had struck her as unassuming,

almost shy, but according to her sister-in-law Lianne, Walker's nerve and quick thinking had
saved the day when the Donovans had conducted
a midnight raid on an island to recover a priceless, stolen jade shroud.

"Tweezers?" Walker asked.

She fished around in another belly drawer and
handed over a long pair of tweezers with an
angle on the pinching ends.

He took the tool without looking up from the
single stone that burned like an ember against
the backdrop of stark white paper. Whistling
tunelessly, he positioned one of the goose-necked
work lamps, held the ruby between his eye and
the intense light, and looked through the loupe.

It was like falling into another universe, an
alien, exquisite universe where red was the only
reality, the only meaning, the only god.

The slight irregularities and "silk" inside the
stone twisted light into new directions. Every
faint impurity reassured Walker. Only man was
obsessed with perfection. Natural rubies were
created from the heart of planetary fire, a volca-
no's seething, secret, molten blood transforming
ordinary rock into something extraordinary, unearthly. Yet traces of the earthly beginnings always remained.

It was those imperfections Walker sought and
savored. Each small flaw, each slight patch of silk,
told him that the bloodred gem he held came

from a distant, ancient mine rather than one of man's clever, high-tech laboratories.

"Well?" Faith asked.

"Nice red."

"I can see that for myself."

"Just enough silk to tell me that it hasn't been cooked by some Bangkok gem chef or created by U.S. labs."

"I could have told you that. The stones were taken from old Montegeau family jewelry."

Walker's dark eyebrows shifted. "Must have been some real wealthy old Montegeaus. South Carolina?" he asked, because some curiosity would be expected. Archer had already filled him in on the basics.

"How did you know?" Faith asked.

He tried to think of a short way to explain that the Montegeaus had been the local gentry of his childhood, the rich folks whose house had always glittered like a crystal palace in the long nights when he had stalked the marshes and bayous, hunting for something edible.

"I was a kid in South Carolina. Montegeaus were like gators—worth a lot on the hoof, always around, and sometimes real nasty."

"I thought alligators were protected."

"Sugar, ain't nothing protected from a hungry man."

Faith's head snapped up again. She saw instantly that Walker hadn't called her "sugar" just to yank her chain. He probably hadn't even realized what he said. He was whistling tunelessly again, totally focused on the gemstone burning in the tweezers' delicate steel grip. Idly she wondered how many of his women he called "sugar," and if he did it so he wouldn't have to remember their names. Like Tony, whose all-purpose "baby" had covered a patchy memory for who he was with, especially when he was drinking.

The memory sent a frisson of unease over her, like a chill breath across her forearms. She reminded herself that her life with Tony was over. She had learned her lesson. Picking a man because he was big and brawny enough to stand above her older brothers had been stupid. But she had wanted to prove to her family—and herself—that she could find a mate they respected, just like Honor had.

After her twin married, Faith had felt adrift and alone. She and Honor had shared so many firsts with each other, from bras to boyfriends to driver's licenses. No longer, though. Honor and Jake were a unit, parents of a wonderful little girl called Summer. The sisters still talked, still laughed together, still loved each other as only sisters could, but it was different now. It always would be.

Until Faith had been left behind, she didn't appreciate just how close she and her nonidentical twin were.

"Next one?" Walker said.

He was holding out the neatly wrapped package to her, gemstone safely inside again. Something about the look he gave Faith made her realize that he had tried to get her attention more than once.

"Sorry," she muttered, "I was thinking." She pushed the small box of packets down the bench toward him. "Help yourself."

While he did, Walker wondered what thoughts had dimmed the gleam in Faith's silver-blue eyes and put a downward curve on her soft mouth. He wondered, but he didn't ask. It was none of his business. The fact that he wanted it to be his business just told him how much of a fool he was.

Silently he filed the old packet, took a new one from the box, and removed the gem from its paper wrapper. Moments later he was back in the ruby universe where everything was pure color, glorious light, and reassuring imperfection.

Completely magnificent.

He had nearly been killed in hope of finding untreated rubies of this quality. The irony of discovering them in Faith's belly drawer made him want to swear and smile at the same time.

With a soft, rustling sound, Faith pulled out her sketch pad. Quickly she flipped to the back. Walker's absentminded, oddly soothing whistle told her that he was caught up in the new ruby.

She grabbed a mechanical pencil and began re-
working a sketch for a client who was as fussy
as he was rich. The man wanted something more
"important-looking" than the spare yet lyrical elegance that had become the hallmark of Faith's
designs.

Frowning, she studied the sketch. The customer wanted something lush yet not baroque,
rich but not clunky, "impressive" but not heavy.
The exotic sensuality of Lalique was "too feminine." The geometries of the late twentieth century were "too masculine."

With a corner of her mind, she wondered if
she would end up refusing the commission. Some
clients simply couldn't be pleased.

Grimacing, Faith went to work on a new
sketch. Gradually she forgot where she was, forgot Walker standing only a few feet away, forgot
everything but the compelling curves and shadows of the design she was creating. Flaring lines
suggested ferns uncurling in solid gold, with an
opal moon cradled in the fronds and smaller opal
raindrops caught randomly near the tips of each
frond. The design could be a pendant or a
brooch, a bracelet or a ring, earrings or a belt
buckle. Only the size and delicacy needed to
change.

For a time the only sounds in the room were
the rustle of paper, Walker's low whistle, and the

occasional shout of a self-appointed world saver holding forth in Pioneer Square.

Finally Walker put back the thirteenth packet. He looked at the belly drawer and the elegant blonde who wasn't aware of anything but her sketch pad. When she absently moved the valuable chunk of lapis lazuli to clear more space to draw, he shook his head in disbelief. She really didn't have the faintest idea of what kind of trouble the Montegeau rubies could be.

Saying nothing, he went to the front door of the shop, locked it, and flipped the sign to CLOSED.

"What are you doing?" she asked without looking up from her sketches.

"Not me. We."

Faith's head turned. The gooseneck lamp Walker had abandoned lit her face from the side and turned her eyes into silver-blue diamonds. "Excuse me?"

"I need some equipment from my apartment. I can't be in two places at once, so you're coming with me."

"I have to work."

"Bring the sketch pad with you."

"This is ridiculous! I've spent a lot of time alone in my shop and never—"

"If you have a problem," he cut in, "take it up with your family. I work for them."

She shot out of her chair, unlocked the door,

and flipped the sign around. "I'm not going anywhere."

"Suit yourself, sugar girl," he drawled, "but I'm taking these with me, where they'll be safe."

He scooped up the box of rubies, grabbed his cane, and limped out of the shop without a backward look.

Before he reached the curb, he was on the cellular to Donovan International's security department. If those rubies were half as good as they had looked through the loupe, they opened up a whole new approach to getting around the Thai cartel's stranglehold on the cut-ruby trade: Donovan International could mine old jewelry and thumb their nose at the cartel. The only problem was that when that kind of money and power clashed, danger was a certainty.

You could die just as dead in a U. S. city as in the barren mountains of Afghanistan.

5

Faith looked up as the shop doorbell buzzed. She had wondered who would take Walker's place. Now she knew.

Ray McGuire waited patiently on the other side of the locked door. He was second-in-command of Donovan security, and often guarded members of the family. Lately he had spent a lot of time in her shop. She had objected to Archer that it wasn't necessary. He had pointed out that all the locks, alarms, and safes in the world weren't any good when you locked the shop door behind you, walked to your car, and found a gun in your back. Then you had no choice but to turn around, unlock the locks, turn off the alarms, open the safes, and pray that the guy with the gun didn't kill you. Better to avoid the whole problem in the first place by never leaving your shop except with an armed guard.

She pressed the button that released the front lock, letting Ray into the shop.

"You must have run all the way," she said, looking at her watch. "Walker hasn't been gone ten minutes."

"I drove. I'm always glad to see you." He smiled as he walked around the two small glass cases that displayed samples of Faith's work. Curves of gold and the gleam of silver, flashes of sapphire and opal, diamond and topaz, ruby and tourmaline, pieces of God's own rainbow. It always amazed him that such beauty could come from the ratty, burned workbench in the back of the shop. "You make the best coffee in Seattle."

"Flattery will get you a sixteen-ounce triple americano, no sugar."

Faith abandoned the design that she wasn't making any progress on—she kept seeing lapis lazuli rather than the opals her client wanted—and went to the espresso maker she had installed at the back of the room.

"You remembered," he said, wiggling his salt-and-pepper eyebrows. They matched his short salt-and-pepper hair. "Does this mean you're going to run away with me after all?"

Steam hissed as she worked the machine with the skill of a sidewalk *barista*. "Millie would have my head." Millie being Ray's wife of sixteen years.

"Millie refuses to learn how to make espresso. Says French press is better."

"No problem. I'll teach you how to make espresso."

"Me?" he yelped in mock dismay. "What's it all coming to?" he asked the ceiling. "Men learning to make fancy coffee. Women carrying guns. The last guard we hired was *female*, for God's sake."

"Really? Remind me to ask for her next time."

"Too late." He grinned. "The Donovan beat you to it."

Faith laughed. "That's Dad for you. He'll hover over his daughters like a helicopter and then turn around and hire a woman with a gun to protect him."

"Hey, be fair. Your father hasn't hovered over Honor lately."

"Why bother? She has Jake now. He's a world-class hovercraft." Faith handed Ray his coffee. "Now, sit over there by the espresso machine and pretend to be invisible. I've got some paperwork to clear up before my three-o'clock appointment comes in. Afterward I'm going to close up shop and go rip a bloody strip off Owen Walker and Archer. With luck, I'll catch them together."

Ray knew she would, because Walker had told

him he had a 3:20 appointment with Archer. But that wasn't Ray's business. Protecting Faith Donovan was, for the moment.

He took a sip of the coffee, sighed deeply, and said, "The only thing you do better than making coffee is making jewelry. Those matching rings you designed for my parents' fiftieth anniversary were just plain perfect."

"More flattery? I just made you coffee. You angling for seconds?"

"Not yet. And it's fact, not flattery."

Ray walked over to a chair near the coffee machine. As he sat, he unbuttoned his sport coat so that it wouldn't get in the way of the shoulder harness he wore. Resting his left ankle on his right knee, he shifted around until his gun didn't dig into his ribs. The motions were entirely automatic. He had been retired from Los Angeles PD for four years. Twenty years of detecting all the ways man screwed his fellow man had been enough.

He pulled a magazine from his hip pocket and began reading about upcoming sales of the antique Christmas ornaments that he and his second wife collected.

For a few minutes the only sound in the shop was the whisper of pencil over paper and the creak of the swivel chair Faith sat in. Neither she nor the guard looked up when a lay preacher across the street in Pioneer Square started yelling

about Armageddon. Since the millennium had already turned, there wasn't much of an audience
for prophecies of sacred blood and gore.

The door buzzer rang. Faith looked up and saw
a well-dressed man of medium height standing on
the other side of the break-proof glass door.

"Know him?" Ray asked, eyeing the sleek, expensive leather coat whipping around the man's
calves. Hat and gloves. European, likely. Most
Americans liked their leather coats hip length.

"I've never met the man, but I'm guessing his
name is Ivanovitch. He has a three-o'clock
appointment."

"He's early."

"What's eight minutes among friends?" she
asked dryly. "Let him in. The sooner I'm finished,
the sooner I can get my hands on my brother."

Ray put the magazine aside and went to open
the door. "May I help you?" he asked politely.

"Yes, thank you." Ivanovitch summed up Ray
with a quick glance. A guard, armed, alert. Not
unexpected, but hardly welcome. "I am
Ivanovitch."

As an ex-cop, Ray didn't like overcoats. They
could hide too much, and anybody who wore a
long coat in L.A. probably had a lot to hide. As
a Seattle guard, he had become accustomed to
seeing overcoats. They were no longer a reason
for instant suspicion.

But he still didn't like them.

"Come in, Mr. Ivanovitch," Ray said. "Ms. Donovan is expecting you. May I take your coat?"

"Thank you, no. I have not long to stay."

Ray eyed the man's thick shoulders and the beginning of a belly. Now he really wished he could see beneath the coat. But he couldn't, so he would just watch the leather-gloved hands and the blue-gray eyes and wait for any telltale signs of nervousness.

Smiling, Faith walked forward. When she held out her hand, Mr. Ivanovitch bowed briefly over it instead of shaking it as she had expected.

European for sure, Ray decided. He stepped back a few feet but didn't go back to his chair. He had been trained to fade into the background without moving more than a few inches. He was good at it.

"May I offer you coffee?" Faith asked.

"Thank you, no." Despite a raging case of jet lag compounded by vodka and anger, Ivanovitch managed a creditable smile. "Please excuse. My time is small and my need is big."

She hoped her smile hid her relief. She really didn't feel like courting a customer over coffee and small talk.

"Then I'll do my best to help you quickly, Mr. Ivanovitch. You mentioned something about a carved stone, but not a modern one?"

"A ruby, yes," he said, watching her intently,

seeking any of the usual signs of nervousness. He saw clear skin, a trace of impatience that had nothing to do with nerves, and forthright blue eyes. "A gift, you comprehend? To my mother. She cherishes such things. To celebrate her eightieth name day, I wish to make a proper gift." He leaned forward, measuring every nuance of Faith's expression. "I am told a designer of your high quality has such stones."

Faith ignored the flattery and forced herself not to step back from the man's intense eyes and manner. She felt surrounded by him, almost threatened. She reminded herself that conversational distance varied from culture to culture. Putting more space between herself and her client could easily be interpreted as rudeness.

She held her ground. "I have a few carved rubies. My brothers travel all over the world. They keep their eyes open for special stones for my jewelry-design business."

"Excellent."

"If you'll excuse me, I'll get them."

Ivanovitch nodded in the manner of a man who was accustomed to being waited on. While Faith went to the closet-sized, high-tech safe, he glanced through the contents of her glass cases. Whatever he might have thought of the unusual designs didn't show on his broad face.

Discreetly Ray watched the client when the safe door swung soundlessly open. For all the reaction Ivanovitch gave, Faith could have been opening a closet full of cleaning supplies. Nor did he seem to care that she closed and locked the safe behind her when she brought out a handful of boxes.

Ray moved to a different angle when she set out the boxes on top of one of the glass display cases. He was pleased to note that Faith stayed on the opposite side of the case from the unknown client. Apparently some of his safety pointers had stuck in her stubborn Donovan mind. Or maybe she just didn't like the smell of stale cigarettes that clung to the man's expensive clothes.

Shifting slightly, Ray moved to a position where he could get between Faith and her customer in one step. Not that he expected to. Like unbuttoning his jacket when he sat, it was simply second nature to position himself to be in the right place in case things went wrong.

Ivanovitch noticed and understood every move. Fortunately, he was prepared to buy the ruby at any price. Tarasov had made it clear that he didn't want any incidents, any publicity, any hint that the ruby had ever left the Hermitage. Ivanovitch knew the cost of failing. He had no desire to become wedded to the Neva's icy surface, only to vanish forever with the spring thaw.

"I have only three carved rubies that aren't modern," Faith said. "They're fairly rare. Most of the carvings were done by Mughals or Persians, and they favored emeralds. In addition to being a holy color, emerald is softer, and therefore easier to carve than a ruby. Nothing is harder than a ruby except a diamond. Today, of course, modern machinery allows any stone to be carved. The Germans excel at it.''

Ivanovitch listened politely, but his eyes never left the box that Faith was opening. He was waiting for the first sign that the Heart of Midnight was within reach.

Seeing his intensity, Faith almost smiled. No matter the nationality, a collector was still a collector—avid to acquire something new. She was willing to bet that beneath his expensive leather gloves, his palms were sweating. No matter what he had said before, he wasn't buying a stone for his eighty-year-old mother's name day. He was buying for himself.

He wasn't the first client to use a sentimental occasion such as a wedding anniversary or a birthday in an attempt to shift the bargaining in his favor. At least Ivanovitch hadn't claimed a dying fiancée, as one would-be client had, hoping to get a special price and earnestly swearing to sell it all back to Faith as soon as his poor fiancée died.

Sometimes people really did believe that blond hair had a negative effect on a woman's IQ.

With a subtle flourish, Faith removed the lid of the box.

A glance told Ivanovitch that his search wasn't over. The ruby resting on bronze velvet was perhaps six carats. The gem was much longer than it was thick, and rudely faceted around the edges. The carving was on the back and had to be viewed from the top to make sense, always assuming the viewer understood Arabic.

"This is a quote from the Koran that—" Faith began.

"No," Ivanovitch interrupted bluntly. "It will not do. It is too small. Too pale. You comprehend? I must have a very fine stone."

Without a word she put the lid on the box and set it aside. Some anonymous, long-dead artisan had labored for weeks or months over a hard stone to inscribe a sacred verse that could be read only with a magnifying glass, but that didn't seem to impress the impatient Mr. Ivanovitch.

She reached for the second box. If six carats was too small, she doubted that seven and a quarter would do, but you never could tell. The color of the second ruby was certainly better. Not up to the Montegeau stones, but then, few rubies were.

"This stone—"

"Too small," he said curtly. "I told you. Very, very fine. Please, let us not waste time."

She slipped the lid back over the box. As she put the rejected stone aside, she hoped Ivanovitch had the money to back up his taste. The next stone was nine carats, had good color, light flaws, and would cost him $75,000. The inscription on the back was another verse from the Koran, this one wishing paradise to the holy and eternal misery to the infidel.

Ivanovitch saw the flowing Arabic script and dismissed the stone without a word.

"This ruby is nine point one carats," Faith said, but the client's face had already told her he didn't want it.

"No. Still too small. What else do you have?"

Faith covered the box, put it with the others, and looked at the very fussy Mr. Ivanovitch. "I'm sorry. That's my inventory of carved rubies. If you would like to look at other types of gems, I have several—"

"I was told you had exceptionally fine stones," he cut in harshly.

"I do." Faith was used to being interrupted. It came with having big brothers. Even so, she was getting tired of not being able to finish a sentence around this abrupt man.

"I was assured that you had a stone such as I want. Have you sold one recently?"

"A carved ruby?"

He gestured curtly and nodded. "But of course.

That is what I seek. A fine, large, carved ruby. Have I not told you?"

Ray shifted slightly. He really wished he had frisked this guy. It might have improved his manners.

"I haven't sold a carved ruby for more than a year," Faith said. "There isn't much call for carved rubies except as curiosities or center-pieces for unique jewelry."

Ivanovitch looked at the safe for the first time. "You are certain this is all you have?"

"Yes."

He didn't bother to look convinced. "Please understand me. I can pay you well, very well. I need—want this stone very much."

"That's always good to hear. If you could tell me exactly what kind of stone would suit you, perhaps I could find one for you. I have extensive connections among collectors and buyers of un-usual jewelry."

"Very fine color," he said. "What is known as blood of the pigeon."

Faith nodded.

"Flawless, or nearly so."

She nodded again, and started toting up the cost per carat. Even if all she did was broker the deal for another jeweler, her commission would be very nice.

"The inscription is Mughal and secular," he continued.

Her eyebrows lifted. "Your, er, mother is quite exacting."

Ivanovitch didn't even pause. "Twenty carats."

Faith whistled. "That would be quite a stone. And very, very expensive. Given that size, color, and clarity, your price would be at least one hundred thousand a carat, and could easily be twice as much."

The client's smile was more predatory than warm. "As I said, I can pay you very, very well. Now get the stone from the safe for me, Miss Donovan, and we can discuss price. There is no more need to be cautious. We understand each other, yes?"

"Not quite," she said dryly. "I don't carry multimillion-dollar stones in my inventory, Mr. Ivanovitch. I would be delighted to look for such a stone for you, but frankly, if you're in a hurry, you'd do better to go to Manhattan or London or Tokyo or Thailand. I could give you some contacts that—"

"I was assured that you have such a stone," he cut in. His hazel eyes were narrowed and his mouth looked ready to snarl.

Ray's hand slipped beneath his jacket. There was more than insistence in Ivanovitch's tone. There was real anger, the kind that led to violence.

"Whoever assured you was mistaken," Faith said evenly. "I'd love to have such a magnificent ruby. I don't." She waved a hand. "As you can see, this isn't Tiffany or Cartier."

For a blazing instant Ivanovitch imagined what Faith would look like beneath his knife, bleeding and pleading and so terribly eager to hand over the Heart of Midnight.

But such a pleasure must be delayed. Her guard was far too alert.

Faith watched what could have been temper or embarrassment flare on Ivanovitch's cheekbones. He bowed briefly, turned quickly, and strode out the door.

"Guess he doesn't want me to look around for his, uh, mother's gift," she said dryly to Ray.

"Guess not." He watched until Ivanovitch disappeared around the corner. Only then did his hand move away from his jacket. "Wherever he came from, he's used to getting what he wants."

"And fast," she agreed. "Well, searching for a stone like that will teach him patience." She looked around the shop. "You've got five minutes to finish your coffee. That's how long it will take me to lock up. Then you can follow me to Donovan headquarters and keep me from killing someone."

❧

The man held the phone the way a strangler holds his chosen victim. Plastic is harder than flesh, which was all that saved the black receiver from being crushed like the cigar butts in the ashtray on the bedside table.

"What do you mean she doesn't have it?" Tarasov snarled into the phone. "Offer her more."

The woman next to him—Tarasov's most recent girlfriend—grumbled and snuggled deeper into the satin sheets that felt so soft against her bruised breasts. She had labored hard tonight, keeping him up and pumping like a teenager. It was sweaty, difficult, distasteful, and often painful work, but paid better than hustling drinks and foreign nationals in hope of snagging a husband who could get her out of St. Petersburg's frozen hell to some warm, foreign heaven.

She was careful not to show any interest in the conversation that had interrupted her sleep. She didn't want to know how her lover made the money that kept her in Russian sable, Italian leather, Chinese silk, African diamonds, and French champagne. She was just bright enough to figure out that the less she knew, the longer she lived in luxury. Or lived at all.

As Tarasov listened to his employee's excuses, his normally ruddy cheeks went even darker with anger. With eyes as cold and empty as the frozen river that coiled through the city, he thought of the many pleasurable ways there were to kill a human being. What he tried not to think about was how very unpleasant it would be to find himself on the receiving end of such knowledge.

If that ruby wasn't back in the Hermitage in two weeks, he would find out more than he wanted to know about pain and dying.

"Bring me that ruby in thirteen days or you will wish you had been born dead." He hit the cutoff button and smacked the cellular phone on the bedside table so hard that it nearly cracked the marble.

Half a world away, Ivanovitch stared at the public phone. Seattle's afternoon traffic swirled past him. The wind tugged at his sleek leather coat. Slowly he hung up, hit the button that invited him to make another call, and started punching in numbers with a blunt, nicely manicured fingertip. As soon as the slow, husky voice answered, Ivanovitch started talking.

"She denies that she has the ruby."

Silence, the sound of someone swallowing hard. "She's lying. I sent it to her on consignment."

"Get it back."

"She must have sold it. That's why she's lying. She's trying to cut me out of my share."

"I am not interested in your problems. I will see you in ten days. If I do not have the ruby at that time, I will cut off your cock and push it down your throat."

"But I don't—"

Ivanovitch slammed the receiver down and vibrated with hunger to have his hands on Faith Donovan's pale skin.

6

The medium-size high-rise overlooking Elliot Bay's wind-harried water was a long way from the sultry green jungles of Myanmar. Or Burma, as the stubborn gem traders called it. No one would pay a premium for a Myanmar ruby, but a fine bloodred Burmese ruby . . . ah, that was something worth risking life and limb for.

At least, that was the theory. It was also the reason Owen Walker was presently leaning on a cane. At least the limb in question, his left leg, was nearly healed.

"You summoned, master?" he drawled to the man behind the desk, although it had been Walker who had asked to see Archer Donovan, not the other way around.

Archer slanted him a look, put up two fingers, and kept on talking into the phone. "You told me the same thing last week. Should I just make a tape and play it again next week?"

Hiding a smile, Walker set the carton down on the floor and looked around the office. Archer's desk was almost big enough to hold the papers piled on top of it. Newsletters and magazines that dealt with policy changes in global backwaters were scattered across the low sofa that ran along one wall and curled out in a cozy L. The sleek coffee table nestled along the sofa held art glass in controlled curves and vivid sunset colors. The painting on the wall had the same colors, but it was more elemental, more powerful, sunset like a tidal wave of color devouring the land.

Motionless, Walker forgot the ache in his leg and simply absorbed the painting. One of his goals in life was to have enough money to afford a Susa Donovan landscape. Until then, he didn't mind waiting in her oldest son's office.

"Cut the crap, Jersey," Archer said. "That shipment is four weeks and four days late. Either you deliver in three days or the contract is void and you owe Donovan International six hundred big ones in penalties."

The receiver met its cradle with a soft, final sound.

Walker wondered if the guy on the other end was still talking. Probably. Not that it would have done any good. One of the things people had a hard time understanding about Archer was that he meant what he said and said what he meant.

That was why Walker got along with him.

Archer's gray-green eyes took in the man standing quietly on the other side of the desk. Right now Walker looked like a backcountry gem expert and bush pilot, duties he often fulfilled for Donovan International. Jeans, blue work shirt, fleece-lined waterproof jacket, scarred hiking boots.

And a low-tech wooden cane. Archer had the feeling the cane was a precaution rather than a necessity. Even recuperating, Walker was catlike on his feet. Quick mind, too, though he did his best to hide it behind a good-ol'-boy drawl and dark, close-cut beard. Archer's own beard had a bit more length; his wife liked the way it felt on her skin.

"Faith was burning up the phone lines," Archer said.

"Didn't like my replacement?" Walker asked innocently.

"She's coming here to yell at me in person. And to hear all about how I yelled at you. At least, that's what she hopes I'll do. So tell me, am I going to yell at you?"

Walker almost smiled. Archer wasn't the yelling kind. He got better results without opening his mouth. He had a way of staring at people that made them hunt for a hole to hide in. "Yell away, boss. It will make your little sister feel a whole lot better."

Archer raked his fingers through his hair. "You're pretty cocky for someone who could barely stand less than a week ago."

"I was lucky. Those bandits were too poor to buy bullets for their Kalashnikovs."

Archer smiled thinly. "Kalashnikovs? Russian antiques."

"You load 'em and they shoot real fine."

"They make pretty good clubs, too."

"No argument here," Walker said dryly. "I've got the lumps to prove it."

"You're lucky those clowns didn't have knives."

"They did."

Archer's eyes narrowed. He pulled a thin sheaf of papers out from under a stack of file folders. He flipped through the papers quickly. Three pages summarizing three months of work. Walker was famous for his terse reports. "I don't see anything here about knives."

Walker shrugged. "They didn't cut me, so why waste words?"

"I suppose if you didn't have any bruises, you wouldn't have reported the ambush?"

"You and Kyle are hell-bent on getting some high-quality rubies that haven't been cooked in the Thai cartel's furnaces. My job was to scout the possibilities, not bitch about the conditions.''

Archer pulled out the last page of the report and began reading aloud. " 'Chance of reaching ruby miners and/or smugglers before the Thais do: real slim.' " He looked up, pinning Walker with the kind of look that made most people uncomfortable. Walker didn't react. That was one of the reasons Archer liked him. "Anything to add?"

"Fucking."

"What?"

"As in real fucking slim. I didn't want to offend the data input pool."

"Mitchell does all my private reports. He doesn't offend easily."

"I'll keep that little thing in mind," Walker said, his voice slow and amused.

"Anything else you left out of the report?"

"It's damn cold in Afghanistan at this time of year."

Archer's eyes narrowed. "How far did you get?"

"Just to the mines at Jegdalek and Gandamak."

"Travel conditions?"

"The southern route is still littered with land mines. The northern route is decent enough until you get to Sorobi. Then it unravels into a Jeep trail that swallows itself in dry washes and rock-slides. A lot of the travel is done by the local

equivalent of a mule because you can fuel a crit-
ter easier than a truck. The bandits are real active.
The clans are slitting throats right and left, trying
to catch up from all those years when the Soviets
owned the real estate and the guns."

Archer glanced at the report. Walker's arduous
trip through the backwaters of Afghanistan rated
one line: *Primitive transport and mining conditions.* "How primitive is the mining?"

"A handful of men with pickaxes, a white lime-
stone ledge with occasional nodules of red crystal
showing through in the weathered parts, and a
portable, sixty-pound pneumatic jackhammer that
shakes itself apart once an hour, if they're lucky
enough to find fuel to run the compressor that
long. Dynamite is easier to haul, so that's what
they mostly use. After the explosion it's pick,
hammer, and chisel work."

"Any quality to the stones?"

"The ones that survive the blast?" Walker
drawled.

Wincing, Archer thought of greedy, unskilled
men mining priceless ruby crystals with explo-
sives. The picture was unpleasant.

"Rumor has it that someone is digging on the
sly in the Taghar mine," Walker said. "That's the
one that the mujahideen buried to hide it from
the Soviets. I saw one or two rough stones that
were nearly pigeon-blood quality. One was
twenty carats. The other was sixteen. A good cut-

ter would get ten and eight carats. Fine, really fine stones." Walker shrugged. "By now, they're cooked in Bangkok and wearing a 'Burmese ruby' tag. The other rough I saw varied from good to second rate."

"What was it selling for?"

"The Thais have a lock on the legal output, and if you're pushy and buy under the table, somehow the bandits find out. Bad news, boss. Really bad. Those ol' boys are as hard as the mountain passes they control."

"But you brought out some rough gems anyway."

"That's what you pay me for."

"I don't pay you to get killed," Archer retorted.

"You want good rubies, you pay the going price. Burma's Mogok mines are either played out or locked up tighter than a sultan's virgin daughter. That leaves Cambodia, Afghanistan, Sri Lanka, and Kenya."

"Justin and Lawe are working on Kenya. From what you've told me, the rest belongs to the Thais—lock, stock, and barrel."

"For now, anyway. No cartel lasts forever."

"Tell it to DeBeers."

Walker laughed softly. "They've ridden their diamond tiger real far, haven't they? Been an inspiration to us all."

Archer didn't look inspired. He looked irritated. He and his siblings—and now Jake, Honor's husband—owned Donovan Gems and Minerals, a very loose affiliate of Donovan International, the family corporation. DeBeers's control of the diamond market pretty well limited the rest of the world, including the Donovans, to smuggled or inferior diamonds. The ethnic Chinese Thais had become middlemen to the world for rubies. China and Japan had a stranglehold on pearls. The drug cartel or local warlords had a lock on Colombian emeralds.

At the rate the planet was being carved up into gem fiefdoms, Donovan Gems and Minerals would be lucky to be selling ''cultured'' turquoise in a few years.

''What's on your mind, Walker?'' Archer said. ''And don't bother with that shit-kicking country-boy shuffle. I saw through it the first time you cleaned me out at poker.''

Walker managed not to smile. ''Have you thought about the ruby resale market?''

''The Thais don't leave much room for anyone else to make a profit. Not in America, anyway. We just won't pay as much for quality rubies as the rest of the world will.''

''I've been thinking about that. There's another way to end-run the Thais.''

''I'm listening.''

''Mine old jewelry instead of old mines,'' Walker said simply. ''Buy estate jewelry from all over the world, take out the good stones, recut them if necessary, and sell them loose. You should be able to have a nice little high-end business, because you can guarantee Burmese rubies that haven't been heat-treated. That's about as rare these days as a natural pearl."

For a time Archer was silent. "Is there that much old jewelry floating around for sale?"

"Gems have always been an aristocrat's savings account. Think about all those centuries of European and Russian and Middle Eastern royalty. Think about all those nasty revolutions, wars, and financial crashes. Think about the cold economics and even colder economies of the former Soviet Union. Yeah, there are lots of family jewels for sale. Some of them are well worth buying."

"Interesting idea." Archer looked out at the wind-whipped bay. "Any idea how to go about getting a handle on this resale market?"

"Faith's friends—the ones who sent her the rubies she's working on—might be a good place to start."

Archer glanced at the door to his office. On the other side of it would soon be a sister he loved very much. A sister who was mad enough right now to scalp him with a dull knife. "Yeah, she mentioned something about those rubies. Said you stole them."

"Road apples. She wouldn't come with me and I wasn't going to leave rubies like that in the belly drawer of a bench in an unlocked shop in Pioneer Square.''

"If I sit here long enough, you'll tell me something useful.''

"The rubies Faith's friends sent her are fine, *fine* stones.''

Archer's black eyebrows went up. "How good?''

"The best I've seen outside of museums and royal treasuries.''

At first a soft whistle was Archer's only answer. Then, "How much are they worth?''

"Retail?''

"Wholesale.''

"Every cent of the million she's trying to get them insured for. A lot more, in my opinion. A big Burmese ruby that hasn't been heat-treated is more valuable than any other gemstone on earth, including diamonds.''

"So what's the problem with getting insurance?''

"The GIA appraisers are backed up. They can't guarantee getting the job done in time for Faith to set the rubies and polish the necklace up before the Savannah show. The insurers won't sign on unless the GIA folks certify the rubies' worth. No one wants to underwrite what might be a scam.''

"What kind of scam?''

"The usual. Fake appraisal, fake gems, fake theft, real insurance claim paid off in real cash."

"These rubies came from friends of Faith."

Walker thought about how very dead you could get trusting friends you hadn't seen in a while. He had trusted the man who sent him into ambush. An old friend.

"Whatever," Walker said. "Even if you could get the gems appraised through an approved lab fast enough for the Savannah show, a lot of appraisers are too young to recognize natural Burmese rubies on sight, or even after a bunch of tests. Appraisal is almost as much art as science. You need a natural eye or wide experience to catch the nuances. There aren't that many real, natural, high-quality Burmese rubies floating around."

"But Faith's rubies are real, natural, and high-quality." Though Archer said nothing more, there was a question buried in his words.

Smiling, Walker reached down and began to unload the contents of the carton he had carried in. In short order he set up a binocular microscope, a polariscope, and an ultraviolet light on the low coffee table in front of the couch. Then he pulled out several small boxes. Among them was the one containing the gem packets that he had taken from Faith's shop.

The intercom on Archer's desk buzzed, Mitchell trying to sound a warning. A second later the door to the office opened.

Walker didn't even look up. He already knew that the lady in the black cashmere slacks, ice-blue silk blouse, and black cashmere blazer was mad enough to take chunks out of his hide and never mind the taste of blood.

"I'm over thirty," Faith said angrily, "I own my own business, and I don't need one of your house apes standing over me like an older brother."

"Hello to you, too," Archer said.

"House ape?" Walker asked under his breath.

"The stage at which boys become teenagers with more height than couth," Archer explained.

Walker gave his boss a sideways look. "*Uncouth*, I've heard of. You sure *couth* is a word?"

"Yes," Faith said. "Somehow I'm not surprised you've never heard the word."

"I suppose ol' road apples was a mountain of couth," Walker said, turning back to his equipment.

"Ol' road apples?" Archer asked, one black eyebrow cocked.

Red burned on Faith's high cheekbones. "Never mind."

"Her fiancé," Walker said.

Archer laughed out loud.

"My ex-fiancé," Faith said through her teeth. "Big difference."

"The only one that matters," Archer agreed. "Did you come to hear Walker's explanation of why I should insure those rubies for a million bucks?"

For two seconds Faith thought about how satisfying it would be to grab the rubies and walk out without a word. Then she thought about how dumb that would be. She needed insurance. Archer could provide it. But her brother was a businessman. He wouldn't insure a pig in a poke, even for his sister.

"I came because the instant Walker left my shop with those rubies, they were effectively uninsured," she said evenly. "While I'm certain he's competent enough flying an airplane, most crime in Seattle takes place on the ground."

Though she said nothing more, she looked at the cane resting against the coffee table.

The suggestion that Walker wasn't fit for security duty seemed to amuse Archer. He was surprised that his sister couldn't see the gutter fighter disguised in casual clothing. But then, few people did. Being underestimated was one of Walker's most valuable assets. It allowed him to talk his way out of situations that other men would try to handle with a gun.

"I'll be responsible for the rubies while they're in Walker's care," Archer said.

"But not while they're in mine?" Faith retorted.

"Do you want them insured or not?"

"Of course I want them insured."

"Then let our resident ruby expert explain to me why I should accept his valuation. Because I sure as hell won't do it on the word of some South Carolina dandy who happens to have a jewelry store in the family."

"Don't worry," Walker said. "The gems are real."

"Of course they are," she said.

"Archer is just being careful," Walker said soothingly. "Comes of having to do business with countries where the old order gave way to new criminals."

"Since when has Donovan International done business with criminals?" she asked her brother.

"You have a touching trust in elected politicians," Walker muttered.

She ignored him.

"If you want to do business in what was once the Soviet Union," Archer said, "and Donovan International does, one way or another you deal with the various *mafiyas*."

"They must be making a lot of long spoons in Russia today," she said dryly.

Archer gave a crack of laughter.

Smiling, Walker looked up at Faith. "Sure enough. Folks who sit down to eat with the devil don't want to get their pinkies burned."

She blinked, surprised at the change a simple

smile made in his looks. Not that he didn't usually smile, but this one was different. She couldn't say just how it was different. Warmer, maybe, like the one he gave Summer.

The idea that Walker genuinely enjoyed her sense of humor both surprised and charmed Faith. It was like being with her family.

"Exactly," she said, grinning back at Walker. Then she realized what she was doing and stopped. She was supposed to be angry, but it was hard when she was smiling. She groaned. "Now I see why fraternizing with the enemy isn't allowed."

"I'm not the enemy, sugar."

"That remains to be seen, *sugar*."

"There you go," he said. "See, we've already reached an understanding, exchanging pet names and all. Next thing you know, we'll be setting a date to get matching leg shackles."

Faith shook her head in exasperation. Walker must have been taking lessons from her brothers. It was hard to stay angry at him.

Smiling, Walker bent over the microscope and finished positioning the first gem. "Ready for a thumbnail education on rubies, Archer?"

"I'm always ready to learn."

"That was the second thing I noticed about you," Walker said.

"What was the first?" Faith asked.

"That your brother hadn't come up against a better poker player in a long time."

"You're better than Archer?"

"Hate to admit it, but it's true," Archer said. "We got grounded by weather out beyond the Brooks Range in Alaska, looking for the Alaskan version of those Canadian diamond mines. By the time the storm cleared, I was down to my Jockey shorts and the parka he lent me at an exorbitant interest rate."

"It's the drawl," Walker said, focusing the microscope with great care. "Gets you Yankees every time. Y'all believe something so soft and slow just has to be dumb as a stump."

Faith snickered and looked at her older brother. If he had any hard feelings about being trounced at poker, they didn't show. He was smiling and shaking his head at the memory.

"Okay, boss," Walker said, straightening. "Take a look."

Archer sat on the couch, leaned over, and looked. After a few moments he asked, "What about those cloudy patches?"

"They're called 'silk' in the trade," Walker said. "Or if you want to be technical, they're tiny exsolved inclusions. Too many and you have an opaque stone."

" 'Silk' works for me."

"Works for the color, too," Walker said, "if you have just the right amount. See, when it comes to faceting, rubies are touchy. If you cut the facets too deep or too shallow—and Thai cutters do it all the time to get the maximum carat weight from each piece of rough—then you get windows and extinction along some of the facets."

Faith came around the table and peered down at the tiny, intense scrap of red Archer was examining through the binocular lenses of the scope. She couldn't see the inclusions with her unaided eye.

Archer could see them, but not the rest of what Walker was talking about. "Windows? Extinction?" Archer asked. "Try it in English. Pearls are my specialty, not hard stones."

"Windows happen when light just goes through a faceted gem without being refracted," Walker explained. "The stone becomes a windowpane. The result is a pale spot in the gem where the window is. Extinction is when light coming into the stone escapes out the side rather than being refracted back into the center. It makes a dark spot. What you want is an even distribution of color. With rubies, it's a bitch kitty to get."

Coming closer, Faith leaned past Walker to look at the ruby glowing like a live ember in the steel grasp of the microscope. She put her hand on her brother's shoulder and nudged, but he didn't take the hint.

Walker didn't move either. He just savored the warmth and scent of Faith standing inches away from him. Then he dragged his thoughts back to the rubies.

"A good cut minimizes extinction," Walker said, "but nothing stops it. It's just the way rubies are. The beauty of Burmese rubies, and what makes them so valuable, is that their natural silk transmits light to facets that might otherwise dim out because of extinction. The result is a softer 'feel' to the color. It's warm and velvety, like a woman's mouth."

Faith gave him a startled look, but he didn't seem to notice.

"Don't Thai rubies have silk?" Archer asked.

"Not like Burmese rubies from Mogok. Nothing does. Even the really good Vietnamese rubies. Great color, but every faceted stone shows dark areas of extinction, no matter how carefully they're cut. Here. Look at this through the loupe."

Archer shifted his attention to a faceted red gem Walker held in a pair of long tweezers. When Archer used the loupe on the stone, he saw that not all facets were equally bright, equally red. Viewed by itself, the stone was still quite beautiful. But compared to the Burmese ruby . . .

There was no comparison. Once you had seen

a high quality Burmese ruby, the others were simply cut red stones.

"When you add the Burmese ruby's natural fluorescence," Walker said, "you've got the gem of fables, the stone that glows with its own internal light. It's *alive*. There's nothing in the world like it, nothing at all."

The certainty and passion in his voice made Faith take a long look at him. She felt the same way when she finished a sketch that she knew would create beauty out of a handful of metal and stones. There was no high to equal that. The memory of that exhilaration kept her going even when everything else in her life was flat. The idea that Walker could feel that depth of emotion about anything was both surprising and intriguing.

He was right. That southern drawl was like quiet, deep water; it concealed a lot more than it revealed about whatever lay beneath.

"Watch this," Walker said.

He took the tweezers and put the second stone over the UV light source. Then he unwrapped another of Faith's stones and did the same. The first ruby showed no change. The Burmese ruby burned with an unearthly crimson light.

Faith gasped softly.

"Fluorescence," Walker said. "Burmese stones fluoresce very strongly in the red to orange range. Red is more valuable because it deepens the desired color. This stone is fine. Really fine. Nice size, too. It should fetch forty thousand a carat, wholesale. More if the buyer is eager."

"What would a twenty-carat stone of that quality be worth?" Faith asked. "One with a Mughal inscription. Secular only, please. Nothing religious."

Walker's eyes narrowed. He had some carved Mughal rubies in his own collection, but nothing more than ten carats, and nothing of the quality of the Montegeau ruby. "Any particular reason for asking?"

"A man was in the shop today, looking for one. He was irked when I told him I didn't have one. He was sure I was holding out, trying to drive up the price."

"Why?"

"Apparently someone assured him that I had a high-quality inscribed ruby."

"Who?"

"He didn't say."

"Did you ask?"

Her eyes narrowed at the cross-examination. "No. Does it matter?"

"Likely not," Walker drawled. "It's just that I collect ruby oddities. Maybe I could help him out with something of mine. What was the guy's name?"

"Ivanovitch, Ivan Ivanovitch."

Walker and Archer exchanged a swift look. Ivanovitch was the Americanized Slavic equivalent of Johnson—Son of John. A generic sort of name. Common as dirt and just as forgettable.

In all, a great name to hide behind.

7

"Let me know if this Ivanovitch comes back," Walker said after a moment. He worked to make it sound like an easy request rather than a demand.

Archer's steel-colored eyes said that he felt the same way, but nothing useful would come of letting Faith know it. After Tony, she fought every request from a man, no matter how reasonable it might be.

"How much would a stone like Mr. Ivanovitch wants be worth?" Faith asked. "Millions?"

"A gem is always worth whatever you can sell it for," Walker said neutrally. "Don't worry. If I come up with one for Ivanovitch, I'd give you a finder's fee."

"You bet your butt you would," she retorted.

Only Archer's presence kept Walker from saying she could have his butt any way she wanted it, including naked, if she'd return the favor.

Archer went back to comparing rubies. "How could an appraiser ever mistake Burmese rubies for any other kind?"

"Easy," Walker said, forcing his thoughts away from Faith and bare butts. "You're looking at an *anyun,* which is the name in the trade for a top-quality Burmese ruby that is two carats or more. An appraiser could go a lifetime without seeing one. The lesser Burmese stones are easily confused with other rubies, especially if they've been cooked. If I hadn't spent a few years dealing with ruby goods from all over Asia, I wouldn't be able to spot the difference so fast."

"Cooked?" Faith asked Walker.

"Yeah. Literally. It's an old practice that, until a generation ago, was the ruby trade's dirty little secret. Like showing rubies against a bronze plate in order to make the red look more intense."

"What does, uh, cooking do to a stone?"

"Changes the color for some stones, the clarity for others. Often both." He reached into one of the other small boxes he had brought and took out some faceted red stones. He lined them up on the table.

"Rubies?" Faith asked skeptically.

He nodded.

"They look dull," Archer said.

"And too . . . blue," she added.

"Right on both counts," Walker said. "Eight hundred years ago, I'd have cooked them for anywhere from an hour to a week. Rubies were originally formed in the earth's fire. Sometimes you can clean them up in a man-made fire."

The idea caught Faith's imagination. Fire creating. Fire cleansing. Fire transforming. Beautiful red fire . . . "How does it work?"

"Too much heat destroys the ruby, so you have to be real careful," Walker said. "The right amount of heat changes the chemistry of the stone itself. The blue tinge is literally burned away, leaving only the red. Same for some inclusions and flaws. Too much silk? No problem. Cook it and drive the clouds away. Of course, you screw up the fluorescence, too, but the end result is still more valuable with heat treatment than without."

"Wonder who discovered it," Archer said.

"The first woman who built a cooking fire on dull alluvial gravel and found cold, bright red embers in the ashes," Walker suggested dryly. "As long as there have been rubies, there have been primitive ways of making them look clearer, brighter, and redder. Today's high-tech labs can do a lot more about 'finishing up' inferior stones than the clay stoves of centuries past."

"Then heat treating isn't considered cheating?" Faith asked.

"Not so long as you tell the buyer. But remember, when you're buying gems, you're buying rarity as much as beauty. Fine untreated stones are far, far more rare than fine-treated stones." Then Walker shrugged. "But today, everybody in the trade assumes that all rubies are cooked. Therefore, there's no point complaining. As in, don't mention it to the customer and maybe the fool won't think to ask."

"So it's like money," Archer said. "The bad will drive out the good."

"Or like pearls," Faith said. "Cultured pearls have driven natural pearls out of the marketplace."

"Pretty much," Walker agreed unhappily. "Natural Burmese rubies are damn near as rare as uncultured pearls. But there still is room at the high end of the gem trade—the very high end— for untreated stones." He glanced at Faith. "Like the ones your friends sent you."

Her honey-colored eyebrows shifted in a frown. "Davis didn't say whether or not they were treated."

"What did he say?"

Faith hesitated.

Walker's casual tone was at odds with the bleak intensity of his eyes.

Archer sensed the sharp edge to the question,

too. He gave Walker a narrow look, wondering what was on his independent employee's mind.

"All Davis told me is that he and his son have a business buying and selling estate jewelry," Faith said. "That's in addition to other family businesses."

"So that's how he got these rubies?" Archer asked. "Estate goods?"

"If he did, it wasn't recently. He said these rubies had been in the family for a while and he decided to celebrate the birth of the next generation by making a pretty necklace for his future daughter-in-law. I gather that the Montegeaus are big on family continuity. Davis has only one child, Jeff, who is my friend Mel's future husband."

"Make a pretty necklace, huh?" Walker said softly. "You bet. As in pretty damned spectacular. Especially with you doing the design."

She blinked, surprised. Everyone in her family seemed to take her skill for granted. Or if they noticed it, they rarely said anything to her about it. But then, her mother was an internationally recognized artist. Next to that, the daughter's accomplishments might seem hardly noticeable.

"Okay, he says they're old family goods," Archer said. "You can date diamonds by their cut. Can you do the same for rubies?"

"Sorry, boss. Asians cut for maximum size, even if that means irregular, clumsy facets. Their methods of cutting and polishing haven't changed in a thousand years. Corundum paste and a wheel driven by foot treadle as often as by electricity."

Archer grunted. "What about the rest of the Montegeau rubies? Are they all this good?"

"All of Faith's rubies sure are. Basically the stones have great color, clarity, and fluorescence. Size, too. The smallest is over two carats. If the Montegeau stones were recut to maximize brilliance, it would increase their value by half, at least. I can't speak for whatever else old man Davis might have buried in the bayou."

"Excuse me?" Faith said.

"Old southern custom, like pecan pie. You take the family proud-ofs and—"

"Proud-ofs?" she cut in.

"Sure. Like that classy silver and aquamarine pin you're wearing. Back in the bayous, that's a proud-of. You're proud of it. Local legend has it that the Montegeaus buried the good stuff in one of the bayous, along with folks who asked too many questions. Lots of Yankee ghosts howling through the marshes and swamps of South Carolina. A few Montegeaus, too, if half of what I heard is true. They have some real skeletons in their attic."

"What would you know about local legends?" she asked.

"I was born three miles from Ruby Bayou.

Lived there until I was sixteen and went to West Texas.''

"You know the Montegeaus?'' Archer and Faith asked simultaneously.

He smiled thinly. "The way a peasant knows gentry.''

"Somehow I can't see you bowing and yanking on your forelock,'' she said.

"Yeah, well, that's what I like about working for your brother. He doesn't think kissing anybody's butt is part of the job description.''

"Still important, though,'' Archer said blandly.

"Then I'll never be CEO. I flunked butt kissing in every grade from kindergarten through eleven.''

"What about grade twelve?'' Faith asked. "Finally get it right?''

"In a manner of speaking. I quit going. Never had a problem with it again.''

Though Walker's tone was mild, she sensed the automatic defiance beneath. He was standing in a room with two university graduates and he didn't even have a high school diploma.

Yet he was the one teaching them.

Archer went back to the microscope. "Pretty, but a million bucks for thirteen badly cut rubies is still a bucketful of money.''

"Fourteen if you count the one that's Faith's fee.''

"Her fee is going in the safe at home. Tonight."

Faith started to argue, then decided it didn't matter. The condo safe was just as good as the one in her shop. Better, actually. Kyle had designed the security electronics with skilled twenty-first-century thieves in mind.

"That leaves the thirteen for the necklace," Archer continued. "A million is still a lot of cash."

"Yeah, I thought you might feel that way." Walker turned back to the table and opened another small box. "In order for you to appreciate just how fine, and how rare, those Montegeau rubies really are, I want you to look at some samples of ruby rough taken from mines all over the world."

Faith and Archer looked at the unassuming pebbles Walker was spreading out across the table. The stones came in all sizes from unpopped popcorn to crab apple. The colors were variations on the theme of red—dilute pink, deep pink, red-brown, red-orange, red-blue, red-purple, and others that were less red than they were brown or blue. Some stones were clear. Most weren't.

Walker glanced at Faith and Archer, saw the disappointment in their expressions, and smiled slightly. They both specialized in pearls. Their idea of "rough" was a pearl fresh from the oyster, which was a lot more finished than any gemstone fresh from the mine.

"Rubies start as crystal formations," Faith said, nudging a pebble with her fingertip. "Why are some of these round and some sharp-edged? Or when you say 'mine,' do you mean placer gravels as well as hard-rock mining?"

He gave her a surprised look.

She gave him a look back that said he shouldn't be surprised. She was, after all, a Donovan.

"Both," Walker said. "Many of the famous Mogok mines of Burma are little more than holes dug through the dirt of the jungle floor to the underlying gravel layer. These miners are still in the Stone Age. Skinny guys with breechcloths dig in a pit wide enough for one man and a bucket on a rope. Not enough room to swing a cat, as we used to say back home." He shook his head.

Archer grimaced. He wasn't fond of small places.

"The poor bastard at the bottom of the pit is usually at least knee-deep in muddy water," Walker said, "hour after hour, in a jungle that's hot enough to cook meat. The pit is as deep as the gem gravels or the last cave-in, whichever comes first."

Silently Faith touched a packet where a cold crimson ember burned within, legacy of an unknown man's risk and toil. She looked again at the various shades of ruby rough spread in front of her. "Are any of these from Mogok?"

"No. But the placer stuff—" he gestured to the stones that were rounded like pebbles "—all came from pretty much the same kind of mine. Real primitive." He rolled some of the darker pebbles in his palm, the ones that were tinged with brown. "These are what used to be called Siams."

"What are they?" Faith asked.

She bent closer to see, so close that her hair brushed Walker's chin. When he breathed in, the scent of gardenias came to him like a lazy southern night. He couldn't help taking in and letting out another breath. Deeper, slower. Her blond hair gleamed above the elegant curve of her neck. His breath stirred the fine gold strands at her crown.

He closed his eyes and reeled in his body's unruly response to her scent, her grace, her heat radiating subtly against him.

"Thai rubies used to be called Siams," Walker said, his voice almost curt, "which was another way of saying inferior goods. That was when Burmese rubies were the only ones worth owning."

"These are too dark," Archer said. "Not enough red."

"Too much iron," Walker said absently. His eyes were open again. He was counting the pulse just beneath the soft skin at the base of Faith's throat. It kicked faster, as though she was as aware of him as he was of her.

"What?" Archer asked.

"All sapphires and rubies are made of the same basic thing, corundum," Walker said, dragging his attention back to his boss. "Pure corundum is colorless, like a good diamond. Add impurities and sapphire comes in every color of the rainbow, except red. If it's red, it's called a ruby. You with me?"

Archer nodded.

"A ruby's color comes from the presence of a small amount of a certain impurity—chromium— at the time of crystal formation," Walker continued. "The blue sapphire's color comes from titanium and iron. Other sapphire colors—"

"Okay," Archer cut in. "I get the idea. Thai rubies have different impurities than Burmese rubies."

"Close enough. If I cook these just right, I'll change the color to a purer red. I'll lose softness of color in the process, but you can't have everything. Next to uncooked Burmese rubies, Thai rubies look hard. Cold, despite their color."

Archer looked at the varieties of ruby rough spread out on the table. He pointed to a bright red piece. "That one's pretty just the way it is."

Walker smiled. "It's spinel. Used to fool a lot of folks, including royalty. One of the British crown jewels is spinel."

Faith pointed to another piece. It was one of the pebbles. "I like that color."

"You have a good eye. When it comes to color, that's the best of the batch. Too bad it's man-made."

"Glass?" Archer asked.

"Nothing that unsophisticated. It's made in a furnace that imitates the conditions that create natural rubies. The labs make them flawless for ruby lasers. The crooks make them with flaws for the gullible."

"Same chemical composition as a natural ruby?" Faith asked.

"Exactly."

"Then how can you tell the difference?"

"Under a microscope. Man-made rubies grow in curves instead of straight lines, and the tiny gas bubbles are stretched out rather than rounded. This one was churned in a rock tumbler and passed off as placer goods, along with some genuine and inferior stones."

"You buy them?" Archer asked.

"Yeah. It's called a learning experience. I had lots of them for the first few years as I worked my way around the ruby trade. I have a whole collection of fakes. I try not to add to it," he said, deadpan.

Smiling, Faith sorted through rounded pebbles of ruby, both synthetic and natural. "They're heavy for their size."

"Like gold," Walker agreed. "That's why rubies sink to the bottom of rivers and from there
down through gravel made of lighter rocks.
When the rivers gradually shift their courses and
the jungles move in, the gravels stay behind, buried beneath triple-canopy greenery, waiting for a
man shrewd or desperate enough to risk his ass
digging in a narrow, unshored, dirt-walled pit."

She stared at the rough bits of color in her
hand. Time and rivers flowing, changing, becoming jungle, and only hard bits of crystal remaining
changeless, timeless, forged in elemental fire . . .

Teasing hints of design swirled in her mind, as
untouchable as silk within a fine ruby.

"This looks like a good hunk," Archer said. He
lifted the rock, which was white studded with a
red crystal the size of his thumb. "Color isn't
bad."

"Afghanistan, from a hard-rock mine. The
white is marble. The red is ruby, but the stone
itself is good only for cabochons. Too riddled
with fractures and flaws. Strictly low-end-jewelry
stuff. They have better rough in some of the
mines, but damned little of it."

Faith looked at the stone with new interest,
imagining what she could do with it. She loved
the unfaceted cabochon cut. It gave a soothing,
satiny glow to any stone, no matter what its
value.

"But you're right," Walker agreed. "The color

is good. Too bad they get so few clear ones in the Afghani mines. And most of what they get isn't fine. Too orange."

While Archer listened and Faith dreamed of designs, Walker went through each piece of rough, explaining its origins. Kenya, Sri Lanka, Cambodia, Myanmar, India, Brazil, Afghanistan, Thailand; names and descriptions came easily, concisely, as did the list of each locality's limitations when compared to the fabled pigeon-blood gems from Burma. To make his point even more clearly, Walker put a cut and polished—and cooked—version of each locale's ruby in front of the rough. Many of the gems were quite red, quite clear, quite beautiful.

Then he put one of Faith's badly cut Burmese rubies in front of the others. Light seemed to flow into it, fill it, and shimmer out like a dream.

Archer grunted. "It's like the difference between dyed Akoya pearls and a fine South Seas natural. Once you see the real thing, you'll never go back."

With a sigh, Faith agreed. Nowhere in the world was there a ruby to compare with the Montegeau stone. She groaned.

"What?" Walker asked.

"You've ruined me for other rubies, and I can't afford my taste as it is."

He smiled slowly. "If things work out, you'll

see plenty of these beauties. I'm sure your brother will give you a good price."

"Okay," Archer said. He stood and went back to his desk. "I'll insure the thirteen Montegeau rubies for a million. You go with Faith to Savannah and see if you can cut some kind of deal with her friends on any family jewelry they want to sell, plus any they have in inventory from other estates. Start hitting estates yourself. If that doesn't pan out, get a really long spoon and head for Eastern Europe."

Her brother's words yanked Faith out of her concentration on the extraordinary ruby. "I don't need Walker to go to Savannah. I can—"

"If you want me to insure those rubies," Archer cut in without looking up from a handful of papers, "you'll go with Walker and you'll do everything you can to help him."

Once she would have argued furiously, stormed out of her brother's office, and kept fighting until reality set in. She was older now. Reality was her constant companion. She needed those stones insured. Archer was the only one who could do it fast enough.

"Fine," she said through gritted teeth.

Three seconds later the office door closed behind her. Softly. Too softly.

Walker whistled. "I've seen wet cats in a better mood."

"She'll get over it."

"Easy for you to say. You don't have to spend the next week or two with her."

Archer grinned. "Yeah. Good luck, Walker. You're going to need it."

8

That night Walker sat in front of his computer with a pizza dripping grease in one hand and an icy bottle of beer next to the keyboard, as he scrolled once more through the lists of stolen rubies. Nothing had changed. Nothing had been added.

There were no inquiries about a missing twenty-carat ruby with a secular Mughal inscription.

Frowning, he sipped at the beer. Then he chose another web site, the one he privately referred to as suckers.com. This site was dedicated to gem history, lore, and modern twists on the ancient idea that anything as beautiful as a gem had to be good for whatever ailed man. Having trouble with your boss or your mother-in-law or your pecker? No problem. There was a gem to cure your ills. Just leave your credit card number, and your own personal miracle would arrive by UPS within ten business days. Faster if you wanted to pay for next-day air service.

He searched through the chaff until he came to a link that led to a compilation of more or less legitimate gem legends. Using "ruby" and "carved," he searched the data pool. Most of the references were in Hindi or Arabic, neither of which he could read. Same for Chinese and Russian. He dumped the information into his best translation applications and went on to read the few that were in English.

They all sounded like they would have suited Faith's fussy client. Big, bloodred, and flawless. A few were accompanied by solid documentation—appraisals, detailed descriptions of size, color, clarity, and source. Those stones were presently in public collections or in anonymous private ones. The rest were simply legends that had been passed down through time, with or without the accompanying gem.

Walker took another drink of beer and read through the translations of other ruby myths as they appeared. Some of the machine translations were hilarious, some were inscrutable, but all of them gave enough information for his purposes. Not surprisingly, many of the rubies had ended up as gifts to royalty, as tribute, or as spoils of various wars. Some of the files were accompanied by sketches that were as fanciful as the legends.

Only two of the rubies were described as having been inscribed in India in the time of the Mughals. Only one of them was the right size.

The Heart of Midnight.

He had read that name somewhere on the myths and legends page. He was sure of it. He went back, scrolled until he found it, and read carefully.

According to legend, the Heart of Midnight first appeared in a sixteenth-century Mughal emperor's court. One of his daughters had a mysterious lover who came to her only at midnight, masked in darkness, and left the same way. After a time, deeply in love and angry that he wouldn't reveal his identity, the princess agreed to wed a distant prince. The next night, her lover came to her in her dreams as a dead man whose heart had been cut out.

In the morning the princess was discovered in bed, quite dead. An inscribed blood-red ruby the size of a baby's fist lay in her cold hand. The elegant inscription read: *Beware the Heart of Midnight.*

The stone, replete with its legends of love and death, and the mysterious fire that only the finest rubies own, came to Catherine I from Peter the Great, whose mistress and ultimately wife she became. The ruby was believed to be part of the spoils of the campaign during which Peter the Great conquered the Ottoman Empire. No drawings or paintings of the stone are known to exist. No mention of it has been found since the seventeenth century, when it became part of the Russian imperial collection, though undoubtedly many royal princesses wore the gem to various official functions.

As with many other gems of such size and quality, dire prophecies attach to anyone who dares to own the Heart of Midnight. Perhaps that is why it fell out of favor in the Russian court.

For a long time Walker stared at the computer screen, wondering who had told Ivanovitch to look for a deadly legend in Faith's jewelry shop in Pioneer Square.

And why.

Across the street and up a block, Ivan Ivanovitch, dressed in shabby clothing he had purchased at a Goodwill store, approached one of Seattle's homeless drunks. The man had staked out a recessed doorway as a shelter from the cold, searching wind.

"Move on," the Russian growled. "I need this place."

"Fuck you, asshole," the drunk replied. "I found it first." He raised a shaking fist that was wrapped in rags because he would rather spend the money he got panhandling on booze than gloves.

Ivanovitch stepped inside a staggering punch and seized the drunk by the throat. The stench of cheap wine nearly made him gag as he slid the long, narrow blade of a dagger between the drunk's ribs. The point of the knife found the man's heart. The Russian twisted the blade, maximizing the damage. The victim gasped, more in surprise than in pain. Blood spilled out of the pericardial sac, filling his chest. As he bled to death without spilling a drop, his legs collapsed. He would have fallen to the concrete but for the powerful hand that held him erect.

"Come along, my friend," Ivanovitch murmured quietly. "I told you I needed this place."

The drunk, now all but dead, didn't weigh much. It took little effort to carry him around the corner of the old brick building into an alley filled with trash Dumpsters. To the rest of the world, the two men looked like old friends scuttling off to share a bottle of fortified wine.

Thirty seconds later, Ivanovitch returned alone and took up his watch post in the grimy doorway. He was wrapped in a heavy coat that was cleaner but no less tattered than the blanket he had stolen from the homeless drunk. Like the corpse he had left in a trash bin, Ivanovitch appeared to doze, but he was far from asleep. Beneath the brim of the thrift-store hat, he watched the closed, barred, yet brightly lit window of Timeless Dreams.

Faith Donovan was in her shop, working on a piece of jewelry. A guard was with her, the same competent man who had been there earlier. It would be too risky to try to grab the woman and slice the truth out of her. He had not risen within the deadly world of St. Petersburg's *mafiyas* by yielding to the hot thrill of murder at every opportunity. If the occasion arose, excellent. If not, there were other ways to assure himself that the Heart of Midnight wasn't locked in the woman's shop. One of those ways involved another skill of his: burglary.

Ivanovitch's personal transition from poverty to wealth had occurred in the chaos of a society that was trying to change from a corrupt tyranny to a quasi capitalism. His rapid rise was due to a real skill for violence and early training as a locksmith. He understood locks and safes in the way that a doctor understands metabolism. It made him an excellent burglar. St. Petersburg's elite spent millions on steel and concrete vaults and safes which Ivanovitch happily plundered, contributing to the social turmoil and violence that had created him.

He didn't really care about the ultimate outcome for Russian society—capitalism, socialism, communism, or chaos—because he was confident of his own niche. There were thieves and murderers in every culture.

He was both.

Cold wind gusted, eating through the second-hand socks and running shoes he wore. As a street urchin, he had lost three toes to frostbite. Their stubs, and the remaining whole toes, were exquisitely sensitive to chill. They ached in stabbing time with his heart. He ignored it. He had suffered much worse in St. Petersburg before Tarasov recognized his value. After that, he had risen swiftly from the icy gutters. The trail of blood he left behind only added to his reputation as Tarasov's man.

It was nearly midnight when the lights in Faith Donovan's shop went out. As if by silent command, a car pulled around the corner and stopped in front of Timeless Dreams. The door of the shop opened. Faith's husky voice and soft laughter drifted through the icy rain as she said something to her guard. An emotion that was both lust and something much darker shot through Ivanovitch. He watched the pale flash of her legs beneath her coat as she walked the few steps to the car and slid into the front seat beside the driver.

When the car drove off, Ivanovitch dreamed of the last time he had had such a woman in his bed, under his knife.

Then he dreamed of the next time. Of *her*.

An hour passed, then another, before Ivanovitch decided it was safe to leave the doorway. When he dragged himself to his feet, he didn't have to fake a drunken stagger. His muscles were cramped from making a cold bed on the cement. Carrying a garbage bag full of "possessions," he stumbled into the darkness, using the brick wall of Timeless Dreams for support. Anyone who saw him would assume he was looking for a place to piss.

The cold wind off Elliott Bay had swept the homeless from the alley behind the store. Two or three bare lightbulbs scattered shadows through the night. Bricks, metal pipes, trash bins, and trash gleamed wetly. Leaning against a building that smelled vaguely of urine and grease, Ivanovitch looked around, assuring himself that nothing had changed since he had first checked out the alley.

Everything looked the same. He set down his

trash bag, sorted through its contents, and went to work.

The building had been wired early in the twentieth century. Service lines and alarm circuits were exposed. Even with fingers stiff from cold, Ivanovitch was able to wire a bridge circuit around the alarm box in less than five minutes. After that, breaking in was a matter of force rather than finesse. The back-door lock had a dead bolt and a locking knob. He was through both in less than ninety seconds.

The safe inside was a model familiar in Europe. Ivanovitch knew its strengths. More important, he knew its weaknesses.

Twenty minutes later he was opening smooth steel drawers. His pinpoint flashlight gleamed on gold, silver, and platinum, as well as every shade of the gemstone rainbow. Each time a bloodred stone glittered, the Russian's heartbeat quickened, only to slow again.

The Heart of Midnight was not there.

With one ear listening for sirens or footfalls, he yanked open drawer after drawer. He saw many gems, beautiful gems, gems both loose and set in striking curves and wings of precious metals. They stirred his admiration and his greed, but none of them answered the need that had sent him rushing to America.

When all the drawers in the safe had been ransacked, he went through the drawers in the workbench, through the filing cabinets, through the containers of polish, the tools, the bathroom supplies, the coffee, scattering all of it in growing anger.

He found nothing but polish, tools, toilet paper, and coffee. With a thick Russian curse, he went back to the safe. Quickly, almost indifferently, he took a selection of set and unset gems and stuffed them in his pocket. The finished pieces were too unusual to pawn, but it would be expected that a thief would take some of the biggest pieces. He would dump them in a trash bin and keep the loose gems for pawn.

America was a very expensive place to visit. Some extra cash would be welcome.

The peekaboo light of sun between low, wind-driven clouds flashed through the front window of Timeless Dreams, revealing chaos inside. Walker and Faith could see the mess from the sidewalk out front. Drawers open, safe ajar, equipment and stock scattered everywhere. She made a muffled sound, anger and dismay rolled into one inarticulate growl.

"No." He snatched the keys out of her fingers as she reached for the front-door lock. "There may be somebody still inside. Call the police. Then call Archer."

When the first squad car arrived, the questions began. Faith wanted to scream as the senior officer took notes with fingers that were slowed by chill. She was desperate to be inside her store, taking inventory, finding out how bad the loss was.

Walker was more patient. At least he seemed to be. He leaned on his cane and went over it all again twice, three times, as many times as he was asked.

Archer showed up just as the cops finished securing the scene. Faith didn't notice that he was wearing his shoulder holster under his Levi jacket. Walker noticed and said nothing.

"I'm going to print out an inventory and get to work," Faith said grimly.

"Help is on the way," Archer said, "just as soon as baby-sitters are rounded up."

"Thanks." With a weary smile, she went to the computer and began tapping on keys.

"Leave that for Kyle," Archer said. "You've got a necklace to finish and a trip to pack for."

"I can't go to Savannah now," Faith said impatiently.

"You don't have to leave for three days."

"I still can't go. There isn't enough time."

Archer ignored her, turned to Walker, and spoke softly. "Don't let her out of your sight until you hand her off to Kyle or me. Somebody just found a body a few doors down. A derelict, killed last night."

Walker's eyes narrowed. "I hear you."

"I want her on that plane to Savannah," Archer continued in a low voice. "She'll fight it, but she'll lose."

Walker nodded.

"Anything happens, let me know first," Archer said.

"I will."

Archer didn't doubt it. He headed for the front door with the stride of a man looking for some butt to kick.

Walker was grateful it wasn't his.

"I can't go to the show and leave this mess!" Faith called after Archer. "And if I clean up the mess, I won't have time to finish the necklace!"

"Finish the necklace," Archer said. "I'll take care of the cleanup."

"But—" She was talking to the door. She kicked an empty can of polishing grit, sending it flying with a clatter against the bench. *"Damn.* I can't just leave my shop!"

"The guy who's paying the bills outvoted you," Walker said easily.

"But—" she began again.

"Relax, sugar," he interrupted. "You promised Mel her necklace and you promised you would be at her wedding. And you worked your butt off for this show. You're the only designer west of the Rockies to be invited. You should be there smiling and charming the buyers, not wringing your hands in Seattle over something you can't change."

"How did you know about the invitation?"

He wiped his grit-covered hands on his jeans and began putting tools back on the workbench. "Archer loves bragging about his clever, beautiful little sister."

"Beautiful? Yeah. Right." She raked one hand through her hair. She had slept badly and had barely taken time to put on mascara before rushing to work. "What does he call me—a swizzle stick with boyish charm?"

Walker glanced at her over a handful of tools. Faith didn't have the expectant look of a woman fishing for compliments. Whatever she saw in her mirror didn't look beautiful to her.

And what Walker saw sure as hell didn't look like a swizzle stick.

"They say love is blind," he muttered. "Lordy. The average woman looking in a mirror can't see worth spit."

"What?"

"Archer thinks you're beautiful," Walker said clearly.

She smiled and ran her fingers through her short hair again. The nails were clean, short, and freshly buffed. She didn't wear polish if she could avoid it. Ten minutes at her workbench usually destroyed a thirty-dollar manicure. "Since Hannah, Archer thinks the world is beautiful."

"Don't kid yourself. His teeth are as hard and sharp as ever."

Faith didn't answer. She was drumming her fingers on the workbench and looking around, making mental lists.

"Whatever is missing, your insurance will—" Walker began.

"It can't replace my inventory," she cut in. "Most of my stones, like all of my designs, are one of a kind."

"Which will just make it easier to find anything that's stolen and then fenced. Kyle will spam the Internet and the local shops with descriptions. There's nothing you can do to help except go to this show, blow them out of their designer socks, and get a million bucks in orders."

"You make it sound so simple."

"With your talent, a million *is* simple."

Slowly she turned and focused on Walker rather than her trashed shop. She had become quite good at picking out lies from truth, thanks to her ex-fiancé. Walker was telling the truth as he saw it.

He really admired her work.

"Thank you," she said simply. "I needed that. You're a nice man, Owen Walker."

"There you go."

He smiled and hoped she kept on believing

that. It would make the job of keeping her out of trouble so much simpler if she didn't fight him every inch of the way.

❧

The Federal Building in Seattle looked like what it was, a workplace designed and executed by bureaucrats. Beige, beige, beige. Square. Beige. There was a different-colored stripe of paint at eye level on each floor. It was supposed to provide visual relief, but instead added the final institutional touch, making the place feel like a hospital or jail.

Behind boring doors and down boring corridors, reams of boring papers were shuffled, stamped, copied, and filed. A few of the doors led to interesting offices whose files weren't copied and whose budgets weren't approved by Congress.

One of those offices was run by a lithe, dark-haired woman named April Joy. She wasn't nearly as lighthearted as her name.

She looked up from a fax that had just arrived, a list of stolen gems forwarded to her by a contact in the Seattle Police Department.

"The fool! The fucking idiot! Why did he put his ass on the line for a handful of gems?"

Maxmillian Barton listened with an assassin's blankness. He had worked for April Joy long enough to know she would be furious when she learned that the right-hand man of her best *mafiya* contact was on the verge of being arrested for burglary.

"I think he was looking for something else," Barton said quietly. "When he didn't find it, he tried to make the job look like a routine burglary to cover his tracks."

"But why didn't he just flush the goddamn stones down the nearest manhole?" the woman demanded. "Why did he run right out and try to hock them?"

Barton shrugged. "Maybe the pawnshop squad doesn't work so fast in Leningrad. Or is it St. Petersburg? I forget."

April Joy shot him a look that would have wilted the ordinary federal bureaucrat, but Barton didn't flinch. He liked his fiercely temperamental boss, as a colleague and as a woman. Despite her small, slender build, she had the strength of a fine samurai sword, with a tongue and temper to match. Today she wore a red pantsuit that fit real well. Even the electronic ID card hanging around her neck didn't detract from her sensual impact.

"This guy is Tarasov's chief lieutenant. He came in yesterday afternoon on the Aeroflot flight from Magadan carrying a passport in the name of Ivan Ivanovitch, U.S. citizen," Barton said. "Somebody made him at Customs in Anchorage, but we let him come through, just to see what he was up to. I had him followed to his hotel and from there to Faith Donovan's shop down in Pioneer Square."

April Joy grimaced. "Donovan again. Christ. Every time I turn around I'm tripping over one of them. What did the Russian want with her?"

"A present for his mother's name day."

"Bullshit."

Barton smiled like what he was, a middle-aged, balding shark whose teeth were still deadly as ever. "That's his story and he's sticking with it. He's cute. Really, really cute. After he met with the Donovan woman, he checked into the Olympic, slipped the bellman a hundred bucks to have a girl sent up. My guys kept watching the room, figuring he wouldn't go out until after the girl left, but apparently he paid her five hundred bucks to spend the night alone."

April was swearing softly, but she was listening.

"In the meantime, he slipped out disguised as a maintenance man. He had the run of the city until an hour ago, when we made him coming back. He had the pawn tickets for a bunch of stolen gems in his pocket, plus a couple grand in cash. Just about the time we popped him, Seattle PD began circulating that list. The pawn tickets and the list match."

"Have the cops tumbled to him?"

"Not yet, but it's probably only a matter of

time before somebody does. Kyle Donovan papered the city with descriptions. He's offering a reward for the goods and a bigger one for the thief."

"Ivanovitch is a bloody stupid bastard," April said. "If he needed money, he should have come to us."

"Maybe he heard about government budget cutbacks."

"Maybe he's just a bloody stupid bastard. Make sure the pawnshop doesn't try to collect the reward from the Donovan family."

"Already taken care of. I redeemed the goods myself."

"Any sign that the shop owner tried to call the Donovans?"

"If he did, it was on a secure phone. We didn't pick it up."

"Good enough. Send Ivanovitch in to me. Then get Tarasov on the line. When you do, put him through to me and stay on the line. I can handle Russian, but all these thugs talk Chechen when they want to be discreet."

Ivanovitch walked in a few moments later. He had disposed of his thrift-shop wardrobe and was once again dressed as a well-off *mafiya* lordling—Italian leather overcoat, gloves, navy-blue French wool suit, and a slate-gray silk shirt handmade in Hong Kong. Sleek Italian shoes, a charcoal hat, and an impressive diamond ring finished off his ensemble.

He didn't remove his hat.

"Why did you rob Faith Donovan?" April asked coolly.

"I was—how do you say it?—framed."

"I'm not—how do you say it?—stupid," she shot back. "You're one answer away from having your smart ass deported. Now, try again. Why did you rob Faith Donovan's shop?"

He shrugged and continued looking her right in the eye. "Money. Why else?"

That was progress, of a sort.

"My assistant is getting Marat Borisovitch Tarasov on the phone," she said. "If I don't like his answers any better than yours, I'm putting you on the next flight for Siberia." She smiled. "And I'll make certain that Dmitry Sergeyev Solokov meets your plane."

For a fraction of a second, Ivanovitch looked uneasy. This woman was well informed. Solokov was Tarasov's worst enemy, closest competitor, and the man who was presently trying to hang Tarasov with a noose called the Heart of Midnight.

April's feline smile told Ivanovitch that April Joy was following his thoughts as easily as if he had spoken them aloud.

"I will talk to Marat Borisovitch," Ivanovitch said after a moment.

"You do that, babe." She looked up as Barton came into the room. "You get him?"

"Line three. He's impatient. He was on his way to dinner."

"Missing a meal might save him a coronary."

She sat behind a gray steel desk that looked like it came from Navy surplus and picked up the phone.

Ivanovitch waited with outward patience until April put the conversation on the speaker phone. For several minutes she listened while the Russian in Seattle tried to explain his predicament to a Russian six thousand miles away. The more April heard, the more she smiled. She had been waiting a long time to get a really good hook into Marat Borisovitch Tarasov. The Heart of Midnight would work just fine.

And if Faith Donovan was caught with a stolen piece of Russian cultural heritage in her hands, it would be the answer to April Joy's prayers. She would finally have a twist on the Donovan family. No more trading occasional favors—Uncle Sam would flat damn own the Donovans.

But first April had to get the Donovans to do her a favor. She would give them a day or two to get over the shock of the robbery and begin to total up the losses. Then, when she appeared with the stolen goods, Archer Donovan would be in a mood to listen.

"You're smiling," Barton said as the door

closed behind Ivanovitch, one more wolf sent out to play among the civilian lambs.

"Yeah."

"You really think the Donovans are handling hot jewelry?"

"As long as I can put a collar and a leash on that family, I don't give a damn what they traffic in."

A steaming cup of coffee appeared underneath Kyle's nose. He had been staring at computer chips and motherboards for eighteen hours straight. He blinked and looked up. Slowly Archer's face came into focus.

Kyle grabbed the coffee. "I need this more than you do."

"You're welcome. Faith leaves tomorrow for Savannah. How does your gut feel about it?"

Kyle pushed his chair away from the mess of electronic components that covered the table of his workshop, which occupied the floor just above the parking garage in the Donovan condo. To other people, the room looked like the aftermath of an earthquake, hurricane, or explosion. To Kyle, it was the one place where things stayed wherever he put them, no matter how illogical that place might seem to anyone else. In this room he had no problems finding whatever he wanted, whenever he wanted it. For instance, the rat's nest scattered across the metal table would soon be a complex, high-tech alarm system for Timeless Dreams.

Faith had finally agreed to let her brother do what he had wanted to do since she had opened the shop—make it secure.

"My gut is still unhappy," Kyle said. He wrapped long fingers around the mug, sipped, and sighed.

"Is your gut better or worse than before?"

"Worse. Why?"

"I talked to the police. They agree that it was an unusual burglary, but not that unusual."

Kyle grunted. Blond hair fell over one eyebrow. He tossed his head impatiently and wondered if Hannah would cut his hair. She sure kept Archer's trim. "So?"

"When I pointed out that a drunk was knifed the same night just a few doors down from Faith's shop, they shrugged."

"Shit happens?" Kyle asked.

"Yeah. I couldn't talk about the professional knife work without letting them know that we have had access to their investigative files."

"The cops think it was just a lucky stab, is that it?" Kyle said dryly.

Archer's eyes looked less inviting than the winter night outside the window. "A hit that killed almost instantly and spilled less than a teaspoon of blood on the sidewalk? That isn't luck. That's something that scares the hell out of me."

"I imagine it scares the hell out of Walker, too, since he has the bodyguard duty on our unruly little sister. Maybe she should stay home instead of going to Savannah tomorrow."

"Would that make your gut feel better?" Archer asked.

Kyle hesitated, swore, and set the coffee aside. "I doubt it. I think trouble might be following our Faith."

"Why?" Archer asked sharply.

"If I knew, really knew, I'd be picking lottery numbers, not messing about with chips and circuit boards." With that, Kyle went back to the project on his bench.

Archer watched, but in his mind's eye he could see again the postmortem photo of the dead drunk on the autopsy table. The knife work had been precise, bloodless, and very, very final.

It was the calling card of a professional assassin.

I think trouble might be following our Faith.

Savannah

Faith had been in the rented Jeep Cherokee twenty minutes before she finally lost her temper. It wasn't the strange city or lost baggage or traffic jams or any of the usual annoyances of traveling that made her angry. It was a soft-voiced, easy-moving, polite, and impossibly stubborn southerner called Owen Walker.

She had been able to ignore him while she was working sixteen hours a day to complete the Montegeau necklace. But she was finished now, and Walker was still there, still close, still getting under her skin like nettles or dreams.

Despite the anger seething through her blood, her voice was even as she turned toward him. "You're being completely unreasonable."

"Your brother gave the orders, not me. Talk to him."

"He's in Seattle."

"Always knew that boy was shrewd," Walker drawled.

She locked her teeth together, then carefully forced her jaw to relax. If she kept grinding her teeth, she would have hell's own headache. Just one of the small, memorable lessons life with Tony had taught her. She took a slow, deep breath. Then another. Then a third and a fourth and a fifth.

If arguing with Walker would have changed anything, Faith would have jumped right in. But she really needed to yell at Archer, and he was out of reach. Walker wasn't necessarily being an idiot. He was just following idiotic orders.

While Walker waited at a stop sign for a catering truck to clear the intersection, he eyed Faith warily. All the Donovans he had met, except her, had enough temper for two people. But it was looking like Faith was a Donovan through and through. She had a real temper. She was just a hell of a lot more careful about exercising it than her siblings.

He wondered why. The Donovans were very much a fight, hug, and make-up type of family. None of them liked to sulk and fester.

"Why," Faith asked finally, her voice cool and calm, "should I come to a lovely, historic city like Savannah and then stay in some soulless modern hotel? Especially when I've already told my professional contacts that I can be reached at the Gold Room of the Live Oak Bed and Breakfast?"

Walker decided that he would rather have had an explosion than the remote politeness that frosted every word she spoke. The silvery blue of her eyes reminded him of glacier ice high in the mountains of Afghanistan. Cold enough to freeze a man's nuts if he got too close.

"Everyone who knows where you are also knows where the rubies are," he said. "It's after six. The sun is down, the banks are closed, and the jewelry exposition building won't be open until tomorrow."

"There's a safe at the Live Oak B and B. I made sure of it before I made reservations."

"Uh-huh," he agreed, not impressed a bit. "I've seen those antique safes with their black doors and fancy gold lettering. Any ol' boy with sensitive fingers and brass balls could have those rubies in less time than it takes you to put on makeup."

"First that ol' boy would have to know the rubies are in the safe," she retorted.

He stifled a smile. "Amen. That's why we're going to—"

"A different historic inn," Faith cut in. "Savannah is full of them."

He thought about arguing, then decided to save his energy for a fight that really mattered.

"Sure thing, sugar," he drawled. "Got any particular place in mind?"

"I'm working on it, *sugar.*"

She turned on the overhead light and flipped quickly through the Savannah guidebook she had purchased at the airport bookstore. Riverfront sounded good. She looked at the map in the center of the book, then at the next street sign she saw. The historically accurate streetlights were elegant and atmospheric, but they didn't illuminate much. The park squares were even darker. Finally she located her position on the map.

"Turn left at the next corner," she said.

"Nope."

Her head snapped up. "Why not?"

"One way. The wrong way."

"Oh." She looked at the map and adjusted quickly. "Turn left at the block after that one. If it's still going the wrong way, just take the first one that isn't."

"Where am I going?"

"Is that the opening gambit of a philosophical discussion?"

He smiled a flat kind of smile. "Folks that don't finish high school don't have much use for high-flyin' discussions."

She winced at the really strong twang in his voice. She was discovering that his accent deepened when he was irritated. Which meant that, once again, her sense of humor had pissed off a man.

The good news was that she wasn't dating Walker. If that sometimes seemed like the bad news, too, she had better get over it, fast. Any non-Donovan man who could make her lose her temper without even trying was someone she should avoid.

"If lack of a diploma bothers you that much, why don't you do something about it?" she asked neutrally.

"It doesn't." Not usually. But somehow it bothered Walker with Faith. He would have to think about that. "I've met a lot of dumb folks with advanced degrees. I've met some smart ones that never finished middle school. And vice versa. It's the person, not the paper, that matters." He turned left. "I hope this is the street you wanted. Master Oglethorpe must have been sucking up bourbon and branch water when he laid out this town."

She looked at the street sign. "This is the one. And what do you mean? The old part of town is beautifully laid out. The squares are magnificent. Centuries-old oaks and magnolias and all that lovely moss, plus flowers and monuments and even some fountains. According to the guidebook, there will be azaleas and camellias blooming everywhere in a month or so."

"The squares are nice enough if you go for that sort of thing," he said, giving her a sideways glance to judge how well she was taking the bait, "but you have to zigzag around them like a drunk to get from one place to another. Damned inefficient, if you ask me."

" 'Nice enough if you like that sort of thing,' " she repeated under her breath.

She started to explain to him about barbarians who couldn't appreciate civilized amenities such as historic, shady squares interrupting and slowing down modern traffic. Even as she opened her mouth, she sensed the leashed anticipation in him. At that instant he reminded her of her closest brother, Kyle, when he thought he was going to sucker one of his sisters into a just-for-the-hell-of-it argument.

"Yes," she said smoothly, "I guess they are. Keep zigzagging like a drunk until you find a way down to the riverfront."

"Where are we going?"

"It's a secret. You might find a way to steal the rubies if I tell you ahead of time."

"Have you forgotten that I'm, uh, wearing the rubies right now?"

Humor flickered through her as she remembered where the ruby necklace was—wrapped in a chamois pouch that was tucked in a smuggler's pocket in his underwear. He didn't clang when he walked, but he did look a little like he had spent his youth on horseback.

"Hardly," Faith said. "Brings new meaning to the concept of family jewels."

He smiled a slow, easy kind of smile. "Sure does. Are you going to put that on the exhibit card in the show?"

"I don't think there's a category for most unusual method of transport."

"Nothing unusual about it. An old Pakistani taught it to me. And it's not the worst place in the world to carry contraband. In fact, smugglers sometimes get much more, uh, *personal* about hiding small stuff."

"I'm not going there," she said firmly.

"Neither is your necklace."

Struggling not to laugh, she let go of a long breath and the subject at the same time. He had topped her again. With or without diplomas, Walker was quicker on his verbal feet than anyone she had ever been around but her siblings.

That shouldn't have surprised her. Someone who could clean Archer out in a poker game was hardly stupid.

Walker turned off the boulevard onto a steeply slanting cobblestone street that looked as old as some of the massive oaks. The Jeep bumped along happily, more at home on an uneven surface than on city streets.

"There," Faith said, pointing to the right.

She directed him onto a narrow cobbled roadway that dropped down the face of a stone revetment. The rock face held an eroding bluff in place. On the other side of the narrow road, a row of two- and three-story buildings lined the lower bank of the Savannah River. At one time the buildings had been riverfront factories or warehouses chock-full of goods and cursing stevedores. Now they had been converted into pricey inns, shops, and restaurants.

Walker parked beside a white Cadillac, directly in front of a no-parking sign. Before he even turned the engine off, Faith got out and headed for the black awning and beveled glass doors of the Savannah River Inn.

"I'll stay here and guard the goods," he told the empty car. "Yeah, I'll just do that little thing. No, no problem. We're here to serve."

He turned the key enough to kill the engine, keep the radio awake, and run down the automatic windows. A whiff of southern river floated in over the hot pavement and engine smells. Savannah was enjoying a run of unseasonably warm weather. Not enough to bring the bugs out yet. Just enough to begin thickening the sky with humidity, forerunner of the blazing quicksilver heat haze that settled each summer over the Low Country like an insistent lover.

Little white lights danced in the winter-bare branches of the ornamental trees on either side of the inn's entrance. Up on the bluff, a live oak spread its massive arms, embracing the night. Streetlight picked out the resurrection ferns that clung like orchids along the broadest branches. Right now there was nothing pretty about the ferns. Shriveled, withered, brittle with drought, the ferns were curled in on themselves, waiting numbly for life-giving rain. When water finally came, the ferns would stretch and grow green, rippling gracefully with renewed life.

But that was a month or two away. Tonight the ferns simply waited and hung on to the half life that was all drought permitted.

A car cruised slowly up the alley. Automatically Walker watched the vehicle close in. Then he saw the light bar across the top of the American sedan.

The cop ignored the illegally parked Jeep. He was used to late check-ins, and Savannah had learned to make allowances for tourists, especially in the off-season.

The gentle, warm, humid breeze flowed through the windows, as familiar to Walker as the shape of his own hands. The air smelled of the boundary where freshwater met salt, where pines gave way to marsh grasses, and hot days became velvet nights. Except for the city sounds and the lights blocking out the stars, he could have been back in Ruby Bayou, soft-footing it through the night with a .22-caliber rifle in one hand and hunger in his belly.

He and his brother had fished, shrimped, oystered, and trapped crawdads with equal success, but even allowing for the fact that Lot was four years younger, Walker always had been the better shot. It was a matter of patience. Lot didn't have much.

The lack had killed him.

Walker closed his eyes against a shaft of pain that had dulled but never vanished in the years since Lot's death. Walker had stood over his brother's barren, windswept grave and vowed never again to be responsible for any life but his own.

He had kept that vow, despite the loneliness that echoed through him as surely as drought through the crumpled resurrection ferns.

"Wakey, wakey," Faith said.

He opened his eyes. The fairy lights of the inn silhouetted Faith in rippling gold and turned her bright cap of hair into a halo. Her eyes were a silver mist shot through with twilight blue. Her gardenia-and-woman scent brought everything masculine in him to full alert.

He felt the smuggler's pouch between his legs with painful clarity. "I'm awake."

Walker's husky voice tickled Faith's nerves like a warm, teasing breeze. She realized she was leaning too close, as though she was going to nuzzle his sleek dark beard to see if it felt half as velvety as it looked. Startled by her own thoughts, she straightened and drew back, but not before she caught a scent of soap and vital, warm male.

"They didn't have any adjoining rooms," she said.

"That's the nice thing about soulless hotels, they—" he began.

"So I took the last room," she cut in. "It's a suite. We flipped for the foldout bed. You lost."

"I don't remember flipping any coin."

"Memory is the second thing to go."

"Do tell," he said. "What's the first?"

"I forget." She smiled at the look on his face and then laughed out loud. "Come on. You can see the river from the window and there's a great big ship coming up the channel. It looks like it's close enough to touch."

Walker thought of all the huge freighters that came and went from Elliott Bay. Anyone with eyes could look out of the Donovan buildings and count ships from all over the world. But Faith was excited, as though she lived in a desert and never saw anything bigger than a puddle. Her enthusiasm was contagious. Like her smile.

"Besides, there are two other conventions in town," Faith said, "so the place is jammed. We wouldn't have gotten this room if someone hadn't canceled at the last minute."

"Speaking of that, you should—"

"I canceled the B and B as soon as I took this room," she said quickly.

"Did you leave a forwarding address?"

She almost had, but she wasn't going to admit it. "Just the booth at the jewelry show. And I called home, of course."

Walker wasn't worried about the Donovans knowing where Faith was. It was the greedy folks who knew she had a million in anonymous rubies that worried him. "Good. I'd hate to have to drag you off to some less historic place out on the highway just to get a night's sleep."

"When you talk to Archer—"

"Who says I'm going to?" Walker asked quickly.

"Experience," she retorted. "Remind him that I'm billing Donovan International for the deposit I lost at the Live Oak place, just like I'm billing DI for the whole trip to Savannah."

"You're not going to split it down the middle?"

"If Archer wants things his way, he can damn well pay the freight."

"There you go. Do they have a safe here?"

"Yes, but there's a ten-thousand-dollar limit on their insurance."

Walker sighed. Wearing a ruby necklace next to his skin—no matter how carefully wrapped the jewelry might be—wasn't comfortable. The necklace was beautifully articulated. It folded into a remarkably small packet. But he was sensitive in the places that the chamois bag was hidden. More sensitive at moments like this than he wanted to admit.

Faith's lips shifted into a smile. "Is something, um, chafing?"

"I've lived with worse. At least Archer isn't insuring the rest of your jewelry for this soiree," Walker said. "If I had to wear any more of your creations this way, I'd have to hop down the street like a rabbit."

He eased out of the car and shut the door behind him. He walked stiffly toward the back of the Jeep. His leg hadn't liked being crammed into an airline seat.

Faith reached past Walker into the cargo area. She grabbed her suitcase and the custom-made aluminum case that held the other pieces she would be displaying at the Savannah Modern Jewelry Exposition.

"I'm not too crippled up to carry your baggage," he said.

"Neither am I."

"This is the South. Women don't carry their own things."

"Men carry purses here?" she asked, widening her eyes dramatically.

Giving up, Walker got out his duffel bag and cane and followed her up the short, steep porch stairs to the inn entrance. He beat her to the door handle, opened it, and gave her a hard grin as she walked by. She gave it right back.

"This way," she said.

Memorizing every detail of the access to the inn, he followed her to a numbered door at the end of a short hall. Two other rooms opened off the hall. The lock on their suite wasn't as old as the building, but it wasn't modern, either. He would have preferred an electronic dead bolt.

The chain lock was no better. One swift kick would pull the puny screws out of the casement. In the South, history meant dry rot. Walker preferred up-to-date steel.

"Beautiful," Faith said, looking around. "Rose and green and cream. Such elegantly textured wallpaper, like silk. And the wainscoting looks original."

"Doubt it. Old riverfront factories were real short on frills even when they were new. This paneling probably came out of an old hotel teardown or some new outfit that specializes in historical reproductions."

She barely heard the southern pragmatist talking beside her. This was her first taste of the historic South and she was enjoying it. "Look at the ceiling. The edges are sculpted with floral designs. Do you suppose it's the original plaster?"

"Hope not. This climate rots plaster almost as fast as meat. The floor is original, though."

Glancing at her feet, Faith saw only a lush,

modern wall-to-wall carpet. Expensive, very taste-
ful, but not a bit of flooring was in sight. "How
can you tell?"

"The way it drapes over the support beams.
You don't get that kind of sag in less than a
century."

"You really would have preferred soulless
modern."

"Wrong. But that doesn't mean I don't know
the difference between a level floor and this
one."

Walker looked at the overstuffed, subtly flowered couch that would be his bed. He hoped
that the fold-out mattress was harder than the
cushions, but he doubted it. Absently he rubbed
the stiff muscles of his thigh. "Next time I flip
the coin for the bed."

She bit her lip against a smile until she turned
and saw that he was kneading his hurt leg. Guilt
washed through her. She was angry with Archer
for being unfair in wielding his corporate power,
yet she was punishing Walker for her brother's
arbitrary decision. Talk about unfair.

"I'll take the couch," she said. "I wasn't
thinking."

There was a flash of deep blue as Walker's
glance cut back to her. "What weren't you thinking about?"

"Your leg."

"It's fine."

"You're rubbing it."

"Want to do it for me?"

Her eyes narrowed. "I should take you up on it, just to watch you squirm."

"Anytime, sugar."

"Okay. Right now. Facedown," she said, pointing toward the floor.

"What?"

"Facedown on the floor." She flexed her hands and smiled in anticipation. "I just finished a three-month course in deep-muscle massage."

His dark eyebrows shot up. "Why?"

"Same reason I took courses in metallurgy and Celtic art and ancient roses and Sun Tzu's theory of war and the migration pattern of birds."

"And that reason would be?"

"I was curious."

Walker laughed softly. "I'll bet you get lost on the Net for hours at a time."

"Net? As in computers?"

"Sure."

"Not a chance. I had all the computer I'll ever need in college. I called it the Antichrist. That's when I was feeling good about it."

"You really do all your design work by hand?" he asked, surprised.

"Beats having three weeks of work booted into the ether because the Antichrist burped." She shrugged. "Kyle got the computer gene in our family. He can make them sit up and do tricks that I'm sure are illegal."

Walker had firsthand reason to know that some of Kyle's skills could land him in federal prison, but didn't say anything to Faith about it. Sometimes ignorance was indeed bliss.

"Facedown," she said. "I'll have that leg loosened up in no time."

"This is going to hurt, isn't it?"

"What makes you think so?"

"Your alligator smile."

"Maybe I'm just dying to get my hands on your body."

"Yeah, and alligators cry," he said. But he eased himself onto the floor. Even if it hurt, it had to feel better coming from her hands than from his own.

"Where does it hurt?" she asked.

"Everywhere."

"Well, that sure helps." She knelt beside him and began running her fingertips over his left thigh, testing for soreness. "Where does it hurt the most?"

Walker didn't think she wanted to hear about the ache in his crotch, and he was damn well sure he shouldn't be talking about it. "Midthigh, in front, and just above the knee."

"Gotcha."

He drew a sharp breath as her fingers closed around his upper thigh. "I said the *knee*."

"If I started there, you'd go through the roof. Some things have to be worked up to."

Walker bit his tongue and settled in to endure an interesting kind of torture.

10

She awoke to terror.

Steel fingers dug into her throat, choking her. Her cheeks burned even as something hot and wet slid thickly down to the lace-trimmed sheets. Something sliced down her arm in a trail of fire. She couldn't move, couldn't cry out, could only lie rigid with fear while a rough voice demanded over and over: *"The ruby! Where is it! Tell me or you will die."*

She told him all that she knew.

She died anyway, painfully, watching her killer's fixed, glittering eyes.

On the opening day of the Savannah Modern Jewelry Exposition, Faith and Walker were up early. She turned on the TV and headed for the shower while Walker went out and scrounged breakfast. He was back before she was finished drying her hair. He balanced the coffee and doughnuts, opened the door, and kicked it shut behind him. The TV and the hair dryer competed for his attention.

"This just in from reporter Barry Miller, live from the murder scene at Live Oak Bed and Breakfast, one of Savannah's most exclusive B and Bs."

Swiftly Walker went to the set and turned down the sound. He didn't want Faith to over-hear, but he sure was interested.

The TV picture switched from the cheerful, well-scrubbed news reader to a suitably rumpled and solemn-looking field reporter. Behind him, several police squad cars and detective units were parked haphazardly, blocking a street. Yellow crime-scene tape was strung in several directions like a modern cliché. Barry Miller held the microphone and looked directly into the camera.

"Words can't describe the savagery of the act. The knife-wielding murderer, or murderers, apparently came in through the bedroom window of the Gold Room, tortured the victim, and finally killed her. Ironically, the victim, whose name is being withheld pending notification of

family, had obtained a room only because of a last-minute cancellation.

"Police are baffled by the brutal crime. No one saw anything or heard anything. Though the victim's wallet was taken and the downstairs safe was robbed, the police aren't saying that was the motive for the murder. They are presently seeking the victim's former husband and ex-boyfriend for questioning.

"We'll stay with this story and bring you updates as they happen. Barry Miller reporting from the murder scene at the Live Oak Bed and Breakfast. Back to you, Cherry."

The picture cut back to the studio. Walker flipped quickly around the channels, found nothing more, and turned off the set. The hair dryer shut off a moment later.

"Why did you kill the TV?" Faith asked as she came out of the bathroom. "I wanted to see if the expo got any local news coverage."

Walker looked up and was forced to swallow hard. Faith was dressed for work. Heels skyscraper-high. A cool silk blouse that matched the silver-blue of her eyes, rough silk skirt and jacket of a darker shade of blue, and sleek hair the color of a summer sun. She wore a pin of her own creation, combining opals and a beautiful baroque black pearl in a design that was neither shell nor sea, but suggested both.

"I thought you'd like to sit out along the river

and have a quiet breakfast before the mob scene," Walker said. "It's real pretty out."

She grabbed her purse and headed for the door. "What are you waiting for?"

The riverside walk was warm by Seattle standards, but the dew point was so high that Faith and Walker could see their own breath. Over her objections, he took off his sport coat and made a clean seat for her on the bench, telling her that she couldn't show beautiful jewelry wearing a dirty skirt.

Anticipating the turmoil of the trade show, Faith was grateful for Walker's easy, silent companionship. She didn't have to worry about making conversation or entertaining him. He was content with the morning and his own thoughts. In blissful peace, she ate her crumb doughnuts and drank the cinnamon latte he had brought her.

Where sunlight managed to spear through the evergreen leaves of live oak and the lacy scarves of Spanish moss, the sun had enough intensity to make Seattle skin tingle. Walker didn't notice the intense sunlight. He was thinking about the TV news. Nothing he was thinking made him smile, but he was careful to conceal that from Faith.

"What was the name of the B and B you were planning to stay at last night?" Walker asked idly.

"Live Oak. I had the Gold Room, reputed to be identical to a southern belle's bedroom in the 1840s." She took another sip of latte. "Why?"

Yawning, Walker stretched and let the sun beat down on his face. It didn't warm the ice in his gut. "Archer will expect a report and I couldn't remember the name." Not quite true, but close enough to pass muster. He would be reporting to Archer shortly, and the name of the Live Oak B and B would definitely be part of the conversation. "You about ready to go?"

"Another sip or two."

Walker gathered up his paper coffee cup and their paper napkins and stuffed them in the doughnut bag. He moved more easily than he had yesterday, thanks to Faith's skilled, surprisingly strong fingers. The fact that it had taken him hours to fall asleep afterward was his fault, not hers. She had never offered anything more sensual than a therapeutic massage.

He kept telling himself it was better that way. His mind believed it. His body didn't.

Faith drained the last of her latte, licked her lips, and sighed. Somehow, in a city of iced tea and drip-coffee drinkers, her unwanted escort had found an espresso place and then begged the cinnamon from the inn's kitchen. For himself, he drank the bitter brewed southern coffee with every evidence of pleasure. Of course, he had been raised on the stuff.

"Ready as I'll ever be," she said, crumpling her cup.

"Not quite."

"What?"

Walker's thumb brushed lightly over the corner of her mouth. "Crumbs."

Faith's heartbeat hitched. Then it raced. The touch had been casual rather than seductive, yet the warmth of his skin against hers made her head swim. She wondered what it would feel like to be his lover. She had wondered the same thing last night, while she probed and smoothed his surprisingly muscular thigh. "Er, thanks. How's my lipstick holding up?"

His dark blue glance moved lazily over her mouth, making her feel as though she had been touched again. Slowly.

"Looking good from here," he said after a moment. "But you might want to check for yourself. Your lips have so much color it's hard for me to tell where you leave off and the lipstick begins."

She stood up briskly. "People will be looking at my jewelry, not me."

"The women, sure." He grabbed his sport coat, shook it out, and put it on. "The men are going to love that outfit. All pale and silky and touch-me soft. And those high heels . . ." He shook his head slowly. "Sugar, what those shoes do to your legs is downright sinful."

She looked at herself. She had picked the outfit because it was comfortable and had a matching jacket in case the main room's thermostat was set for men wearing suits. The shoes were left over from a time when she had tried to please Tony by wearing heels high enough to give her legs a sexy curve.

"What they do to my arches is sinful," she said. "By the end of the day I'll be whimpering."

"Then why wear them?"

"They make my legs look less skinny."

"Skinny?" Walker couldn't have concealed his surprise if a big poker pot had depended on it. "You had your eyes checked lately?"

"Yes."

"Try another optometrist. Your legs are—" *enough to make a man's palms sweat* "—just fine the way they are. Both feet touch the ground, right?"

"Last time I looked."

"There you go. What more could anyone ask?"

She smiled and held out her hand to him before she could think better of it. "C'mon. You can help me set up my booth."

He had been prepared to insist on just that and was relieved it wouldn't be necessary. The longer he was around her, the more at ease she became. By the end of the day, she would be treating him like one of her brothers.

If that irritated him as much as it made his job of protecting the rubies easier, he would get over it. They would be living in each other's pockets until she went back to Seattle. Better that they play at being brother and sister than lovers.

Yeah. Right.

All he had to do was keep telling himself that, just as he had kept telling himself last night that he couldn't hear her undress, couldn't smell gardenias and woman whispering out to him, couldn't count her breaths slowing and deepening until she fell asleep.

He really should have let her close the door to her bedroom. That way he might have gotten some sleep, too. But he doubted it. Falling asleep with a hard-on was a bitch.

Walker stood up, moving more slowly than necessary. He sensed that at some unconscious feminine level, Faith was reassured by his appearance of physical weakness. The only reason he could think of for that made him want to have a short, brutal chat with her ex-fiancé.

With subdued anger, Walker stuffed the remains of their riverside breakfast into a trash can. He picked up his cane in one hand. With the other, he casually took Faith's hand. Instead of interlacing their fingers hard and deep the way he wanted, he squeezed gently before releasing her.

"C'mon," he said. "Let's go show those folks at the expo what quality jewelry looks like."

He picked up the aluminum case that held nine of the ten pieces she would display in her booth. The tenth piece—the ruby necklace—was where it had been since Seattle, tucked right next to the Walker family jewels.

Which, at the moment, felt as hard as stones. Those shoes of hers really should have been outlawed, right along with her sexy fragrance and her wary, fallen-angel eyes.

"Is your leg still stiff?" Faith asked, eyeing Walker's drawn expression.

He almost asked her which one. "It'll ease up."

"I'll work on it again tonight."

"No need."

"Don't deprive me. I enjoy watching you grit your teeth and suffer in macho silence. It gives me a feeling of great power to make a grown man cry."

"I knew you were a sadist." But he was smiling. His leg really did feel better.

Even before Faith and Walker left the bench, sparrows flitted out of the trees and started vacuuming crumbs. The tiny birds all but landed on Faith's toes.

"Bold, aren't they?" she said.

"They can't afford to be shy. The bigger birds will be along real quick. Then the sparrows are slam out of luck."

"Hardly seems fair."

He gave her a sideways look. "Whatever made you think survival was fair?"

She opened her mouth, sighed, and said, "I keep hoping, even though I know better."

The corner of his mouth kicked up. "Hope all

you want, sugar. Just keep your eyes wide open while you do."

❧

Walker leaned against the classy rose and gold wall at the back of Faith's booth. The showroom was the size of a big hotel lobby and laid out in much the same way. Business was conducted around the edges of the room. In the center there were flowered, overstuffed couches and chairs flanked by ornate mahogany or cherry tables that were either European antiques or excellent knockoffs. Flower arrangements as big as fountains sent messages of spring and gracious living throughout the room. Champagne and fresh fruit waited at the far end of the room, strategically placed to make certain that hungry show-goers had to walk through the displays to get to the bubbly. A discreet string trio played Bach— fugues mostly, so the customers wouldn't feel any need to raise their voices.

But there was no mistaking the room's true purpose. Beneath the lush décor, business was the order of the day.

From where Walker stood, he could watch each person who approached the booth. The show was not yet open to the public, but exhibitors and discreetly dressed security personnel mixed and mingled. Jewelers circulated, greeting old friends and checking out new competition. The security folks just circulated and kept their mouths shut.

At the moment, Faith was bent over her own display case, fussing with the layout of jewelry she had brought. As far as Walker was concerned, the view was breathtaking. Literally. Long, long legs with silky thighs half revealed by a hiked-up skirt. Slender hips that were just the right size for a man with big hands to span and squeeze, testing the resilience of feminine flesh. Soft. Hot. Shadowed.

"I need the necklace," Faith said.

"Coming right up." Walker reached for the zipper on his one pair of good slacks.

Her head whipped around toward him. "You wouldn't dare. Not here!"

He laughed until her cheeks turned as pink as her lips. He shouldn't enjoy teasing her so, but he did. It was like touching her without actually doing it.

"Get out of here," she muttered, shoving him none too gently. "Shoo. The door opens in five minutes and I need the merchandise."

He didn't want to leave her, but it would never be safer than it was now, before the public was let in. Picking up his cane, he walked around the beveled-glass case and headed toward the men's rest room. The deep pile of the faded yet still colorful Persian carpet swallowed the sounds of footsteps.

On the way out of the showroom, he collared one of the plainclothes guards and nodded toward Faith. "She's been having trouble with a stump-dumb sonofabitch who just won't take no for an answer," Walker drawled. As he spoke, he simultaneously shook the guard's hand and passed over a ten-dollar bill. "Keep an eye on her until I get back, would you? Just be a minute."

The money disappeared into an ill-fitting dark suit. "No problem, suh. My pleasure."

The glint in the man's faded blue eyes said that beneath the white hair, jowls, and paunch beat the heart of a southern gentleman who would protect—and appreciate—a shapely pair of legs until the day he died.

Walker headed down the hall for the men's room, but before he reached it, he ducked into an alcove and pulled one of the Donovans' cellular phones out of his coat pocket. It had been modified to accept a built-in scrambler.

Archer answered on the first ring. "This better be good."

"It's Walker. Did I get you up?"

On the other side of the connection, Archer looked down at Hannah. Warm and sleek beside him, she was testing his belly with her teeth. "I was already up. What's your problem?"

"Could be I'm paranoid."

"I'm listening." His breath sucked in. Hannah was smiling like a cat. And like a cat, she was licking him.

"The B and B where Faith had a reservation was burgled last night. The room she would have had was tossed, then the downstairs safe was drilled and cleaned out. The woman staying in the room was murdered by a guy who loved his knife."

"Christ."

Hannah looked up, concerned. Forcing himself to smile reassuringly, Archer ran a fingertip over her sultry mouth. She put her cheek against his belly and contented herself with nuzzling his arousal.

"Most cat burglars don't come prepared to do safes and . . . such," Archer said carefully. "Not big safes, anyway."

"Do tell," Walker drawled.

"Who knew where Faith was staying?"

Hannah nibbled what she had been nuzzling.

Archer stopped breathing.

"The show organizers knew," Walker said. "So did the Montegeaus, the Donovans, and anyone else who cared enough to ask someone who knew."

Archer grunted. "You're not helping me here." Even he couldn't have said whether he spoke to Hannah or Walker.

"Sure I am, boss. I'm the soulless bastard who

wouldn't let her check into that genuinely historic B and B in the first place. I'm also the one who spent the night crucified on a foldout couch in one of Savannah's finest renovated riverfront warehouses while your little sister slept in magnolia luxury on a bed straight out of *Gone With the Wind*."

Archer swallowed a strangled sound. His eyes warned Hannah that she was going to pay for every bit of the torment she was putting him through.

Her smile said she could hardly wait.

"Good catch on the B and B," Archer managed. "I owe you one. A big one."

"It's what you pay me for."

"Remind me to give you a raise." His breath caught and all but groaned in his chest as his wife's warm mouth closed around him.

"Give me a raise, boss. And tell Hannah to stop teasing you. I'm getting all hot and bothered just listening to you trying not to pant."

Archer gave up and laughed out loud. "Anything else?"

"Have Kyle check whether burgled B and Bs and dead lady tourists are the latest rage in Savannah. I'd do it myself, but I'm not letting Faith out of my sight."

"Ah . . ." Archer tightened all over as heat lanced through him, slicking his skin with sweat. "Anything else?"

"You have a complete inventory on her shop yet?"

"Check your e-mail after dinner." Archer moved suddenly, flipped Hannah over onto her back, and pushed deep into her steamy, welcoming body. Smiling like a pirate, he handed the phone to her and began to move. "It's Walker, sweetheart. Say hello."

❦

The guard gave Walker a nod when he passed by on the way to Faith's display.

"What took you so long?" she said impatiently "I only have a minute before they open the door."

"Phone sex."

Her eyes widened. "Excuse me?"

"Phone sex is better than none a'tall." *Like hell.* "Here."

The weight of the chamois bag dropped onto her outstretched hand. The warmth—and the realization of just why it was so warm—hit her. Embarrassment and something much more unnerving tinted her cheeks pink. She turned away and began unwrapping the necklace as though it was too hot to touch, but it was her thoughts rather than the gleaming swirls of gold and ruby that were burning her.

The Montegeau necklace held center stage in

her display. She had chosen a simple backdrop of pale aqua silk to set off the open curves of gold and provide a cool contrast to the brilliant, intense color of the Burmese rubies. The hand-made links that joined each of the thirteen un-even segments of the necklace articulated in a way which allowed the jewelry to lie gracefully against any surface. The three magnificent rubies that made up the pendant could be detached and used as a brooch. The pendant held its rubies within subtle arcs of gold, like burning dewdrops condensed on the flickering edge of flame.

Even without the fiery rubies, the necklace was a showstopper. No matter how many times Walker looked at it, he saw something different. It was fluid, feminine, powerful, both natural and the essence of a decorative art that had been re-fined through all the ages of man.

Walker traced his fingertips over the necklace without actually touching the glass.

"You look like you're wishing you lived in a century when men wore necklaces," Faith said.

His smile was a quick, bright curve against his dark beard. "This one would be wasted against a hairy chest. But looking at it still makes me feel like I'm hearing the first bird of dawn after a long night in the swamp."

She couldn't think of anything to say. Even if she had, she couldn't have spoken around the sudden closing of her throat. Walker kept on taking her by surprise. No one had ever said anything about her work that touched her so much.

"If you don't get the purple ribbon for that," he said, "there's no justice."

"Justice, huh?" she said huskily. "There goes my purple ribbon."

He laughed and wished he could hug her. Then kiss her. Then— He reined in his impulses and settled for flicking a fingertip down Faith's aristocratic little nose the way he had seen Archer do once or twice. "Yeah, I suppose so."

"Besides, you can't hand out awards until you've seen the competition."

He looked at the twenty widely spaced display areas. Each held the cream of a designer's work. Each had its fans and collectors. Each was radically different from anything else in the show. The designers were a show in themselves. Their clothing varied as wildly as their jewelry creations.

"I figure I need a native guide or a secret password or a special handshake to get close to some of those folks," Walker said dryly.

She grinned and made a here-I-am gesture with her hands. "*C'est moi.* We'll do a turn around the room when I take a break. Until then, you'll just have to —Ah, here it is."

Walker looked past her to the same white-haired guard he had spoken to earlier. He and another man were carrying a plush wing-back chair covered in a heavy silk with rose and pale gold stripes. The chair was big enough to seat a man in comfort.

"Put it against the wall," she directed. "Thank you. He's too thickheaded to ask for one himself, and his leg is stiff."

"Our pleasure, ma'am." The guard's grin said he didn't mind getting a close-up look at the face that went with those legs, but he was careful to include Walker in his smile. "If y'all need anything else, just holler."

"Not literally," Walker said to Faith when she looked a bit startled at the idea of yelling across the refined room to get the guard's attention. "It's what the university types call a figure of speech."

She gave him a sidelong glance. "Stuff it."

"Another figure of speech. At least, this ol' boy sure hopes it is."

"I prefer to think of it as a tantalizing possibility." Faith looked away from Walker's laughing, dark blue eyes and tried not to laugh herself.

A ripple of subdued conversation washed through the room. The guards had opened the doors. The first of the collectors, dealers, and tourists came inside in an eager rush. Though their style of dress varied as dramatically as that of the exhibitors, the clothes had one thing in common: they were expensive.

"Sit over there and behave like a good southern boy," she said. "It's show time."

Obediently Walker sat, shifting so that he could reach beneath his jacket easily. Being the bad southern boy that he was, he had a knife handy, and guileless blue eyes that memorized the face of everyone who walked by Faith's display.

He was betting that one of the folks looking at all the fancy goods was the murderer who had burgled the Live Oak B and B.

11

After four hours on duty, Walker was thinking about the Low Country joys of cold beer and a pull-pork sandwich. Doughnuts just lacked staying power. But he doubted that the expo would have anything as ordinary as brew and barbecue on hand. He had seen nothing more substantial than melon balls and lettuce sandwiches on the buffet table.

Faith was discussing gold alloys with a fellow designer, a long-haired, sun-toasted California surfer dude in a red silk shirt and pegged pants. When the man finally moved on, Walker began to have hopes of a lunch break.

Before he could mention his rumbling stomach, a woman slid up to the display. She wore heavy makeup to hide deep acne scars and a Rolex big enough for a man's wrist. Her outfit was European. It was set off by an emerald pin from a late-twentieth-century designer—a rectangular stone set within a rectangular frame of platinum with diamond-studded spikes jutting out in carefully uneven geometry.

There was an intensity about the woman that caught Walker's attention. Her accent could have been Russian or perhaps Hungarian. He moved closer to Faith, just in case.

"The three-sided emerald," the woman said. "How did you set such a stone?"

"Very, very carefully. Emeralds shatter if you look sideways at them." What Faith didn't say was that her globe-trotting twin brothers, Justin and Lawe, had both threatened fatal retribution if she chipped their glorious stone while she was setting it. "The triangle is an unusual shape for any emerald, much less one of more than four carats. The unique possibilities of this emerald are what drew me to it. That's a very fine emerald you're wearing, by the way. Colombian?"

"But of course." A wave of the woman's manicured hand dismissed her own jewelry. A scarlet nail tapped on top of the beveled-glass case. "This brooch you have here, this triangle stone, it is stable now, yes?"

"As stable as emeralds ever are. The setting is more than a year old."

The woman studied the deceptively simple silver shape. A few curves, two inverted vees, and the jeweled green wink of the emerald like a single eye.

"It is a cat, yes?"

"Yes."

"It feeds well, I think."

Faith smiled. "Very well."

The woman looked intently at the brooch. "Is for sale, yes?"

"Yes." The price was $47,000, but Faith wasn't going to bring that up until the woman asked.

The woman nodded so abruptly that her red hair jiggled. "I will think." Her red nails tapped on the glass case. "The necklace. Rubies like blood. They are of Burma?"

"Yes."

"How much?"

"I'm sorry. It's not for sale."

The woman flicked away the words. "All is for sale. Only the price changes."

"In this case, I don't own the necklace. However, the 'cloud suite' over here—" Faith gestured to a bracelet, ring, and earrings done in textured platinum "—has very fine rubies and—"

"Yes yes," the woman cut in impatiently. "The necklace. Who owns it?"

Faith's smile began to ache at the corners. "I'll be glad to put you in touch with the owner, although I have to say I don't think he'll sell. It's a wedding gift for his future daughter-in-law."

"Name?" the woman asked.

Demanded, really.

Faith told herself that the customer probably didn't mean to be rude. Different cultures simply approached business in different ways. She went to her purse, withdrew a business card, and handed it across the glass.

"Montegeau Jewelry," the woman read aloud. "Established in 1810. This shop. It is where?"

"Someone else will have to help you with local directions. I'm from Seattle."

With a last, measuring look at the smug cat, the woman moved on to the next display. She gave it only the briefest of glances before walking on.

"Rude, but she has good taste underneath all that war paint," Walker said.

"What do you mean?"

"She passed right by that clown in the next booth."

"That, uh, clown is one of the most respected designers in America."

"Which century?"

She looked into Walker's bottomless blue eyes and thought of a well-fed cat. "Late Jackson Pollock."

Walker laughed loud enough to draw a few

amused glances. "Explosion in a paint factory, huh?"

"Has anyone ever mentioned that you're a well-read good ol' boy?"

"Nope. Somehow they seem to forget the part before 'good ol' boy.' "

"Amazing," she said, wide-eyed. "You wouldn't do anything to help them underestimate you, would you?"

"No, ma'am. Misleading good folks is a sin. Praise be that the Lord didn't make too many good folks for me to fret over too much misleading."

She snickered. "You could pour that country boy act into a spoon and lick it up like honey."

Walker was saved from having to answer when a young woman in a floaty, ankle-length black skirt and a long-sleeved pink silk blouse walked up to the display. Her skin was pure magnolia blossom and her hair was the color of sunlight. The ID badge clipped to her collar identified her as Meg. "Ms. Donovan?"

"Yes?"

"Your assistant requested this morning that someone sit with your display while you have lunch. I'm free now, if that's agreeable to you."

"My assistant?"

"That's me," Walker said easily. "Pack up the necklace. We're fixin' to find some real food."

"But the Montegeau necklace is the center-piece of my display," Faith objected.

"The rest of your jewelry is insured by an out-side company. The necklace is my responsibility. It goes where we go, and we're going to eat something more filling than lettuce sandwiches and fruit salad."

Muttering, Faith removed the necklace from the glass case, wrapped it carefully in thin chamois, and slid it into the equally soft chamois bag. She handed the package to Walker. He picked up her purse, put the bag in, and closed it.

At least, that was what it looked like to anyone watching. Only Faith was close enough, and quick enough, to spot his sleight-of-hand pass of the chamois bag from one hand to the other to his pocket, instead of her purse.

"Is that how you beat Archer at poker?" she whispered.

"I was never foolish enough to sharp him," Walker said. "And since he hired me, I haven't had to worry about losing a few bucks."

Walker handed Faith her purse before he took her elbow in a grip that was as gentle as it was unbreakable. He picked up his cane and made a show of needing it. "Thank you, Miss Meg," he said, nodding to the young woman. "We'll be along in an hour or so."

"Y'all don't rush your food." Her warmth was genuine. So was her careful, feminine appraisal of Walker and his welcome-to-hell smile. "Things will get real slow around here now, until about three," she said. "Then the lookers will start worrying about letting something special slip through their fingers."

"We'll definitely be back by then," Faith said.

As they strolled out, Walker caught the eye of the white-haired guard, who came over immediately.

"Yes, suh?"

"Where's the closest real barbecue place?" Walker asked.

The man's eyes crinkled. "Have to go all the way down to Tybee Island for that, suh. Barbecue ain't fancy enough for downtown Savannah no more. Now, if it's fresh shrimp you're lookin' for, there's a place along the riverfront folks seem to admire."

"Do you eat there?"

"No, suh. I go to Cap'n Jim's Fish Shack, down t'other end of the waterfront. Those boys own their own shrimper."

Walker's mouth watered at the thought. Truly fresh shrimp was almost as good as Low Country barbecue. "Tell me how to get there."

The guard looked doubtfully at Faith. "It's not a, uh, fancy sort of eatery."

"I'll tie her bib on personally."

The guard gave them directions and Walker took Faith's arm. They began working their way through the crowded room. Without seeming to, he kept an eye on the people behind him.

It didn't take long to spot their tail. The man was too aggressive shouldering his way through people. No subtlety, just muscle. He acted more like a professional knee breaker than a cat burglar.

Walker frowned. Playing with all the unhappy possibilities, he left Faith by the registration desk and told her to make a show of depositing the rubies in the safe at the exhibition office. While she went through her charade, he ducked into the men's room and returned the necklace to its safest hiding place.

Faith went through the motions of transferring an imaginary packet from her purse into the safe. In the privacy of the security booth, she rummaged through her belongings and finally dropped a tin of aspirin, lip liner, and a ballpoint pen into the box. While she watched the box being locked behind thick steel, she tried very hard not to think about what Walker was doing with the rubies that were supposedly now in the expo's safe.

On the other hand, thinking about Walker's method of guarding the Montegeau neclace took her mind off her whimpering feet.

Walker reappeared and handed her into the rental Jeep with automatic southern politeness. Faith kicked off her shoes, the better to flex her aching feet. He took one glance at the graceful arch of the foot she was massaging and forced himself to look away. Stockings that made a woman appear more naked than bare skin should be outlawed right along with perfume that smelled like gardenias and a night of slow, sultry loving.

Trying to look everywhere but at his passenger, he drove out of the parking lot. After a few minutes of massaging her feet, Faith sighed and let her head drop back against the headrest. She knew she should be admiring the stately, moss-draped squares and beautifully renovated mansions that flowed by on either side of the car, but she just didn't have the energy. Four hours of selling herself and her jewelry was more exhausting than four weeks of real work.

Some designers loved the sales end of their job. Faith wished she was one of them.

Walker divided his attention between the driving mirrors and the cars ahead. Savannah wasn't big enough to have much traffic, particularly in the off-season. There were plenty of white Cadillacs in this part of the South, but it was easy enough to pick out the one that turned squares every time he did.

"Are we lost?" Faith asked without lifting her head from the headrest.

"Not yet," he said. "Why?"

"This is the third time we've been past this corner."

"And here I thought you had those fallen-angel eyes closed."

"Fallen angel?"

"Misty blue and deep enough to lure a poor country boy into sin."

"Then I guess I better stick to rich city boys."

His quick, husky laughter made her want to lean over and nuzzle against his neck, then bite him just hard enough to make him take her seriously as a woman. The thought startled her almost as much as it intrigued her. Tony had always complained about her lack of sexuality. She never got hot enough, fast enough, to suit him. The harder she tried to be what he wanted, the worse the sex got. And the angrier he got.

Don't go there, she told herself automatically. *He was as much at fault as I was. It takes two.*

Sometimes—more and more often, lately—she believed that. When she didn't, usually in the middle of the lonely nights when her memories echoed with Tony's disappointment and rage, she simply poured herself into her work. There, she was sure of herself. Whatever her lacks as a woman, she could create ageless beauty by transforming her dreams into jewelry.

And when she got hungry to hold a baby or to heft the growing weight of a child, there were her nieces and nephew. They didn't get impatient when she wanted to cuddle and nuzzle and just absorb the miracle of another life, another laugh, another heartbeat close enough to feel.

"Now, that's a pure angel smile," Walker said.

"I was thinking of Summer and Robbie and Heather."

"That Summer is a pistol. Jake and Honor better get busy on another, or that kid will be too spoiled to breathe."

Faith gave him a lazy, amused glance. "Says the man who brings Summer a stuffed animal every time he sees her. Which, according to Honor, is almost every day since you got back."

"Hey, an almost-uncle has privileges."

"Only when you arm-wrestle the other uncles." Her smile widened. "I never thought I'd see the day when Justin and Lawe fought each other to hold a baby."

"Good thing Archer sent them to Africa or the rest of y'all would never get within touching distance of Kyle's twins."

Faith laughed. "Lianne cleverly had one of each sex, too. I wonder what it would be like to be twin to a male."

"About like it would be for a man to be twin to a female."

"Interesting."

"That's one way of putting it. I figure Robbie is going to be the artist and Heather is going to run Donovan International and anything else she gets her hands on."

"She'll have to go through Summer first."

"Nope. Summer is a wanderer. She'll be back-packing over foreign mountains before she's out of college."

"Do you spend much time peering into your crystal ball?" Faith asked curiously.

"Not enough, or I'd be as rich as your brothers."

And Lot would still be alive.

It was something Walker tried to remember whenever his pants started to fit too tight in the crotch just because he was listening to or looking at or talking with Faith. She was a Donovan. He was a trusted Donovan employee who had vowed over Lot's grave never to tie himself to anyone else who might die trusting him. End of story.

Or it had been until Archer made protecting Faith's rubies part of Walker's job. To protect the rubies, he would have to protect her, too.

The thought was enough to send cold sweat down his spine. The last person he had been responsible for protecting was buried in the lone-liest grave he ever wanted to see.

"Money can't buy the important things," Faith said.

"It sure can take the cuss off being poor."

The cool neutrality of Walker's voice told her that the subject was a tender one. She looked at the square that was sliding past her window. Same Confederate general. Same horse. Same pigeons whitewashing both.

"Fourth time is the charm, right?" she asked.

"You lost me."

"The question is, have you lost the guy who's following us?"

He slanted her a quick glance. "What makes you think we're being followed?"

"Are you telling me that you normally drive in circles?"

"Squares, actually."

"Or, to borrow a phrase from Jake, turning squares." She faced Walker with a coolness that matched his. "As in doubling back to flush out or sneak up on a tail."

"Smart man, that Jake."

"Evasive man, that Walker."

"Yeah. We're being followed by some clown with a white Caddy and a cell phone."

"All the way from the expo?"

Walker nodded.

"Well, damn," she said. "Why?"

"I don't know."

But he was afraid he did. Someone hadn't bought the diversion with the rubies and the expo safe. *Shit.* He never should have left the expo hall. His taste for real food had put Faith at risk. Now he would have to carry the damn purse himself.

"Guess," she said in a clipped voice.

"Maybe he wants to find the best fish shack in town."

"Maybe I'm built like Miss February."

"I'll have to take your word for it, sugar. Play-girls aren't my style."

She wanted to believe him, and she knew she was an idiot for wanting. Every man alive lusted after the playgirl body, even if it came complete with scars from a surgeon's scalpel. "Such convincing lies. Must be those lapis lazuli eyes. No, it's that honeyed drawl."

Those lapis eyes narrowed. "We'll get along better if you smile when you call me a liar."

"White lies don't count."

"Counting has nothing to do with it. I know what I like. You don't."

"Right," she muttered. "Like you aren't a man. Is he still following us?"

"Yeah. Hell's fire. I just drove by it."

"What?"

"Cap'n Jim's Fish Shack."

"So turn another square."

Instead, Walker made an illegal U-turn and slid into a parking place in front of the café. It was the only parking spot along the block on either side. There was nowhere for the white Cadillac to hide. It continued on down the two-lane street, giving Walker a good look at the driver.

He was in his mid-twenties, black hair, sunglasses, no smile, and one big hand locked hard on the wheel. His other hand was fisted around a cell phone. From the look on his face, he didn't like what he was hearing.

The bad news was that their tail was wearing a black leather jacket despite the heat of the day. He was either a clotheshorse or he was armed.

Silently Walker swore at the complication.

"Sloppy," he said.

"What do you mean?"

"A pro would have changed his look. Different glasses, a hat, different jacket or no jacket at all. A pro would have had a partner to hand me off to the first time I started turning squares."

Silently she absorbed what Walker had said. And what he hadn't. "No wonder Archer trusts you. You must have led an interesting life. Like his, before he quit."

"I was never a professional like your brother or your brother-in-law, Jake. I'm just a real cautious country boy. That's why I'm still alive."

And why Lot wasn't.

The realization of loss and rage and guilt was always fresh, and always bit deep with teeth that never dulled.

With an edge to his expression that was as grim as his thoughts, Walker grabbed his cane and slid out of the car. Faith had the door open and was standing on the sidewalk before he got around the Jeep's square butt. Her smart, slim black purse dangled from its shoulder strap to her hip.

"I'll take that." He slipped the purse from her shoulder.

"You're joking."

He stuffed the purse into his sport-coat pocket. It didn't quite fit. "Am I smiling?"

The look in his eyes made Faith think better of the hot words crowding her tongue. "You think he knows that the rubies left with us? Probably in my purse?"

Walker grunted.

"My brothers taught me how to defend myself," she said evenly.

"You do that little thing, sugar. I'm being paid to defend the rubies."

12

Faith stalked into Cap'n Jack's. The smell—fish and hot oil—rolled over her, but both were fresh, clean smells, not stale. Her salivary glands reminded her that a crumb doughnut and a cinnamon latte wasn't much breakfast for a woman who had just spent four hours on her feet answering the same questions over and over again. And smiling. Smiling until her face ached.

No wonder she felt like attacking something. Owen Walker, for example.

From the corner of his eye, Walker watched Faith's reaction to a hole-in-the-wall eatery whose décor could most charitably be described as modest. Worn linoleum floor. Faded beer advertisements on dingy walls. Fifteen cracked tables with mismatched chairs and randomly sized paper napkin holders, ketchup, and tartar sauce squeeze bottles.

The place was packed like fish in a tin with carpenters and painters, plumbers and workers whose hands were freckled from the sun and scarred from the tools of their trade. The men, and a few women who had wedged their way into blue-collar jobs, were up to their lips in the kind of deep-fried sin your doctor warned against. The customers' faces said that like many things sinful, the experience was divine.

The only polish in the place came from people sliding into and out of the plastic chairs. Not that Cap'n Jack's was dirty. It wasn't. It just looked like it had been bought at a neighborhood rummage sale and would be sold the same way. There was no hostess to seat customers, no server to take orders. Folks waited in line in front of a counter that was just big enough to hold a cash register. That was all Cap'n Jack accepted. Cash.

Despite the ruby necklace in his shorts and the woman's purse in his coat pocket, Walker felt right at home. He had been selling his catch to fish shacks like this before he got out of fourth grade.

In her expensive clothes, Faith looked as out of place as a princess at a demolition derby. If that bothered her, Walker saw no sign of it. She studied the chalkboard menu as though it held the answer to the meaning of life.

"Well, that security guard was right about the fancy part," Walker said. "From the way folks are chowing down, looks like he was right about the rest."

She was too busy trying to choose among the handful of menu items to do more than nod absently. Fresh shrimp, steamed or fried. Two kinds of fresh fish. Oysters, raw or fried. Scallops. She groaned, unable to make up her mind. "I'll have one of everything and two of the shrimp."

He laughed, pleased that she didn't object to the shabby décor and grubby, hardworking customers. "If you like shrimp that much, I'll order fish and fried oysters and we can share."

"Make it shrimp, then."

"Steamed or fried?"

"Steamed. Two pounds."

His eyebrows shot up.

"Don't look at me like that," she said. "I know all about 'sharing' with older brothers. It's like sharing a lamb chop with a hungry wolf."

Before Walker could answer, she spotted three men getting up to leave. She shot over to the vacated table, politely cutting off two carpenters in stained Carhartt coveralls. Grabbing a handful of napkins, she wiped up spilled cocktail sauce and emptied the heaping ashtray into a trash container as though she did it every day. Then she looked expectantly at Walker.

Smiling, he went to order for them. When he came back, he was carrying a pitcher of cold tea and two empty plastic glasses that had the opaque finish that comes only from long, hard use. He set the pitcher down with a thump.

"What's that?" she asked.

"Sweet tea, the house wine of the South."

He poured a glass and handed it to her. She sipped, swallowed, and cleared her throat.

"It's an acquired taste," he said. "Like beer."

"I'd rather have beer."

Walker would rather have had beer, too. He drank tea anyway. Only a fool started sucking up alcohol when some Low Country knee breaker was parked outside, sweating in the unseasonable heat and waiting for Faith to reappear.

But that didn't mean she had to suffer along with everyone else. "I'll get you a beer," Walker said.

He rose to order one, only to stop when her fingers locked with surprising strength around his wrist.

"No thanks," she said. "I'd fall asleep before we got back. I'll stick to, um, the house wine." She took a second sip. "Suppose they have any lemon?"

"Doubt it, but I'll ask. Around here, folks use tartar sauce rather than lemon on fish."

"Wait." She took a third sip, then a fourth. Cool, clean, brewed, and undeniably sweet, the tea was refreshing. "I'll drink it straight up, just like the natives."

It didn't take long for the gravel-voiced counterman to call their number. As one, Faith and Walker headed for the food. He picked up the plastic baskets of fries, coleslaw, fish, and oysters, and a fistful of plastic silverware. She balanced a plate mounded with unpeeled shrimp and a plastic carton of shrimp sauce. When everything was unloaded onto the table, he tucked her chair beneath her. She was already stripping off her jacket and rolling up her silk sleeves.

"Don't touch anything just yet," he warned her. "I forgot something."

As soon as his back was turned, she dove into the mound of shrimp and started peeling, dipping, and eating. After the first bite, she began making noises that were half hum, half purr. The shrimp was pure ecstasy—succulent, sweet, perfectly cooked.

"I told you to wait," Walker said when he returned.

Without looking up, she made noises that roughly translated into "Do I look stupid?"

Smiling, he shook out the clean apron he had borrowed from the kitchen. "Stand up and hook up, sugar. We don't have time to go back to the inn for a change of clothes."

"Mmph." She swallowed, licked her fingers, then tried and failed to wipe them clean on a paper napkin. Hastily she stood, turned her back to him, and held her arms away from her body. "Go for it."

After an instant of hesitation, he took the neck strings and tied them in place. He tried not to notice the warmth of her skin and the exotic mixture of gardenias and cocktail sauce that tantalized his senses. When he reached around her for the waist ties, he discovered they were hip ties on her. Even after he wrapped them around twice, he still had enough left over for a big double bow.

While he worked, he told himself that he didn't enjoy discovering just how good she felt in his arms. He even tried to believe it. He tried really hard. Then he sat down in his own chair, shifted and shifted again, and decided that sometimes, just sometimes, testosterone could be a literal pain in the ass. Sitting down to eat with a woody and a ruby necklace stuffed into your shorts was one of those times.

And if she kept licking her fingers and making sex-kitten noises, he was going to do something stupid. Like grab her and start doing some serious licking of his own.

Instead, he forked up several fried oysters, bit into them, and then went still as the memories of childhood washed over him, drowning him.

The sounds of the swamp, deep to shrill, and the echoing silence that followed a noisy misstep. Raking oysters in the salt marsh, the rich smells of mud and brine and shellfish, the cruel slice of shell through careless flesh. Sun like a million burning daggers. Bayous steeped in heat and silence and time. Swamps alive with the pale flash of herons. Dark water shimmering with the slow, rippling wake of an alligator. The elation of finding his net squirming with fish or his pots bristling with crabs. Hunger. Cool glide of water over sunburned skin. Warm mud squeezing between bare toes. Sunrise like a silent explosion. Surprise at discovering that few of his schoolmates knew what possum or alligator tasted like.

And his dead brother echoed through every memory, every scent, everything. Ragged pants and reckless grin. The first one to take a dare and the last one to give up a losing game. Black hair, golden eyes, handsome as sin and twice as hard to live without. Smart about women before he had to shave.

Fool enough to believe his older brother walked on water.

Come on. We can do it. Hell, Walker, you can do anything. You got us out of Colombia alive. What are a few Afghani tribesmen next to that? Think of the adventure!

It had worked just the way Lot said it would.

For a while. Then Lot trusted his brother to get him out of one too many jams.

And Lot died.

Faith watched Walker power through oysters as though they were an enemy to be vanquished. If she wanted any, she had better move fast. "You're not holding up your end of the bargain here."

Walker's mouth turned down in a sour twist. "That's the problem with me, sugar."

She made an unladylike sound. "I doubt that."

"Don't."

The darkness in his eyes told her that he wasn't teasing any more than he was talking about dividing up the lunch. Despite that, or perhaps because of it, she smiled brightly and began forking some of his food onto her plate. "Then I'll just have to take my fish and oysters up front, won't I?"

He looked at her for a long, tight moment, seeing both her concern and her offer of companionable laughter. Reluctantly the corner of his mouth turned up. "There you go."

As she cut into a delicate, fragrant grouper filet, she wondered what scars lay beneath Walker's easy drawl and slow smile. Then she told herself that it was none of her business. It certainly wasn't her business to take him in her arms and simply hold him until the bleak pain faded from his eyes.

Yet she wanted to do just that.

Deliberately Walker looked only at the food he was eating. Not at the brutal mistakes of the past that added up to his brother's early, rocky grave. Not at the mistakes he had to avoid in the future. And certainly not at the woman whose simple, sensual pleasure in the Low Country lunch made his whole body tighten with a hunger that no amount of food would satisfy.

He was way out of line. He had no business thinking about how much fun it would be to peel her like a shrimp, lick her, taste her, suck on her, swallow her whole and get swallowed in turn, the two of them slick with sweat and rolling over and over like a roadside gator wrestler who had bitten off more than he could chew. Hell, a gator would be nothing next to a woman like Faith Donovan. Sensing the elemental sex beneath her coolly expensive exterior aroused him to the point of pain.

With a silent curse, he went to work on his fish and fries. Both were equally hot, tender-crisp, and fresh. The tartar sauce and the spicy cocktail sauce were homemade and good enough to lick right off your thumb, which was what he did when he made a miscalculation. The coleslaw was pure blue-collar—heavy on the mayonnaise and light on the greens.

Walker concentrated on the fish. As he ate, he couldn't help noticing that despite a slow start,

Faith was getting the hang of peeling shrimp. An uneven mound of translucent pink shell fragments was growing on one side of her plastic basket. Some of the time she dipped the shrimp into the fresh, spicy cocktail sauce. Most of the time she just ate the tender beauties in her own messy but increasingly rapid fashion, using her tongue on any scrap that was in danger of getting away from her.

Watching it was making him nuts.

"That's your finger you're working on, not a shrimp," he muttered.

"That's why I'm licking and not chewing."

He grabbed a wad of paper napkins from the scarred metal holder in the center of the equally scarred table. "Try these."

"Why? No one else in here is."

"I am."

"Are not," she retorted with the ease of a younger sister. "You're licking your fingers, not wiping them daintily."

"I'm a man."

Her tawny eyebrows arched. "Last time I checked, there was no sex difference in tongues and fingers. One and ten each, male or female."

Walker had the losing end of this conversational tug-of-war and he knew it. Part of him wanted to laugh. Part of him wanted to swear. Most of him wanted to grab her and show her just what a man could do with his one tongue and ten fingers.

With great care, he wiped his hands on the napkins she had refused.

She went back to the slowly shrinking pile of shrimp.

"Are you fixin' to share those shrimp with me?" he asked, taking the last bite of fish.

"Sure. The way one pig shares with another."

This time he did laugh. Then he reached out and scooped up a big handful of shrimp. It had been years since he had earned money peeling Low Country shrimp, but the skill came back quickly. Soon he was drawing even with Faith in the shrimp eating. Then he was pulling ahead.

She started to peel and eat faster, then faster.

Smiling like a pirate, so did he.

Soon the conversations at the closer tables faded to silence as folks watched the silk-shirted lady in the oversized counter apron and the rough-looking man in the black sport coat race each other through two pounds of shrimp.

"Five on the classy blonde," one young man said.

"Done," said the older man who was eating with him. "Git out your wallet."

"Why? It ain't done yet."

The other man lit a cigarette, took a hard drag, and smiled as he exhaled a long plume of smoke.

"I peeled shrimp as a boy. From the look of him, so did he."

"She's got a head start."

"She's gonna need it."

More money appeared on the other tables. The younger customers bet on the blonde. The grizzled pragmatists went with Walker.

Shrimp shells flew every which way.

"You have to eat them, not just peel them," Walker said, stuffing another shrimp into his mouth.

"Says who?"

"God."

"Prove it," Faith retorted.

"Prove he didn't."

"She."

Walker gave a crack of laughter and nearly choked on a shrimp. "Sugar girl, if you can prove that, you win it all."

But even while he laughed, chewed, or choked, his fingers worked so quickly the separate motions blurred into one quick unzipping of flesh from shell. Despite his speed, the shrimp emerged whole and clean, no missing pieces and no prickly legs clinging to sweet meat. He peeled and ate two shrimp to her one, then three.

It didn't help Faith's cause when a shrimp squirted out of her fingers, plopped into Walker's tea, and bobbed there like a pink cloud over a muddy swamp. She snickered, tried not to, gave up, and began laughing so hard she could barely hold on to the next slippery shrimp, much less pull it whole from its shell.

He grabbed the last handful of shrimp and dumped them onto his side of the table.

"No fair," she said between laughs.

"All's fair in love, war, and shrimp shucking," he drawled. "Besides, you haven't peeled the one that's doing backflips in your fingers, much less the one that's facedown in my sweet tea. You get to those and I'll see about sharing whatever's left of mine."

Ignoring him, she swiped some of his shrimp and went back to work, peeling and eating and peeling and eating, with side trips into the cocktail sauce. A line of concentration appeared between her eyebrows. She couldn't get the hang of shelling the slippery beasties in one quick swoop the way he did.

When her cheek itched, she rubbed it against the back of her knuckles rather than break her rhythm in tearing off shells and eating shrimp. Sauce from her knuckles smeared under her cheekbone like cheap blusher. She didn't even notice it.

Walker's rich laughter destroyed her concentration. She looked up and realized that he was finished. Even a little sister had to admit that his pile of shells looked bigger than hers.

Naturally, that meant nothing about conceding victory.

"I've got the most," she said smugly.

"Wrong, sugar."

"Okay. We'll count 'em. The one with the most *pieces* wins."

The café echoed with laughter, Walker's included. Everyone with eyes knew that Faith had shredded her shrimp shells rather than unzipping them in one neat piece as he had.

"Put your money away, boys," Walker said to the men at the next table. "Looks like the lady and I both win."

Feeling triumphant, she stood up, whipped off her apron, and bowed. There were cheers and catcalls and applause. When she turned back toward Walker, he was standing about two inches away. The look in his eyes was amusement and something much more intense. She knew right away that it wasn't outraged male ego. Unlike Tony, Walker could laugh at himself and truly enjoy the joke.

She grinned back at him. Then her breath wedged when his hand lifted to her cheek. His thumb skimmed and pressed caressingly just below one cheekbone. He brought the thumb to his mouth and licked, removing the cocktail sauce.

"That's right tasty rouge you're wearing," he drawled.

"Yeah?" Despite the sudden racing of her heart, she dipped her fingertip in the sauce and splatted some on his cheek just above his beard. "Doesn't look as good on you." She leaned close, licked the sauce off with comic thoroughness, and said, "Yum. Spicy. Got any shrimp to go with it?"

"You're fixin' to get in trouble, sugar."

"I'm terrified," she said blithely. She dipped a napkin in her water and finished cleaning his cheek. "There you go, sugar boy. All bettah." Her tone was a close imitation of his drawl.

She was still grinning when she sauntered out the door, her jacket slung jauntily over one shoulder.

"Hold on," Walker said. "I—"

Faith screamed.

It was the kind of scream that could be a weapon, ripping flesh and making bone ache.

13

The man in the black leather jacket grabbed Faith's hair in one hand and waved a knife in front of her eyes with the other. "Gimme the fucking purse."

When the door swung open, he glanced at the man with the cane and dismissed him as a threat.

"The purse, bitch!"

The instant the mugger looked back at Faith, Walker hooked his cane around the attacker's knife hand and yanked the blade aside. At almost the same moment, Faith's stiletto heel sliced down his shin. She ducked out of his grasp, set to give him her knee on the return trip, but the cane beat her to it, stabbing into the mugger's crotch.

The man fell to his knees. Walker gripped the
cane like a bat and pretended the man's head
was a baseball. The cane was too light to break
the mugger's skull, but it was heavy enough to
ring his bell. The skin on the side of his head
split open. Blood spilled onto the shoulder of his
fancy leather coat. He stretched out on the sidewalk like a man planning to take a nap.

"You okay, Faith?" Walker asked without looking away from the attacker.

"Yes." She didn't mention her torn jacket. She
was still shocked about the amount of damage a
man could do with a few thrusts of a cane.

The door to the café burst open. Three burly
men barreled outside, saw that the situation was
under control, and looked more disappointed
than relieved. One of the men was the grizzled,
sunburned carpenter with fingers like steel cable
who had put his money on Walker in the shrimp
contest. The carpenter looked at the big man
thrashing around on the dirty cement and smiled.

He clapped Walker on the shoulder. "Nice
work, son," he said as he flipped his cigarette
butt into the gutter. He picked up the folding
knife the attacker had dropped and flipped it end
over end with an agility that told its own story.
"Round here, trash like this sometimes trips on
their own knife and end up gutted like a fish."

Walker ignored the knife and the sideways

offer. He didn't trust himself with either one. He was furious with himself for putting Faith at risk.

"Is the cook calling the cops?" Walker asked the carpenter.

"Yeah."

"You recognize this trash?"

The three men looked at each other and came up empty. "Not a local boy," the carpenter said, lighting another cigarette. "Dresses like some Yankee slick."

Walker swore under his breath. He had been hoping he was wrong. "Faith?" he asked.

She took a closer look at the man. "I think he was at the expo hall."

Walker knew he had been.

The sound of a siren crying in the distance told Walker the cops were on their way. He knelt beside the thief and dug a wallet out of the hip pocket of his slacks. A New Jersey driver's license in the name of Angelo Angel. Maybe fake, but Walker doubted it. Only a mother could make up a name like that.

He nudged the mugger with the cane. The prod was hard enough to focus the man's attention.

"What do they call you?" Walker asked. "I'm thinking it can't be Angel boy."

The thief muttered something that was lost against the sidewalk.

Walker poked him in the ribs. "I didn't hear you."

"Buddy. They call me Buddy."

"You ain't mine," Walker drawled. "Who sent you?"

"Fuck you. I want my lawyer."

Before Walker could ask more forcefully, two squad cars pulled up at the curb. Doors shot open, uniforms jumped out, and Savannah's finest took over.

Walker leaned on his cane and looked obliging.

❦

By the time Faith and Walker returned to the expo hall, she was ready to scream. Part of the feeling was the result of adrenaline, the rest was reserved for slow southern drawls and even slower bureaucracies.

"I hope our little southern blossom hasn't abandoned ship," Faith said. "I've got to make some sales to cover the expenses of this trip."

"Seems like a pin or two would do it and then some." Walker's drawl was deeper than ever. Adrenaline seemed to slow him down instead of put him on a hair trigger like normal people.

"Most of my valuable stones are on consignment from members of my family or from other jewelers," Faith snapped. "I don't make as much as you think on each piece."

"You don't have to make anything at all."

"Because my daddy's rich?"

"Don't forget your ma," Walker said wryly, offering Faith his arm. If the easy way her fingers curled around the crook of his elbow meant anything, she was getting used to having him beside her. "One of Susa's paintings costs more than the national debt of some third-world countries."

"It's my parents' money. They earned it starting from nothing at all. Until I was in junior high, we gave each other underwear and gym clothes for Christmas." She caught the flicker of Walker's surprise. "That's right. The Donovans haven't always been rich. As far as I'm concerned, the kids still aren't. Except maybe Archer. His half of Pearl Cove must have been worth a bundle, not to mention Hannah's. And Jake has his own business, in addition to being a full partner in Donovan Gems and Minerals."

"You're a partner, too. So is Honor."

She shrugged. "After a fashion. No wages. I take my share of the profits in unusual gemstones. Honor used to, but now she puts most of her share aside for building a home in the San Juan Islands. She doesn't want to raise kids in the city. When she's not working on her own designs, I pay her to execute some of mine, especially in amber. She has a real feel for that material. She could also make a bundle painting portraits."

"Why doesn't she?"

"Susa casts a long shadow. She doesn't mean to, but . . ." Faith shrugged. "I don't think Honor has any idea of how good she is, how much she has accomplished. She keeps comparing herself to Mother."

"Must run in the family," he said blandly.

"What does that mean?"

"You have your own business and a flair for jewelry design that's getting you a national reputation, yet you seem surprised when someone compliments you on your skill."

Faith pushed Tony out of her mind, Tony who had wanted her to give up her "stupid hobby," get pregnant, and spend her life raising his babies while he traveled all over the world as a "media adviser" for Fortune 500 companies.

Tony, who hadn't found her sexy enough to be faithful even when they were engaged.

Sometimes when she thought of how close she had come to succumbing, to giving up everything that was important to her just to have the appearance of a marriage, she still could get a sick feeling in her stomach.

"You're good," Walker said calmly. "Really, really good. You had as much traffic past your case and more real interest than the strutting idiot at the display next to us."

"I'll tell myself that the next time I wonder how I'm going to juggle all the bills, buy another casting furnace, fix the leak in the shop sink, and still dress expensively enough to reassure potential customers that I don't need their money. Why is it that when you don't seem to need money, people can't wait to give it to you?"

He smiled thinly and opened the door to the expo hall. "First rule of banking: Don't lend money to people who really need it. Poverty just breeds more poverty."

A few steps inside the door, Walker nodded to the guard who had sent them to Cap'n Jack's for lunch. "Thanks for the tip on the seafood place. Best shrimp I've had in years."

"You're welcome, suh. You folks missed all the excitement round here, though."

Walker looked at the knots of people gathered around the room. There was tension in the voices that hadn't been there before. "What happened?"

"Some stickup artist with solid brass balls—excuse me, ma'am—robbed the expo safe at gunpoint. Taped up the poor gal, left her on the floor, and got away before anyone knew what happened."

Walker whistled between his teeth. "How much did he get?"

The guard grinned, showing teeth stained by nicotine. "Just some trinkets. The good stuff was all out in the hall on display. Damn fool should have waited and hit it after the show was over for the day."

Faith glanced sideways at Walker, then at the guard. "Seems like the fair city of Savannah is going through some growing pains," she said. "I was mugged just outside of Cap'n Jack's."

The guard's eyes widened in shock. "Are you all right?"

"My jacket is torn, but other than that, I'm fine."

"She's deadly with those stiletto heels," Walker said. "Opened up his shin like it was a mullet."

The guard shook his head. "Believe me, ma'am. Savannah ain't like this. Oh, we have our trash, sure enough, but we make a point of keepin' it separate from decent folks."

"I'm sure you're right," she said politely. "I'm going to the booth, Walker. You mentioned the rest room, I believe?"

He got the unsubtle hint. She wanted the ruby necklace on display. "I'll be right back."

Lights twinkled and winked in the bare-branched trees outside the inn, casting uncertain shadows over the glass. From outside the open window at one end of the suite, a ship's horn sounded. Like the smell of the river and the murmur of traffic, the ship's warning was low and distant, dreamy rather than urgent.

Walker felt anything but dreamy. Frowning, he stared at the screen of his laptop computer. He had just downloaded an inventory of the gems that were missing after the Seattle burglary. They had already known about the loss of the most significant gems before they left, but the final count wasn't going to make Faith smile.

"Tell me if it's as bad as I think it is," she said tightly, pacing barefoot over the soft carpet. It had driven her crazy to work on the necklace and ignore her family putting her shop back together under the unflinching eyes of an insurance adjuster. "I can deal with anything but not knowing."

"You got off pretty light. Ten or twelve loose gems. None big enough to make a ripple in the marketplace when they're fenced. The finished pieces all turned up in the bin out back. Apparently the burglar decided they were too unusual to pawn."

"The carved emeralds and the three Pearl Cove baroques didn't turn up?" Faith asked.

"Nope. But Kyle already put the word out on them. They'll stand out like neon lights in a pawnshop."

She let out a long breath. "Okay. A few glitters more or less, I can live with. Gems, even the carved ones, the unique ones, can be replaced one way or another. I was just afraid . . ."

Her voice faded. She didn't know how she

could explain the aching sense of loss and anger that came at the thought of having some of her beautiful creations stolen by a thief who didn't understand that the true value of the jewelry lay in the marriage of gem and design, rather than in the value of the gems alone.

Yes, she could always re-create a design, but it would never be the same. Creation only came once. Attempted duplication simply never turned out as well.

"Yeah," Walker said, quickly reading through the inventory again, "I know what you mean. The thought of some brain-dead thief yanking stones out of settings and dumping your art in a trash bin would sure send me out hunting some serious butt to kick."

"Exactly!" Pleased, she spun around and planted a smacking kiss on Walker's cheek just above the soft, nearly black beard. "My hero."

He slanted her a look that was at odds with his off-center smile. "Don't count on it. I keep telling you—"

"Buddy Angel tripped and fell on your cane," she cut in. "Right. Do you think the cop believed that?"

"Why not? It's the truth."

"I got the feeling that Savannah's finest didn't like having some Atlantic City bad boy on their turf."

Walker's smile thinned to a razor slash of

white. "Especially a clumsy one who terrorizes pretty tourist ladies. No telling how many times Buddy is going to trip again before his fancy lawyer gets him out of jail."

"Out? But he had a knife! Surely armed robbery is worth more than a few hours in jail?"

"Depends on the lawyer." And on how thoroughly the cops checked Buddy's knife. A good crime lab might find bloodstains on it, bloodstains of a type that matched the dead tourist in the Live Oak Inn. Walker knew that the investigators had received an anonymous call suggesting such a link. He knew because he had placed the call himself. But he wasn't sure the cops would follow up.

"Buddy's leather coat cost a thousand bucks, easy," Walker said. "The ring on his pinky was a three-carat diamond. My guess is he'll make bail on charges that are reduced to a misdemeanor purse snatching, unless they find something else to hang on him. Then they'll throw his sorry ass in jail and let his lawyer howl."

"If Buddy has that much money, what's he doing snatching purses?" She made a quick, disgusted sound. "Never mind. Forget I asked. Dumb question. A better question is why he didn't believe the Montegeau necklace was in the expo safe."

"Offhand, I'd say a pal of his taped up that

expo gal, went through the safe, came up dry, and called Buddy on the cellular."

Neat white teeth pressed into Faith's lower lip. "That means they watched us. They followed you to the desk. They thought I put the necklace in the safe because we were going to lunch."

He nodded. "That's the way I figure it."

"So you think they just waltzed past all the exhibits, saw that the Montegeau necklace offered the best return on a fast grab, and went after it?"

"I don't know. I didn't have enough time to, uh, question Angelini."

"Angelini?"

"Buddy. He's mob, sugar. It's all over him like itch on a chigger bite. He might have changed his last name to Angel, but his daddy or granddaddy was an Angelini for sure."

She thought of Buddy's sleek black hair, hard black eyes, and Mediterranean complexion. "Wonder what his pal's name is. Guido?"

"It could be Mick Mulligan or Jack Spratt. The Mafia might have started in Sicily, but in twenty-first-century America, organized crime is an equal-opportunity employer—you want to break laws for them, you're hired."

Slowly Walker rotated his shoulders. Beneath his laconic style, he was still tense. He could close his eyes and see how damned close the steel blade had been to Faith's throat. If he had lagged one more step behind her, he would have had fresh blood on his hands, and this time it would have been Faith's, not Lot's.

Too damned close.

"Will they try again?" Faith asked.

That was the million-dollar question. That, and whether Buddy's knife had sliced up the lady tourist. "Depends on how bad he wants the necklace."

"Do you think they know where we're staying now?"

"I'm guessing they do."

She sighed and turned away. "I've been dreaming of that deep, jet-powered bathtub all day. Oh, well. Maybe the next place will have one. I'll start packing."

"Good. I'll take you to the airport. Gulfstream makes their executive jets down here. They'll have one available for charter. You can be back home in Seattle tonight."

Spinning around, she stared at Walker. His eyes were more sapphire than lapis right now. Crystalline. Darkly blue. Emotionless. "What do you mean?"

"Someone else can sit behind the display for you and make nice with all the customers. You'll be safer in—"

"No." The refusal was as curt as her voice.

"Why not?" he asked reasonably.

"I came here to make contacts that are vital for my future as a jeweler."

"If the next thug that goes after those gems gets lucky, you won't have a future."

"I understand that it's asking too much of you to risk your life for—"

"Shit, that's not—"

Fists on her hips, she talked right over him. "—a handful of gems. You signed on to carry gems, not to risk your life for them."

"I've guarded gems in places a hell of a lot more dangerous than Savannah, Georgia."

Curiosity warred with irritation. Curiosity won. "Where?"

"Anywhere they're selling rubies worth buying. Go soak your aching feet and let me do the worrying."

She could feel her grip on her temper slipping. She didn't know what it was about Walker.

"We'll talk about this again after I take a long soak," she said coolly.

"Sure thing." He turned back to his computer and started surfing the Net. "Bet your feet hurt almost as much as your tongue from biting it."

She made an exasperated sound and went to the bathroom. He was right. Her feet were screaming at her. Tomorrow she definitely would have to wear a different pair of shoes.

And yes, her tongue had skid marks on it from biting back her temper.

14

As soon as Walker heard the thunder of water into the big tub, he switched from random Net surfing to the hot-gems page. A few new rubies had been listed, but none of the stones matched the description of the big carved ruby Ivanovitch was after.

Walker picked another site and surfed to it. This site concentrated on gems people wanted to acquire. The section on loose rubies hadn't changed. A great many people still wanted to buy a three-carat Burmese for the price of a fish sandwich and a side of coleslaw. There was no listing for the Russian's stone at any price.

Knuckling his beard thoughtfully, Walker sorted through the events of the past few days.

Then he reached for the Donovan cellular phone with its built-in scrambler and called one of Archer's private numbers.

It was picked up on the third ring.

"Jake here. What's up, Walker? Easy, Summer, that ear is attached to your ever-loving daddy."

Walker heard Summer's squeal of delight and knew that she had grabbed her daddy's nose instead. "What are you doing at Archer's office?"

"Baby-sitting. We sent Mitchell home early and took the place over."

"Palace coup?"

"Kind of. We're still trying to plan for the party. The only place we could catch Archer was here. No, Summer. Your cousins aren't dolls. You touch little babies the way you do your kitty. That's it, honey. Real soft. Just the way you like to be touched when your tummy hurts."

Summer's giggle made something ache deep inside Walker. He could see Jake now, knee-deep in kids, slightly harried, his hard face laughing and his pale eyes full of light. A lot of Walker wanted just that, kids and love and laughter.

Yet the thought of it terrified him.

Life was so fragile. Death was so final. The double-edged blade of guilt and survival never lost its bite.

I can't go through it again, Walker acknowledged bleakly. *If that means no family, so be it.*

A man who can't take care of his own doesn't deserve to have them.

The fretful cry of a very young baby came through from Jake's end of the line. "Uh-oh, Summer. You woke Heather up and she's going to want food. Hang on, Walker." Jake flipped an intercom button and spoke into the microphone. "Heather's tuning up. Robbie won't be far behind. Where's lunch?"

"Dinner," Lianne corrected.

"Whatever. Bring it on the run."

"I'm already there."

True to Jake's prediction, Robbie tuned up. The wailing, husky cries of tiny babies gained in volume. The two infants seemed to compete. One cried and the other cried louder.

With a half smile on his face, Walker waited patiently while Lianne—and Kyle from the sound of it—came from Archer's office and took their babies off to be fed.

Immediately Summer started fussing. Her volume and intensity were startling.

"Turn her loose, Jake," Kyle said loudly from across the room. "If she starts hollering, no one will be able to hear themselves think. Not since Faith have I heard a scream like that."

Walker overheard. "Let her go," he agreed quickly. His head was still ringing from Faith's scream earlier in the day.

"Okay, Summer," Jake said, setting his daughter down. "You can watch the twins eat, but only if you're very, very, very quiet."

He waited while his daughter half crawled, half staggered over to her cousins, using whatever piece of office furniture her little hands could grab on to for balance. As an exercise in locomotion, she was breathtaking to watch. Each instant guaranteed disaster, but somehow it never arrived.

"Home safe," Jake said into the phone, sighing. "Okay, I'm ready to speak adult."

"You sure you remember how?"

"Now, yes. In the middle of the night, I goo. Kyle is worse. He goo-goos."

Kyle gave Jake a casual middle finger.

"Goo-goo." Walker snickered at his end of the line. As he did, he realized how much he had come to enjoy being a satellite of the Donovans' sprawling, growing family. Being with them wasn't anything like the tension and anger and loneliness he remembered of his own childhood.

"Well, goo over this, sugar boy," Walker drawled. "Somebody wanted the Montegeau rubies bad enough to pull off a daylight raid on the expo safe."

"Mother," Jake muttered. "Archer's not going to like making good on that million."

Another line rang. Someone in Archer's office picked it up.

"No problem," Walker said. "The rubies are still tucked in right next to the family jewels."

"Ouch."

"I've carried worse," Walker said, shifting slightly in the chair. He didn't mention that the real problem was the semiarousal that seemed to be a permanent state when he was around Faith. Though Jake was only a brother by marriage to Faith, he protected her as fiercely as any blood brother would.

"You're certain it was the rubies they were after?" Jake asked. "There are a lot of other gems on display at the expo, aren't there?"

"Yeah. Lot of crap, too, but all the prices are solid platinum."

"You know what they say about art—like beauty, it's in the eye of the beholder."

Walker grunted. "Thing is, I set up an elaborate switch so that anybody watching Faith's necklace would think it was in the hotel safe. Truth be told, the rubies had lunch with us."

Jake waited. He knew that there was a point to the story. For all his drawl, Walker didn't waste time on unnecessary words.

"And after the expo safe was cleaned out, a guy named Buddy Angel jumped us and grabbed Faith outside the place where we had lunch."

"*What!* Is she all right?"

Kyle looked up sharply from the diaper he was putting on a squirming baby.

"She's fine," Walker said. "Sliced the guy's shin open with a stiletto heel and was going for his balls when I got in a good lick or two with my cane."

Jake gave a thumbs-up to Kyle, who went back to changing the baby.

"There was no damage, I hope," Jake said. His smile was as thin as a blade. Walker was a gutter fighter after his own heart.

"None to us. The bastard had a knife. He might be the one who sliced up a tourist the night before. That happened in the same room that Faith had reserved, then canceled."

"Archer's not going to like this," Jake said tightly.

Understatement of the year.

"I don't care much for it myself," Walker drawled. "That room was the only one ransacked. Then the burglar opened the safe. How many second-story residential prowlers kill a woman, then slide downstairs and light-finger their way into a big safe?"

"Never knew of one. You're sure Faith is all right?"

"Only thing hurting is her feet."

"Four-inch heels?" Jake guessed.

"At least."

"Still trying to be as tall as her brothers."

"She's near enough eye to eye with me in those stilts," Walker drawled.

"That's because you're short."

"There you go."

Jake laughed. Walker stood more than six feet tall, short only in the company of the Donovan brothers and Jake. "So, in light of the robbery in Seattle," Jake said, "and the, uh, problems at that lovely little historical inn, you don't buy the idea that the safe job at the expo and the purse snatching in Savannah are a coincidence?"

Kyle started working faster. He wanted to hear both ends of this conversation.

"Throw in the fact that the purse snatcher was wearing a thousand-dollar leather jacket and a ten-thousand-dollar watch," Walker said. "He was from Atlantic City and his name ended in a vowel. Did I mention that?"

"Shit."

"Yeah."

"What's the connection between rubies and the mob?" Jake asked.

"I was hoping you'd know. Or some of your past buddies would."

"You've got some of the same buddies."

"Not officially. Not since I used to take visiting firemen into the back country of Afghanistan for a close-up look at how the local guerrillas were cutting throats. All my contacts are international. If this is mob, we need domestic specialists."

Jake grunted. "FBI. So you want Archer to call in Uncle?"

"Uncle?" Kyle asked sharply. "As in the government?"

Jake nodded.

Kyle slid Robbie's jumpsuit into place, wrapped his son in a clean blanket, and headed for the inner office door. "That does it, boys and girls. This just became a conference call."

He went to Archer's office and entered without knocking. "Walker is talking about bring—"

Curtly Archer held up his hand, cutting off his brother's words.

Kyle's odd, hazel-green eyes narrowed. Archer held the phone as though it was a snake.

"I'm listening, April Joy," Archer said. His voice had the deadly neutrality that came only when he was hanging on to his temper by a slippery thread. "I'm just not hearing anything that makes sense."

Kyle muttered something under his breath. April Joy was bad news, the kind that came with the full might and majesty of the federal government behind it.

"It's pretty simple, slick," April said. "We have the cretin who ripped off your sister's shop."

"Have him? As in custody?"

"He's more useful to us on the street. Really useful. It will be even better when we put a long leash on him and send him home."

"Where is that?"

"Russia."

Archer shifted the phone, trying to loosen his grip on the receiver. "His name wouldn't happen to be Ivanovitch?" He sensed a change at the other end of the line. April Joy was poised over the phone like a cat over a fat mouse.

"How do you know that?" she demanded.

"Ivanovitch was in the shop earlier this week. We did a little checking of our own, traced him back to the once-a-week Aeroflot flight from Magadan to Seattle, with a short Customs stop in Anchorage. The rest was easy."

April laughed. "Not much gets by you, does it?"

"Not when it comes to family. What did he want with Faith?"

"What he got. Jewelry."

Archer was certain that April Joy was lying. But he didn't know why. "You're aware that some poor drunk was murdered about the same time as the robbery, and in about the same place."

It wasn't a question.

"Some poor drunk is always getting sliced up somewhere," April said impatiently. "It's a national shame. Read about it in the *New York Times* over your bagel."

"Coincidence, huh?"

"Listen, slick. I'm not a nun and I don't work for a national church. But if you find out Ivanovitch did the drunk, let me know. Murder is a better twist on him than fencing stolen goods. Or do I have to explain to you why we need all the twists we can get on whichever Russian *mafiya* type we get our hands on?''

Archer didn't need to be told. The *mafiya* was the most active smuggler of the former Soviet Union's nuclear technology. The various *mafiyas* would sell nukes to any paranoid world saver with the money to buy them.

Ivanovitch might be a piece of shit, but he was Uncle Sam's. If April lost him, she would have to start from scratch with another *mafiya* lowlife. Better to keep the devil you know than go hunting in hell for another.

''E-mail me a photo of this Ivanovitch,'' Archer said.

''Why?''

''Because you want me to help you.''

''You'll have it in half an hour.''

''I'll talk to Faith,'' Archer said.

''Thanks. I owe you one.''

Archer's smile was hard as a knife. ''Yes. You do.'' As he hung up and switched to a secure cellular phone, he said to Kyle, ''Whatever it is will have to wait. I have to talk to Walker first.''

''He's on the phone with Jake right now.''

Archer shot out of his office and looked at his brother-in-law Jake. ''I need Walker.''

Jake handed over the cellular. A wise man

didn't argue with Archer when his eyes looked like cold-rolled steel.

"Walker?" Archer said.

"Right here, boss."

"You have any Russians following you?"

"Not that I've seen."

"Keep your eyes peeled. I'll e-mail you a photo as soon as I get it. April Joy had her hands on the guy who robbed Faith's shop, but she let him go because she wants sources in Russia more than she wants a burglar with an accent. At least that's what she hinted. She probably has other irons in the fire as well."

"Ivanovitch?"

"Yeah. He's Russian *mafiya*."

"Which one? They've got hundreds. It's a national sport, like baseball or soccer."

"Ask him which team he plays for the next time you see him," Archer retorted. "Just be damn sure you see him before he sees you. It's possible he's the knife artist who did the drunk. I just saw the final autopsy report. He's very, very good with a blade."

"My, how those mob boys love their sharp toys. We ran into one who fancied Faith's purse."

"What?"

"Don't worry, boss. She's fine. But this guy is sloppier than your friend out there. Nobody's been able to prove it, but I suspect he was behind that very messy murder the night we got here."

"Wait. Start over, at the beginning," Archer said curtly.

Archer didn't like it any better the second time.

❦

The Hilton Head condominium was large, airy, and very expensive, but shouts still echoed in it, drowning out the soothing lap of the Atlantic's ankle-high surf. Perhaps it was all the marble and glass that enhanced the echoes. Perhaps it was simply that even in his declining years, Sal Angel had the voice of a rutting gorilla.

"What kind of a grandson are you?" Sal demanded in disgust. He stabbed his grandson's chest with a sharp index finger. "A crip and a woman. A simple grab and you fuck it up. Twice!"

"Hey, last night wasn't my fault! Shit, there was blood all over the place! You expect me to—"

"I don't expect nothing, and that's good, cuz that's what you are, nothing! You have the guts to whine to me about a little blood and how your leg hurts because some babe stepped on you. I thought you were a man. Looks like I'll have to wait for the next generation to find a successor—"

his finger stabbed again, harder "—but first you gotta stay home with your wife long enough to fuck her. Anything you forgot to tell me?"

Staring at the top of his grandfather's shiny pink head, Buddy Angel bit back a smart remark. His sweet wife was a sack of ice in bed, but he was stuck with her because her grandfather was one of Sal's cronies from the old days, when they ate spaghetti and fought gang wars together. Buddy knew better than to cross the old farts. They still ran the East Coast rackets.

There were days Buddy wished he had become an accountant. But paying taxes just didn't leave enough at the end of the month to live on. It was easier to prey on the chumps than to be one of them. So he put up with his father and grandfather yelling and thumping on him. Sooner or later they would die and he would be king of the Angels. Then he would kick ass instead of kiss it.

"I told you," Buddy said through his teeth. "The guy with her looked like a pussy, but he didn't fight like one."

"Yeah yeah yeah. Whine some more, like I haven't heard enough already. Shit, do I have to show you how it's done? I'm seventy-seven, for the love of Jesus! Young people. *Huh.* Can't even beat off without help."

Buddy doubted his grandfather could beat off under any circumstances, but he kept that little nugget to himself. His head was still spinning from the clout he had received as a grandfatherly greeting.

"Go home to your sweet wife," Sal said. "Go on. I'm sick of looking at you and thinking that the best part of you ran down your mother's leg. *Huh*."

"Leave my mother out of this! She's a saint!"

Sal itched to point out that a saint wouldn't have spread her legs for a dog like Sal's youngest son. But the old man kept his mouth shut; the only good thing about Buddy was his respect for his mother.

"Go home," Sal said gruffly. He gave his grandson a half slap on the cheek that passed for affection. "I'll call you later. And don't forget to collect from that asshole on the docks. No more sob stories. He don't pay, break a knee. People start thinking I'm going soft and there won't be no more money coming in, understand?"

"Yes, sir."

Sal waited until Buddy's footsteps faded. When he was sure he was alone, he picked up the phone and punched in a number.

"It's me," Sal said when the call was answered. "You didn't say anything about a cripple with a cane."

"What about 'im?" The man at the other end slurred his words. He was drunk already and it wasn't even dinnertime.

Sal grimaced at the whiskey-roughened sound of his partner's voice. He should have known better than to trust a drinker. On the other hand, he didn't know any teetotalers. "He damn near crippled my grandson, that's what."

"But he got the rubies, right?"

"Wrong."

"What? I can't pay you unless—"

"Shut up," Sal cut in ruthlessly. "This is how it's gonna be. You're gonna get that woman to your place and lift the necklace yourself."

"I can't do—"

"I said shut the fuck up! You like breathing, you'll do it the way I tell you. Get those rubies or you'll be attending your own funeral. A week, no more. Unnerstand?"

His partner understood. "Yes."

"All right," Sal said. "I'll send you a package. Just follow the instructions and the cops won't know it's an inside job."

"What's in the package?"

"You'll know when you open it. Don't fuck up. I been too nice lately. People think I'm going soft. I ain't."

Sal broke the connection.

His partner hung up and put his head in his hands. After a few long, shaky minutes he poured another drink and wondered what else could go wrong.

15

"Hurry up, Faith. Archer isn't feeling real patient right now. Do you want me to bring the phone to you?"

"Keep your shirt on. I'm just drying off." Faith muttered a few more words as she let the still hot water out of the tub. She had really wanted to soak out the aches of the first day of the expo and wash off the feeling of that man's hands on her.

"Faith?"

"I'm coming, I'm coming," she said loudly. "I could have called Archer back, you know. I'm running late for dinner as it is. I could call from the restaurant."

"You could talk here much easier."

Walker preferred the security of a scrambled line to a restaurant phone, but he saw no point in worrying Faith by bringing up murders and federal agents and such. So he waited almost patiently until she emerged from the bathroom and he could hand over the phone.

Grimacing at him, listening to Archer, Faith sat down on the inn's overstuffed couch and adjusted the big white terry-cloth robe the hotel had provided. Light from the lamp on the end table washed over her like liquid gold. Her wet hair stuck up in spikes.

She glanced at her watch. Less than thirty minutes before she was supposed to meet Mel at what had been advertised as a "trendy new Italian restaurant." She had to get dressed and dry her hair. Instead, she was talking on the cellular with Archer.

Listening, to be precise.

Across the room, Walker watched with eyes so blue they were almost black. He knew he should be thinking about Russians, not about the gentle swell of her breasts between the loose lapels of the robe, and certainly not about the long, bare legs that showed beneath the garment's hem.

Breathe in. Breathe out. Shadows and light and softness shifting, inviting.

He was thinking, all right. What he was thinking was that there wasn't a damn thing he could do tonight about Buddy Angel, the well-dressed mugger, or Ivan Ivanovitch, the customer who had come back after dark and helped himself to the inventory of Timeless Dreams. As for nuzzling the shadow between Faith's breasts, Walker knew he should stop thinking about it, and about what her skin would feel like, whether her nipples would rise eagerly to his tongue, and if she would be soft and hot and finally wet between her thighs, wanting him the way he couldn't stop wanting her.

The next time Archer needed a bodyguard for Faith, he could get some happily married man. Or a woman.

Or a marble statue.

"Wait," Faith said to Archer. "Back up. I'm not going anywhere. Send a bodyguard to hover over me if you feel you have to, but I'm staying in Savannah until the show is over and the necklace is delivered to the Montegeaus. And don't forget the wedding. I haven't. I promised Mel I'd be there."

"Tell her there's an emergency and—"

"No, it's my turn to talk and yours to listen. I've lined up three new outlets already and I've taken high-end orders from four clients. Everyone who sees the necklace at the wedding is a potential client. I'm not blowing that just because April Joy got a wild hair and called you."

"April Joy doesn't have a wild hair on her,"

Archer said dryly. "She's a first-class agent with a world-class mind. She's asking us a favor. We would be smart to grant it."

"She wants me back in Seattle?" Faith asked. "Is that what she said?"

Her oldest brother sighed. "No. She wants you not to press charges against Ivanovitch, whose true name is indeed something else."

"The bastard robbed me, Archer! I'm supposed to smile and let it go?"

"You'll be repaid for any losses."

"Well, yippee." Fingers combed through hair, making it stand up at new angles. "Oh, hell. Sure. Why not? Let him go. Make April smile."

"Thanks. I owe you, because now she'll owe me."

"Oh, please." Faith rolled her eyes. "Get real."

"Do you want me to send another—a body-guard?" Archer corrected quickly. He wondered if his little sister had finally discovered that Walker was more than a soft drawl and a shy smile. Since Tony, Faith had been very skittish around men. Yet from the way she looked at her nieces and nephew, it was clear she wanted a family of her own. As far as Archer was concerned, that meant she had to get used to being around men who weren't related to her by blood. Walker was a good place to start.

Archer liked Walker. His sister could do a lot

worse than that smart country boy—as Hannah, Honor, and Lianne had all pointed out.

"No bodyguard," Faith said. "Please. It's hard enough to find suites with one sofa bed. Two would be impossible."

"You sure? I worry about you."

"Archer, in case you haven't noticed, I'm a woman fully grown."

Amen, thought Walker as he listened and watched. Then he closed his eyes. It was that or start running his tongue down the shadow between her breasts.

"Why did April want this Russian to walk on the grand theft charges?" Faith asked.

Walker's eyes snapped open. That was a question whose answer he wanted to hear.

"She didn't precisely say," Archer said.

"But you want me to do the favor anyway."

"Yes. Please."

Faith's frown turned into a smile. " 'Please,' huh? Watch it, older brother. Summer was the first one to turn you into mush. Then Hannah. You're becoming a closet pussycat."

Archer gave a crack of laughter. "I'll remind Hannah of that the next time she gets mad. Let me talk to Walker again."

"Only if you promise not to tell him anything you didn't tell me."

"You really want to know about the assay reports on—"

"Forget I asked," she cut in. "My hair dryer is calling me." She held the phone out to Walker. "He wants you again."

"Probably to chew butt."

"Nah. He doesn't do that anymore. He's a pussycat."

Walker stared at Faith as she walked away. "What planet is she living on?" he muttered into the phone.

"I've always been a pussycat with family," Archer said.

"Now, it's a real shame I'm too old to adopt. I suppose I could just start calling you Pa and—"

"You're fired."

"Ma?"

Archer gave up and laughed. "Is Faith running that hair dryer yet?"

"Just fired it up."

"Okay. April Joy—you remember her?"

"Beautiful and deadly. Like a coral snake."

"You remember. Kyle followed your advice and put out the word on the Internet with color photos and complete descriptions of what was missing from Timeless Dreams. Then we printed out photos from the on-line inventory you set up for Faith. We wallpapered Seattle and every West Coast jeweler with a fax."

Walker listened to the hair dryer with one ear and his boss with the other.

"I still don't know how or where April got into the loop," Archer continued. "She didn't say."

Walker said something under his breath. "Did April mention a fine ruby the size of a baby's fist, or at least twenty carats?"

"No."

"The Montegeau necklace?"

"No."

"Well, hell. This thing has more legs and less brains than a trap full of crabs."

Archer didn't disagree.

"What are the chances of Ivanovitch having connections in Atlantic City?" Walker asked. "You know, sort of like professional courtesy among the international brotherhood of mobsters?"

"Possible," Archer said slowly, "but not high on my list. That kind of international summit stuff requires a more dependable hierarchy than the Russians have managed with their various *mafi-yas*. They're still at the stage of clan warfare. But I'll ask April to check it out, if you want."

"Not yet. I'd rather keep Uncle on the credit side of the Donovan ledger."

"So would I."

"Can Kyle get into Savannah PD's computer, and the Georgia motor vehicle licensing division, too?"

"I'm not sure I want to hear this."

"Then put your brother on."

"And let you corrupt him?"

"One of life's little pleasures," Walker drawled. "That boy purely loves being corrupted."

"Kyle," Archer said away from the phone, "your public is calling."

❧

Walker gave a last look at the rearview mirror. No doubt about it. They had been followed to the restaurant. A man and a woman following a man and a woman. Even if Walker and Faith split up and went out rest-room windows, they were covered. This mixed pair of shadows were parked down the street in a beige Ford Taurus that fairly screamed, *Your tax dollars at work*.

Walker consoled himself with the idea that no one would have to call 911 if things went from sugar to shit again.

He slid his computer under his seat and went around to open Faith's door. The laptop was filling up with important information. He didn't want to lose it to Buddy Angel or to any other jerk who made his living ransacking tourist rooms.

"Really, you didn't have to come to dinner with me," Faith said as he held open the passenger door of the Jeep.

"I get hungry around this time just like normal folks." He looked sideways at her and saw the

telltale edge of her teeth against her lower lip.
He had seen the Donovan women often enough
to know that there were times when the company of men wasn't appreciated. It put a real
damper on girl talk.

"Don't worry. I won't hang around. I'll be at
the bar, drinking sweet tea and eating shrimp
and grits."

Slowly Walker opened the restaurant door,
gave a fast glance around, and saw nothing immediately suspicious. Lots of smoke from the bar.
Lots of noise. Stepping aside, he politely gestured
Faith into the room.

"How did you know La Cucina had a bar?" she
asked, wrinkling her nose at the wave of smoke.

"I called and asked. Do you see Mel?"

Before Faith could answer, a slender brunette
in navy-blue maternity clothes and medium heels
rushed toward them.

The woman seemed out of place in this southern setting. Even in pregnancy she had a tanned,
outdoorsy look. Her dress was midcalf, the con-
servative South's answer to women wearing
pants. She was several inches shorter than Faith
and wore a three-carat Burmese ruby as an engagement ring. Against the wide, beaten gold of
the engagement band, the stone glowed on her
finger like molten blood.

Mel wrapped Faith in a big hug that was returned with enthusiasm. The silver-blue of Faith's

eyes gleamed with pleasure and a faint sheen of tears.

"My God, it's been years!" Mel said, smiling widely. Her accent was California rather than Georgia. She held Faith at arm's length. "Let me look at you. You haven't changed a bit. Still as slim and pretty as ever. Seattle must be full of blind men if none of them have snagged you."

"Can't see for the rain," Faith said wryly.

Mel rolled her big, dark eyes like the actress she once had studied to be. "Well, that explains it." She turned to Walker and held out her hand. "Hi, I'm Mel Montegeau, or I will be in a couple of days, anyway. And if you're hoping to get a word in edgewise tonight, you're out of luck. It's been much too long since I've talked to Faith."

"A pleasure," he said, shaking her hand gently. "Call me Walker. I've been around Faith and Honor long enough to know a country boy like me doesn't have a chance once they get to talking. I'm fixin' to sit at the bar until y'all are done talked out."

Faith heard the South rolling thick through Walker's voice and wondered if he wanted Mel to think he was a Low Country working stiff. Perhaps his accent thickened with exposure to live oaks and magnolias.

"You're a family friend?" Mel asked.

"I know the Donovans one and all," Walker drawled. He smiled almost shyly and leaned on his cane. "I'm helping Faith run her little jewelry show at the expo, watching customers and such so that she can do the real work. Now, if you ladies will excuse me, I'll be among the smokers."

"Nonsense," Mel said. "We'll tell the maitre d' to set a third plate at the table."

"Thank you, ma'am, but it wouldn't be right. Y'all would feel funny talking about growing babies and such, and listening to you would make me feel like my collar was too tight."

Laughing, Mel looked at Faith, silently asking her if she agreed that Walker should eat alone.

"If you get bored watching Sports Center, give a holler," Faith said to Walker.

"Yes, ma'am, I'll do that."

"Walker," Faith said sweetly, "if you 'ma'am' either one of us one more time, I'm going to beat you over the head with your cane."

"Whatever you say. Sugar."

Mel snickered and watched while Walker made his way, limping, through the crowded room to the bar. "Is it permanent?"

"Walker?" Faith asked, startled.

"The limp."

"A recent accident."

"Good. That is one prime hunk of man. Hate to think of anything spoiling all that smooth and easy muscle."

"Down, girl. You're married. And expecting."

"Doesn't affect the vision." Mel hooked her arm through Faith's and headed for the small table. "Is Kyle as handsome as ever?"

"Yes. The proud father of twins—boy and girl—and husband of a woman who can sometimes beat him in karate."

"You're just saying that to make me cry. I had the worst crush on him when I was a freshman."

"So did every girl who saw him. Unless they saw Lawe, Justin, or Archer first."

"Nobody is better-looking than Kyle."

"If you like blonds."

"What's not to like?" Mel pulled in her chair and leaned across the table confidentially. "Or is it that soft-drawling, dark-haired southern boy at the bar who made you switch to brunettes?"

Faith thought about explaining Walker—employee, not boyfriend. Then she thought of the endless follow-up questions. "I'm off men since Tony," she said, taking the easy way out.

"Tony?"

"My ex-fiancé."

"Whoa. It *has* been too long. I've been so wrapped up in the Montegeau family saga that I've let everything else go."

"No," Faith countered quietly. "It's my fault. Tony didn't like it when I had friends he didn't know. So I gradually stopped having friends. He probably would have resented my family, but he was hoping to do business with them."

"Possessive, you say?" Mel smiled at the host-ess, who handed them menus.

"Very."

"Glad you dumped him. I bet he wore tank tops that showed off his muscles."

"How did you know?"

"In the South we call them wife-beater shirts."

Faith buried her face in the menu. Mel had made a joke, but it was too much like a good guess. Faith didn't want anyone to know why she had ended her affair with Tony, because if any-one else knew, word would get back to her brothers. When that happened, there would be more trouble than a loser like Tony was worth.

"Any recommendations?" she asked Mel tightly.

"It's all fantastic. And I could eat all of it. God, I'm never going to be a size eight again."

"Good for you. Men like women with some curves."

"Easy for you to say. You can eat anything you want."

"I could if I wanted my butt to drag on the floor," Faith retorted. "Only my StairMaster knows what I go through over an extra piece of pizza. Now, if those inches would only go on top, I'd eat pizza three times a day. With ice cream."

"You're making me drool. Since I stopped throwing up, eating a pizza sundae is one of my secret dreams."

Faith threw back her head and laughed. She had forgotten just how much she enjoyed Mel. The realization reminded her of how much she had let slip away because of Tony. Looking back at her eagerness to please him was both frightening and sickening.

Silently she repeated the mantra she had spoken as she lay on the floor of Tony's apartment, her ears ringing from his casual blow. *It's over. Finished. Done. It never should have been. It's over. Finished. Done.*

But the experience hadn't been a total loss. She had learned an important lesson. She would never again make the mistake of giving a man that kind of control over her life.

"So what's this about the Montegeau family saga?" Faith asked, turning the conversation away from herself.

"Ohmygod, the Montegeaus," Mel said, leaning over the table confidentially. "It's so southern."

"Seems reasonable. This is the South, after all. Are we talking Erskine Caldwell southern or Tennessee Williams southern?"

"And the difference would be?"

"Poor trash versus rich trash."

Before Mel could answer, their server came. The slender young man looked good in his tuxedo. He put down a saucer of olive oil, grated Parmesan cheese into it, and ground fresh pepper on top. Then he repeated his litany of specials, pasta, fish, and meat, and withdrew.

Faith dipped in a bit of bread and made a humming sound of surprised approval. She was still occupied with the tastes and her conversation with her friend when the front door of the restaurant opened and another couple entered.

The hostess started to turn them away, but then the man said something that must have changed her mind. She surveyed the dining room, then signaled the busboy and instructed him to set up a table. It was a tiny table. It had to be in order to fit into the space immediately adjacent to the table that had been reserved for Faith and Mel.

Walker watched the whole transaction from the corner of his eyes. He had expected to see money change hands. It had. But it had been preceded by a leather folder holding a badge. The move had been smooth, discreet.

He was certain the FBI had just joined them for dinner at La Cucina.

16

Faith laughed, then shook her head slightly when the server offered her more wine. "The Montegeau founding father was a pirate?" she said to Mel. "You're kidding. That's definitely not Tennessee Williams."

"Oh, I don't know. You'd be amazed how much old money came from tainted wells." Mel eyed the bread and olive oil hungrily, thought of her merciless scale at home, and took a sip of mineral water instead. "Anyway, Jacques 'Black Jack' Montegeau was a straight-out brigand. No special privateering license from a queen or king, no political overtones or undertones, just full-on rape and pillage. If he could run down your ship, you belonged to him. Mostly he took the valuables and killed the passengers, unless they were worth ransoming.''

''Wow. Talk about a black sheep. I thought the Donovans were doing well with their Scots outlaws, witches, horse thieves, and men who shot first, last, and always.''

''Sounds like the Montegeaus.'' Mel spotted the salads coming toward them in the arms of their very graceful, very pretty male server. She leaned toward Faith and said quietly, ''If I had that boy's eyelashes, I'd burn mine.''

Faith bit her lip against laughing out loud while the server, who indeed had improbably long eyelashes over artificially colored green contact lenses, positioned a salad plate in the precise center of each place setting. After a few expert grinds of the pepper shaker, he left them alone again.

''You can buy those eyelashes at any beauty supply house,'' Faith said, but she was careful to keep her voice down.

''Oh, the disillusionment.'' Mel pouted spectacularly. ''Like finding out your scale counts calories that you just *know* shouldn't really count.''

''Tell me something cheerful. How many people did Black Jack Montegeau kill?''

Mel waved her fork airily. ''Thousands. Well, hundreds. Twenty or thirty for sure.''

''Then they caught him and hung him high?''

''Never caught him. He bribed the local authorities with a few chests of loot, got a sweeping pardon, and married a local beauty whose family needed money more than respectability. Her only dowry was a ruby brooch the size of a chicken."

"Poor thing."

Mel shrugged. "Save your sympathy. She made that old pirate's life a living hell. He smoked on the back stoop with the servants just to get away from her."

"Any children?"

"Two to speak of. A lot more, if legends hold true. The ones the family talks about were sons. They went to England to school, became ship's captains, and took up dear old Dad's career. Or was that the grandsons? Great-grandsons?" Mel shrugged. "Whatever. The tradition continued."

"Piracy?"

"You got it. Only, the offspring were smart enough to get a license to steal. One of them was hanged anyway. Couldn't keep his hands off a juicy ship no matter what flag it was flying. The other son married and had kids. Legend is that the daughter went to sea with her brothers, but no one will talk about her. Must have taken after the first Mrs. Montegeau, she of the chicken-sized ruby brooch."

Smiling, Faith let Mel's conversation wash over her.

"Somewhere about then, they got into the jewelry business and Ruby Bayou came into the family," Mel continued, eating neat bites without pausing, "only they didn't call it Ruby Bayou until later. Family legend has it that the land was ransom for some rich planter. If it was, he got the last laugh."

"Why?"

"This was just before the Civil War. Nobody sold much cotton for the next few years, but somehow the Montegeaus not only hung on, they managed to build a big mansion. The place came to be called Ruby Bayou because supposedly the mansion was financed by selling off some of the family jewels that had been hidden in a nearby bayou. Or were those the rubies stolen from the jewelry store?" Mel made a frustrated sound. "It's hard to keep all these gory details straight. Anyway, the family jewels were hidden somewhere and then sold to build the house."

Faith thought of Walker and his uncomfortable means of carrying gems.

"Stop snickering into your salad," Mel said. "I wasn't referring to *that* kind of family jewels."

"Too bad. I imagine some governments would have paid a lot to see the end of the Montegeau line."

"That was then. The Montegeaus went kind of respectable in the nineteenth century and mostly respectable in the twentieth. Jewelry, shrimping, farming."

"How do you define 'mostly respectable'?"

"Well, they still keep a loaded shotgun in the library—supposedly the same one that killed Jeff's grandfather—but they gradually switched from privateering to importing."

Faith's fork paused over the last of her salad greens. She decided to let the shotgun go and pursue more recent topics. "Privateering to importing. That's quite a jump."

"Not really. They specialized in jewelry and art goods from the Continent."

"Gotcha. The very things they used to steal."

Mel winced. "Don't let Daddy Montegeau hear you say that. He's real sensitive about the black sheep in the family. Every time Tiga—"

"Who?"

"Antigua Montegeau, Jeff's maiden aunt. His father's sister. You know—the obligatory nutcase."

Faith swallowed salad before she choked on it. "Excuse me?"

"The batty older relative. Every family has to have at least one. In the South they're considered local landmarks. The government should have a special historical register just for them. Same for the ghosts."

"I'm floundering."

"Welcome to the South. It took me months to sort the Montegeaus out, dead *and* alive." Mel licked her fork clean. "If I reach for your wineglass, smack my fingers. Even though the doctor says a sip or two now and again won't hurt the baby, I'm determined to do it right."

"It?"

"Being a mother."

Faith watched the flicker of sadness on Mel's pretty face and reached across the table to take her friend's hand. Mel's childhood had been miserable, thanks largely to a mother who couldn't open her mouth without criticizing her daughter. Miraculously, Mel had turned out as a glowing mirror image of her caustic mother; from the day Faith met her, Mel had been a generous spirit, easy with her smiles and her compliments.

"You'll do very well," Faith said, leaning forward to grip her friend's hand for a moment. "You'll teach your baby to laugh and enjoy life and be careful of other people's feelings."

Mel sighed and smiled slightly. "Thanks. I worry about it. Being like her, I mean."

"Your mother could find fault with God. Tell me about your new family. They sound much more interesting."

"Oh, once they gave up robbery and mayhem, they turned out pretty normal, if you don't count ghosts and the odd one locked in the attic."

"Ghosts in the attic?"

"Yeah, but they only locked in the nutty live ones. And only when important company came."

Laughing, Faith shook her head. "I've missed you, Mel."

"Really? Is that why it took a jewelry expo to drag you to this side of the continent?"

"Guilty as charged."

"I'd love to see the expo, but Daddy Montegeau has kept me hopping the whole time. He wouldn't even let me take off enough time to meet you for lunch. Had a fit when I suggested it to Jeff. Why, even my future husband sided with his father. It really made me mad."

Faith hid her smile in a glass of wine. She suspected that the Montegeau men didn't want Mel to see the ruby necklace before the wedding. In any case, it was just as well Mel hadn't come to lunch. The food had been wonderful, but the mugging afterward had taken the shine off the day.

"I married the last of the slave drivers," Mel muttered while the server removed salad plates.

"Really?"

"What? Oh, no. I didn't mean it that way. There might have been some Montegeau slaves before the Civil War, but I kind of doubt it. The family fortunes came and went like an express elevator, and slaves were really expensive to buy."

"An express elevator, huh?"

"Rags to riches to rags to riches to rags to upper middle class," Mel said. "Or it might have been riches, riches, rags, ri—"

"I get the point," Faith cut in. "Every generation was pretty much its own thing. From the looks of your engagement ring, Jeff is on the upswing generation."

Mel hesitated. Something close to fear shadowed her beautiful brown eyes. Then she smiled with more determination than conviction. "Even at seventy-one, Daddy Montegeau keeps a firm grip on the reins. Jeff mostly takes orders."

"Must make for some lively family conversations. Sort of like a prince waiting for the aging king to step aside."

The understanding in Faith's voice warmed Mel's smile. "Jeff is nearly forty. He's real tired of waiting. But Daddy Montegeau has vowed to make the Montegeaus wealthy again."

"Back to rape and pillage?" Faith suggested dryly.

"Nope. Real estate."

"Ah, modern pirate stuff. Don't walk the plank, just give me your life savings for this loooovely piece of waterfront property. Only you have to visit just at the lowest of the low tides, because otherwise you'll have surf in your mouth."

Mel's laughter was as rich as the chestnut brown of her hair. "Wicked child! Don't say anything like that in front of Daddy. He doesn't have a sense of humor, especially about real estate and money."

"Don't worry. I won't even be meeting your father-in-law."

"Oh, but you will. After the expo ends. We want you to stay at Ruby Bayou until the wedding. You're coming to the wedding, right? Please say yes." Mel's smile threatened to slip. "When Jeff got his wildly romantic idea to get married on Valentine's Day and at Ruby Bayou instead of Savannah, I had to change all my wedding plans. A lot of people aren't going to be able to make it on such short notice, but I guess it doesn't matter because the library can't hold more than ten or twenty anyway."

Faith could see the anxiety and sadness in Mel's eyes. She suspected her friend wasn't happy with the changed wedding plans. "Of course I'll come to the wedding," Faith said, "but—"

"Oh, good," Mel said eagerly. "And Owen Walker. We want him to stay at Ruby Bayou, too. Daddy Montegeau said it was the least we could do, because you've done us a real big favor. He didn't say what it was. Is it a secret?"

Dinner arrived, saving Faith from having to make an immediate answer to any of the questions. She knew that Walker would be more than willing to go to Ruby Bayou, because he wanted to talk to the Montegeaus about buying some family rubies. She wasn't quite as pleased by the prospect. The thought of living in Walker's pocket for another few days unnerved her.

Up until now, she had found the idea of going without the male of the species to be quite wonderful. Walker was making a shambles of her vow.

He actually seemed to like her. He even laughed at her jokes. And the flashes of heat she sometimes saw in those lapis eyes made her curious.

Or something.

"Your shrimp smells divine," Mel said, tearing into her swordfish and polenta.

"Trade bites?"

"Sure thing. It really was Daddy's idea, by the way, if that makes any difference."

Instantly Faith thought of the beautiful ruby necklace. "What was?" she asked cautiously.

"Having you come and stay for a few days at Ruby Bayou. He knows how much I was looking forward to seeing you." Mel grimaced. "Actually, Jeff and I had a row over the no-lunch bit. Daddy must have heard, because he suggested that you come out to Ruby Bayou and stay with us until after the wedding."

"I don't want to get you in trouble with Jeff."

"If Daddy says do it, it gets done." Hearing herself, Mel winced. "That makes him sound like a tyrant. He isn't. Not really. He's just, I don't know, a bulldozer. He knows what's right for the family and that's that. He means well, and he's a snuggly gruff old teddy bear with me.''

"Sounds like The Donovan," Faith said, referring to her own father.

"Mmm. He still fighting with his sons?''

"Only every other day.''

"And then they make up, open some beer, and bond in front of an NFL game, right?''

Laughing, Faith tore into her shrimp. "I forgot. You have brothers.''

"Only two. Younger and bigger than I am. Too bad Mother and I couldn't pop open a beer and bond over dishes.''

Privately Faith doubted that Mel's mother could have bonded with superglue.

"Well, that's old news," Mel said. "Let me tell you about Tiga and the Montegeau family Blessing Chest. Much more interesting.''

"Tiga," Faith repeated. "That would be the dotty aunt?''

"Dotty? She phases in and out of reality quicker than one of the old 'Star Trek' characters. Kind of sneaky, too. Every time I looked around she was there. Quiet as a cat and three times as curious. Jeff told me to ignore her. Everyone else pretty much did. Then I got used to her, like the wallpaper in the parlor. Oddest shade of green you ever saw.''

Faith swallowed a laugh and took a sip of wine. "That leaves the Blessing Chest.''

"For what?"

"Explanation. As in yours to me."

"Ah. Gotcha." Mel's brown eyes gleamed with mischief. "It must have been fun, growing up with a sister. Sharing secrets and jokes and boyfriends."

"Not boyfriends. No way. Honor and I were smarter than that." Faith smiled rather wistfully. "Yes, it was fun. And times change. My twin and I are still very close, but she's a wife and mother now. Different worlds in many ways." Faith shrugged as though it didn't really matter, as though she hadn't gotten engaged to Tony because she felt left behind. That had been her biggest mistake, but she had learned from it. No man could make her feel good about herself. Only the person in the mirror could do that. "About that Blessing Chest?"

Mel forked a shrimp from her friend's plate. A long strand of linguini trailed after. She sucked it up with surprising neatness. Smiling behind her napkin, Faith decided she wouldn't demand a bite of swordfish in return. Obviously Mel was one hungry woman.

"This is where the ghosts come in." Mel dabbed at her lips with her napkin, leaving a faint smudge of bronze-plum lipstick behind. The shade exactly matched her long fingernails. "By the time the first Montegeau paid off everyone who could have hanged him, he was down to seeds and stems, lootwise.''

Faith blinked, hung on hard, and followed the thread of Mel's meaning. It was a skill left over from their university freshman days when they had been assigned to each other as roommates.

"At least, that's what he told everyone,'' Mel added. "It might even have been true. But one chunk of wealth remained. It was a solid silver casket, elaborately carved after the Spanish fashion. The casket was either four or eight inches wide and eight or sixteen inches long, depending on how hopeful you're feeling.''

"Either way, that's a lot of silver.''

"Hey, it should have been gold.''

"It should?''

"Sure.'' Mel waved an empty fork. "What good is a legend about silver? Gold is the stuff of myths. You ever hear about a world-changing *silver* rush in History One-B?''

The empty fork swooped down, speared another of Faith's shrimp, and departed in the direction of Mel's plate, trailing a banner of linguini. Shrimp and accompanying pasta disappeared neatly.

"Be grateful it was silver,'' Faith said. "If it was gold, one of the Montegeaus on the downward curve of prosperity would have hocked it by now.''

"They still might if they could find it.'' Mel

eyed the handful of shrimp remaining on Faith's plate and decided to keep her fork close to home. Friendship only stretched so far. Not to mention the waistband of maternity clothes.

"Do you mean that the Montegeaus lost their Blessing Chest?" Faith asked.

" 'Fraid so. Someone came into the house and shot Jeff's grandfather, Rich. The thief either stole the Blessing Chest or killed the only one who knew where it was hidden, that being Richmond Montegeau. Whatever. It hasn't been seen since. Jeff's grandmother, Bess, went a little nuts after her husband was murdered, but not enough so she had to be locked in a closet or anything. A genteel nervous breakdown followed by a five-year slide into death. Antigua, who must have been about fourteen or fifteen at the time her father died—"

"This is Jeff's aunt, the one who phases in and out like a 'Star Trek' character?" Faith cut in.

Mel nodded. "Tiga might have seen the murder. No one knows and Tiga never talks about it, or if she does, nobody can figure out what she's saying. But Tiga wasn't ever the same after Rich, her father, died. She kept it together enough to finish raising her brother—that's Daddy Montegeau now—while her mother was going nuts, but Tiga was a little weird even back then."

Faith blinked, sorted through the conversation,

and grabbed a thread. "I take it Tiga didn't improve with age?"

"Depends on your definition of improvement. For all I know, the ghosts think she's better than a pizza sundae. So when you come to Ruby Bayou, just treat her like a pet cat. If she wants to talk to you, listen and try not to look confused. If she doesn't see you and talks to dead Montegeaus instead, I'll give you a genealogy so you know who's answering. Or what." Mel paused, "Is a ghost a what or a who?"

Faith gave up trying not to laugh out loud. "Ask them."

"I'll leave that to Auntie Tiga. Where was I? No, no hints. I figure if I talk fast enough, you won't have to kill me for stealing all your shrimp. Let's see. The Blessing Chest," she said triumphantly, looking away from the temptingly full plate across the table from her nearly empty one.

Biting her lip against a laugh, Faith forked a shrimp and its attendant linguine onto her friend's plate.

"You're a saint," Mel said. "The calories don't count if someone gives them to you, right? God, why does everything that's bad for you taste so good?"

"Shrimp is good for you."

"Minus the olive oil and pasta, sure." She closed her eyes, savored every morsel of forbidden food, and whimpered. "No more. Even if I beg and drool like Boomer."

"I'm almost afraid to ask. Who's Boomer?"

"He's a what. A big mixed hound that Jeff found hurt along the side of the road. We fixed him up and took him home. Our apartment in Hilton Head was too small once Boomer got well—that's how he got his name, booming around the apartment—so we gave him to Tiga and Daddy. What's a creaking southern mansion without a hound?"

"Blessing Chest," Faith said firmly, feeling the conversation sliding away from her again.

"Oh. Right." Mel took a drink of mineral water, pretended she was full, and went back to talking. "Every generation was supposed to add a special piece of ruby jewelry or a particularly fabulous loose ruby to the Blessing Chest. Kind of a tradition and a superstition at once. The generations that fed the chest rubies and other goodies got rich. The ones that took without giving back got poor."

Faith suspected that Mel's wedding necklace would have ended up in the Blessing Chest in a previous generation.

"Of course, Daddy Montegeau never got a chance to add to the Blessing Chest, because it was stolen. He blames the loss of the family heirloom for his money problems."

"What does Jeff think?"

"That his father is a lousy judge of real estate. So Jeff runs the Hilton Head jewelry store and Daddy keeps trying to make a killing in real estate and Tiga runs Ruby Bayou after her own wacky fashion. A good cook, though. She can do scattered, smothered, and covered with the best of them."

"You lost me."

"Scattered, smothered, and covered?"

"Yeah."

"Potatoes scattered with onions, smothered with cheese, and covered with gravy," Mel said longingly. "It's a style of southern breakfast. Heavy on sin and real light on fresh fruit."

"Have another bite of shrimp."

"If I close my eyes, the calories won't count, right?"

"Um," was the kindest thing Faith could think of to say. As though she was feeding her niece, she tucked a shrimp between Mel's eager lips.

Mel chewed slowly, swallowed, sighed, and opened her eyes. "Next to Jeff, fresh shrimp is the best part of being in the South. How soon can you come to Ruby Bayou? The show ends tomorrow afternoon, doesn't it?"

"Yes, but I can't promise anything. Especially for Walker."

"Then we'll let the man speak for himself."

Mel stood up and walked over to the bar. Even six months pregnant—or perhaps because she was so gloriously pregnant—she moved with a feminine confidence that drew men's eyes.

She leaned dramatically on the bar next to Walker and fiddled with his jacket collar. "What's a good-looking guy like you doing in a bar like this?"

Walker's eyes crinkled at the edges. "Waiting to get lucky?"

"Consider yourself got." She tugged at his collar.

"You sure? I don't want to get in the way of ladies' night out."

"Positive. We're ready to move on from labor-room horror stories to the all-time great fights in the NHL."

The smile spread from his eyes to his mouth. "Should I bring my own barstool?"

"If you limp hard enough, our server will get the point."

"There you go."

Sure enough, the server beat them back to the table. The fact that he managed to cram a chair between the other two without upsetting Faith's plate into her lap assured his tip.

Any reluctance Walker might have felt about intruding vanished when he saw Faith. At the beginning of dinner, she had been as pale as bone china. Now her color had returned and laughter danced in her silver-blue eyes. She was finishing the last of her shrimp and twirling pasta around her fork with obvious enjoyment.

Relieved, he settled into his chair. "You're good for her," he said quietly to Mel.

"What do you mean?" Mel murmured.

"The mugging shook her more than she wanted to admit."

"Mugging?" Mel's shocked voice carried easily to the FBI agents seated nearby.

"At lunch," Walker said.

"Today?" Mel asked, horrified.

Faith shot him a *nice-going-champ* look.

"Oops," he said. "Guess Faith didn't get around to telling you."

"That does it. You're coming to Ruby Bayou tomorrow night, if not sooner."

Out of the corner of his eye, Walker saw the agents look up sharply. The thought of Uncle's best-dressed agents crawling around Ruby Bayou at midnight made Walker grin like a gator.

"I never argue with a beautiful lady," he drawled. "We'll be there."

17

After the expo awards were handed out, dozens of customers and designers prowled the aisles of the exhibit hall, taking stock and keeping score. At least ten uniformed, obviously armed men circulated among the lookers. After the brazen robbery yesterday, the management was taking no chances. It had hired off-duty policemen and to hell with being discreet about showing weapons.

Faith and Walker mingled with the crowds. Today she was wearing a sleek pants suit whose deep red echoed that of a prime Burmese ruby. Her killer heels had been replaced by simple, sinfully expensive black Italian shoes. They were even more comfortable than they were costly, which was all she cared about at the moment.

Walker was dressed in his same dark sport coat, a different pale blue shirt, no tie, and dark pants, all of which were calculated to be as close to invisible as clothes got. The less people looked at him, the more he could watch what was going on without being obvious about it.

His personal nomination for "Most Ridiculous" entry in the expo was a piece of jewelry that looked like a dropped fried egg. A very expensive egg, to be sure, with fancy yellow diamonds as the yolk and colorless diamonds as the white, but still your basic model hen's egg. Offhand he couldn't think of a woman who would want to wear a half million dollars worth of breakfast on the front of her business suit. However, he was just a country boy. He didn't know what moved women in Manhattan or Los Angeles.

"Stop snickering," Faith said to him without moving her lips.

"Why? Whoever voted that pin Best in Show must have had a keen sense of the ridiculous."

"This isn't a dog contest. The award is 'Most Inspired Design,' not 'Best in Show.' " Leaning over the case, she read the judges' card that accompanied the award. "The pin is a 'droll post-postmodern statement of the everyday trivia that lies at the heart of even the most glamorous life.' "

"So's a pile of road apples."

She bit her lower lip, hard, and tried not to

laugh out loud. That would only encourage him. But it felt very good to remember the real indignation on his face when the Montegeau necklace was awarded an Honorable Mention "for our talented western jeweler, Ms. Faith Donovan." He had all but growled at the balding professorial type who had handed Faith her framed certificate with such fine condescension.

"This particular design association," she said mildly, "began on the East Coast. Their idea of important designs is firmly grounded in the academic."

"No professor could afford that fried egg."

A snicker escaped despite Faith's teeth leaving marks on her lower lip. "That's not the point. The winning design will be documented in every modern-jewelry design text for the next decade."

"Documented, huh? Just like it was really important."

"It is. If, after a year, the piece itself doesn't sell to a museum or a private collector, the gems will be removed and reused in other pieces."

"I'll look forward to that part of it."

"You're a bad dog," she said under her breath.

"There you go. Want to scratch my belly?"

She squeezed his arm and made a soft, shushing sound. "From a designer's point of view, the interesting thing about the fried egg award is that the era of sandstone and stainless steel is pretty well gone."

"Back up. You lost me."

"The last decades of the twentieth century were full of jewelry designers who wanted their artistic vision to set the price of the piece, rather than the market value of the materials themselves. Like painters or sculptors. Oils and marble aren't valuable in themselves; the value is in the creation. So the jewelry designers used common stones and base metals in their pieces instead of gold, platinum, and precious stones."

"A lot cheaper," he agreed. "But the final price didn't reflect that?"

"Nope. It was a return to the Renaissance idea of jewelry, before we learned to facet, and therefore covet the beauty of, truly hard gems. Back then, the value of the jewelry was in the design, not solely in the worth of the gems. Then we learned faceting, and the role reversed. Gemstones became the heart of important jewelry, and design was secondary, at best. While the, um, 'droll postpostmodern' piece isn't to my personal taste, at least it represents a fusion of materials and design as equal partners in determining the value of the finished piece of jewelry."

Walker tilted his head slightly to the side, studied the glittery piece again, and nodded. "Okay. If you look at it that way, it's not bone-deep silly. But if you're looking at jewelry that way, you should have the card next to your work, not that guy's. All of your pieces are a fusion of gem value and intelligent, elegant design."

"I take back what I said about you being a bad dog. You're a love. It's nice to be appreciated." She smiled, stood on tiptoe, and kissed him on the cheek above the beard as though he was Archer.

But he wasn't her brother. Walker's heartbeat quickened. He could think of some other ways to appreciate her, but he doubted she wanted to hear about them and he damn well was certain he shouldn't be thinking about them.

"You're worth appreciating," he said casually. "So, what's your interpretation of this?" He gestured to the next display, which held a small, jeweled sculpture that looked to him like a Chihuahua plugged into an electric socket. "Nope," he said, covering her eyes. "No fair reading the card."

She was still laughing when a guard approached. "There you are, Ms. Donovan. A Mr. Anthony Kerrigan has been looking for you."

Walker felt Faith's body stiffen. He removed his hand from her eyes. Her skin was pale as bone, the way it had been when she sat down to dinner last night. A shudder went through her that could have been fear. For an instant she leaned toward Walker as though seeking shelter. Then she straightened and turned to the guard.

"Tell Mr. Kerrigan what he already knows,"

she said in a clipped voice. "I have no desire to see him. Ever."

It was too late. Tony was shouldering through the crowd with the carelessness of a man who was used to being bigger and stronger than anyone else around.

"Hiya, babe," Tony said, reaching toward Faith with the obvious intention of grabbing her for a big kiss. "I had business in Savannah and saw your name in the papers. Lots of fancy jewelry. Bet you could use a little protection."

She sidestepped him in a move that took her farther away from Walker. She sensed that Walker, like her brothers, was protective of her. Unlike her brothers, Walker was five inches shorter and at least eighty pounds lighter than Tony. Worse, Walker was injured.

And she had bitter experience with how Tony dealt with those who were weaker than he was.

"Good-bye, Tony," she said.

"Now, don't pout. You know I hate it when you pout."

"Do I know you?" Walker asked idly.

"Don't let it bother you," Tony said, dismissing the other man without looking away from Faith. "This is between me and my fiancée."

"I'm not your fiancée," Faith said.

"Nothing has changed, baby. I love you and you love me."

Rage sizzled through Faith, burning away anxiety and fear. She wished she was big enough to pound Tony into paste. "You're wrong. I don't love you and you don't know how to love. It's over, Tony. Good-bye. Don't bother me again."

Though Faith hadn't raised her voice, heads began to turn. Tony's voice carried well enough to be its own PA system.

"Hey, hey," Tony said, smiling despite the narrowing of his light blue eyes. He reached out as though to take her arm in his ham-sized hand. "You've had enough time to get over your mad. If you haven't, it's because you won't talk to me, listen to my side. Now, this isn't the best place to do it, but you're not giving me any choice."

Faith didn't want to be humiliated in front of a room full of fellow professionals. Tony's grin said he knew that as well as she did.

Walker hooked his cane over his own arm and reached out as though to shake Tony's hand. Considering the result, Walker's movement was remarkably subtle. Only the guard noticed and understood why Tony's face lost color. The lumbering nose tackle sucked air through his teeth in reaction to sudden, blinding pain. The guard smiled slightly. Looked like the guy who was harassing the pretty jeweler had bitten off more than he could chew.

With a few steps, Walker "encouraged" Tony to turn his back on Faith. "Hi there. My name is Owen Walker." Smiling, pumping the other man's big hand, Walker put more pressure on Tony's thumb, bending it back and under until it almost touched the big man's wrist. "Good to meet you. Faith is kinda busy right now, but I'd really like your autograph. I hear you used to be a big football hero. You can tell me all about it outside."

Tony's mouth opened, but no sound came out.

"Great," Walker said genially. Against the cover of his body, Walker switched hands without releasing Tony from the nearly paralytic pain of the "come-along" grip. To the people standing around, the big man appeared to be helping the smaller man with the cane walk to the door. "C'mon, pal. I'll buy you a beer."

Faith watched Tony and Walker leave. She didn't know how Walker had managed to hustle Tony out without a fuss, but the proof was in front of her eyes. He and Walker were going out side by side, with Tony leaning down as though to hear whatever the smiling, soft-voiced Walker was saying.

Even when they were on the street outside the hotel, Walker maintained his grip on Tony's hand. He turned and faced the much bigger man. To anyone watching, they still looked like two friends having a chat on the sidewalk.

"Let me tell you how it's going to be." Walker's voice was as gentle as his hold on Tony's hand was agonizing. "Faith already knows what you are, so you're not going to apologize to her for being a sorry asshole. You hearing me okay, boy?"

Tony was sweating, but he managed a nod.

"That's real good," Walker said. "Apparently you didn't hear what Faith told you, so I'm going to go over it again, just to make certain you get it through your thick head. Faith is finished with you. Don't call her. Don't e-mail her. Don't write her. Don't bump into her anywhere in the world. If you see her coming anywhere, anytime, haul your lard butt in the opposite direction. You hearing me?"

Tony nodded. He could still hear, even if he couldn't speak.

"Just so you don't make a mistake as stupid as you are big," Walker continued easily, "you got the nice one with me. Yesterday Faith put down an Atlantic City mobster with one swipe. She would have ripped off his balls, but I stepped in. Blood makes me puke, you see? So if you're thinking of catching her alone, think again. Her brothers have taught that lady some purely nasty tricks. They work best on big, slow, beefy types like you. Of course, if there was anything left after she was finished with you, I'd feel honor-bound to finish the job, and I purely hate yakking up my guts. Sure as sin, I'd take it out on you. You still with me?"

"Let—go," Tony managed hoarsely.

"You still with me?" Walker repeated, squeezing.

Tony nodded jerkily.

"Good boy," Walker said, as though congratulating a particularly dim hound on remembering not to pee on the floor. "This is the only warning you'll get, and one more than Faith wanted you to have. You see, she was looking forward to tearing off your pitiful pecker and shoving it up your nose. Followed by your pea-sized balls. Hear me?"

"Esss."

The sound was more a hiss than a word, but Walker understood. He waited for a long three-count before he released Tony's hand. Then he watched to see if the other man was truly as stupid as he was big.

Color trickled back into Tony's face, then flooded it with red. "Who the hell are you?"

"Faith's."

"Her what?"

"Now you're catching on."

Tony looked at Walker's calm, measuring blue eyes and took a quick step backward. Tony was used to rough-and-tumble games like football.

Walker wasn't playing games.

"I could break you in two," Tony said.

Walker waited for him to try.

"But I don't fight smaller men," Tony sneered.

"Just women? Boy, you're a real grade-A chickenshit, aren't you?"

Tony's face darkened. "You're lucky I don't take you apart."

A gentle smile was Walker's only answer.

"Anything Faith got, she asked for," Tony said. "Damn, but you are *dumb*."

Walker moved as though to turn away. As he did, his cane swung out carelessly and tangled in Tony's feet. A quick jerk, and both men fell in a surprised heap.

At least, that was what it looked like to anyone who was watching. To Tony, the world suddenly turned upside down, his feet flew up, and he was flat on his ass on the concrete, wheezing while Walker tried to scramble back to his feet, using Tony as a floor. Elbow to the throat, knee to the balls, a flying hand to the nose. The seemingly accidental blows all connected before Walker managed to stand upright again.

"You okay?" Walker asked anxiously, bending over Tony for the benefit of the few bystanders who had stopped to watch. "I'm awful clumsy with that cane. Can't seem to get the hang of the damned thing. Here, let me help you up."

Dazed, Tony let himself be levered to his feet and dusted off with a force that left him breathless. Blood ran from his nose. He couldn't stand straight for the pain throbbing up from his groin in sickening waves. His kidneys ached in a way that told him he was just starting to hurt.

"Let me call you a cab," Walker said. "You don't want to be walking in this heat."

Raising his cane, he signaled for a cab and bundled Tony into it. Walker gave the driver a twenty and an address in the roughest part of town before he smiled at Tony. "Good talkin' with you, boy. Say hi to the folks back home."

Walker slammed the door, smiled at the nice people gathered around, and was careful to limp heavily all the way back into the building.

When Faith saw Walker, she rushed over and put her hands on either side of his face. Her eyes searched him for signs of injury. All she saw was smooth skin, dark silky beard, and eyes the color of lapis lazuli. "Are you all right?"

"Sure thing. Why?"

"Tony can be . . . very difficult."

"That ol' boy?" Walker smiled and looked surprised. "He was purely apologetic about interrupting you. Said he won't do it again. He was just hoping you were over your mad."

"I'm not. I never will be."

Walker smiled despite the rage simmering in his gut when he remembered Tony's words: *Anything Faith got, she asked for.* Those were familiar words. His stepfather, Steve Atkins, had used them every time he slapped Walker's mother around. The excuses for the beatings had varied from a late dinner to T-shirts that weren't clean enough, but the result was always the same. *Anything she got, she asked for.*

"Sometimes a good mad is the only thing that gets the job done," Walker said. "You deserve a lot better than that pile of road apples."

Faith's smile was shaky, but real. "Yeah. I finally figured that out for myself."

"I'm surprised one of your brothers didn't figure it out for Tony," Walker muttered.

"I'm old enough to make my own mistakes and to clean up after them, too."

Privately Walker thought that Tony was out of Faith's weight class, but he knew better than to say it aloud. She resented the unfairness of life that made men stronger than women. "There you go."

"This must be my lucky day," she said. "I just sold that emerald cat and Tony finally got the message."

Walker smiled. "The cat, huh? To the woman with makeup and scars?"

"No. Some guy who needed a birthday present for his niece."

Walker's eyebrows went up. "Quite a present. Was it really for his niece?"

"He was seventy years old if he was a day. What do you think?"

"I think his niece is blond and built."

"So do I."

18

The jewelry show closed at noon of the third day, which gave the exhibitors plenty of time to pack up and secure their valuables before heading home. Walker spent every minute trying to talk Faith out of going to Ruby Bayou to deliver the necklace and hang around for Mel's wedding.

Kyle's gut was in overdrive. So was Walker's. The more he thought about the dead Seattle street person, the dead Savannah tourist, and the fact that Buddy's knife was clean of everything except steak juice, the less Walker liked any of it. But he didn't want to tell Faith that a murderous knife artist might be after her, so his hands were tied when it came to good arguments to get her to leave.

Faith ignored all of his arguments, good or bad or ridiculous.

Walker didn't give up. He spent the short drive to Hilton Head Island and Ruby Bayou trying to talk her into leaving.

"It's not too late to get you on a plane," he pointed out. "Hilton Head has a nice little airport not two miles from here. Modern, good landing strip, plenty of room for one of the small corporate jets. I'll deliver the necklace. You can check your shop's inventory personally, just like you were screaming to do before we left."

"I know what's missing."

"Kyle and Lianne might have overlooked something. Nobody knows what's in that shop as well as you do."

"When I tried to stay home in the first place, you and Archer kept pointing out how I promised Mel I'd be at her wedding."

"That was then. This is now."

"Now, there's a reasonable argument if I ever heard one."

"How about this one?" Walker's back was to the wall. "The same folks who knew you were at the expo know you're going to Ruby Bayou. You're safer in Seattle and so are the Montegeaus."

"I pointed that out to Daddy Montegeau on the phone, just before we left the inn, but he wouldn't hear of it."

"Neither one of you is thinking real clear."

Faith ignored Walker, just as she had ignored all his attempts to ship her back to Seattle. She had no intention of going home. There was too much to see, to feel, to absorb right here. Designs shimmered and condensed in her mind as she studied the exotic landscape of salt marsh and palmetto alternating with live oak, pine, and deciduous trees on the drier ground. At low tide the marsh had a heady, earthy, primeval scent, as though time had slowed to the speed of a big reptile sunning on the side of a drainage canal.

"That alligator looks like a big truck tire that's come unwrapped," Faith said as they passed a road-killed gator.

Walker sighed and knew he wasn't going to get any further on the subject of her going back to Seattle. "Tires don't have teeth."

"I didn't say I was going to walk up and pet it."

"Well, thank God for small favors."

"Someone I know is in a snit."

"Shit," he hissed under his breath.

"No, *snit*."

Smiling despite himself, Walker reached out and tugged lightly on her hair. "You're a brat."

"Thank you." Then she laughed softly and reveled in the freedom of being able to tease a man and not worry about his tender ego. "You're fun,

Owen Walker. Like having a brother without years of baggage to juggle.''

Walker's smile turned down slightly. ''That's me, sugar. Everybody's brother.''

Faith smiled out at the winter-brown marsh basking in the sun, but her smile faded when she remembered that she once had asked Walker if he was an older brother. He had answered, *Not anymore.* At the time she had let the subject drop. But now she didn't want to. She wanted to know more about Walker with an urgency she didn't question.

''You never talk about your family,'' she said.

He didn't answer. He was still wondering how long he would be able to keep his hands off Faith. Not long enough, he was afraid. Not unless she went back to Seattle real soon. An hour, max.

Just the scent of her nearby in the car had made him hard as stone.

''Walker?''

He bit back a searing curse. This was what came of letting her think he was a kind and smiling brother type.

He shouldn't want her.

He shouldn't touch her.

And he wouldn't be able to put her off the subject of his family without making her mad, which he couldn't afford to do and still stay close enough to do his job.

"My parents gave up on each other when I was twelve," he said flatly.

She waited, but he didn't say anything more. "Did you stay with your mother?"

"Yeah."

"Did you see your dad much?"

"Not until I was sixteen."

"Then what?"

Walker gave her a narrow look. "What do you think?"

"If I knew, I wouldn't ask."

He hissed a word under his breath and concentrated on his driving. Silence grew until it was a living presence inside the car. Walker wanted to put his fist through the windshield, but he controlled the urge without really noticing it. Faith had done nothing to earn his anger. She sure hadn't asked to have him panting after her like a dog after a bitch in heat.

"Steve, the guy who moved in after Ma and Dad split," Walker said carefully, "didn't like having two teenage boys underfoot, eating food and such. So she bought two bus tickets and dumped Lot and me on Dad."

"Lot? You have a brother?"

"Not anymore."

This time Faith didn't let Walker's bleak expression warn her away. "What happened?"

"He died."

She closed her eyes. "I'm sorry."

"So am I," he said bitterly. "But sorry doesn't get him back, does it?"

When the silence in the car began to eat at Walker, he glanced toward Faith. The stricken look on her face made him feel lower than a gator's tail for lashing out at her over something she had nothing to do with. His fingers clenched around the wheel. Slowly he forced them to relax.

"It was a long time ago," he said finally.

"I don't think—" Her voice broke. She swallowed and tried again, only this time she forced herself not to visualize her own family, the pain of losing someone who was as much a part of her as her own blood and bone and memories. "I don't think there's enough time on earth to get used to losing a sibling."

Walker couldn't disagree, especially when he had been to blame for Lot's death.

"Was he like you?" Faith asked softly.

"Like me? How?"

"Smart. Gentle. Good-looking. Dark. A smile like a flash of light."

Walker let out a long, silent breath. Later he would sort out how he felt about being smart, gentle, and good-looking. For now it was all he could do to allow himself to remember his younger brother.

"Black hair," Walker said, his voice huskier than he knew. "Yellow cat eyes with eyelashes so long they tangled. Too mean to be pretty, but still almost beautiful. The devil's own looks. Tough in a lean, long-boned way. Street-smart in some ways and dumber than a rock in others. Women started staring at him when he was twelve. When he was thirteen he found out why. He was twenty when he died."

"Jealous boyfriend?"

"A deal that went sour." Walker's voice warned her not to go any further.

Faith ignored the warning. "What kind of deal gets a kid killed?"

"The kind where he's counting on his older brother to cover his ass and his older brother fucks up big time and the trusting younger brother dies with a surprised look on his face."

"I don't understand."

"Lucky you."

Walker turned down one of the narrow, winter-dusty side streets that led off into the Hilton Head Island scrub. Pine straw clung to everything like long, spiky brown moss, covering roofs and overflowing the gutters of ramshackle houses that were half hidden by overgrown vegetation.

A high, sheer veil of clouds condensed across the sun. Wind stalked the marsh and pounced on the narrow channels that wound among clumps of man-high grass. The road turned sharp angles along old property lines and climbed up on a low, sandy ridge that was covered with wicked palmetto and vine-shrouded trees. Pools of brackish water winked like alligator eyes in the scrub, marking the slow dissolving of land into marsh and marsh into sea.

Another turn, another low rise, and live oaks bearing burdens of shriveled resurrection ferns and silvery Spanish moss appeared among the palmetto and pines. Pools of black water became a slow creek coiling across the nearly flat land, imprisoned like an immense snake between banks of dense trees. Then the marsh took over. Sometimes there was only mud marking the margin of the creek. Sometimes oysters clung to every wet surface like dirty white ruffles.

Bronze, shimmering, dark, secretive. The winter salt marsh was all of that. It was also as graceful as a dancer, as untamed as the flight of a hawk.

"It's beautiful," Faith said softly.

Walker grunted. "Tell me that when you're covered in bug bites."

"Don't you like it? You were born here."

He shrugged. "The Low Country is like family. Doesn't much matter how you feel about it. It's bred into your bones."

Her smile came and went as quickly as a cat's-paw of wind. "It helps if you like it."

"I went hungry too often to like it."

"After your parents divorced?" she guessed.

Absent fathers too often forgot about supporting their children.

"Even before. Pa was a drinker, a mechanic, a plant thief, and a gator hunter. Ma was a waitress at a shrimp shack. Sometimes she stole food for us when hunting was lean."

Faith almost flinched at the deadly neutrality of Walker's voice. "Good for her. What does a plant thief do?"

"Steal plants."

"From?"

"Marshes. Swamps. Government land, mostly. Wherever the rare plants grow, the endangered species, the ones people will pay money to collect or to grind into folk remedies for everything from gallstones to brewer's wilt."

"Gallstones, I know about. Brewer's wilt, I don't."

"That's when too much beer wilts what a good ol' boy is most proud of."

Faith blinked, then laughed as she understood. "Brewer's wilt, huh? Never heard it called that. So your dad helped out men where they, um, needed it the most."

Walker's smile flashed briefly. "Looked at that way, he was a real do-gooder. Pa figured the various government agencies had enough plants so that they wouldn't miss a few here and there. Mostly they didn't."

"What happened when they did?"

"Ma worked double shifts until the fine was paid or Dad got lucky hunting gators."

"Which was also illegal, right?"

"You bet. They paid real good, though. Tasted good, too."

"So does anything, if you're hungry enough."

"We were hungry enough to eat mud. I had a trapline when I was six. What I caught, we ate. When the traps were empty I caught the kind of licking that taught me not to come home without food for the table."

She heard the simple truth underneath Walker's casual tone. The thought of him as a lonely, skinny boy haunting the swamps for anything edible sent a shaft of sadness through her. She didn't like thinking of him as hungry, poor, caught between a drunken father and the need to survive.

"It got a little easier after Lot was old enough to have a trapline of his own," Walker said, remembering. "Then I could concentrate on hunting. Pa wasn't much account when he was drinking, but sober he was a fine hunter and a better mechanic. He took off for Texas when I was twelve. Said he would come back and get us when he found work."

"Did he?"

"Find work?"

"Come back."

"What do you think?"

"I think you didn't see him until your mother

bought you and your brother bus tickets to Texas."

"You're learning, sugar."

She looked out the window, but she no longer saw the countryside. She kept thinking of a young boy taking on the swamps and bayous and marshes in order to eat.

"Don't look so grim," he said finally. "It sounds worse than it was. Lot and I had some fine old times hunting and fishing and hell-raising. We weren't long on polish, but we knew the country better than the teacher's pet knew multiplication tables. When Steve was riding a mean, Lot and I just went out in the swamp until he was too drunk to make a fist."

"Your mother's boyfriend beat you?" Faith heard her own shock and said quickly, "I'm sorry. That's sounds so naïve. I'm not. Not really. It's just the thought of a man raising his hand against children and their own mother allowing it . . ."

Walker shrugged again, although it cost too much to be casual. He had never understood his mother. In time, he had given up trying. "Ma needed a man nearby, and she didn't mind a drinker. That's why when it came time to choose, she chose that drunken, woman-beating son of a bitch."

Faith gave Walker a quick glance. There was nothing gentle about him now. Even his beard couldn't conceal the hard line of his mouth. "You were better off with your father."

"Wasn't much choice when it came down to it. The night I stomped Steve into the mud, Ma bought Lot and me bus tickets and sent us off before he came to. Took me three weeks, but I tracked down Pa. He was working at a ragtag little airport on the Gulf. He taught me about engines. One of the flyboys taught me about airplanes and books. I took to it like fire to pine straw."

She looked again, drawn by the change in him. He loved flying. It was there in the easing of his drawn face, in the huskiness and pleasure vibrating in his voice, and in the gentle, remembering curve of his lips.

"By the time I was nineteen, I was shuttling stuff in and out of Central America and the Caribbean," Walker added. "It was the first real job I had."

"What kind of stuff?"

"Supplies and mail and medicine, most of the time. Some missionary pamphlets and Bibles. The occasional rich eco-tourist. That sort of thing." He gave her a sideways glance. "No drugs. I was young, but I wasn't stupid. I left that to my brother." Walker's smile was like his memories, bittersweet. "Lot had enough young-and-dumb for both of us."

Walker didn't mention that he had also run

guns for the U.S. government or its surrogates from time to time. It wasn't something he talked about. The pay had been good. The numbered bank accounts fattened on schedule. That was all a ragged twenty-year-old who was supporting his father and younger brother could ask.

A gust of wind moved over the marsh like an invisible comb, making grass bow and sway in rippling lines. Walker lowered the window and let the soft air run through his hair. Out on the water, a shrimper was coming in. Its working arms, the two long booms that held the nets, now were folded straight up like a butterfly's wings. Drying nets added to the illusion of something winged at rest.

"If we had time," Walker said, "I'd take you down to Tybee Island to watch the shrimpers come in. They sail in under a bridge so low that they have to put down their trawling arms to get under the span. A pretty sight at sunset, with the pelicans lined up on the pilings like kids watching a parade."

"Really?"

He smiled. "God's truth. But it's the dolphins that really put on a show. Somehow they always know when a boat is coming in to unload at the packing house. The dolphins come pouring in from the ocean and start leaping and rolling and playing along the wharf. They know that when the shrimp tanks are flushed, a lot of juicy tidbits will be washed right into their lazy, grinning mouths."

Faith laughed. "I'd like to see that."

He smiled at the sound of her laughter. It was like the air, soft and warm and alive with possibilities. "I'd like it, too."

She smiled at him in return and decided not to ask any more right now about his brother and childhood and death. "How much farther to Ruby Bayou?"

"Just up around this corner."

The Jeep turned past another property line, rattled over a rickety wooden bridge that crossed a creek, and bumped onto an overgrown drive lined with oaks that had been tall before the first shot of the Civil War was fired. With fields stretching away on either side, the driveway wound for a mile between moss-laden oaks. On a low, windswept rise, a huge two-story white plantation house faced the sea to the east and a dark, narrow bayou on the south. To the west and north lay fields, scrubland, and gardens.

Walker glanced at the fallow fields that were slowly, silently being reclaimed by native scrub. Beyond them, the Montegeau mansion rose high and white. It had double galleries supported by pillars around both stories of the house. The lower gallery was screened in. The upper had been left open.

Though nothing looked dangerous, there was

a definite sag along one side of the lower gallery. Like the roof, the screens needed repair. Gardens ran wild in a riot of wisteria and gardenia, azalea and magnolia, with climbing roses threaded through. Though still beautiful, both the grounds and the house needed the kind of maintenance only money could bring. A lot of money.

Walker grunted. "Looks like Crying Girl still hasn't led the Montegeaus to the Blessing Chest."

"Crying Girl?"

"One of the Montegeau ghosts."

"Mel didn't mention her."

"Not surprising. Like most things about the Montegeaus, it's not a happy story."

"What do you mean?"

Walker leaned back in the seat and turned toward Faith. "Murder, incest, adultery, extortion, madness," he said. "You name it, the Montegeaus have it somewhere in their history. Crying Girl is just one of the legends."

"Go on."

"I'm not talking bedtime fairy tales here."

"That's fine. I'm a big girl."

Walker could hardly argue that. He shrugged. "Seems like one of the Montegeaus took a fancy to his own daughter."

Faith grimaced.

"Yeah," Walker said. "Not pretty. Depending on which legend you believe, Crying Girl is either the child of that incest or the betrayed daughter herself. She walks the dark places at midnight, looking for her lost soul or the baby that was taken away from her at birth by her own mother and drowned in the marsh.''

Faith let out a long breath. ''Lovely.''

Walker's smile was as sardonic as her voice had been. ''Welcome to Ruby Bayou, sugar. Welcome to hell.''

19

Ruby Bayou

Jefferson Montegeau was worried, and nothing his father said was making him feel better.

"Wait," Jeff said, cutting off Davis Montegeau. "You said you were going to explain why the wedding had to be moved from town to here and rushed through to Valentine's Day. Well, explain. Faith and her boyfriend will arrive any minute, and I damn well want to know what was so important that you felt you could ruin the beautiful wedding Mel wanted."

Davis Montegeau looked longingly at the nineteenth-century mahogany library table where a whiskey decanter waited. The Montegeaus had acquired many decanters in two or three centuries of drinking, but this one was special. This one was filled with Davis's favorite bourbon.

His fingertips tingled. He could almost feel the slight hesitation as crystal rubbed over crystal in the instant before the stopper came free. The cool liquid sound as whiskey splashed into more gleaming crystal. Then the hot bite as liquor burned down his throat and into his brain, a sweet red haze that veiled a blinding world.

"Dad?"

Sighing, Davis rubbed his face. He hadn't shaved today. Bad form. When he was a boy, he had known the old man was on a drunk when he showed up with gray whiskers at the breakfast table. Davis patted his thinning thatch of white hair with fingers he couldn't keep from trembling. His hair was a little mussed, but not bad. Like his clothes. No one could tell that he hadn't bathed today, could they? Or that he had slept in the clothes he was still wearing?

"Dad!"

Fuck it, Davis thought. He needed that drink.

Abruptly he stood up, went to the mahogany table, and yanked out the crystal stopper. The decanter clashed against the rim of the glass as he poured, but he didn't care. All he cared about was the numbing burn of high-test whiskey. It hit his throat and then his brain like Lucifer's own benediction.

When Davis started to pour another, Jeff's

hand clamped around his father's wrist. "That's enough."

Davis focused on the tall, blond son who had once been a towheaded toddler hardly able to navigate across the library's thick rug. "Wha' chu—" He stopped and carefully untangled his tongue. "What are you talking about?" he asked with great precision.

"Liquor. You've had enough."

"No such thing, boy. If I'm breathing, I haven't had nearly enough. Leggo—*let* go of my wrist."

Jeff looked at his father's bloodshot gray eyes. They glittered with more than booze. There was an animal kind of fear. Jeff had been uneasy about his father's condition for weeks. Now that nagging premonition crystallized into certainty. It settled in his gut like a ragged ball of ice.

"Talk to me, Dad. For once, treat me like an adult. Let me help with whatever is bothering you."

His father's laughter was worse than his smile. "Sure thing, boy. Got a half million dollars, cash?"

Jeff's clear gray eyes widened. "You're joking."

"I'm fixin' to die laughing."

"You're not making sense."

Fiercely Davis rubbed his face. "I'm making too damned much sense. I need another drink."

"No."

Davis made a grab for the elegant crystal bottle.

Jeff picked up the decanter and threw it into the old stone fireplace. Crystal exploded against sooty brick. Amber whiskey darkened ash to black. The pungent smell of alcohol spread through the room like an echo of the explosion.

With a hoarse shout, Davis lunged at his son. Jeff made no move to avoid the first blow. Then he took his father down to the faded, intricately patterned rug and pinned him there beneath the oak pegs that held the shotgun that had killed his grandfather.

Rage sobered Davis with a temporary storm of adrenaline. "Goddamn you! Let me up!"

"Not until you tell me what's going on."

"I need a drink, that's what's going on!"

"Not a drop. Not until you tell me."

Davis stared at his son in disbelief. Jeff had always been a dutiful, obedient—if only marginally competent—son. "What's got into you, boy?"

"I'm nearly forty." Though anger burned on Jeff's otherwise pale cheeks, the hands holding down his father were as gentle as possible. "I have a mate. In a few months I'll have a child. Since mother died nine years ago, all you've done is drink and hatch one money-losing real estate scheme after another while I worked like a donkey to keep the jewelry business alive."

"Who got you all the jewelry, boy? You tell

me that! Who bought all the baubles and brought them back to you to cut up and sell?''

"You did. Then you took the money I got from talking sweet to faded grannies and fancy ladies and you blew it all on bad land deals. No more, Dad. It's over. I have a wife and family to think of. The lawyer drew up papers that give me power of attorney. You're going to sign them. I'll be handling all the money from now on.''

Davis stared at his son's face. Clean bones, thick blond hair, eyes as clear as rain, handsome as a god. It was like looking back through time at himself. It made him want to laugh and cry and drink until he was blind. *Laurie, Laurie, why did you have to die? Damn, but I'm tired of being old and alone.*

"You're crazy," Davis said finally. "Why would I sign those papers?"

"Because until you do, you don't get a drink."

"How you going to stop me?"

"I already am." Sickness and determination fought in Jeff's stomach as he waited for the brutal truth to sink in. "Listen to me, Dad. I'll do whatever I have to for my wife and my future child. All these years I tried going along and getting along with whatever half-assed scheme you came up with.''

Davis twisted, but he was no match for his son's sheer strength.

"I figured you would give it up finally," Jeff

continued relentlessly. "Even a drunken fool could see that everything you touched turned to shit. But you didn't see it. No matter how much you lost, you always had another plan that would make us all rich. So you squeezed the jewelry business and the shrimp business and wrung them dry and blew all the money on useless property. It's time to get off that pony. The ride is over."

Davis started to argue, but the sight of the tears running silently down his son's face was more effective than a gag. Booze had kept his worst fears at bay, but now, suddenly, he saw them burn through, hot and bright as the southern sun. For an instant Davis saw with savage clarity what he had done.

"I need a drink."

Neither man recognized the hoarse, trembling voice.

Both knew a defeated man had spoken.

Jeff reached into his suit coat and pulled out a sheaf of neatly folded papers. "Sign these."

Numbly Davis nodded. As though looking through the long end of a telescope, he watched himself sign on each line as Jeff pointed. When it was over, he took the stiff drink his son poured and finished it in one long, ecstatic shudder.

Now he would have enough courage to tell Jeff just how badly things had gone wrong.

Maybe his son could pull all the chestnuts out of the fire before nothing was left.

❧

Despite Walker's bleak description of Ruby Bayou and the Montegeau legends, Faith was impressed with the landscaping. Even run-down and overgrown with weeds, the shabby formal gardens echoed with past glory. She could easily imagine a time when the local gentry sipped homemade lemonade and aged bourbon at the cool feet of oaks while crickets sang and the heady, sensual fragrance of gardenias and magnolias breathed through the soft summer evening like a lover's sigh.

"It must have been spectacular," Faith said as she turned in a slow, full circle.

"It was." But not as spectacular as Faith herself, standing in a shaft of moonlight like a princess made of spun silver and impossible dreams.

Walker was careful not to say anything about what was on his mind. Bad enough that he was thinking it. Even worse, he felt it to the soles of his feet.

An unpruned rose grabbed low on Faith's back, beneath her soft suede jacket.

"Hold still or you'll snag the lining." He hoped she didn't notice that his voice had thickened with plain, unvarnished desire. He slid his hands beneath the jacket hem and began to work the thorn free. "I used to sneak up that bayou in a skiff and watch all the fancy folks drink and dance beneath the colored lights. Laurie Montegeau knew how to throw a party."

Faith couldn't answer. Though the intimacy wasn't intentional, the feel of Walker's fingers brushing against her hip stole her breath. His body heat seemed to burn through her jeans.

"The women looked like clouds of butterflies whirling through the garden," he continued huskily.

And not one of them had been as beautiful to him as Faith Donovan was now, standing in her jeans and running shoes and butterfly-soft leather jacket, surrounded by moonlight and a ruined garden. But he didn't say anything about that either.

"It must—" Her breath broke. *Surely he hadn't caressed her hip.* "It must have been hard for you to sit out there hungry and watch—watch all the—"

"No," Walker said, lightly stroking the swell of her hip for a third time before reluctantly freeing her. "It was just the way it was." Knowing he was a fool and too hungry to care anymore, he turned her slowly until she was facing him. "Like you and me. Are you going to let me kiss you? Or are you going to keep me out in the dark, watching everything beautiful that I can't touch?"

"I've sworn off men." But even as Faith spoke,

her arms slid around him and she tilted her face up to his kiss.

"According to my fourth-grade teacher, *men* is a plural," Walker said. "There's only one of me."

The last words were breathed over her lips. She shivered and leaned closer to his warmth. "Yes."

"Yes what?" His lips brushed like moonlight over her face.

"Just yes." She turned her head to follow his tantalizing, warm mouth. "Kiss me, Walker."

When his head dipped, she expected a quick, thrusting kiss and fast hands all over her. What she got was a slow, savoring kind of caress, as though he was absorbing every texture of her mouth. Absorbing her.

She lost herself in the soft brush of lips over lips, the silk of his beard and the heat of his breath and the hard edge of his teeth in gentle, knee-loosening nips that circled the edge of her mouth. When he finally let her taste him, she made a low sound and arched up against him. He tasted like a Low Country night, dark and warm and alive with secrets. She couldn't get enough of him.

Walker felt the same about her. He told himself he would stop soon. Real soon. The next breath.

Then he wondered how long he could hold his breath.

She was burning in his hands, in his mouth,

against his aroused body, trying to get inside his skin the same way he wanted to be inside hers. Her hungry little sounds went through him like electric shocks. No whiskey could be stronger, no sugar sweeter than her mouth, no fire hotter than the promise of her thighs pressing close and her whole body an arc of desire curving into him.

He forced himself to lift his head and dragged in air. "We shouldn't be doing this."

She took a broken breath. "Why?"

The huskiness of her voice licked over him. His body clenched with a hunger so raw and deep it caught him by surprise. "I'm not ready for this."

"You sure feel ready," she said without thinking. Then she thought of Tony's anger when she had once suggested that he slow down and let her catch up. "Sorry. I didn't mean to imply that you're, um, too fast off the mark."

"Is that what you were implying?" His voice was deep and amused, because he was undoubtedly ready, willing, and fully able against her belly.

And the Montegeau necklace was damned uncomfortable in a smuggler's pouch that was suddenly too small.

"No, I wasn't implying anything," she said quickly. "It's just that you're obviously, um, capable and I'm, um, slow."

For a moment Walker was too astonished to

speak. She had damn near set fire to his shoes with a single kiss and she called herself . . .

"Slow," he said, not sure he had heard right for the blood pounding in his ears.

She bit her lip and nodded. "Slow. But it's okay. I know men and women are different and I—" she took a quick breath "—I'm okay with it. I enjoy anyway." *Some of the time,* she admitted silently. *Well, not much, not really.* But it sure had been nice before Walker started talking. She had never been kissed like that, as though she was a rare treat to be touched and sampled in tiny little bites and slow tastings.

"Different, huh?" Walker said. He looked into her beautiful, earnest eyes. "Am I'm getting the ripe smell of ol' road apples here?"

"What? Oh, Tony. Well, he's a man."

"I'll take your word for it."

"And I'm a woman—"

"Amen."

"—so I know that I have to make allowances for different sexual drives, that's all."

He lowered his forehead until it was resting against hers. Then he breathed softly against her lips, "Bullshit."

She snickered. "But it's true."

"Sugar, ain't nothin' true all the time and ain't nothin' always a lie. There are some times you couldn't get a man hot with a blowtorch and vice versa. Trust me, tonight wasn't one of those times."

"Sugar, huh?"

"Sure enough. If you were any sweeter, I'd just have to slide you out of those clothes and lick you all over."

The lazy intensity of Walker's voice sent ripples of heat through Faith. The thought of that kind of love play stopped her breath.

The combination of curiosity and desire was clear on her face, so clear that for the space of two slamming heartbeats, Walker thought he was going to do just that—strip her naked and lick her until she melted in his mouth.

"You better hope we don't have adjoining rooms," he said, his voice almost hoarse.

"Why?"

"Because I'm supposed to be too smart to seduce my boss's baby sister," he said bluntly.

Her eyes narrowed. "Yeah? What if she seduces you, just sneaks in your bed and starts—" Her voice broke at what she was thinking, Walker naked and herself all over him like a warm rain. The idea had never appealed to her before. With him, it was different. She didn't know why. She just knew it was. Like the heat shimmering hot and sweet beneath her skin. Different.

Walker told himself he wouldn't ask Faith to finish her sentence. It wouldn't be smart. Like standing so close to her that her breasts brushed against him with every breath she took. And she was breathing fast.

"Starts what?" he asked before he could stop himself.

"Licking you all over," she whispered.

He opened his mouth. Nothing came out but a soft, rough, hungry sound. His arms tightened around her until neither one of them could breathe. "This is the dumbest thing I've ever done."

But even as he spoke, he was slanting his mouth over hers.

Suddenly a pale blur moved at the corner of his eye, white cloth fluttering where there was no breeze.

Faith saw it at the same instant. "What—"

His hand covered her mouth. He shook his head, silently telling her to be quiet. She nodded. He lowered his hand and they turned their heads toward the bit of motion.

At first they saw only moonlight and darkness, heard only silence. Then something moved at the end of the garden, where roses ran in a tangle toward the bayou. White flickered like cold flame before it was snuffed out by the weight of night.

Breath held, Walker and Faith waited.

Moonlight, darkness, and then the low, keening wail of a girl buried in grief like moonlight smothered by night.

Cold prickled over Faith. She started to speak.

She couldn't. Her mouth was too dry, her throat too tight with a sorrow that wasn't her own. Even after she swallowed, all that came out was a whisper.

Walker understood. "Crying Girl," he explained softly. "She walks Ruby Bayou. She's real early tonight. Usually it's midnight when she roams."

"That was a *ghost*?"

"You don't believe in haints?"

"Haints?"

"Spirits. Ghosts."

"Er, no, not really."

"I usually don't, either. Crying Girl is different. I make allowances for her. I was seven when I saw her for the first time. My first night alone in the bayou, too."

"You were *seven*?"

He nodded.

"My God," she said, trying to imagine what it must have been like for a young child alone in the dark with that unearthly wailing rising like black mist through the silence. "What did you do?"

"Wet my pants." He smiled slightly, remembering. "But I got used to her. Came to think of her almost like company. Hardly ever saw her after Lot started swamp-crawling with me. He was too noisy. Crying Girl likes her solitude."

Cold still prickled down Faith's arms and

spine. Warily she peered out toward the edge of the garden. No pale flash of white. No feeling of someone or some*thing* hovering just at the edge of awareness.

"Well, I'm happy to give Crying Girl all the solitude she wants," Faith said briskly.

Walker took her cool fingers and lifted them to his lips. After a brushing kiss, he put her palms against his neck, warming them. Then he thought of some other things that would warm both of them to flash point. Slowly he pulled her soft hands away from his skin, kissed her knuckles, and released her.

"Come on," he said. "Folks in the house will be wondering where we are."

"I don't think they saw us drive up."

He didn't think so either, but he knew if he didn't get her out of the garden real quick, they would find out if those overgrown weeds had stickers that poked through clothes.

The wind shifted in a long sigh, as though the marsh itself was breathing slow and deep. A moment later a deep, belling cry came from the house. It was the call of a hound that has just caught a scent.

"Boomer," Faith said. "Mel's dog."

"He sure is."

"No, that's his name."

"Good nose on that boy," Walker said, judging their distance from the house. The dog must have caught their scent the instant the wind shifted. "Helluva doorbell. I'll get the luggage."

"I'll help."

By the time they had unloaded their bags, someone in the house had called off the hound. As Walker and Faith climbed the front steps, a light came on in the hallway. Then the porch light came on. Or rather, the porch lights. There were strings of Christmas lights wound on the tall Doric columns. The columns supported porches that wrapped around both stories of the house. The once colorful lights had been all but bleached out by the relentless southern sun. Most of the bulbs had burned out. None had been replaced.

Walker had already noted the weeds growing between the bricks of the driveway. The walkway to the house couldn't decide if it was stone, gravel, or more weeds. The stately columns loomed pale and straight in the moonlight. Paint peeled from them. The porch wasn't dangerously rotten, but it needed work real soon. Privately he thought that the Montegeaus would do better to sell the rubies in Mel's wedding necklace and put some money into the old mansion before it crumbled under the weight of neglect and time.

"It's as sad as Crying Girl," Faith murmured.

"It won't be the first old house to rot back into the land." But Walker's voice was a lot softer than his words. Setting down his luggage, he picked a brittle flake of paint off a column and remembered twenty-five years ago, when the Montegeau house was a magical white palace shimmering with light and music and wealth.

"You feel it, too," she said.

It wasn't a question, so he didn't answer. He opened his fingers and let the bit of old paint drift down to the porch where other flakes lay like dandruff circling the pillar.

The ten-foot doors with their intricately designed leaded glass panels seemed to shudder. Finally one door came open with a reluctant squeal of hinges. Light shifted and changed over the glass before spilling out onto the porch. Faith's hair burned bright gold and her eyes shone gray.

The woman who had opened the door took one look at Faith, said a choked word, and fainted.

20

Walker kicked aside the luggage and caught the woman before she hit the floor. Like a bayou heron, she was long-limbed and weighed very little. Though she was wearing a midcalf dress of shiny, pale cotton, she smelled oddly of marsh and crab pots as well as baby powder and some innocent floral fragrance. Her hair was a mixture of gray and blond. It looked as though she cut it blindfolded, with a dull pocket knife.

"Is she all right?" Faith asked anxiously.

"She's breathing. Her pulse is okay." Walker shifted her into carrying position in his arms. "Looks like just an old-fashioned genteel fainting spell."

Ignoring the luggage, Faith held the door open

so that Walker could carry the woman inside.
He moved so easily that Faith wondered how he
managed it with his hurt leg. Then she wondered
if he was being stoic for her benefit. "Should you
be carrying her?"

"Sure, why not?"

"Your leg."

"It's just stiff, not really hurt."

"Did you understand what she said before she
fainted?" Faith asked.

"Ruby."

"Ruby?" She followed Walker in and shut the
door behind. The hinges squealed again, making
her wince. Surely someone in the house had oil
or silicone spray. Even soap would work. "Do
you suppose she knows about the necklace?"

Walker shrugged despite his burden. With a
twist of his body, he shouldered open the massive door that led to the parlor just off the entry
hall. Here, in lemon-scented splendor, properly
dressed visitors once had been entertained. Now
the smell of must, dust, and curtains brittle from
too much sun filled the room.

"See if you can find a light switch," he said.

Faith fumbled around for a few moments before she found a set of switches. When she hit
the right one, an extraordinary crystal chandelier
scattered rainbows through years of dust. Another switch set off a Tiffany lamp, which sent
spears of colored light out from a dark corner of

the room. Tarnished silver bowls of potpourri sat in the middle of each end table on either side of the elaborate, faded velvet couch that was styled after the court of Louis XIV.

Walker laid the woman on the uneven cushions and propped her feet on the high arm.

Mel's voice came from the back of the house. "Tiga? What was Boomer carrying on about? Boomer, quit shoving. Stay! Was that Faith?"

"We're here," Faith called out. "Tiga—"

"Hang on," Mel interrupted. "Let me untangle myself from the hound."

Mel grabbed a double handful of Boomer's warm, loose scruff and hauled back. The hound's nose had been wedged in the barely open door leading from the kitchen into the dining room. He looked up at Mel as though asking what all the tugging was about.

"Jeff, Daddy, are you in there?" she yelled in the direction of the library, which was opposite the parlor but toward the kitchen end of the house. "Tiga answered the door!"

Boomer wagged his yard-long whip of a tail against Mel's legs and gave her a big wet swipe across the mouth with his tongue.

"Bleh! Dog kisses," she said, but she was laughing. "Jeff," she yelled, "we've got company, Boomer wants to make friends with them, and I don't know if they're dog people."

"Let 'er rip," Walker called back. "Tiga just fainted. We're in the parlor."

"Oh, no!" Mel cried. "Jeff, I need you!"

She yanked the kitchen door fully open, Boomer took off, and the library door swung wide at the same time. Looking disheveled and hunted, Jeff ran out of the library. Dog and man collided, skidded, windmilled.

Jeff caught himself and the hound with the ease of long practice. "Settle down, you big mutt."

Boomer woofed softly and licked Jeff wherever he could reach him. Jeff strengthened his grip on the dog's collar and thumped his barrel amiably. He and the hound strode toward the front of the house.

"Didn't you tell them to come in the back way?" Jeff asked as Mel hurried to catch up with him. "I don't even know if the lights still work in front."

"I forgot to tell them. Tiga fainted." Mel hurried past her husband and the dog. "They're in the parlor."

Jeff cursed under his breath. "Leave it to Tiga to put on a show for company. Heel, Boomer."

The dog wagged his tail and leaned harder into his collar.

"You've forgotten everything we taught you," Jeff complained to the hound.

"That would have taken all of five seconds," Mel said over her shoulder.

"Slow down, darling. You might slip. Tiga's all right. You know what she's like."

"That's why I'm worried about our guests."

After his chat with Daddy, so was Jeff, but he didn't say anything. He was still reeling between disbelief and fear. He felt like a chicken thrown into an alligator pond. Until he figured a way to get out of it, he didn't have energy for frills like strategy. Survival was all that mattered.

As Mel hurried into the parlor, Tiga moaned and opened her eyes. She saw a dark beard, a hard-edged mouth, and deep blue eyes that were watching her intently.

"Are you a pirate?" she asked in a little-girl voice.

"No." He smiled gently. "I'm just an ordinary Low Country boy, Miss Montegeau. How are you feeling?"

"Quite well, thank you. And you?"

"Fine. Do you remember fainting?"

"Did I faint?" She let out a long breath. When she spoke again, her voice was that of an adult. "Oh, dear. I thought it was one of The Dreams."

Walker raised his eyebrows at the capital letters in her voice. "The dreams?" he asked politely.

"Tiga, don't you dare," Mel said quickly. "You

promised you wouldn't, uh, dream when we had company."

"Did I? What was I thinking of? I don't choose the time to dream, child. It chooses me."

Mel turned and looked over her shoulder. The eager Boomer had just towed Jeff into the ornate, faded parlor. The dog's nails scrabbled on the hardwood floor and then fell silent as soon as they bit into the beautiful old carpet.

"Hi, I'm Jeff Montegeau, but things will sort out faster if you meet Boomer first," he added.

Faith looked up and saw a man who could have modeled for any up-scale men's fashion magazine, but it would have taken a woman to really appreciate his lithe build and beautifully sculpted face. Gray eyes. Blond hair. A smile that made you believe he meant it. A voice as supple and beguiling as a cello. She gave Mel a look that said, *Nice going, roomie,* and then turned back to Jeff Montegeau.

"I'm Faith," she said, smiling at him. "That hundred-pound wonder is Boomer, I take it?"

Hearing his name, Boomer lunged forward, tail thumping against everything within range.

Just as the dog wrenched loose from Jeff's grip, Walker reached out and snagged the big hound's collar.

"Easy, boy," Walker said, bracing himself. He jerked once on the collar. Hard. "Sit."

The dog's butt hit the floor and he panted happily up at Walker.

"Good dog," Walker murmured, running his hands appreciatively over the hound's short, smooth coat. "You're a handsome feller, aren't you? Long, strong legs for swamp running. Deep chest for stamina. Short fur to make it easy to find ticks, widely spaced eyes, enough forehead for the brains you never use." As he talked, he squatted on his heels next to Boomer and scratched the hound's long, silky black ears.

Boomer's eyes glazed with adoration.

Walker glanced up at Jeff, who was almost as pale as his aunt Tiga. Nervous, too. "I'm Walker. What is he—black-and-tan, redbone, bluetick?"

"Yes," Jeff said dryly.

Walker smiled. "One hundred percent hound. Two hundred percent knothead."

Boomer's tail slapped the rug in happy agreement.

"How do you feel about dogs?" Walker asked Faith.

"Envious of everyone who has the time to take proper care of one." She walked forward and savored the soft whuffing sounds as the loose-lipped hound sniffed her hand. When he began to lick intently, she laughed and petted him.

"I wouldn't get up just yet, ma'am," Walker said, sensing movement behind him.

Tiga ignored him. She sat up and stared at Faith. *"Ruby."*

Mel rolled her eyes at Jeff, who sighed and tried to deflect his aunt before she got off into one of her loopy, semi-rhyming monologues.

"Aunt Tiga, this is Faith Donovan," he said. "No one by the name of Ruby lives here anymore."

Tiga gave her nephew a pitying look. "There are none so blind as those who won't see."

"The original Ruby died more than two hundred years ago," Jeff said patiently. "Ruby wasn't her real name. It was just a pet name her father gave her."

Tiga shuddered. "She hated him. It was a different Ruby, anyway. She went away so long ago, far away, good-bye, I never got to know you. I'm a child, too, you see." With a heartbreaking smile, Tiga turned to Faith. "I'm glad you came home to me, Ruby. I was so angry when Mama took you away. I looked for you a long, long . . . so long, good-bye, hello, now I'll know and you never will."

Her laugh was gentle, musical, and gave Faith goose bumps even as tears burned against her eyelids. Tiga was fascinating, eerie, and frightening by turns. Her eyes were twilight gray, haunted by something unspeakably sad, unspeakably terrible.

Faith wanted to believe it was simple madness.

"Tiga," Davis said from the door of the library. "Are you being silly again?"

Tiga jumped as though slapped. "Papa?"

Pain flickered across Davis's lined face. "Papa died, Tiga. I'm his son. Your brother."

"Oh." She sighed. Blinking as though coming into light after long darkness, she turned to Faith again. "Have we met?"

"I'm Faith Donovan," she said gently.

"I'm Antigua. People used to call me Miss Montegeau, but now everyone just calls me Tiga. May I call you Faith?"

"Please do."

Tiga nodded and stood with the agility of a woman half her age. "Dinner at eight." Then she walked out of the room as though no one else was there.

When Davis heard pots and pans clash toward the back of the house, he let out a sigh of relief. "Welcome to Ruby Bayou, Ms. Donovan, Mr. Walker. Please excuse my sister. She means no rudeness. She isn't entirely . . . here. This hasn't been one of her better weeks."

Davis was an older version of Jeff, more puffy and more hunted. His eyes were the same fog gray as his son's, but the whites were a road map of red blood vessels. His white hair was just beginning to thin on top. His skin was pale except for a flush that could have been embarrassment, fever, or booze.

"No problem," Faith said, forcing herself to smile despite the emotions still ripping at her. "Sometimes things get a little hectic around the Donovan family, too."

"Hectic." Davis smiled like a man not accustomed to it. "Well. I'll show you to your rooms. After you freshen up, we'll eat. Tiga might be, uh, scatterbrained about some things, but there's no finer cook in the Low Country. We don't dress for dinner anymore. If you'll follow me?"

Don't dress for dinner . . .

For a moment Faith had visions of everyone sitting down naked to eat. Walker's grin told her that he knew what she was thinking. She didn't look at him, afraid she would laugh or blush. She didn't look at him when she saw that they had connecting rooms, either. If she had, she *would* have blushed, remembering her own threat to sneak into his bed and lick him all over.

Biting her lip, she concentrated on the accommodations. The suite had been designed for a visiting family. There were bedrooms on either side of a shared sitting room. A bathroom had been added on to the larger bedroom forty years ago, according to their host. That was when Mrs. Montegeau had been alive and they had entertained nearly every week.

"I'm afraid you'll have to share the bathroom," Davis said apologetically. "The other ones on this floor just aren't reliable anymore, except for the suite Mel and Jeff use, which is on the opposite side." With a hand that had a fine tremor, he gestured toward the far reaches of the second story.

"This is wonderful," Faith said quickly. "It's very kind of you to have us on such short notice."

Davis closed his eyes for an instant. The visions of disaster he saw awaiting him weren't pleasant. He opened his eyes and looked at the likeable young woman who was his future daughter-in-law's old friend.

And perhaps his own salvation.

In the meantime there was whiskey. With enough of it, he wouldn't think about all of his mistakes coming back to haunt him.

"My pleasure, I assure you," he said softly. "We have drinks in the library before dinner, if y'all would care to join us."

"Thank you," Walker said. "We'll be down as soon as we have a chance to freshen up."

"I'll bring up the luggage," Faith said after Davis disappeared.

Walker was already out in the hall, heading downstairs. "You're in the South, remember? I'll get it."

"But—"

"Unless you're wanting company in that bathroom," he drawled, "you better hurry along. I'm not fixin' to be late to a Low Country feed cooked by Antigua Montegeau.''

❧

Faith was relieved when the cocktail hour was over. She no longer wondered about the cause of her host's flush. Despite lethal looks from Jeff, Davis had consumed two whiskeys in short order and was hard at work on a third. Mel was looking strained beneath her generous smile. Walker was impassive, as though the sight of a man drinking way too much was familiar. Considering the little that he had told Faith about his childhood, she was pretty sure Walker's thoughts weren't happy, no matter how bland a face he put over them.

Exactly at eight, Tiga picked up an antique crystal bell and swung it briskly. Sweet sounds rang through the hall leading to the dining room.

Boomer had been curled asleep in front of the unnecessary but attractive fire. At the sound of the bell, the hound scrambled to his feet, bolted out of the library, and took up his station at one end of the table, just beside Davis's tall-backed captain's chair.

Except for dust on the extravagant chandelier, the dining room was much cleaner than the parlor. Time and use had turned the intricate, elegant lace tablecloth from white to gold, but the delicate threads were mostly intact. While the huge mahogany table, sideboard, china cupboard, and eighteen chairs could have used a good polishing, the woven seat covers were relatively fresh and glowed with rich jewel tones in the candlelight.

Despite tarnish, the ornate silver candelabra and silverware added to the warm light of the pale beeswax tapers. They looked like living satin glowing from within. The bone china was either as old as the house or an excellent reproduction. Faith guessed the former because the intricately designed gold border on each plate had been dulled by use. Cut-crystal pitchers filled with icy mineral water waited by each place setting.

No matter what the status of the present Montegeau generation, there had been real money around in the past.

Or real pirates.

Walker caught Faith running a thoughtful fingertip around the gold-rimmed crystal wine goblet and smiled. She didn't have to hear his low murmur of Black Jack Montegeau's name in her ear to know what Walker was thinking. The bad old days had been very good to some Montegeaus.

The dark, ostentatious, gilt-framed portraits on the wall announced just who had benefited from the legacy of piracy. Every generation of Montegeaus since Black Jack's had been painted in turn, except the two most recent.

And each woman was wearing one piece of ruby jewelry that would have suited an empress.

"None of them are the same," Walker said, following Faith's glance at the portraits.

"What?" she asked absently.

"The rubies they're wearing. Either the necklaces weren't passed down or each generation designed new settings."

"You have a good eye," Jeff said. "The tradition was that after each portrait was painted, the jewelry went into the Blessing Chest to assure the fortune of that generation and the next. Once in the Blessing Chest, jewelry could be worn but never sold without bringing bad luck. At least, that's the family legend."

Walker whistled softly and looked at the portraits with new interest. "That would be a chest worth opening."

"Tell me about it." Jeff's voice was bitter. "It disappeared in my grandparents' day." He looked up as his aunt handed him a platter heaped with deviled crab that had been stuffed back into individual shells. "Thank you, Tiga."

She nodded and took her seat. Though there were only six people at the big table, she sat down alone at the far end, opposite her brother, Davis.

"People were still talking about that when I was a boy," Walker said. "A sad occasion all the way around."

Jeff smiled slightly. "I thought I heard Low Country in your voice."

"Born and mostly raised," Walker agreed. He took a bite of deviled crab. "Lordy, Lordy," he murmured. "Miss Montegeau, it's God's own miracle some man hasn't up and stolen you for your cooking skills."

Tiga's smile was as fresh and sweet as a child's. "You are very kind, sir."

"A lot of folks will be relieved to hear it," he said, and winked at her. "Bet you have angels sneaking down from heaven just to get a taste of what you put on this table."

Tiga giggled like a girl who still was learning what it was to catch a boy's eye. And hold it.

Faith smiled down at her food. It was much smaller than the Dungeness crab of the Pacific Northwest. Though this Low Country crab flared to wicked-looking points on either side of the "shoulders," its shell would have fit in the palm of her hand. There had to be at least twenty of the little beasties piled on their backs on the platter. Maybe thirty.

Silently wondering if crab was the main course rather than the appetizer, Faith took a bite. She closed her eyes with unconscious delight and made a murmuring sound of approval. "Sea-tasting and steamy, creamy and succulent," she murmured, "with just enough spice to hold your attention."

Walker swallowed hard and tried to think pure thoughts.

"It's perfect." Faith opened her eyes and gave Mel, who was sitting across from her, a look of sympathy. "No wonder you're worried about gaining weight."

Mel sighed and ate another carefully rationed morsel of the rich crab. "I tell myself that a few bites won't hurt, despite the cream. Besides, I know dessert is coming."

"Don't tell me what. Let me dream."

"As long as you're dreaming of sugar pie, pecan pie, lemon refrigerator pie, and Key lime pie, some of your dreams will come true. Unless we're having Tiga's own version of Chocolate Sin. Then you just can't have more than one helping."

"Stop! I'm drooling."

"You can afford to," Mel retorted. "You're not fighting your waistline."

Some of the tension around Jeff's mouth and eyes eased as he smiled at his pregnant lover and soon-to-be bride. "When she moved out here, Mel thought she was going to miss West Coast fusion cooking. After she ate one of Tiga's meals, she never looked back. Sometimes I think Tiga's cooking is the reason Mel agreed to marry me."

Mel gave him a slow smile. "It wasn't Tiga who made me fat, now was it?"

Walker snickered. Faith kicked his foot under the table. He winked at her.

Davis finished his first glass of wine as though it was the bottled water. When he reached for the decanter, Jeff beat him to it. He topped off everyone's glass—except his father's—and set the decanter down on the floor beside his chair, out of his father's reach.

Boomer sniffed the top of the decanter, sneezed, and moved to the other end of the table in a huff.

The narrow glance Davis gave his son told Walker that Jeff was going to pay for the stunt.

"Yes, my dear papa lost the Blessing Chest," Davis announced as though someone had asked. "That old son of a bitch lost everything but the way into his zipper."

"Eat fast," Walker muttered to Faith. "The storm is about to break."

21

"I don't think our guests want to hear about Grandfather Montegeau," Jeff said.

"I was almost ten," Davis said. He fiddled with his empty wineglass and looked pointedly at Jeff's full goblet. For a price—a glass of wine—Davis would be happy to set the family history aside.

Jeff ignored him.

Davis started airing dirty Montegeau laundry. "My papa wasn't like me or Jeff," he said to Faith. "He was a sure enough hell-raiser and skirt lifter."

"Dad—"

"Shuddup. 'S rude to innerupt your elders." Though the words were slurred, they were quite understandable.

With eyes accustomed to drunks at the family table, Walker measured Davis Montegeau. The old man was angry, but not violent. Not yet. Maybe not at all. Davis lacked the bone-deep coldness of a truly violent man.

Walker helped himself to another crab and did the same for Faith. "Mel?" he asked.

"No, thank you. I'll wait for—"

"Papa liked 'em young," Davis said loudly, interrupting Mel. "Just budding, he used to say, when their nipples were near as big and tender as their breasts."

Tiga stood with a speed that made candle flames jerk. "It's time for the chicken."

"I'll help you," Mel said quickly.

"Mama was 'bout thirteen, near as I can tell, when he wed her," Davis continued. "From the wedding picture, I can't be sure she was even bleeding regular."

Faith took another bite of crab. The fingers of her left hand dug into the heavy, lavender-scented linen napkin that was in her lap.

Beneath the table, Walker's hand closed over hers gently. The simple warmth and comfort of the touch loosened the tension around her lungs. She laced her fingers through his and breathed deeply.

"Took him a while to breed a baby on her, but she finally caught and held."

Jeff looked grim.

His father kept talking and fiddling with his empty wineglass. "Antigua came along before mama was sixteen. I came along a little more than four years later. One child died in between us. Maybe two. I forget. What with all the babies and the miscarriages, Mama was looking a whole lot older than twenty. Papa started lifting skirts. Girlish ones."

"Pass the salt, please," Jeff said to Walker.

Walker did. "Pepper?"

"Please. How did the show go, Faith?"

"Very well. I—"

"He got caught with a sharecropper's daughter," Davis said loudly. "She was thirteen and—"

"I sold most of my pieces and made some excellent connections," Faith said, pitching her voice above her host's. "There is one piece in particular that I would like—"

"—money changed hands, so there was no lawyering. The nex' time, the gal was barely—"

"—to deliver to its owners," Faith said, giving Jeff a meaningful look. "It is very, very valuable."

"—twelve, and there was a royal pissing match over that, but Papa—"

"I understand your problem," Jeff said, and hoped his expression didn't give away just how much more he understood.

"—paid off the family with some rubies from the Blessing Chest and stayed out of—"

"But," Jeff said, "I believe it was made clear that the transfer wouldn't occur until—"

"—jail. Then there was a sweet little gal—"

"—the night of the ceremony, correct?" Jeff finished grimly.

"You haven't lived until you've eaten Tiga's buttermilk chicken," Mel announced, coming into the dining room with a flourish that made her dark hair swing jauntily against her lipstick-red blouse.

"—daughter of a local shrimper. Papa always denied—"

"I should have worn clothes the color of cream gravy," Mel said as though her father-in-law wasn't in the middle of a loud monologue about the seamy side of the Montegeau family. "It's all I can do not to roll in the heavenly stuff."

"—he was the bastard's father, but a few months later the little gal sold off a ruby brooch and—"

"Buttermilk," Walker said. The reverence in his voice was almost like a prayer. "I haven't had really good buttermilk fried chicken since I was sixteen."

"Help yourself." Mel put down the platter, shot Jeff a *do-something* look, and went back out the door.

Jeff took a sip of wine.

"—went to Atlanta with her older sister,"

Davis said, smiling coldly. "I was near eight then, plenty old enough to remember the fights. Mama might have married young, but she grew—"

"Gravy?" Tiga asked brightly. Her pale, work-roughened hands clutched a priceless tureen that was brimming with cream gravy. She looked as though she wanted to throw it at her babbling brother. "This is for soup, but everyone loves my gravy, so I make—"

"—teeth," Davis said over his sister's voice. "Mama chewed him up one side and down the other for giving away Montegeau rubies to hussies."

"—so much that I serve it in the tureen," Tiga said in a rush. "Makes for less running back and forth to the kitchen. Mr. Walker? You look like—"

"Things quieted down for a few years," Davis continued, looking hard at Jeff, "but that didn't mean Papa kept 'er zipped, just that he was—"

"—a man who enjoys gravy," Tiga said, keeping her haunted gray eyes on Walker as though he was her one promise of life ever after.

Walker usually preferred his gravy over potatoes instead of straight up, but he said, "Yes, ma'am, I sure do."

"—never caught. Least, that's what the police figured," Davis said. "The night before Tiga's birthday—"

"Oh, good. Here." Tiga shoved the tureen into

Walker's hands, gave Davis a terrified glance, and fled.

Walker thought about dumping the tureen over his host, but decided it was a waste of what smelled like sublime cream gravy, the kind a Low Country boy would hitchhike across hell to eat.

Faith passed Walker some chicken.

"—Papa musta needed some more rubies to pay off some other outraged father, cuz he—"

Walker ladled gravy over his chicken and looked at Jeff. "Gravy?"

"—had it out from its hiding place when—"

"I'll wait for the potatoes," Jeff muttered.

"—someone came in, blew a hole in him with his own shotgun, and—"

"Might be a long wait," Walker said neutrally.

"—took off into the night. We never saw the damned Blessing Chest again!" Davis shouted at his son. "It was gone and so was our luck! I need a drink, damn it!"

Davis stood up so fast that his chair slammed over backward and sent Boomer scooting out of the way with a surprised yelp. Davis lurched against the table hard enough to make wine goblets sway. Without another word, he straightened and staggered from the room. A minute later the library door slammed hard behind him.

Silence expanded in the dining room like a relieved sigh.

Jeff put his elbows on either side of his plate

and massaged his temples with both hands. Mel went to stand behind her future husband. She kneaded his tight shoulders as if it was something she had to do often.

"Please accept my apologies," Jeff said in a rough, muffled voice. "My father and I argued earlier. He's very upset with me."

"No need for apologies," Walker said. "Though I must admit, it was the most long-winded grace this ol' boy ever heard spoken over a good hot meal."

Faith snickered, then gave up and let out her tension in a laugh. So did Mel. After a moment, even Jeff lifted his head and smiled wearily.

Tiga tiptoed in with a bowl of potatoes and whispered, "Is Papa gone?"

Jeff started to explain that it was her brother, not her father, who had left in a drunken snit, then decided it wasn't worth the trouble. "Yes. He's gone."

"Oh, good." She smiled with the transparent glee of a twelve-year-old. "I brought the potatoes. Is there any gravy left?"

"Not more than a gallon." Walker got up, took the potatoes from Tiga and set them on the table, and then seated her like a princess. "Allow me to serve you, ma'am. You've done enough for one night."

"Thank you, sir."

"It's the least I can do for the best cook in the Low Country."

"You've only had a bite or two," she fretted.

"I'm fixin' to make up for that."

She looked at him closely. "You're nice. Have we met?"

"Owen Walker, ma'am."

"Do you like gravy?"

Faith looked at her plate. Only three days until the wedding. With a muffled sigh, she took a bite of chicken. Like the dinner, it was extraordinary.

For food like this, she could put up with a little family eccentricity.

❦

Mel and Walker were laughing over some story from his Low Country childhood. Faith told herself it was just as well. She was tired and a bit too relaxed after two glasses of wine. If Walker came upstairs with her, she doubted that she would sleep alone. Part of her quickened at the thought. Another part of her wondered if she was crazy.

Just as Faith started up the stairs for bed, Jeff pulled her aside. "Do you have a minute?"

"Sure."

With a tip of his head, he indicated the library.

Faith hesitated. She didn't want to see Davis Montegeau again while he was drinking.

"Don't worry. Daddy has long since staggered off to bed and passed out." Though Jeff's voice was mild, love and bitterness clashed just beneath the calm. The lines around his face and eyes were deeply cut, telling of emotional turmoil.

She followed him into the library without saying anything. There were no words to lighten the suffering of the child of an alcoholic.

Like the dining room, the library was clean if not polished. The smell of whiskey was almost overpowering. When she saw the sparkling fragments of a decanter lying jagged in the fireplace, she remembered Jeff's words at the dinner table. *My father and I argued earlier. He's very upset with me.*

It wasn't hard to figure out why.

Jeff closed the door. "I know it's an imposition to ask you to keep the necklace until the wedding, but Daddy insured it separately from our normal policies. Coverage won't begin until after Mel and I are married. Normally I wouldn't worry about the lapse of a few days in the coverage, but—" he laced his fingers together and squeezed "—the Montegeau luck hasn't been very good lately. If anything happened and the necklace wasn't insured, it would be the final blow." He smiled, but it turned upside down. "I would very much appreciate your understanding in this. I don't want anything else to spoil Mel's wedding."

Faith said the only thing she could. "Of course. When would you like to have the necklace?"

His mouth flattened, then softened. "Daddy wants to put it on Mel just before she walks down the aisle. It's his gift to us."

There was sadness in Jeff's voice, the complex yearning of a son for a father. It twisted Faith's heart. She wished she knew him well enough to give him a hug. "I'll see that he gets it."

"Just before Mel walks down the aisle."

Obviously Jeff didn't trust his father with a million dollars worth of rubies. Faith couldn't blame him. Compassion turned her eyes into silver-blue mist. "Of course."

"It—it won't be a problem?" he asked almost reluctantly.

"No."

"You don't have to go back to Savannah to get it?"

"No."

"Good. I was afraid you were counting on me to pick it up or something."

"Don't worry. The necklace is here." She thought of its resting place in Walker's underwear and smiled. "It's quite safe."

"If you say so. I worry about valuables kept in luggage. We have a safe in the library." He gestured to a massive painting of Black Jack Montegeau with the Blessing Chest gleaming in shades of silver at his feet. "It's behind there."

"What about your father?"

"What about him?" Then Jeff realized what Faith was delicately trying to say. "Oh. Yes. Well, I doubt if he even remembers the combination. Other than the family Bible and some documents, there's nothing inside the safe now. It's fireproof, you see. I'd be happy to let you use it."

"I'll suggest it to Walker."

Jeff's eyebrows lifted slightly.

"The necklace is his responsibility," Faith explained. "He's sort of a walking insurance policy."

Jeff cleared his throat and looked uncomfortable. "Well, if you feel that's safer than metal and combination locks . . ."

"That will be up to Walker. My brother Archer is insuring the rubies. Walker works for Archer."

"Ah. I see." He shrugged jerkily. "Well, as long as the necklace is secure, that's what counts. But I'd really feel better if it was in the safe. Would you mention it to Walker? I'll be working in here for another hour or so. It wouldn't be any trouble at all to put the necklace in the safe. And you have pieces of your own, don't you? You're welcome to put them in as well."

"Thank you, I will," she said, wanting Jeff to feel as though he had done something to make up for his father's behavior. "I'll get them now and talk to Walker about the necklace." She smiled and touched Jeff lightly on the shoulder.

"Don't worry. You and Mel will have a wonderful wedding and a beautiful baby. That's what you should be thinking about, not your father and his problems."

Jeff smiled grimly. "When it comes to family, it's hard not to worry. But thank you, Faith. You're as nice as Mel said."

❦

Walker wasn't in the living room when Faith came out of the library.

"He went up to bed," Mel said. "I think his leg was bothering him."

"I wish he would let me help him."

"How?" Mel yawned. " 'Scuse me. He's too big to carry."

"Deep muscle massage."

"Mmmm. Sounds like fun."

"That tells me you've never had it," Faith said dryly. "It does good, but it doesn't *feel* good."

"Forget it," Mel said with a grimace. "I'm into being pampered." She smiled at Jeff, who had followed Faith into the living room. "Take me to bed and pamper me."

"As soon as Faith brings a few things downstairs to put in the safe. Go on up, darling," he said to Mel. "If you're asleep, I'll wake you up."

"It's a deal, but only if you kiss me good night now."

Smiling, Faith made her exit. As she climbed the stairs, she admired the broad banister, polished by generations of hands, and probably by generations of knee pants and pinafores. The lovely, centuries-old Persian carpet was still colorful and thick enough to muffle sounds in the hallway. Flower-shaped brass sconces and flame-shaped lightbulbs gave the sculpted plaster ceiling a golden glow. Dust and jasmine potpourri competed to scent the air. If time had a scent, it would smell like the hall.

The sitting room was empty when she arrived. She hesitated, then got the jewelry case and set it on a chair. Stretching long and hard, she wondered idly if Walker had already gone to bed. Then she heard the muted thunder of water filling the master bedroom's big claw-footed tub. She knew from her own earlier bath that the tub was a more comfortable reproduction of the original Victorian model. Longer, deeper, wider, with a slanted ledge running all around the back that was just right for propping up your head. She hoped that Walker enjoyed it as much as she had.

Then she thought of his leg and how slippery wet tile was. A long soak might take out the aches, but it wouldn't make his leg any stronger on a treacherous floor.

Frowning, she went to the spun-aluminum case that looked as out of place as a spaceship in the faded elegance of the Victorian sitting room.

Opening the locks on the case, she looked inside at the three pieces of jewelry that remained. They weren't her most valuable pieces—the emerald cat and the Montegeau necklace were—but the iridescent Pearl Cove baroque black pearl set against a ruby-rimmed platinum cloud was irreplaceable. She had sold the earrings from the suite of platinum and ruby jewelry, but not the ring and bracelet.

Her own fault, really. The rubies, while richly colored and clean, weren't in the same class as the incomparable Montegeau rubies. She shouldn't have displayed them in the same case.

The sound of water stopped. Out in the darkness toward the bayou, something large called out with a sound that was a cross between a boom and a grunt. She wondered if it was an alligator or a bullfrog the size of Nebraska.

A night breeze lifted the gauzy privacy curtains and moved over her like a sigh. Walker had opened the French doors leading to the second-story gallery. The unseasonable heat the Low Country had been enjoying felt like the tropics to Faith. She was accustomed to Seattle's bracing, sleet-laced winters.

For a moment she was tempted to open the decanter of brandy that sat on the small cherry table at the end of the couch. It would be lovely to stand barefoot on a second-floor gallery in

February and sip brandy while the mild, salt-scented air caressed her.

But first, the necklace.

She went quickly to the bathroom door and knocked. "Walker?"

"C'mon in, sugar."

She distrusted the barely subdued anticipation in his voice, just like one of her brothers before he sprang something on her. "Are you decent?"

"We're all born decent."

"Uh, right. Does that mean you're wearing what you were born in?"

"Sure does. Plus a tub full of bubbles."

"Bubbles?" she asked, startled. The thought of the bearded Walker awash in froth was . . . piquant. "You're having a bubble bath?"

He laughed low and soft. "Sure am. You going to call the macho police and turn me in?"

"Nope. It's a family secret, but The Donovan, Kyle, and Lawe all love soaking in suds. It hasn't dented their macho a bit."

"There you go."

Faith found herself grinning at the heavy mahogany door with its ornate crystal and brass handle. "You still wearing the necklace?"

"That would be above and beyond the call of duty."

"Darn. I was having this nice fantasy of you wearing suds and rubies."

"Well," he drawled, "I wouldn't want to get

in the way of a nice fantasy. I'll have them on in no time at all."

She snickered even as her breath shortened. She shouldn't tease him this way—and herself—but it was just too delicious to resist. "You going to shave your chest, too?"

There was silence followed by the sudden wash of water over porcelain sides. "How do you know I don't already?"

"The shadow under your shirt."

"Dirt," he said quickly, muffling a laugh.

"Sugar," she drawled, tracing the dark grain of the wood with her fingertips, "that's an out-and-out lie. I know what dirt smells like. It doesn't smell like coffee and soap and a spicy, special kind of musk."

Walker told himself he wasn't going to stand up, open the door, and haul her into the tub with him.

"You fixin' to come in and see the family jewels?" he asked. "They're ready and waiting."

Faith didn't doubt it. Temptation swept over her, hotter than any Low Country breeze. "Thanks, but I'm supposed to take all the jewelry downstairs and lock it in the safe. It's Jeff's way of apologizing for not taking delivery of the necklace right away. And for a few other things, as well."

Walker grunted. "His safe, his house, his insurance?"

"No. His father took out a separate policy on the necklace. It won't go into effect until the night of the wedding."

Walker scooped up a double handful of suds and stared into the mound as though it was a crystal ball. His eyes were almost as dark as the night beyond the etched-glass window.

"Tell you what," he said finally. "Jeff has enough on his plate with his dear old daddy. I'll keep track of the necklace until the wedding."

"Jeff's going to feel bad about that. He really wants to do something nice to make up for his father's performance."

"So don't tell him. Just take your case down, smile sweetly, and ask him to leave you to it."

"What he doesn't know won't hurt his feelings, is that it?"

"That's one of the things I like about you. You catch on real quick."

"What's the other thing you like about me?" she asked before she thought better of it.

"Your sweet, unquestioning nature."

"I walked right into that one."

"Sure did."

"Just for that, you're not getting out of it tonight."

"Out of what?" he asked warily.

"More deep work on the leg."

He laughed despite a rush of desire. She hadn't given him a sexy little massage the other night, but it had loosened up one leg . . . and made another one hard as hell. "I'm beginning to think you're a closet sadist."

"You just keep thinking about it, sugar. I'll be right back."

Walker let out a breath and reached for the cold-water tap.

One of them had to start being sensible.

22

When Faith emerged from the library with an empty aluminum case, Jeff was waiting at the foot of the stairs. Boomer stood at his side, looking like a hound ready to find a soft nest for the night.

"All set?" Jeff asked.

"Yes, thank you. I spun the dial for you and pushed the portrait back in place. Everything's locked up tight. I even turned off the lights."

"Thanks." Jeff yawned, easing the taut lines in his face. "Funny how things like that weigh on a man. It's only money, after all, and no matter what, one way or another, everything is insured, right?"

"Right."

He smiled slightly. "I guess all the family history is nagging at me. I have to keep reminding
myself that even if something happens, it's the
insurance company that loses, not us, and the
good Lord knows they have money to spare."

"Mel would lose, too. That's a beautiful necklace, if I do say so myself."

"I'll take your word for it," he said rather
grimly. Up until today, he hadn't even known the
combination to the wall safe. That had changed
hands along with the power of attorney. "Daddy
never showed anyone your drawings. He kept
them in the safe and then burned them after the
necklace was done. He wanted it to be a complete surprise. He's the only one at Ruby Bayou
who has the least idea what it looks like. Other
than you and Walker, of course."

Faith smiled. "No matter how beautiful the
necklace is, you'll only have eyes for Mel."

He grinned suddenly and looked ten years
younger. "She's wonderful, isn't she?"

"Yes. You're a lucky man."

His smile shifted, but held. "I hope so. I surely
hope so. The Montegeaus could use a change in
their luck."

"Papa was greedy," Tiga said from behind
them. "He didn't put any souls in the Blessing
Chest."

Faith made a startled sound. Jeff didn't even
flinch. He was used to Tiga's soft-footed ways.

"Rubies, Tiga," he said mildly, yawning again. "The Blessing Chest holds rubies."

"You've never seen them in moonlight. Sometimes they sing. Sometimes they laugh. Mostly they just weep for all that happened before souls bled and turned into red stone."

The calm reason in Tiga's voice was so at odds with her words that the hair on the nape of Faith's neck moved.

Tiga walked forward and put a cold, brine-scented hand on Faith's cheek. "I would have loved you, but they took you away. Pretty little baby girl. Are you safe from him now? I put something very special in the chest for you, for me. A soul to set us free." She looked at Jeff. "You must do the same. Thirteen souls. If enough rubies weep, your generation won't."

"Tiga," he said wearily, "it's time for you to be in bed."

"Haven't I told you about time? It comes and goes like moonlight. You can never tell, never tell, wishing well, souls wishing, sighing, crying, never dying." She smiled at him. "Breakfast at eight. Pancakes, Papa's favorite. Sugar pie and Fourth of July. Pecans for Thanksgiving. Thanks be I'm not a ruby, I think. He drinks. I'm not just rubies, am I?"

With a sigh Jeff took Tiga's arm and led her off toward the family wing of the house. Boomer followed, nosing the older woman's slack fingers as though to remind her that she was indeed flesh and blood. Gradually the sound of her voice faded into silence.

Faith rubbed her hands up and down her arms to smooth away the primitive ripple of unease that came in the presence of madness. Suddenly she understood why tribes made shamans or spirit doctors of the insane. There was an eerie feeling of larger truth woven like a glittering black thread through Tiga's irrationality.

After a moment Faith shook herself and went back upstairs. She needed Walker's wry sanity and laughter.

The bathroom was silent. The door to his bedroom was closed. She stood just outside it and called softly, "Walker?"

There was no answer.

After a few moments she quietly turned away. She opened the door to her own bedroom and saw the single snifter of brandy sitting on her bedside table. The message was clear: she would be sleeping alone. Ignoring the stab of disappointment and something very close to sadness, she kicked off her sandals, grabbed the snifter, and went back to the sitting area.

There was no reason to feel hurt and rejected. It wasn't like she had propositioned him or anything.

Yet she felt rejected just the same.

Are you going to let me kiss you? Or are you

going to keep me out in the dark, watching everything beautiful that I can't touch?

Apparently Walker had decided he would rather be alone in the dark.

Faith turned off all the lights and went out onto the gallery, in the dark, and thought about everything beautiful that she couldn't touch.

Some women weren't good at sex. She was beginning to accept that she was one of them. She had always been able to take it or leave it. Tony had known. That was why he had sex on the side. That was why they argued. That was what drove him to hit her.

That was why she hadn't married him.

Obviously Walker didn't want her. Not really. Not the way she wanted him. Once he had cooled down from that surprising kiss in the garden, he had managed to avoid her quite easily.

I'm supposed to be too smart to seduce my boss's baby sister.

Yeah? What if she seduces you—just sneaks into your bed and starts licking you all over?

Brave words. But she wasn't feeling very brave right now. She was feeling weary and worn and sad.

"Ruby Bayou blues," she whispered. "Maybe I could put it to music and have a hit. Single, of course. Always single."

Moonlight glinted back at her from the marsh on one side of the point and the seamless ocean

on the other. Moonlight full of shadows and misty
secrets. She wondered if Tiga knew the secrets
of the night, and if the night knew hers.

The rich yet astringent fragrance of brandy
curled up to Faith's nostrils and stung her eyes.
She took a sip and told herself the slow tears that
felt first hot and then cold on her cheeks came
from the bite of the brandy and pity for Jeff. Jeff,
who was caught between the love of a child for
his parent and the reality of an adult who was
hurt by a parent who was acting like a child.

Not enough people had grown up the way she
had, with parents who loved each other and their
children. Having known that kind of love, it was
hard to think of the emptiness that must lie at
the heart of Jeff's childhood memories. Davis and
Tiga had been even more badly savaged by their
father. Had that father been raised cruelly, too?
And his father? Did it go all the way back to
Eden, one cruelty begetting another, world without end, amen?

Then there was Walker, with his dead brother
and his childhood out of a social worker's file.

Yet Walker wasn't cruel. Except for her family,
she had never known a strong man who was so
gentle. He had handled Tiga with the tenderness
of a son rather than a casual guest.

Faith had been drawn to Walker even before
that. Now she was very much afraid she could
fall in love with him. Given her track record with

men, that would be quite stupid. He wasn't like Tony, the kind of man a woman would easily forget.

Yet Walker had made it clear that he could forget her.

Night air swirled around the balcony and breathed over her like a sigh, drying some of her tears. She took a deep, ragged breath. The night smelled of salt and mystery and something elemental, musky, spicy, warm.

Walker.

"You'll get cold standing out here in your bare feet," he said quietly.

His voice came from a point only inches behind her.

She nodded, but didn't turn around, didn't speak. She didn't want to have to explain her foolish mood.

"Everything locked up?" he asked.

She nodded again.

"Enjoying the moonlight?"

She nodded.

"Cat got your tongue?"

Her breath caught on something that wasn't a sigh or a laugh, but in between. Something painful.

Walker hesitated, yet couldn't ignore the ragged breath he had heard. He put his hands on Faith's shoulders and slowly turned her around. Faint silver trails gleamed on her cheeks.

"What's wrong, sugar?" he asked.

The tenderness in his voice made her eyes sting all over again, blurring the outline of the man who stood in front of her, naked but for a pair of smuggler's shorts and a million dollars worth of rubies.

"Don't be nice to me," she managed, smiling just a bit. "I'll just cry more."

"Want to talk?"

Her smiled turned upside down. "About madness and the sins of the fathers? No, thanks. I spent dinner with them."

Without a word, Walker closed his arms around her and rocked her gently from side to side. He tried very hard to ignore the warmth of her against his bare chest, but it was all he could do not to groan with a combination of tenderness and desire.

"I should have put you on that plane," he said huskily.

"I'm a big girl. And contrary to myth, big girls *do* cry. Some things are worth crying about. The Montegeaus are one of them."

"No argument there." His hand moved soothingly over her hair and down her back in slow sweeps that asked nothing, gave everything. "If it helps, I'll bet it isn't always as bad as tonight for Jeff."

"What makes you say that?"

"If Davis had been like this when Jeff was

young, Jeff wouldn't care anymore. Kids are survivors. They have to be."

"You were." Her arms stole around Walker and she leaned into his warmth. The smell of him was like the night, warm, rich with possibilities and secrets. "I like you, Owen Walker. You're a gentle man."

He brushed his lips over her hair. "Don't you believe it. I'm mean to the bone."

"Whatever you say."

"Now, don't go all agreeable on me. I won't know what to do with you."

She smiled against his chest. His thatch of soft, dark hair felt intriguing against her mouth in a way that Tony never had. She didn't know what the difference was. She only knew that it was as real as Walker and her response to him.

Standing on tiptoe, she pressed her lips against his neck just below his beard. The leap of his pulse beneath her lips was a revelation.

A harsh cry came out of the night.

"What was that?" she asked, stiffening.

"Shitepoke," he said absently. He was still trying to control his response to her almost sisterly caress. At least, that's what he was telling himself. Sisterly.

Yeah. Right. And he was a fairy godmother.

"What's a shitepoke?" Faith asked.

"What my ma's granny used to call a blue heron. Something disturbed the bird on its roost.

Those city boys aren't much good in bayou country."

"You're making almost as much sense as Tiga."

Walker smiled against Faith's forehead as he thought of the FBI out there right now, blundering around with the mud and the bugs and the gators. But he didn't want to talk about that with her. Not when the moon was up and her breath was warm against his bare skin. He didn't want to think, because if he started thinking, he would stop doing what felt too good to stop.

"Did you drink all that brandy?" he asked.

"Not yet."

"Feel like sharing?"

She looked into his eyes. Like the night, they were dark, mysterious, waiting. "Do you?"

"I shouldn't," he said bluntly.

She waited.

He let out a rough sound. "Damn, sugar. I wanted you the first time I saw you nineteen months ago. Now I want you more. I want you the way I want to breathe. That taste of you in the garden just about dropped me to my knees."

Her heartbeat doubled as heat shimmered out from the pit of her stomach. She reached for him. "Let's see what a second taste will do."

Afraid that Walker would change his mind, wanting to be hot enough, fast enough to please him, Faith pulled down his head and gave him a deep, hungry kiss that promised immediate sexual oblivion.

His masculine, multilayered taste almost distracted her from her single-minded pursuit of pleasing him. His mouth was hungry and vital, salty and secret, heady and male. Avidly she explored the velvet roughness of his tongue, the satin sleekness beneath, and the edgy warmth of his teeth. Her hands kneaded down his naked back to his hips, then slid over the front of his shorts. He was hard, hot, ready. She took a deep breath and hoped she would be enough woman for him.

For Walker it was like being caught in a whirlwind. Any thoughts of savoring and seducing after all the nights of hungering for her were blown away in the whirlwind of her tongue and hands demanding his response. Only the certainty that they were under FBI surveillance kept him from yanking off her clothes and burying himself in her right where they stood.

Without lifting his mouth from hers, he dragged her back into the room. Then he pulled her down onto the floor, stripped off her jeans and underwear with a few quick motions, and started to take her.

Her actions had screamed to him that she wanted sex and she wanted it *now*. Her body sent a different message. There was heat, yes, and the promise of slick passion. But it was only a promise.

With a shuddering groan, he brought himself under control. If he took her now, she wouldn't enjoy it nearly as much as he would. He might even hurt her. He had never been so full and hard for a woman as he was for her right now.

"What's wrong?" Faith asked, lifting her hips against him.

When he spoke his voice was rough with the effort of controlling the driving need to take what she was even now offering him. "You're not ready."

Chill washed over her skin, a preview of the ice that would settle in her belly when he told her just how lacking she was. Yet she had felt different with him, flares of heat and possibility that were as exciting as they were unexpected.

"What are you saying?" she said. "I'm as ready as I've ever been."

Walker remembered what she had said in the garden about how men and women were so different and that she enjoyed anyway. "Humor me," he said thickly.

"But—"

He stopped her argument with a kiss that was as gentle as it was hungry, filling her warmth with his flesh in the only way he would let himself right now.

Faith wasn't prepared for Walker's kiss. It devoured her tenderly, completely. Her breath unraveled in a long sigh that became a low sound of pleasure. It felt so good to have his body against her and his tongue rubbing deeply, rhythmically over hers. Close, warm, intimate. Like sex without the self-consciousness and anxiety and discomfort.

When Walker finally lifted his head, Faith realized that she was lying back on the rug, awash in surprise and pleasure, rather than running her hands all over his body and making the sexy demands that men expected.

When she tried to move her hands, she discovered that she couldn't. Her arms were pinned above her head, her wrists locked within the grasp of his left hand. His right hand was opening her blouse and bra.

"I can't touch you this way," she said. Her voice was light, rushed, breathless.

"Yeah." His breath wedged. Her nipples were neither pink nor coral. They were both, like the rarest of rubies, the color called *padparadscha* by those few people privileged to ever see it.

"But—"

"You touch me right now and I'd go off like a skyrocket."

She frowned. "Isn't that the whole idea?"

"It's half the idea. We're working on the other half."

"What—" Coherent thought splintered.

His tongue was licking over her breasts like a kid with two ice cream cones. Tasting, swirling, sucking, nibbling, devouring her with the same total sensual concentration he had showed with his kiss. Then he took one nipple deeply inside his mouth, rubbing over her sensitive skin with a slow, firm rhythm that foreshadowed the feast to come.

Sensation tightened like fine, hot wires from her breasts to her core. Her body clenched and shuddered with pleasure. She made a sound that was surprise and his name combined. He bit her with exquisite restraint, then sucked until her back arched and she twisted in slow motion against his mouth. She tried to tell him how good it felt, but all that came out was a gasp as something burst inside her, drenching her with heat.

Walker felt the change in Faith, smelled the primitive, heady musk of feminine arousal, and knew she would be worth every instant of the frustrated agony she had put him through. Not that he was blaming her. It wasn't her fault that a man took one look at her long legs, high breasts, and pouting lips and thought of nothing but raw, hot sex.

On the other hand, there was nothing wrong with thinking about it, either.

Smiling, he took his mouth lower, biting, licking, tasting, letting her essence infuse him until his head was spinning and she lay open to him, her mind stunned by pleasure. He liked having her that way, liked the dazed look in her half-closed eyes and the humming heat of her body. He teased her as long as he could bear it before he gave in to his hunger and nuzzled with his mouth into the center of her soft heat.

At first she didn't understand. Then the unexpected, silky probing of his tongue made her arch like a bow. Her hands were free now. She would have lifted them, but she was too weak. She made a broken sound and shifted. Even she couldn't have said whether she was moving toward his hungry mouth or away. She knew only that she had never felt anything as sleek, as hot, as wild, the world spinning away until she was twisting, crying, falling, turning. The tender, merciless greed of his mouth never let her catch her breath, her mind, herself.

The hoarse, shattered sound she made when she came was nothing like the measured whimpers she had manufactured for Tony. It was a cry torn from her soul, shock and discovery and ecstasy intertwined. He drank it as he drank her, consuming her even while she lay slack and trembling, destroyed, reborn.

Distantly she heard herself call his name again and again, not knowing what she wanted, only that saying his name was more necessary to her than breathing.

This time when Walker entered her, the joining was as smooth as it was hot. The sultry core of her gave sweetly around him, then clasped him like a wet velvet fist. Slick. Tight. God, she was tight. So good. Too good. The pulses of his climax were already bursting at the base of his spine.

Walker's groan sounded a lot like Faith's. He knew he wouldn't be able to hold on long. Nothing in his life had felt as good as her clinging to him, gliding and sliding over him, sleek and eager and utterly seduced. No matter how far he pushed into her, she welcomed him, pulsing, pleading, demanding that he take her as hot and deep as he could.

With a throttled shout, he gave her what they both needed, locking himself hard and deep within her until not a single drop of ecstasy remained.

His sudden, slack weight felt wonderful to Faith. Her hands stroked down the valley of his spine in languid motions. She laughed softly when she discovered that despite being deep inside her, he was still wearing his smuggler's shorts.

"You laughing at me?" he asked, his voice muffled and lazy against her breasts.

"You're still dressed. Kind of."

"So are you. Kind of. Wanna get naked?"

She glanced aside. A pale blur in the moonlight told her that her blouse and bra had ended up under the claw-footed side chair. She had no idea where her jeans and underwear had gone. "What am I still wearing?" she asked idly.

He shifted until he could nibble up the side of her neck. "Gold earrings. And me."

"In that case, I don't want to get naked."

Walker's chuckle was another kind of caress, for he moved inside her with each laugh. Sensation danced up from her core like sparks lifting from a fire. She made a murmurous sound of pleasure and nuzzled against his neck. Sighing, nibbling along the edge of his ear, she wondered how a woman thanked a man for the best loving of her life.

"Maybe you should just keep on wearing the rubies," she said, smiling to herself.

"Why?"

"You deserve them."

He rolled over onto his back, taking her with him, still locked deep inside her. "Is that your way of saying you wouldn't mind going another round?"

She shifted and slid down on him more fully. "Anytime. Anywhere. Anyhow."

"You sure?"

She knew he was remembering her worried, headlong approach to sex. "I'm very sure. You make me feel wonderful. Sexy and female and alive."

"That's because you're all of those things."

"Not before tonight." She put her cheek against his warm, sleekly muscled chest and sighed. It was wonderful to be intimate with a man she respected, liked, enjoyed, admired, trusted . . . everything. The sexual freedom he brought to her was rooted in her feelings for him, not simply his technique. She hoped she brought the same level of freedom and pleasure to him. "You're good for me, Walker. I hope I'm good for you."

Pleasure and pain sliced through him like a silver razor. The pleasure came from hearing the trust and contentment in her voice. The pain came from the same source. Just the thought of having someone trust him that completely made Walker cold to his soul. He didn't deserve that kind of trust. Not after failing his brother in such a final way.

He caught Faith's face between his hands and kissed her very gently before he released her. "Enjoy me, but don't depend on me. That kind of trust makes me real nervous."

Slowly Faith let out a long breath and smoothed her cheek against the soft mat of hair on his chest. At least he wasn't like Tony, lying about love and happily ever after in order to get close to the Donovan bank account. Surely she was adult enough to take what Walker offered and not sulk because there wasn't any more.

And if she wasn't adult enough, she could keep it to herself. "Okay," she said.

"What does that mean?"

"Just that," Faith said simply. "Okay. What we just had was more than I ever expected with a man. I'll take it for as long as it lasts."

Her words should have made him feel better. They didn't. Instead, he felt like something was sliding out of his grasp. "Sugar, I didn't mean to hurt you."

She lifted her head and looked him in the eye. "Then take off those rubies."

"What?"

"They're digging into me."

There was a moment of startled silence, followed by his soft laughter. "Why don't you take them off for me?"

"Good idea."

"I have a few other ideas," he offered as she shifted position.

"Mmm." Her tongue traced the line of his ribs. "Don't hold back, sugar."

He didn't.

23

Jeff got up as quietly as he could, but Mel made an unhappy sound and rolled toward his side of the bed as though already missing him. Murmuring reassurances, he touched her. After a few moments her breathing deepened. She was back asleep again and wouldn't even remember almost awakening.

The house was so quiet he was sure he could hear the sweat breaking out along his spine as he bent down to pick up the clothes he and Mel had abandoned halfway to bed.

When Boomer's nose nudged his master's bare butt, Jeff almost jumped out of his skin. He bit off a curse before it became a sound. With shaking hands and drumming heart, he pulled on his slacks. Maybe he could talk his father out of this craziness. Surely there must be another way to raise the money. The shrimp boats. The jewelry store. Ruby Bayou itself.

Anything but this.

Taking care to avoid all the squeaky boards, Jeff went down the hall to his father's room. Boomer padded alongside, pleased to have company in the middle of the night. Behind his father's door, thick snoring vibrated through the walls. Jeff knew the Marine Marching Band wouldn't have awakened Davis Montegeau.

The door was closed, but the crystal knob turned beneath Jeff's damp palm. He had a flash of memory more than thirty years old . . . *a young boy racing down the hallway, pursued by nightmares, flinging himself through the door. His parents welcomed him, held him, soothed him, tucked him into bed between them. His mother smelled of jasmine, his father of the seaweed fire he had built to steam crabs and corn for a beach picnic that night. The child snuggled between his parents' big bodies. With his hand cradled in his father's, he slept deeply, certain that he was safe.*

God, it was so long ago.

And it was yesterday. He could close his eyes and smell the powdery jasmine scent of his mother. He understood her absence, her death, but he didn't understand where that boy had gone.

Or where the boy's father had gone.

"Daddy?" he whispered.

The oblivious snoring of a drunk answered him.

Impatience and anger snaked through Jeff. Some of it was for himself. The boy of his memories was as dead as his jasmine-scented mother. Now the boy was a man with his own child to protect. And if the man wished he could crawl into bed right now with his parents as the boy had that long-ago night, too bad. The world wasn't going to go away. Ever. That was what being an adult was all about.

Abruptly, viscerally, Jeff understood why his father drank. It made the world go away.

As his hand closed around the doorknob, he thought he saw something from the corner of his eye. He spun toward the pale blur that he had sensed more than seen.

Nothing was there but the closed door of Tiga's bedroom, and the doors of rooms that were no longer used. He looked at Boomer. The hound was completely at ease.

Jeff let out a soundless breath. Though he had occasionally seen Ruby Bayou's resident ghosts, he really didn't want a spectral experience tonight. He had all he could handle and then some.

Opening the door fully, he walked into his father's bedroom. It reeked of stale whiskey. At a gesture, Boomer followed Jeff inside and flopped down on the thick rug.

Quietly he shut the door and moved to his father's bed. Nothing but the sheets had been changed since his mother died. The same perfume bottles reflected tiny shards of moonlight on the vanity table. The curtains with their big magnolia flowers and trailing vines were so faded that the pattern existed only in his memory. The rug was faded, too, but it had happened two hundred years ago. Like driftwood, the rug had a silver dignity that time couldn't steal.

It was a pity that men weren't rugs.

"Daddy," Jeff said in a normal tone of voice.

Nothing.

"Daddy."

Still nothing.

Jeff turned on the bedside light, shook his father, then shook him again. Hard. The snoring subsided into grumbling complaints. He kept on shaking the slack body that was so unlike the sheltering parent of his memory.

"Wha'? Wha'? Jeffy, wha' you want, boy? You have a nightmare?"

Pain sliced into Jeff. He hadn't been called Jeffy since he turned thirteen. Knowing that his father remembered him as a boy didn't make the present any easier to bear. It made it worse.

"Wake up, Daddy. We have to talk."

Davis blinked, then blinked again. Slowly he focused on the face of the man who had once been his little boy. With returning memory came a desire to escape back into sleep or booze, whichever blacked him out first. He rubbed his gritty eyes and tried to get past the dead skunk taste in his mouth. He didn't have nearly enough saliva to do the job.

"Need a drink," he muttered.

"That's the last thing you need," Jeff said impatiently.

"Need a drink!"

"We need to talk about how to raise the money for Sal. I'm going to mortgage Ruby Bayou, the shrimp boats, the jewelry store—whatever it takes."

Davis looked at Jeff as though he was speaking in tongues. "You can't."

"Watch me," Jeff shot back. "That's what power of attorney means."

Davis shook his head, winced at the lancing headache, and said simply, "They're already mortgaged."

For a moment Jeff didn't believe it. "The land, the house, the boats, the—"

"Everything," Davis interrupted hoarsely. "That's how I raised the money to go into partnership with Sal."

Jeff looked around the room as though it already belonged to somebody else. If he didn't carry out his father's bizarre scheme, it would. He would be forty years old with no job and a crazy aunt, a drunken father, and a pregnant wife who all depended on him for food and shelter.

The jaws of the trap snapped shut hard enough to make his bones ache.

Davis groaned. Too many memories, each one sharper and more painful than the last. "I really fucked up, Jeffy."

Something like grief twisted through Jeff, but he couldn't afford it. He had a woman and child to think about. Unlike his father, they were innocent.

Yet they would pay along with the guilty.

"Yes, Daddy. You really fucked up."

Davis didn't hear. He had dropped back into his drunken stupor. Before Jeff left the room, snores were shaking the air.

It was after midnight when a dark figure slipped through the shadows of Ruby Bayou. Nobody upstairs heard the muffled crack of glass and old wood giving way to blunt force. Nobody heard the dark fumbling as four-by-five-foot Montegeau portraits were lifted off the library wall and left leaning drunkenly against the old, polished wainscoting. Finally the cool steel of the safe came through the person's thin rubber gloves. Sensitive headphones picked up the secret slide and click of tumblers.

Left. Right. Left. *Missed it.*

Left. Right. Left. Now right again.

Click.

The big safe door opened for him like an old lover. With trembling hands, he raked around the interior.

He found nothing but paper, a heavy Bible, and air.

With a muffled sound, he dragged out the papers and dropped the Bible on the floor. Nothing met his frantic, searching fingers but the smooth steel walls of the safe.

Empty.

Completely. Empty.

With the silence of a man raised hunting in the dark, Walker moved along the upper gallery just as the first light of day started to tint the eastern sky. The luminous pink-coral color reminded him of Faith's nipples all wet and proud from his mouth. The memory sent both heat and ice through him. The heat was easy to understand, for he had never enjoyed a woman as much as he had Faith. The ice came from the same source: He had no business becoming her lover. She was a woman for sunlight and babies.

He was a man for the night, responsible for no one but himself, hurting no one but himself with his mistakes.

Walker paused and listened for the click of a dog's nails on wood. He didn't think Boomer would worry about a restless guest, but he sure didn't want to surprise the hound into baying. The house was silent. Boomer was either sleeping hard or out chasing something in the swamp.

Walker eased out onto the gallery that ran along the face of the second story. Moving with great care, he went to the place he had selected earlier. Beyond the house, lost in darkness, spread the garden and the bayou, marshes and sea. In front of him, a blacker piece of night, stood an old oak tree.

Lightly he went over the railing and settled his weight onto a thick branch. Resurrection ferns crunched and crumbled softly beneath his weight. Soon he was against the trunk, feeling with his foot for the next branch down. Like riding a bike, tree climbing was a skill no one ever forgot.

He dropped to the ground with a gentle thump. The air was cool and damp, smelling of sea and earth. No songbirds trilled. No frogs sang throatily for mates. Even the crickets were quiet. Nothing disturbed the silence but the raw cry of a seagull and the distant cawing of crows as they rose from their nighttime roost.

A wide, sandy beach lay just a hundred yards from where Walker stood, but there was no sound of surf, for there was no wind to build waves. Hushed, seamless, expectant, the air seemed to hold its breath in anticipation of dawn.

With the ease of long practice, he became part of the landscape. He didn't need fancy camouflage clothes or high-tech equipment to blend in. He simply wore a slate-colored shirt and black jeans that were old and so soft they had become silent. The rest was a matter of skill and patience. He had both.

He also had a gunnysack full of peace offerings for the FBI.

Even in the darkness, it took Walker less than ten minutes to find where the surveillance team had made its cold camp. The watchers were right where he would have been if he had their job— on the dry land above high-tide line yet below the worst tangle of vegetation. The position gave them a view of the long, winding driveway and the floating wharf where two battered oyster skiffs were tied in the brackish water of Ruby Bayou. No one could come or go without being seen.

One of the agents was rolled up in a light sleeping bag behind a screen of brush. Another blended perfectly into the scrub but was betrayed by the sounds he made as he pissed vigorously against the thick trunk of a palm. Being polite,

Walker waited until the sounds stopped before announcing his presence.

"Mornin' in the camp," Walker drawled. "Rise and shine, gents. You've got company."

Agents cursed and dived for cover and their weapons, but they must have realized instantly that there was no danger. If the man out in the tangle of palmetto and trees had wanted a gunfight, they would already be dead.

After a moment, a female voice called out from a position deeper in the palmettos. "Nice going, Farnsworth. Were you asleep or what?"

"I was wide-awake, but I didn't hear a thing," Farnsworth called back. He turned toward the darkness where Walker stood. "Who the hell are you and what do you want?"

"Put away the sidearms. I came here to talk," Walker said dryly.

"Do it," the woman said wearily. "It's too dark to shoot anyway."

Farnsworth let out a disgusted curse. The sound of steel sliding into leather was soft but quite distinct. So was the sound of a zipper being yanked upright.

Walker stepped into the open, carrying the half-full gunnysack. He made sure his hands were in full view.

"Have a care coming out of those palmettos, ma'am," Walker said when he heard rustling sounds. "They can slice like knives."

"No shit," she muttered.

Walker managed not to grin. Barely. "May I give you a hand?" he asked neutrally.

"Shove it, cowboy."

"I'll pass on your kind offer, thanks just the same," he drawled.

The man named Farnsworth swallowed a snicker. It had been a long time since he had seen his spit-and-polish partner looking less than professional. He rather liked her this way.

Cindy Peel clawed her way out of the vegetation and stalked toward Walker. She was about five foot six inches tall and wore her salt-and-pepper hair in a short, no-nonsense cut. She was mad as a cat in a rainstorm.

She looked familiar. She was. Walker had last seen her in the Savannah restaurant, but she had been dressed quite differently. Then she had worn a businesslike dark jacket, cream blouse, and dark skirt. Now she wore a dark all-purpose coverall of the sort that most agents carried in the trunk of their cars. The Bureau uniform of suit and shiny shoes was still required for the office, but the practical agent expected to encounter messy crime scenes and unlikely beds on stakeouts.

But Walker doubted that the surveillance team had come prepared for a night in the scrub. That was why he was counting on the barter value of the goods in his gunnysack.

Peel swept debris and dirt off the legs of her black coverall. "Big help, Pete. Real big. Get your beauty sleep?"

Farnsworth held up his hands in self-defense as he approached her. "Honest, Cindy, I was wide-awake."

"He was, ma'am," Walker said.

"How do you know?" she retorted.

"A man his age doesn't usually piss in his sleep."

"Oh, good, a comedian. This is my lucky day."

"It could be," he agreed, "if you feel like exchanging a little information."

"Information? About what?"

"About why you're here."

"I'd sooner have a root canal without anesthesia."

He wasn't surprised. The FBI wasn't noted for their eagerness to share information.

In the increasing light, he could see dark, thin scratches on the backs of her hands, palmetto cuts. "You're bleeding, ma'am."

"It's a long way from my heart."

Walker grinned. "Archer says that from time to time."

"Archer who?" Peel asked.

"Faith Donovan's older brother, the guy I work for."

"Faith," Peel muttered. Then the morning haze in her brain cleared. "Faith as in a woman's name rather than a religious belief. Faith Donovan. She was with Melany Soon-To-Be-Montegeau at the restaurant. Are you the guy with the famous cane? Savannah PD is still talking about the damage you've caused."

"I left the cane at the house," Walker said.

"Then your name is Owen Walker," Cindy said curtly. "What's your relationship to the Montegeaus?"

"If you know my name, you know as much as I do about my background. The FBI is real thorough about things like that."

"What makes you think we're FBI?" she demanded.

"What makes you think I'm stupid?"

Walker's voice was so gentle that at first the agent didn't believe she had heard correctly. Then the strengthening light gave her a decent look at his eyes. She swore under her breath. "Search that gunnysack, Pete."

Walker opened the sack. "Nothing in here but a peace offering or two," he said. As though to prove it, he dipped in and produced a thermos bottle and a roll of toilet paper.

The woman looked at the two items for a long time, then shook her head.

"I hate it when the subject is better prepared than we are," she grumbled as she snatched the roll of toilet paper from Walker's hand and stalked away into the scrub.

"Those coveralls must make things tough for a woman in the woods," Walker said after a moment.

Farnsworth looked up from the gunnysack. "Agent Peel is tough enough to piss standing up." With a grunt that said he hadn't found anything lethal, he handed the sack back to Walker.

"I take it she's the senior partner."

"You got it."

"Bright lady."

"You got that, too. Been with her two years. Someday she'll run the Bureau."

"Is that before or after the Second Coming of Christ?"

Farnsworth swallowed a laugh. "The Bureau has changed."

"And your name is Pollyanna."

The agent shook his head.

Walker looked at the man whose features were slowly condensing out of the darkness. Farnsworth was perhaps forty-five, fit, with graying hair, shrewd dark eyes. He was about two inches shorter than Walker. He wore a coverall similar to his partner's. The front was unzipped and Walker could see that he still wore a dress shirt and slacks underneath the coverall. His shoes would have been more at home on a tennis court.

A low, blistering curse came from the bushes.

"Hope she didn't squat on something sharp," Walker said blandly. "She might hurt it."

Farnsworth rubbed his mouth and tried not to laugh.

Walker heard Cindy Peel crashing back out of the bushes and reached into the gunnysack. He produced two plastic cups that went with the thermos. He unscrewed the top of the flask and poured. The scent of coffee curled up like a promise.

"Hope y'all like your coffee black," he said.

"I'll take it any way I can get it." Farnsworth took the cup, drank deeply, and sighed. "Thanks."

Cindy appeared out of the thinning gloom. "If you didn't leave at least one cup of that for me, Pete, you're fired."

"Plenty for all," Walker said.

He handed her a cup, then dug fresh fruit and a paper bag of leftover biscuits out of the gunnysack. The biscuits were still fresh enough to leave dark greasy spots on the brown paper bag.

"Forgot the jelly," Walker said. "Hope you don't mind." Then he waited while the agents wolfed down biscuits and fruit. They were on second cups of coffee before Peel looked ready to talk.

"How long y'all been interested in the Montegeaus?" Walker asked.

Farnsworth looked at Peel. She looked at her coffee, then at the man who moved like mist through the prickly landscape.

"Denying it would be kind of silly," she said carefully. "Look, Walker. We've vetted you. There are a few folks out there who say you can hold your mud. I'd appreciate if you kept our interest to yourself."

Walker said nothing. He simply watched Peel with eyes that were only now beginning to show a hint of deep, deep blue.

"Word also is that you know how to keep a bargain," she said, not quite asking a question.

Walker nodded.

She drained the last of the liquid in her cup and thought hard about how much she wanted to put on the table. Not everything, for damn sure. She had never met April Joy, but she had heard about her. A smart person didn't get in that lady's way.

"No one mentioned that you make a mean cup of mocha java," she said.

He smiled almost shyly. "Thank you, ma'am."

"God," she muttered. "I bet there's a whole world full of people who believe you when you smile."

"Yes, ma'am, I believe there is."

"Can the 'ma'am' routine. Where I come from, 'ma'am' is what we call someone when we're trying to yank their chain. You trying to yank mine?"

Walker looked into her clear brown eyes and knew she was every bit as tough and smart as her partner thought she was. "Where I come from, no one yanks on a chain attached to a junk-yard dog."

Farnsworth almost choked on a swallow of coffee.

Peel laughed. "We're going to do fine, Walker. That's what people call you, isn't it? Walker, not Owen."

"Yeah. My pa was Owen. I never took to being Junior or Little O. Wouldn't answer to either name, never mind how many times they took a switch to me. We all compromised with Walker."

Absently she scratched one of the bites she had picked up since she had spent the night on the ground. "Tough guy, huh?"

"More like stubborn," Walker said easily. "That's why I keep asking the same question until I get an answer. Why are you interested in the Montegeaus?"

Peel studied him over the rim of her coffee cup, trying to decide how much to trust him. "What do you know about the Mafia?"

"Domestic? Damned little."

Eyes narrowed, Peel studied him. Then she looked at Farnsworth. He shrugged, then nodded.

"Tell you what, Walker. I won't reveal sensitive information, but I will tell you what you might discover if you looked through public records long enough and started putting pieces together. How's that?"

"The public record is always a good place to start," Walker said. "Anybody can get information from it."

"Precisely," she said. "For instance, if you go on-line and start checking property tax lists and state incorporation papers, you'll find that your host, Davis Montegeau, is in partnership on a land deal with a New Jersey corporation named Angelini Construction, headquartered in Newark. And if you dig into the New Jersey records, you'll find that Angelini Construction is owned by one Salvatore Angel, nee Angelini. Sal Angel, as he prefers to be called, is a capo in one of the most aggressive crime families on the East Coast."

"Davis and Sal Angel are partners?" Walker asked.

"Real estate partners," Farnsworth said. "On the street, they might even be called crime partners."

Walker grunted. "Go on."

"Not much further to go yet," Peel said. "We're trying to build a racketeering case against Sal Angel. We know he's involved in gambling, prostitution, insurance fraud. He's been capering for years. Now he's trying to branch into legitimate business as a means of laundering all his dirty money."

"And you think this real estate deal is financed with that money."

"We know it is, just as sure as that sun will finally come up in the next few minutes," Peel said, glancing off to the east. "But knowing it and proving it in a court of law are two different matters."

Walker wondered if the agents knew about the attack on Faith by the young thug named Buddy Angel. While he considered the implications of the FBI knowing—or not knowing—a big heron flew by with prehistoric grace. He watched the long-legged bird slant down to land at the edge of the brackish bayou. Instantly the bird froze, as though posing for a sculpture called *Patience*. Dawn washed over the heron in shades of pink and tangerine and gold.

"The Montegeaus are in trouble," Walker said. "How deep?"

"Davis Montegeau likes to think he's a big shot," Peel said. "He isn't. He's just a packager putting together deals. He did one for Sal and another hood named Joe Donatello. The deal went south. Sal and Joe lost a quarter of a million each. They can afford it, but they can't afford looking like schmucks. We figure they're going to even things with Davis. We want to be close by when that happens."

"What good will that do you?"

"Davis isn't a tough guy. He's an old drunk.

When Sal and Joe start breaking knees, we're hoping Davis will get scared enough to roll over for us."

Peel glanced at the thermos. Walker poured her the two swallows that were left.

"Or we might get lucky and tag the leg breaker that Sal and Joe send to do the job," Peel continued. "If we do, and if he rolls over, we've got something. Right now all we have is a few hundred bug bites."

She handed her cup to Farnsworth, who took the final swallow. Walker liked her for that, but he still didn't entirely trust her.

"Were you following Mel or Faith at the restaurant?" he asked casually.

"Mel."

Walker's poker face was in place. He didn't even blink over Peel's outright lie. "Is Mel a suspect?"

"We thought the old man might be using her to courier payments to these loan sharks." Peel shrugged. "Guess not. At least, not last night."

Walker smiled grimly. "I'm guessing Davis isn't making payments. Judging from the shape of the old homestead, he couldn't afford a fresh postage stamp, much less a courier service."

"You're guessing right," Farnsworth said. "He's so close to declaring bankruptcy that his lawyer is drawing up the papers."

"Does he think bankruptcy will protect him from crooks?" Walker asked.

"Magical thinking," Peel said. "Gets 'em every time."

Farnsworth tried to look like he cared.

Walker thought of the magnificent rubies gleaming like blood against curving gold. Even taking a steep discount, the rubies would pay off the Montegeau debt to the mob. Why would Davis be giving that kind of money to his daughter-in-law?

Then again, maybe he was trying to have his cake and eat it, too. Grab the rubies, or have Sal do it, and then go crying to the insurance company.

If Walker hadn't been carrying the rubies, they would have been stolen in Savannah and the Donovans would have been stuck with the loss. Too bad, how sad, life's a bitch and then you die.

The money would have gone from the Donovans to the Montegeaus with profound apologies for losing the rubies. No fingers would have pointed at the nearly bankrupt Montegeaus as possible thieves.

"So what are you doing here?" Peel asked.

"Guarding the rubies."

"What rubies?" Peel asked sharply.

"The Montegeau rubies. Old family heirlooms, or so the story goes."

Peel's dark eyes narrowed. "Keep talking."

"A few weeks ago, Davis called and asked Faith to create a wedding necklace for Mel. Davis would supply the rubies and the gold. Faith would supply the art and the work. As payment, she would keep the smallest of the fourteen rubies he sent."

"Rubies, huh?" Peel frowned. "How much are they worth?"

"A million, easy. That's wholesale."

Farnsworth whistled softly. "Holy shit. Why doesn't he use them to get Sal off his back?"

"Maybe Davis would rather have the rubies and the insurance money both," Peel said.

"That's what I'm figuring," Walker said.

"Where did he get the money to buy them in the first place?" Farnsworth asked. "They sure as hell aren't listed with his assets."

"Could indeed be heirlooms," Peel said. "A lot of them get passed down without being listed for inheritance taxes. Could be stolen, too."

"If they're stolen, nobody has posted them on the Internet," Walker said.

"How do you know?"

"I checked before Archer agreed to insure the gems."

"Archer," Peel said. "That would be Archer Donovan, the oldest son. So he's insuring the gems?"

"Until the wedding," Walker said. "Then they're on Davis's ticket."

Thoughtfully Peel tapped a fingernail against her front teeth. "Valentine's Day. Whatever's going to happen with those rubies will have to happen soon or it won't do Davis any good."

"Likely," Walker agreed.

"You sure the gems are real?" Farnsworth asked. "Davis wouldn't be the first one to insure high-class glass and then 'lose' it."

"They're real."

The agents absorbed Walker's certainty.

"So they're your responsibility at the moment," Peel said thoughtfully. She looked like what she was, a federal agent wondering how she could use a new fact to her own advantage.

"Yeah. They're on my head." Walker began to gather up the remnants of the breakfast he had brought. He knew that Peel was looking for an advantage. He expected it.

They had their agenda, he had his.

He didn't even mind that the agents had lied to him in at least one important regard. He knew that they had been shadowing Faith, not Mel, twelve hours before in Savannah. What he wanted to know was *why* they were lying. He had a hunch that the answer to that question would cost him more than coffee and cold biscuits. Right now he didn't have enough on the table to ante up. Time to fold and wait for a better hand.

Because the important thing was to stay in the game.

24

Walker slipped back into the house as secretly as he had left it. The gallery creaked when he stepped off the oak branch, but Boomer was either snoring too loud to hear or out somewhere chasing raccoons. Everyone else in the house was asleep.

Except Faith.

"Where were you?" she asked the instant he closed the sitting room door behind him.

Standing just inside her bedroom door, he looked in at the pleasantly rumpled sheets and the even more pleasantly rumpled woman. Even in first light, her skin glowed. He knew he never should have touched her, but he couldn't wait to do it again. Smiling, he toed off one shoe.

"Walker?"

The other shoe thumped softly onto the rug. "Did I remember to tell you how beautiful you are?" he asked, walking to the edge of her bed. "Or was I in too much of a hurry?"

Her breath caught at the light and memories in his eyes. "You made me feel beautiful."

"You sure?"

She looked at the fit of his jeans and smiled. "Get undressed while I think about it."

"Sugar, if I take anything else off, I'll be wearing you real quick."

A tingling rush of heat swept through her. "In that case, let me help you."

Walker laughed as though she was joking. Then he felt her fingers tug at the steel buttons on his jeans. Suddenly it was all he could do to drag in a breath. He covered her hands with his own, stilling her busy fingers by pressing them hard against his arousal.

"I'm thinkin' I might just have to tie you to the bed," he drawled.

She looked up, startled and maybe a little bit intrigued. "You are?"

"Sure am. I keep fixin' to take it slow and easy, then you get those clever, hungry hands in my pants and it's all I can do to keep from hiking your heels up next to your ears and seeing how deep and fast I can bury myself in you."

The tip of her tongue worried her lower lip. "Heels and ears, huh? Sounds uncomfortable."

His slow, gentle smile lit fires. "I'd never hurt you in bed, sugar. You know that, don't you?"

She sighed and flexed her fingers against him. The hard, vital surge of his life fascinated her. "If I had any doubts, I wouldn't be here." Unconsciously she licked her lips as she tugged down his jeans. "And I sure wouldn't be, um, fixin' to see how you taste of a morning."

The shudder that ripped through him surprised both of them. He wanted to tell her how sexy she was, but he didn't have the breath or the words. So he kicked off his jeans, ignored his smuggler's shorts, and pulled down the sheets an inch at a time. His mouth tasted what his eyes could barely see in the darkness. Soon she was twisting and crying for him.

Slowly he hooked his hands beneath her legs and drew them up until she was fully open to him. He freed himself from the shorts and pushed against her steamy flesh, parting her just a little. She was a silky fire just barely kissing his sensitive head. He wanted more of that feminine flesh. He wanted it all.

He wanted her.

Slowly Faith's eyes opened. In the dim light they were smoky, sensual, dazed with pleasure and a need that had her shaking. "Walker?"

"Right here, sugar." He tightened his hips to make the point.

She moaned as she felt the sweet pressure opening her, penetrating her. But not enough. He was barely inside her. She knew what it felt like when he was locked deep, filling her. She wanted that.

She wanted it now.

"Why?" she managed.

"Why what?" he drawled despite the sweat sliding down his ribs.

"Why are you waiting?"

"For what?"

"You know!"

He didn't know whether to laugh or swear at the sudden, lithe twist of her hips that almost succeeded in driving him deep. "I haven't a clue, sugar. Tell me."

"You're a tease."

"Now, that's a first. I've been called a lot of names, but—" His voice broke as her hips moved against him, her slick heat demanding its match. He groaned. "You're fixin' to kill me."

"Now you're getting the idea."

"I want to make sure I give you what you want. What do you want?"

The tantalizing touch and withdrawal was unbearably arousing. He never went deeper than an inch, and each time he withdrew she felt like clawing him.

"You," she said roughly. "Damn it, Walker, I want you!"

"You've got me." To prove the point, he nudged against her hot, silky core.

So close . . . and not nearly close enough. She twisted, driving them both closer. "I don't have enough of you."

"How about this?" He penetrated her a bit more deeply and then withdrew. "Better?"

The liquid silk of her response followed him, licking over both of them. She shuddered at the heat clenching rhythmically inside her. "More."

"Greedy, huh? I like that in a woman."

Her fingernails bit into his flexed hips.

"I like that, too," he said. "Go ahead, sugar. Show me what you want."

"Deeper," she said.

He gave her another inch and was rewarded by the silky warmth of her response pulsing over him. Slowly, deliberately, he withdrew. Though sweat gathered in his spine, the inches that had just been inside her felt cold without her. He pushed back in, then forced himself to stop halfway home. The scent and rushing heat of her response made him light-headed.

"Walker," she said hoarsely. "Why are you torturing me?"

"Damned if I know. I never wanted to have any other woman crying for me, but you're different. You're so sweet, I could come just teasing you.''

He slipped her legs over his shoulders and opened her even more, drawing her tight around him. He watched her as he traced her swollen flesh with his fingertips until he was as slick as she was. Then he plucked at the proud nub that had grown out of her softness. He felt the deep pulsing of her response even before he heard her throaty whimper. Shaking with restraint, he pushed deep into the clench and release of her climax, stretching her even more, sending her higher, then higher still.

Only when she was crying his name and her pleasure did he begin to move the way they both needed, hard and deep. She arched up against him and went rigid. He barely covered her mouth with his own before she screamed her release. It was no less intense for him, his shout muffled by her mouth as he pumped himself into her until the world went black.

Slowly Faith became aware of the room, the wonderful weight of Walker lying against her . . . and the fact that she could bite her own knee if she turned her head.

She laughed softly. ''You were right.''

''Mmph?'' Walker asked, too lazy to move his mouth from her neck.

''It didn't hurt. Still doesn't. I hope you don't mind my saying that I'm amazed.''

Reluctantly Walker stirred. "Is this going to be one of those meaningful male-female talk things?"

She smiled and closed her teeth over the edge of his jaw. "Nope. Just an observation. The *Kama Sutra* has nothing on us."

His laughter was silent but obvious, for he moved inside her. Slowly he let her legs slide down his body. Then he shifted until he could nuzzle the tip of her breast. "I don't think that book was on the approved reading list in my high school."

"Never read it, huh?" she asked, stroking his hair.

"In high school? Nope."

"Junior high?"

"Nope."

"Ohmygod. Kindergarten?"

He laughed again and she made a murmurous sound of pleasure at the reminder of how completely they were joined.

"Nope," he said, nibbling over to her other breast.

"I refuse to believe you were reading in the womb."

"First grade."

"Oh, boy. I'll bet it was fun playing doctor with you."

Laughing out loud, Walker wrapped his arms tightly around her and rolled over onto his back. She moved with him easily. When he realized the

perfection of her lithe partnering, her unconscious adjustments to stay close, and the easy intimacy of their linked bodies, his laughter faded.
He had never known a woman like Faith. Businesslike one moment, a dreamy artist the next.
Slashing her heel down a mugger's shin and
weeping silently in the moonlight. Deceptively
fragile. Deceptively strong. Deeply passionate.
She lured him in ways he couldn't describe, and
she terrified him in the same ways.

For the first time he understood at a gut level
why a moth flew into flame: it was better than
staying alone in the cold and dark.

". . . hear that?" Faith asked.

"What?" he said, shaking his head as though
to clear it of his own thoughts.

"It's Mel. I think something's wrong."

Suddenly, faint and yet all too clear, a woman's
scream echoed through the silent house.

"God, I hope it's not the baby!" Faith scrambled off the bed and searched for her clothes.

Hurriedly Walker adjusted his million-dollar
shorts, grabbed the knife in its sheath under his
pillow, and lunged out of bed. Sheath clenched
in his teeth, he reached for his jeans. By the time
he got his pants buttoned, Faith had raced out
the door in the first thing she could grab—his
shirt. He spit out the knife and took off after her.

"Mel?" Faith cried. "Mel, where are you?
What's wrong?"

The thought of Buddy Angel and a deadly Russian thug put wings on Walker's feet. Halfway down the hall, he caught up with Faith and grabbed her arm.

"What—?" she began.

"Stay here until I find out what's wrong," he said curtly, cutting across her protest.

"But—"

"But nothing. This could be an ambush. They might be after you. *Stay here.*"

"What about you?"

She was talking to his back. He went down the stairway like a ghost. When he turned at the landing, light from a sconce spilled over him. She saw him draw the knife and shove the sheath into a hip pocket. There was a shadowy pattern of fading bruises just above his waistband at the small of his back. She didn't know which shocked her more, the knife or the bruises.

She started to call out to him. Then what he had said about an ambush registered. Her stomach rolled over. She bolted back to the bedroom, snatched the little canister of pepper spray from her purse, and raced downstairs on silent bare feet.

Though Walker listened, he heard no second scream, no sounds of struggle. He was still wary. The old house was big enough to absorb all but the loudest noises.

He sensed Faith coming up behind him. Furious, he spun around and glared at her. She glared back stubbornly. Her eyes said that arguing with her was useless.

He hauled her close and said very softly into her ear, "Sugar, if you get any of that shit in my eyes, you won't sit down for a week."

She nuzzled against his ear and spoke with equal softness. "If I get any of this shit in your eyes, *sugar,* you won't be able to see to catch me for a week."

With a jerk of his head, he signaled her to get behind him. Her chin lifted, but she stopped trying to push past him in the hall.

Together they slipped silently through the lower floor of rooms, listening. Together they heard a mutter of voices from the direction of the kitchen.

Walker bypassed the library and headed swiftly for the back of the house. Faith was right behind him. The kitchen door was ajar. He put her on the hinge side and took the open side himself.

They listened.

". . . dead!" Mel cried in a low voice.

Faith started forward. A look from Walker stopped her cold.

"No, he isn't, darlin'," Jeff said. "See? His side is moving real regular like."

"Are you sure?"

Walker eased the kitchen door open to look inside. Mel and Jeff—wearing pajamas—were on the floor beside Boomer. The kitchen lights and the growing daylight showed Boomer stretched out on the linoleum like a thick, limp rug.

"I'm sure," Jeff said soothingly. "Give me your hand. Feel him move? He's breathing long and deep. He's just fine." But there was an edge of worry in Jeff's voice that he couldn't entirely disguise.

"Why didn't he wake up when I tripped over him?"

Letting out a long, soundless breath, Walker sheathed the knife and clipped it to the waist of his jeans.

"Y'all got a problem?" he asked as he walked into the kitchen.

Jeff jerked as though he had been stung. Mel just looked up, tears streaming out of her big brown eyes.

"It's Boomer," she said simply, looking back at the dog. "He won't wake up."

As Walker crouched over the hound, Faith followed him into the kitchen. The pepper spray was in the pocket of the shirt she wore.

"Are you all right, Mel?" Faith asked, kneeling near her friend. "I thought I heard you scream."

"I was hungry, so I came down to the kitchen for some crackers," Mel said without taking her eyes off the hound. "I guess I was so sleepy I didn't see Boomer lying here. I must have yelped when I tripped over him. I know I screamed when I thought he was dead.''

''I came running at the first scream,'' Jeff said, stroking Mel's shoulder as gently as she was stroking Boomer's head. ''Did you fall?''

She shook her head.

''You sure?'' he pressed. ''You didn't hurt yourself or the baby, did you?''

''I grabbed the counter so I wouldn't fall,'' Mel said. ''Why won't he wake up?''

Walker examined the hound with gentle hands. ''No blood. No swelling or broken bones that I can feel. Heartbeat is steady if a bit slow. Same for his breathing. Seems okay, but you should call a vet.''

When Walker stood, he signaled quietly to Jeff to follow. The other man hesitated, looking at his fiancée, before he got reluctantly to his feet.

''Stay with Mel,'' Walker said quietly to Faith.

She nodded.

As soon as the kitchen door closed behind Jeff, Walker asked softly, ''Have you been poisoning varmits lately?''

Jeff shook his head. ''There's nothing worth saving in the garden, and there's not enough poison in Hilton Head to keep the house clean of mice.''

Walker grunted. ''Where's the nearest phone?''

''Library. I'll show you.''

"I think ol' Boomer was drugged," Walker said as he followed the tall blond down the hall.

Jeff stopped in his tracks in the library doorway.

Walker looked past him into the room. "And I think I see why."

He went to the wall where Black Jack Montegeau's huge picture stood propped against the wainscoting. On the wall above, the door to the big, rectangular wall safe stood half-open. Papers and an old family Bible were scattered around.

A pair of small headphones dangled from the safe handle, as though they had been set aside and then forgotten after their job was done. Thin cables ran from the headphones to a small rubber suction cup that had been used to attach an amplifier to the safe.

Archer used a set of earphones just like that when he had occasion to get in somebody else's safe. To his credit, it didn't happen very often.

"Call the sheriff," Walker said after a glance into the safe. "Looks like you've been cleaned out."

25

The veterinarian had come and gone, but the patrol deputies were busy breaking up a family brawl in one of the fancy waterfront condos. So it was Sheriff Bob Lee Shartell himself who walked up the back steps of Ruby Bayou. He was flanked by his chief deputy, a laconic snuff chewer named Harold Bundy.

By then, everyone except the senior Montegeau had showered and dressed. Davis still hadn't hauled himself out of bed. Jeff was relieved. It wouldn't take a sensitive nose to smell alcohol on his father, which would only add to Davis's growing reputation as a drunk. The island was a small place. Word would spread quickly, making it all the more difficult to resurrect the family status.

Fortunately, Tiga hadn't made an appearance yet. Her loopy monologues would just add to the gossip.

The vet had revived Boomer with a shot of something that encouraged him to give a groggy woof when lawmen knocked at the back door.

"Quiet, Boomer," Jeff said sharply. "You'll wake up the rest of the house."

Walker gave Jeff a glance. Despite the expensive slacks and freshly pressed shirt, he looked edgy as a cat in a wolf pack. Not that Walker blamed him. Being dragged out of bed at dawn by your lover's scream, then finding your dog drugged and your home burgled, wasn't a great way to start the day.

But Faith was the one who should have been snapping at everyone in sight. The stolen pieces could be paid for by insurance, but they never could be truly replaced. Despite that, she had kept her worries to herself and had spent her time soothing her friend, since Jeff seemed too upset to do it himself.

Boomer woofed again and tried to get to his feet.

"Stay," Walker said, his voice as calm as his hand pressing the dog's head back to the floor. He pulled the blanket into place again, covering the big hound's shoulder. "Take it easy, boy. Right now you just need to sleep off your drunk."

Boomer huffed, grumbled, and gave Walker's

hand a sloppy lick. He stroked the hound's silky ears. They were warming up. The vet had been right. Boomer was already throwing off the shock of the drugs. He would recover quickly.

"Sheriff Shartell," Jeff said, opening the back door with a jerk, "thanks for coming out so early."

"It's my job," the sheriff said, "but I wouldn't mind coffee if it's handy. One of these days, folks around here will figure out if they want twenty-four-hour protection, they got to pay for more deputies. This here is my chief deputy, Harold. He's taking over for Trafton, who finally got smart and took up bass fishing full-time."

Harold nodded toward the civilians. The deputy was a long, lean drink of water. The sheriff wasn't. He had been a varsity wrestler in high school. Forty years later, his stocky frame was thicker and his light brown hair had thinned to gray wisps. The forty years had also added a measuring edge to his blue eyes and ready smile.

As always, the sheriff admired Mel's casual elegance. Though she wore nothing fancier than dark maternity slacks and a loose red blouse, she looked like a duchess visiting the downstairs help. The kitchen itself was as big as most apartments and showed all the scuffs and odd angles of a room that had been remodeled with every generation except the last. The floor was hardwood and the appliances were thirty years old, scrubbed clean as a young hound's tooth.

"Morning, Miss Buchanan," the sheriff said, touching his hat to Mel, who was sitting on a kitchen chair near the blanket-wrapped hound. "How's the dog?"

"Getting better all the time," Mel said, trying to smile. It wasn't a very successful effort. "How are your wife and grandchildren?"

"Susie's tolerable and the kids are hellions." He grinned. "Everyone says the older boy is just like me. What did Dr. James say was wrong with the dog?"

"Sleeping pills," Jeff said curtly. "But not enough to hurt him."

"That's real good. A lot of these burglars don't care if they kill a good dog on the way to the money."

Jeff flinched. "Have you had many burglaries lately?"

The sheriff shrugged. "Lots of new money on Hilton Head. Money attracts thieves. We keep busy. First time one of the old places has been hit, though. Sure do hope it's not a trend. Scare some of those old widow grannies near to death to find someone creeping around their prize silver."

"I'll get the coffee," Mel said.

"You stay with Boomer," Faith said. "I know where the coffee is." With a nod to the sheriff and his silent deputy, she headed for the coffeepot.

The sheriff looked closely at Walker. Jeans that were neither new nor old. A well-used dark cotton work shirt. A look of easy strength and an intensity that could be either good or bad. A wooden cane that suggested some weakness that wasn't readily apparent. "You're a Walker, aren't you? Owen and Betty's boy."

"A long time ago."

"Not so long when you're my age. You have the look of your father. Good man when he wasn't drinking. That brother of yours always took after his mother's side. How's Lot doing?"

"He's dead."

The sheriff shook his head. "Can't say as I'm surprised. That boy was hell-bent on destruction from his first step. Sure a good-looking kid, though. His smile could put the sun to shame. Pity he had no more sense than a duck."

Faith winced and set down the coffeepot. She knew it was painful for Walker to talk about his brother. "Cream or sugar?" she asked firmly, drawing the sheriff's attention away from the past.

"Both, ma'am," the sheriff said. "Double them up, if you don't mind. I missed breakfast."

"Black." It was the first word the deputy had spoken, but even that single word tagged him as an outsider. Worse, a Yankee. "Thanks."

The sheriff turned to Jeff and said, "Now, what's been going on around here? And why don't you start with yesterday. Any outsiders coming around, besides your guests?"

"The wedding coordinator was here," Jeff said. "Something about measuring the library and shrinking the flowers."

"Her little piano wouldn't fit and it's too late to tune the spinet that's here," Mel said, "so we're going with taped music." Nothing in her voice or expression suggested the disappointment she felt that their plans for a big Savannah wedding had fallen through. She was enough of a businesswoman to understand cash-flow problems.

"That would be Miss Edie Harrison who's doing the wedding?" the sheriff asked.

"That's right," Jeff said almost impatiently. "We're getting married in two days. I thought I made that clear on the phone."

"I understand that you're a bit upset by all this, but it would help if you answered a few more questions. What time did y'all go to bed?"

"Mel went to bed about ten. I went maybe half an hour later. She got up after dawn and went to the kitchen to find some crackers. She tripped over Boomer and screamed. I came running. So did Walker and Faith."

Nodding, the sheriff listened while the deputy took notes. "Who found the open safe?"

"I did," Walker said.

"What did you touch?" the sheriff asked.

"Nothing."

"You sure? Most folks would be fishing around in the safe just to see if it's really empty."

"I watch television," Walker said easily, shifting to let the cane take more of his weight. Nothing reassured a cop like the appearance of weakness. "Didn't want to mess up the crime scene."

"Thank you," the sheriff said as Faith delivered mugs of coffee. Shartell took a long swallow and sighed. She made a good cup of coffee, even if she did dress like a man in jeans and blue cotton shirt. "Just right, ma'am." He turned back to Jeff. "Who went into the library first?"

"I did," Jeff said. "I wanted to use the phone to call the vet. Walker came with me. That's when he saw the open safe and the—what are they, earphones?—dangling from it. He took one look and said we'd been robbed."

"Knew all about that safecracker stuff straight off, did you?" the sheriff asked Walker.

"I knew the safe was open." Walker smiled obligingly and leaned harder on the cane. "I assumed the junk hanging off the dial had something to do with it."

The sheriff made a sound that could have meant anything. "Where was the hound last night, out chasing coons?"

Jeff shrugged. "He started whining about midnight, so I let him out."

"That happen often?"

"Every time he can con one of us into believing he just can't wait," Mel said. "We've got it down to once a night, usually. I think Daddy Montegeau and Tiga just let him run at night, so he's not used to holding it."

"Any sign of forced entry?" the sheriff asked.

"We haven't looked," Mel said, startled. "I'll—"

"Sit down, darling," Jeff said quickly. He went to her, tipped up her chin, and kissed her gently. "Let me take care of everything. I don't want you getting upset." He turned back to the sheriff. "Walker and I checked. The lock on the French doors in the library was broken."

"Anybody hear anything?" the sheriff asked.

"The library is a long way from the bedroom suites," Jeff said. "We didn't hear a thing."

"How about your father or Miss Antigua?"

"They're still asleep. Or Tiga might have gone out already to check her crab pots and fish traps." Jeff made an abrupt gesture. "If they heard anything, they would have awakened us."

The phone rang. Jeff turned away. "Excuse me. That will likely be our insurance agent."

Looking concerned, Mel followed her future husband out of the kitchen. Her voice floated back to the kitchen. "Was there anything valuable in the safe, Jeff? I thought it just held old papers and things."

"Nothing for you to worry about, darling."

The sound of their voices faded when the library door closed.

"Mr. Montegeau told me on the phone that you left some jewelry in the safe," the sheriff said, looking at Faith.

"Yes." Her mouth flattened at the fresh reminder of her loss.

"Valuable, I expect."

"Yes. I have photographs and written descriptions of each piece, as well as separate appraisals of the gemstones. I'll give them to you, if it would help."

"That's real handy, ma'am," the sheriff drawled. "Most people aren't that well prepared for a robbery. Should hurry up the insurance payment."

Walker's eyes narrowed. He had had enough experience with small towns and local prejudice to know that outsiders were guilty until proven innocent. He might not like it, but he expected it.

Faith wasn't so understanding. She turned and looked Shartell right in the eye. "I'm a jewelry designer," she said distinctly. "I always have photographs and descriptions for potential clients. I came to Savannah for a trade show, looking for new clients, so I brought multiple copies of all kinds of pertinent information."

The sheriff grunted.

"She was the only designer west of the Rockies invited to strut her stuff," Walker drawled. "Did real well for herself. Sold all but three of the pieces. Those are the ones she put in the safe," he added, jerking his thumb toward the library.

"The most valuable jewelry of the lot, I suppose," the sheriff said.

"Nope." Walker shifted his weight on the cane and smiled like the country boy he once had been. "The high-ticket stuff went faster than ice cream in August. The small stuff was all that was left. It was a real moneymaking trip."

The sheriff's gray eyebrows shifted as he absorbed the fact that Faith might not have needed the insurance money. "So what are we talking about in the way of losses? A couple hundred? A thousand or two?"

"More like sixty-eight thousand dollars," Faith said. "Materials only. I'm still a relatively unknown artist. No insurance company is going to repay me for the months of work that went into the pieces. So when that burglar opened the safe, I lost three months' pay and three designs. They can't be replaced. They were unique."

"You aren't an unknown artist, not after that show," Walker said. "I'll have a talk with the insurance folks myself. They'll add a zero, maybe two, to get you fair market value."

She gave him a smile that loosened the tight lines around her mouth. "It's not the money, it's just . . ." She shrugged.

"I know," Walker said, taking her hand. He squeezed gently, reminding her that they had agreed not to mention the rash of burglaries and worse that had followed them through the South. He turned to the sheriff. "She's just a little upset," he said. "Nothing pisses a body off so much as being robbed."

"Sixty-eight thousand dollars. Hoo-*eee*." The sheriff shook his head. "And that was just the smaller pieces?"

"Correct," Faith said, her voice clipped. "As Walker said, the trip was profitable."

"When did you put the jewelry in the safe?" the sheriff asked.

"Ten. Just before I went to bed."

Frowning, the sheriff took another swallow of coffee. "Did Davis Montegeau handle it at any time?"

"No. I did."

"Anyone see you?"

Faith's eyes narrowed to glittering silver-blue slits. "No."

"Anyone check it after you did?" the sheriff asked.

"I don't know."

"But you do know the combination."

"No. Jeff was worried about the jewelry. He

opened the safe for me, then left the room. I put the jewelry in, spun the dial, shoved the family ancestor back into place, and went to bed."

The sheriff looked at Walker. "Where were you?"

"Taking a bath. Eases the ache in my leg."

"And y'all heard nothing after that?" Shartell persisted, looking at both Walker and Faith.

Being reminded about last night defused Faith's anger. Remembering Walker and the delight of being thoroughly loved, she didn't know whether to blush or lick her lips in pure feminine triumph.

There had been sounds, all right, but not the kind that the sheriff was interested in.

"Not until dawn," Walker said, but he was remembering the same things Faith was. "Then she heard a scream. She got me up and we went downstairs. You heard it all from there."

"So no one heard anyone coming or going. Y'all just got up and the safe was open."

Walker nodded.

The sheriff looked at Harold, who had been taking notes. Harold put away his clipboard and pen, swigged down the rest of his coffee, and waited for a signal.

"Well, we'll have a look at the safe and the door, but I gotta tell you, these cases are pretty tough to crack," the sheriff said.

"My jewelry designs are quite distinctive,"

Faith said. "When someone tries to hock the pieces, they'll be easy to find."

"Maybe, maybe not." The sheriff finished his coffee and set the cup on the counter. "If the burglar is smart enough to use fancy gear to get into the Montegeaus' safe, he's not some druggie looking for a quick score. He's clever enough to fence the unusual goods somewhere else."

"Then the sooner you circulate a description, the better chance you'll have of solving the crime," Faith said. "I'll get the photos for you."

"Thank you, ma'am," the sheriff said dryly, "but don't get your heart set on seeing anything again. This ain't TV. Out here, the bad guys yank out the stones, junk the settings, pass the stones on up the ladder, and set up the next break-in."

"You're telling me that crime pays," Faith said, her voice equally dry.

"For a while, ma'am, for a while. Then, sooner or later, one of those clever boys gets drunk or high and brags to the wrong person. That's when we nail 'em."

Faith had the feeling that it would be later rather than sooner. A lot later.

If ever.

❦

Walker eased through the scrub, heading for the agents' camp. As soon as he was out of sight

of the house, he walked openly. He hadn't gone
fifty feet when Peel emerged from the deep shadows beneath a pine tree whose needles were
three times longer than her hair. She looked a
little dustier in full light, and a lot more irritated.

"What the hell is going on at the Montegeaus'?" she demanded.

"Try talking to the local sheriff," Walker said
curtly. He had a gut full of badge-heavy cops.

"Pal, I don't talk to locals. They get a case of
the ass every time a federal agent puts a foot
on their turf." She slapped at a mosquito. "Like
anybody who had a choice would want a piece
of this stinking swamp."

Walker tried not to smile at the agent's discomfort. "I hear you. You interested in comparing
notes?"

"You show me yours," she suggested.

"Okay. Somebody cracked the Montegeau safe
last night. Now it's your turn. Did you see anyone
sneaking around?"

"Other than you?"

Walker just smiled.

"We didn't see anything or hear anything until
maybe half an hour after you left. Then we heard
a shout or a scream, activity in various parts of
the house. Fifteen minutes later a panel van pulls
up. A woman gets out with a bag in her hand.
She's inside maybe ten minutes."

"A vet," Walker said. "Somebody slipped the dog a Mickey Finn."

"While she's there, Antigua Montegeau gets in one of those skiffs—don't know why those tubs haven't sunk, they're half-full of water—and goes into the marsh. Twenty minutes after the panel truck leaves, the sheriff arrives. Nineteen minutes after he leaves, Antigua Montegeau comes back with enough crabs to feed an army. Forty minutes later, Davis Montegeau gets in his car and drives off."

"Is that where Farnsworth is, chasing Davis Montegeau?"

"Pete's watching the house."

"How many agents you have working here?"

"As many as we need. What was stolen?"

"Jewelry."

A subtle change came over Peel. She looked a little like a dog catching an interesting scent on the wind. "What kind of jewelry?"

"What kind are you looking for?" Walker asked.

"I can get it from the locals."

I don't talk to locals. Strike two on Cindy Peel. Obviously somebody spoke to the locals and then to her. Walker wondered who, but knew that was one question he wasn't going to ask, because it wouldn't be answered. "The burglar, or burglars, took three pieces of jewelry that Faith didn't sell at the expo."

"What kind of gems?"

"Not the necklace, if that's what you're worried about."

Peel almost managed to hide her relief. Almost.

Strike three, Walker thought with savage satisfaction.

"That supposed to mean something?" she asked casually.

"I can give you photos of the missing stuff, if you like," Walker offered.

"I'll let you know."

"You do that little thing."

Walker turned and vanished into the scrub as quietly as he had arrived. He moved fifty yards through the brush, then withdrew into the shadows and waited, listening.

At first he heard nothing but the faint whisper of air moving through winter-dry grass, saw nothing but the land itself. The dark green of a lone live oak and the dusty green of pines loomed like distant storm clouds above the golden grass and fading green of palmettos. The sky shimmered with humidity, a silver-blue that reminded him of Faith's eyes when their bodies were locked tight together.

The sensation of being watched nibbled at Walker worse than the bugs. Slowly, very slowly, he turned his head. Behind him, in a nameless finger of Ruby Bayou, chartreuse duckweed floated over still black water. Three turtles crouched motionless on a sunny, half-sunken log, their heads pointed toward the morning sun. The reptiles looked freshly scrubbed. The yellow accents on their heads were the color of newly minted doubloons.

Marsh turtles were timid creatures. Nothing had disturbed these three for some time, neither man nor alligator. As if to confirm the impression, an egret glided in on angel-white wings. It settled lightly into the grass, waiting for something edible to make an unwary motion.

The bugs had found Walker by now. They buzzed and lit and bit with abandon. He ignored them. He had been bitten before. He would be bitten again. That was life in the Low Country.

He waited with the patience of a hungry bayou hunter. No sound. No scent. No sudden flight of birds to give away human movement.

Yet he was certain that he had been followed as he left the FBI agents' camp. He was equally certain that neither Peel nor Farnsworth could move silently in the swamp. Maybe the agents had brought in a good Low Country man, but he doubted it. The FBI and the Low Country were about as likely to mix as granite and water.

Ten minutes. Twenty. Thirty.

Walker waited.

Nothing moved but nature itself.

"Must be losing my touch," he muttered.

He stepped out from the concealing shadows and started back to the house.

Behind him there was a pale flash of white, the suggestion of movement sifting through shadows, and then nothing but a primal silence.

26

When Walker returned to the house, he found Faith leaning against the railing of the second-story gallery. The late morning sun spilled over the land and water in waves of very pale, shimmering gold. The sunlight was the exact color of her hair and the tears just barely spilling from her eyelashes.

"Come here, sugar." He turned her in to his arms and held her close.

Her arms slid around him as though they had been together for years instead of days. She knew she should worry about that frightening ease, then reminded herself that this time she knew exactly what the game was, and the score. Walker was an honest man. He wasn't looking for more than sex.

But he was with her now, and she needed him.

"It's been a rough few days for you," he said.

She nodded against his chest, then sighed. "I wasn't getting teary over that."

"Then what?"

"Archer and Hannah just called."

Walker leaned back until he could look in her eyes. "Is something wrong at home?"

"No. Something's very right." Tears glittering against her lashes, Faith smiled up at Walker. "They're going to have a baby."

Although Walker shook his head, his smile was the kind that made her wish he wasn't a solitary kind of man.

"Always knew that boy was brave," Walker drawled.

"That's male-think. It's the woman who carries the baby and delivers it. All he has to do is pace."

"And think of everything that could go wrong, and how there aren't any guarantees, and how it's up to him to keep his family safe."

Faith tilted her head to one side and studied him for a long moment. "You're serious."

"Amen."

"Walker, a man isn't in it alone."

"What does that mean?"

"Say you were confronted by two opponents, one a man who wanted to brawl and the other a woman defending her children. Which fight would you choose?"

He tucked her head under his chin, inhaled the faint gardenia and sunlight scent of her, and wished that life was different. But it wasn't. "Some women aren't like that," he said.

His bleak tone was a caution. Faith remembered his mother's failure to protect her children from a drunken boyfriend. She bit her lip with regret for all that couldn't be changed.

"Most women aren't like your mother, or humans would have died out when meat eaters discovered how slow and tasty we are," Faith said. "Who do you think defended the babies when the men were out hunting or off on some stupid Crusade? What do you think Honor and Lianne and Hannah would do to someone who threatened their kids?"

Walker almost smiled. "Lianne would karate-kick the tar out of anyone who touched those twins wrong. Honor and Hannah would help her, if she needed it."

"She wouldn't. She regularly dumps Kyle on his butt in workouts. She even throws Archer once in a while."

Walker laughed softly. "She's a quick little thing. Fast thinker, too. Wonder if Kyle ever forgave me for seeing her near naked when she distracted those guards."

"I wouldn't mention it if I were you."

"Sugar, I'm a lot smarter than I look."

"Then why are you afraid of kids?"

He pulled back. "What are you talking about?"

"You. You bring toys all the time, and you smile when you watch the babies, but a few days ago at the condo, Archer practically had to hold a gun on you to make you pick Summer up. Why?"

"I'm not used to things that helpless. Makes me nervous."

"Helpless. Needy. Dependent. That's how you see families. None of the laughter, none of the love, none of the sharing. That's sad."

He shrugged uncomfortably. "That's life."

"Your life. Your choice."

Walker clenched against the unexpected twist of pain in his gut. "I told you last night, Faith, don't trust me that way. All I can give you is sex."

"Can, want to, in the end, there's no real difference." She looked up at him and managed a believable smile. "Don't worry, sugar, I'm not designing matching leg shackles in my dreams. I know you don't want any more than we already have. And I'm not complaining. I didn't know it could be this good." She turned her face against his chest and nuzzled the opening of his shirt. "Wonder if they'll have a boy or a girl. Or even twins."

Relieved, Walker accepted the change of subject. "Lord save us. Twins are hell on four legs."

"Oh, Honor and I weren't so bad. Justin and Lawe were the holy terrors."

"You stick with that story. Maybe your brothers will come to believe you."

Faith chuckled against his chest, then remembered the rest of Archer's call. "Speaking of brothers, Archer wants you to call him. He said something about the 'secondary trade,' but he didn't explain."

Walker hoped she didn't feel the adrenaline sliding through him. The "secondary trade" was Archer's code name for the Russian *mafiya*.

"Did you tell Archer about the robbery last night?" Walker asked.

She sighed. "He was so happy about becoming a father. I figured the bad news could wait."

"I'll tell him. He's used to bad news from me. Why don't you slide back between the sheets and take a nap. You didn't get much sleep last night."

"Neither did you."

Walker's slow smile made her tingle.

"I'm trying not to think about that, sugar." He nuzzled her neck, then bit very lightly, very hotly. "If I do, Archer won't be getting his call and you won't be getting your rest."

"Promises, promises."

"You ever hear of a rain check?"

"Yeah."

"I'm giving you a whole book of them."

Half an hour later, Walker was still trying to reach Archer. Faith gave up attempting to sleep and opened her sketch pad. After fifteen minutes of doodling, she put the pad away. She needed to look at new things, new patterns for inspiration. The old house was too steeped in time and emotion. It was hard for her to relax inside its walls.

She felt watched.

"Don't be ridiculous," she muttered under her breath. "No one's here but Walker, and all he's watching is the phone."

Even so, she pulled on her walking shoes and got ready to go out. When she found herself against a wall with her designs in Seattle, she aired out her mind in Seattle's parks and along the waterfront. She could try the same thing here.

She waved at Walker as she went through the sitting room on her way to the hall door.

"Where are you—" began Walker, but he switched in midsentence when an impatient voice came onto the phone. It was Archer, finally. "You need to clone yourself, boy. A man could grow old waiting to talk to you."

❧

Softly Faith pulled the hall door closed behind her. She had been promising herself a walk on the beach. Now was a good time. Nobody needed her. At least she hoped no one did. Mel had been looking too strained and pale. Understandable. No bride—pregnant or virgin—needed a household robbery two days before the wedding.

Once downstairs, Faith was pleased to find herself alone in the big house. Apparently Mel and Jeff were taking advantage of the warm afternoon to catch up on sleep. Davis wasn't back and Tiga had been gone all day.

Faith liked it that way. She needed space, not people.

Quietly she let herself out the kitchen door and took the path past the rickety dock and leaky skiffs, through the scrub, and across a shallow, sandy swale that was scattered with rough-edged saw grass. On the far side, the path unraveled in the loose sand, but now she could hear the hushed breathing of a gentle ocean and the muted cry of seabirds. She was getting close to her goal.

She slogged up a sandy ridge and stood on top. The last of the sea grass stopped just short of the high-tide line, which was marked by a small lip of loose sand. The lip crumbled gently when she put weight on it and she half stepped, half slid onto the beach itself. Here the tidal action had mixed the sand with fragments of broken shells and packed it flat.

The beach was fifty feet wide. Beyond it, the

water was pale blue, surprising after the cold blue-green of Puget Sound. Wavelets no higher than her ankles lapped across the compact, water-dark sand. The smell of brine told her that she was looking at the Atlantic Ocean, but she might have mistaken its calmness for an inland lake.

The quiet water fascinated her. This was open ocean, yet there were no breakers. If she had been on the western shores of Washington or on the ocean-facing side of the Olympic Peninsula, the waves would have been shoulder-high and thunderous.

Kicking off her shoes, she went to the edge of the calm water and tasted it. Salt. The ocean, without question. She wiggled her toes against the packed sand. It was firm yet resilient, a perfect walking surface. As she turned and headed up the beach, exploring, the troubles of the past few days disappeared.

Or so she thought.

❦

Several hundred yards up the beach, where the first condos became a solid glass-and-cement wall lining the water, light flashed off binocular lenses. The watcher sat just below the crest of the low row of sand dunes that separated the buildings from the beach. It was as close as a stranger could come to Ruby Bayou without being obvious. Considering the FBI team staked out in the rough scrub between the condos and the house, the watcher had decided that being obvious was a good way of getting arrested.

Like him, the FBI had night-vision goggles. Theirs were better than the ones he had picked up at the Savannah sporting goods store, but his were good enough, and certainly better than anything he could buy in Russia.

But now, in the daylight, regular binoculars worked quite well. They didn't even attract any attention from the locals. There were a lot of bird-watchers in the area.

This way, little girl. Come to me. Closer. Closer. I promise you it will be quick.

The smile beneath the binoculars was cold. Some promises were meant to be broken.

Faith glanced around uneasily. The feeling of being watched had crept through her, overcoming the peace she had felt for a time. She was sure she was being watched, but the beach seemed empty for at least a mile behind her. With an impatient sound, she looked ahead. The beach soon gave way to marsh. She looked back over her shoulder again, where the sand stretched on for miles, empty but for a scattering of people strolling the tide line, taking in the warm winter day.

Maybe that was why she felt watched. Ruby Bayou seemed very remote, but civilization crowded right up to its boundaries. If she went with the broad, inviting beach, she would soon encounter the condos, hotels, and private homes that lined the ocean side of Hilton Head Island. More people, but no inspiration, only concrete condos.

Sun beat with surprising intensity against her shoulders as she turned away from the condos and headed down the beach toward the marsh. The calm water and strength of the sun kept taking her by surprise. She had been in Seattle too long. Tony had always wanted her to be handy when he came back from a trip, and his schedule was unpredictable. So she had stayed in one place and lost touch with the rest of the world.

Faith took in a deep breath and blew it out, cleaning the past from her mind. She had chosen to do as Tony asked, always, because she believed that was the way to make their relationship work.

Bad choice.

Never again would she settle for a relationship where respect and understanding were a one-way street. She knew now what it was like to have respect flow both ways.

Like Walker respecting her jewelry designs. Like Walker seeing her sadness and holding her instead of scolding her for sulking.

Like her holding Walker and understanding him even when it hurt. Like making him laugh when his eyes were haunted.

A two-way street.

Too bad it was such a short street.

The sharp edge of a shell dug at her bare foot, reminding her that she should look where she was going, not where she had been or where she couldn't go.

She leaned down to pick up the fragment and saw that it was the top of what had once been a whelk. The spiral design of the shell was elegant, like a tiny galaxy spinning against a vast universe of sand. Much of the shell had been broken by tumbling storm seas, but enough remained to reveal the smooth, shiny, curving center that had once supported life. The inner colors were neither peach nor cream, but a luminous mixture of both, like sunrise.

The first, niggling possibility of a design began to form in Faith's mind. She was hardly aware of it. She simply stared at the lustrous fragment as though it contained the answer to an urgent, wordless question.

After a time she put the shell in the pocket of her jeans and walked along the edge of the sea. She made slow progress, because she kept spotting fascinating fragments of shells, shapes that teased her with their mute poetry.

Then, just above the waterline, she came across a long, twisting ribbon of shells. They looked like fragments, yet when she crouched down to examine them more closely, she discovered that they were whole, nearly perfect miniatures of the larger pieces she had already found. Their balanced beauty was breathtaking, a thousand thousand tiny ballerinas spinning gracefully to music only the dancers could hear.

If she could have described the tiny shells in words or song, she would have. But she couldn't. She could only absorb them and let them shape her dreams and designs.

"I knew they would draw you, precious," said a woman's soft voice.

Faith's heartbeat doubled when she felt something caress her hair as lightly as a breeze. She shot to her feet and spun around. She was close to where the beach merged with the marsh. The gentle voice and touch belonged to Tiga Montegeau.

"My God," Faith said, putting her hand over her heart, "you scared me out of my skin."

Tiga smiled. Her graying blond hair lifted in the faint wind like mist off a midnight bayou. Her eyes mirrored the humid, shimmering sky, both shallow and bottomless, unfocused, a pale color that shifted from gray to blue with every turn of her head.

"No need to fear," Tiga murmured, touching Faith's cheek as though they were mother and daughter rather than near strangers. "You know I'd never hurt my precious little baby."

Faith opened her mouth to point out that she wasn't Tiga's precious little baby. Then she remembered Mel's advice: *Just treat her like a pet cat. If she wants to talk to you, listen and try not to look confused.*

"Of course you wouldn't," Faith said reassuringly. "I just thought I was alone."

"Silly, sweet child." Sun-browned, salt-water-toughened hands repeated the ghostly caress over Faith's hair. "We're never alone. Your great-granddaddy hung a man just over there," she said, pointing to an ancient oak growing back toward the house. "You can still hear him screaming when the moon is dark. Guess he didn't like it."

Faith couldn't think of any response.

Tiga didn't notice. "Up yonder," she said, looking toward the marsh and its still, black water, "a girl drowned. Least, folks think she did. She came thirteen and went oystering alone. When there's moonrise and mist, you hear her calling like a bird, *let-me-go, let-me-go, please-let-me, let-me-please.*"

Tiga's soft fluting imitation of a ghostly bird made the hair at the nape of Faith's neck stir.

"She's still there," Tiga said, *"let-me-go, let-me-go, please-let-me . . .* Don't know why she cries. Drowning's easier than hanging, least that's what they say."

"They?"

"The spirits, precious. You hear them."

"Actually, I don't."

Tiga's smile was sad enough to make Faith's eyes sting with tears.

"Of course you do, precious baby," Tiga said, almost touching Faith, almost not touching. "You're one of them. So am I, sometimes. Crying, dying, *let-me-go, please-let-me . . ."*

The certainty in Tiga's voice and eyes held Faith rooted. Desperately she tried to think of Tiga as a pet cat. It wasn't possible. No cat this side of hell had such wise, unearthly eyes.

"Sometimes they wear rubies," Tiga whispered confidentially. "That's how you know."

"Know?" Faith managed.

"Your kin, precious baby. A bracelet wide, cold gold, souls fixed in gold by the hundreds, red tears, red blood. A circle, a crown of thorns, drops of blood at every point, blood frozen to ice and polished to shining, crying, sighing *let-me-go, let-me-go."*

Faith gave up trying to picture a chatty cat. Somehow that was more unnerving than simple human madness. And beneath the madness . . . pain.

She wished that she couldn't sense Tiga's pain so clearly, like darkness at midnight.

"A long ruby rope, burning hate, burning hope," Tiga said, pinning Faith with her uncanny eyes, "twisting round and round, *let-me-go, please-let-me.* Souls as big as pecans, hanged in silver rope, swinging like dead men from her ears. They don't cry, can't sigh, dead as only a hanged man can be. The king of all, or even the queen, too big for a cat or a child to swallow, dear Lord, the *red*, and so cold, so old, surrounded by angels' tears white as blood is red, angel tears for my dead baby. It speaks. To me. Find the rest of the queen's court, the thirteen curves, the thirteen souls, the blaze of hope."

With startling speed and strength, Tiga's fingers wrapped around Faith's wrist. "You must bring it to me, precious. It belongs in the Blessing Chest, not a noose around your neck. I can't bear hearing you scream, *let-me-go, let-me-go. . . .*"

Faith did the only thing she could think of. "Of course I'll find it," she said in a low, soothing voice. "Will you walk with me now, back to the house?"

Slowly Tiga's fingers slipped away. As though orienting herself, she looked at the sea, then the sun, then the marsh. When she looked at Faith again, she blinked in surprise.

"Hello," Tiga said in a normal, if girlish, voice. "What are you doing here? Did you come to play with me? I'm so very sorry. I can't. The crabs are waiting to be blessed."

Tiga smiled vaguely, turned, and walked back toward the marsh. Her strides were long, certain, the movements of a woman thirty years younger. Very quickly she vanished back up the path that led to the ratty skiffs at Ruby Bayou's dock.

Faith blew out a long breath, then another. She wished that Tiga's conversations were completely mad, completely incomprehensible. But the woman's eerie certainty of her own meaning turned her words into a language that only one person spoke. Sound and meaning, yet no possibility of understanding.

On the other hand, Faith wasn't eager to understand a world of hanged men and missing children and souls as red as blood locked in gold.

The image of Mel's engagement ring flashed into Faith's mind, a bloodred ruby set in gold.

Let-me-go, let-me-go, please-let-me . . .

27

"If your assistant interrupts you one more time, boss, I'm going to do something fatal to him," Walker said mildly into the cell phone.

Archer's laughter cracked over the line. "Sorry. The trouble with working for yourself is you're always at work."

Archer looked up as his assistant rolled in with coffee and a snack tray resting on the arms of his wheelchair. Mitchell passed the tray over Archer's desk, spun the wheelchair, and left, closing the door behind him. "Okay, now that we're on a secure phone and Uncle Sam probably can't listen in, what the hell is going on at Ruby Bayou?"

"Someone cracked the safe and cleaned it out."

"The rubies?"

"Still next to the family jewels, but only the three of us know that."

Archer sipped coffee, took a bite of pesto bread, and thought. "So everyone but you and Faith thought the necklace was in the safe."

"Yeah."

"You think it was an inside job?"

"The dog was drugged and the French doors leading to the library were forced."

"That doesn't rule out an inside job."

"You're cynical, boss. It's one of the things I like best about you."

"Thank you. I won't ask for the rest of the list."

Walker laughed. "Smart man. As for the safe, I think whoever opened it expected to find more than three of Faith's beautiful designs."

"Damn! Three of her pieces are gone?"

"I e-mailed Kyle the inventory numbers. He said he'd put out photos and warnings where it would do the most good."

"The insurance company isn't going to like that."

"Neither do I. I could have told her not to put anything in a safe that's as old as Methuselah."

"You think she would have listened?"

"Anything is possible," Walker said wryly. "But I wanted to go fishing and I let her use the stuff as bait."

"Explain."

"Someone wants those rubies real bad. First that Russian shows up looking for a fairy-tale ruby in Faith's Seattle shop. He cases the place, watches awhile to be sure, then goes back and drills out the safe. No necklace, because I was wearing the damn thing."

"Back up. A fairy-tale ruby?"

"Ivanovitch described a ruby that probably never existed, and even if it did, hasn't been seen for centuries."

"So you think he was just fishing for an excuse to get inside Faith's shop?"

"That's the most likely scenario. If he asked for the necklace outright and then it went missing, he would have a lot to explain. This way we're linking him with something that likely didn't exist—the Heart of Midnight—instead of with the Montegeau necklace."

"Okay."

"If that scenario doesn't work, I'll move on to the others. You want to hear them?"

"Only if the first scenario goes bad. All right, we're assuming the Montegeau necklace is the target."

Walker winced. He knew as well as Archer that assumption was the mother of all fuckups.

But you had to start somewhere.

"They hit the bed-and-breakfast where they expected to find Faith, then the exposition safe, and then they mugged Faith trying to get the necklace," Walker said. "Nobody outside of that Russian has said a word about the Heart of Midnight, so the necklace sure seems to be the real target."

Archer made a sound that was closer to a snarl than a word.

"Yeah," Walker said, his voice dangerously calm, "I'm fixing to make someone pay for waving a knife at Faith."

"Sounds like you already did, from what Kyle told me about the jailhouse doctor's report in Savannah."

"Has that boy been hacking into official computers again?"

"Is he breathing?" Archer retorted. "From the official description of Buddy Angel's bruises, contusions, and kidneys, he's going to be whining like a kicked pup every time he pisses."

"He can cry on Tony Kerrigan's shoulder."

There was a heartbeat of silence followed by Archer's opinion of his sister's ex-fiancé.

That was another thing Walker liked about his boss. He could speak gutter Afghani like a native.

"When did you see that son of a bitch?" Archer demanded, reverting to English.

Multiple phones rang in the background at Archer's office. He ignored them.

So did Walker. "He turned up during the show. Said he wanted to talk about old times."

"Christ." Archer's free hand curled into a fist. "Did he bother Faith?"

"Nope. I introduced myself, we shook hands, went outside to chew the fat, and then I paid for a cab to take him where he belonged. And he only had one li'l ol' broken finger when I was done."

One of Archer's dark eyebrows lifted. He would love to read the rest of that official summary in its original long form. Like the way Tony had looked facedown on cement. "They don't have cabs to hell."

"You've never been to Savannah."

"Kyle didn't see a police report about it," Archer said.

"Hell in Savannah?"

"No, your, uh, *conversation* with Tony."

"No fuss, no muss, no bother. It looked to all the world like some poor fool who was so damned clumsy with his cane that he tripped his big friend and then thrashed all over him trying to stand up."

Archer smiled, liking the picture in his mind. "Should I put a man on him full-time?"

Walker thought about it for a few seconds. "No need. If he gets in touch with her again, I'll take care of it."

"Don't get caught."

"Caught doing what?" Walker asked mildly.

Archer snorted. "So the man I assigned to

guard Faith is such a klutz he's put two guys in the hospital. The Montegeau rubies are still safe despite numerous attempts to steal them. Three more of Faith's pieces are stolen at Ruby Bayou, no one was hurt but the dog, and you're voting for an inside job."

"Too soon to vote, boss. I'm still trying to figure out where April Joy's Russian *mafiya* intersects with the Atlantic City mob, which is baying after Faith's jewelry like hounds on a hot scent. Then there's the FBI."

"The FBI? Oh, shit. I'd forgotten about them. Where does the FBI fit in?"

"They claim they're following Davis Montegeau, trying to nail Sal Angel any way they can."

"You don't believe them."

Walker sighed. "Damn, boss, I'd sure like to. It may even be part of the truth."

"But?"

"But we had Uncle on our ass before we ever saw a Montegeau. Two agents followed us to the restaurant, badged the hostess to get a table, and didn't leave until we did, even though Mel was still waiting for her car to be brought around. Yet Cindy Peel—the agent in charge—claims they were following Mel and got on to us after the fact."

"Not good."

Walker didn't argue. He felt the same way.

"Anything else?" Archer asked.

"They've got Ruby Bayou staked out fairly well, but they claim they didn't see anything unusual during the burglary. Course, they aren't swamp rats, so they could have missed something. I sure got close to them easy enough."

Silently Archer absorbed the fact that Walker had tracked down the agents in the swamp. "Maybe they didn't see anything because it was an inside job."

"Maybe," Walker agreed. "The local sheriff seems to think Faith is good for it."

"What?"

"I told him to check out Donovan International before he did anything he'd regret, like saying in public what he was hinting in private."

"Judas Priest, what a cluster-fuck."

"Don't take it personally. I didn't, and he hinted I could have done it, too."

"That's it," Archer said flatly. "I'm flying out."

"Stay with Hannah and celebrate the next generation. And congratulations, by the way. You're a braver man than I am."

"I doubt that."

"I don't. Marriage and kids scare the bejesus out of me."

On the other end of the phone, Archer kneaded his neck and raked his fingers through hair that already was rumpled. His office door opened. He turned to snarl at Mitchell, then saw Hannah. The smile he gave her transformed his face from dangerous to simply handsome. Silently he held out his hand to her.

"Then you're an idiot," Archer said.

"Hey, every man has to be good at something," Walker said.

"Why is the sheriff sniffing after you and Faith?"

Hannah gave Archer an alarmed look. He kissed her fingers, released them, and returned to rubbing his tight neck. She brushed his hand aside and leaned into the job of loosening tight muscles. He tried not to groan aloud with pleasure.

"Down here," Walker said, "everybody blames outsiders."

"I suppose the sheriff never heard of a local pillar of society breaking into his own safe."

"That's the problem. The Montegeaus don't stand to gain anything if Faith's pieces disappear. Ditto the necklace. It's not part of their insurance coverage until Mel wears it at her wedding."

"Even without insurance, the jewelry is valuable."

"Sure, but you have to turn it into cash first. That's not easy, as good old Ivan Ivanovitch discovered when he got tagged trying to fence one of Faith's unique pieces."

"Ahhhh, I get it," Archer said, almost purring with the pleasure of his wife's fingers kneading away the tension. "You're waiting to see where the new pieces turn up."

"Amen. Then I'm going to kick some serious ass."

There was silence at the other end of the line. It didn't bother Walker. He knew Archer was mentally summarizing and filing everything that had been said and not said, done and not done.

Phones rang incessantly in the background. At least two computers beeped impatiently.

Frowning, Hannah kept working on Archer's hard shoulders. Even if she hadn't heard half of the conversation, the tension in his body would have told her that it was family rather than business at risk. He was fiercely protective of the people he loved.

"Get Faith on the next plane out," Archer said finally.

"Short of tying her up and stuffing her in a bag, how do you suggest I do that?" Walker asked calmly.

"Tie and stuff works for me."

"Kidnapping is a federal crime," Walker said. "It's hard to get away with such things when there are federal agents camped on your butt."

"Try sweet reason on her."

"I did."

Archer didn't have to ask the outcome: Faith was still in Ruby Bayou. "E-mail directions to Ruby Bayou to—"

"Kyle already has them," Walker interrupted.

"He didn't say anything to me about it."

"Probably didn't want to rain on the baby parade."

Archer smiled slightly and kissed what he could reach of Hannah's strong, nimble fingers. "Probably not. If the sheriff is as stupid as he sounds, you'll need the name of a good local lawyer. I'll put Mitch on it."

"He took care of it while I was on hold. The woman's name is Samantha Butterfield and she's been in the South since the first mosquito hatched. Knows where all the local bodies are buried, who buried them, who went to jail for it, and who didn't."

"Does she know the damned sheriff?"

"Second cousins."

"Kissing kin, huh?"

"Down here, we're more serious about our cousins than just kissing," Walker said wryly. "We like to keep things in the family. Don't want to spread all that poverty too wide, hear?"

Despite his tension, Archer laughed.

Hannah smiled. Walker was one of the few people who could knock Archer out of full work mode. Then she remembered the circumstances the last time she talked on the phone with Walker. She didn't know whether to laugh or blush. She supposed it served her right for teasing Archer when he was on the phone, but it had been so delicious to listen to him carry on a rational business conversation while she seduced him.

She wondered what would happen if she did it again. Right now. Right here.

He would probably do what he had the last time—pull her on like a glove, hand her the phone to talk to Walker, and then make her forget her own name.

Archer felt Hannah's touch change from medicinal to sensual. His blood heated, his heartbeat kicked, and the fit of his pants changed. He figured he had a minute before she got him unzipped. Maybe two.

He was hoping for one.

"Get Faith on a plane if you can," Archer said.

"And if I can't?"

"Take care of her any way you have to. Lawyers are cheap."

The line went dead.

As Walker disconnected, he hoped that Samantha Butterfield didn't look like the north end of a southbound mule. Unless he got real lucky, he would be spending a lot of time with the formidable southern lawyer.

"Faith?" he called.

There was no answer.

Walker went through the house very quickly. Faith was nowhere to be seen. The gardens were empty. The rickety wharf stood vacant in the sun.

He swore in Afghani with deep conviction and considerable expertise. He knew if he told her not to let him out of her sight, she would tell him to go to hell. So he hadn't given her any orders.

Now she was gone.

Trying to still the rush of adrenaline in his blood, Walker untied one of the battered oyster skiffs and started rowing. Boats were the fastest means of travel in the murky depths of Ruby Bayou.

28

Faith hesitated, trying to remember which path she had taken down from the house. The faint dirt tracks braided their way along the dunes and through the scrub in startling confusion. She was beginning to think she might be lost.

Well, not lost, exactly. She knew where the ocean was. She knew where Ruby Bayou was. She just didn't know how to get from here to there through the knife-blade grass, waist-deep mud, and brackish water so dark it could have been a mile deep. Or an inch.

"Faith?"

She jumped before she recognized Walker's voice. He was calling from somewhere out in the tall marsh grass.

"I'm over here."

"Yeah, I figured that out. But I'm damned if I can figure out how you got there."

"Me too," she admitted.

"Stay put and keep talking."

"What about?"

"Anything you wouldn't mind seeing on the front page of the local paper."

"Darn. And here I was fixing to talk dirty to you."

"Just as well. My poor old heart couldn't take it."

Faith's laugh was as silky and hot as the sun pouring over the uncertain margin between ocean and land.

"Talk to me, sugar," Walker said.

"I'm trying to think about something that wouldn't get us arrested."

"Good idea. Bondage only works in books."

She snickered, drew a breath, and memories came flooding back. She didn't know why the restless breeze and the earthy smell of wet ground called up an incident that had happened years ago and thousands of miles across the continent, but at least she had something to talk about.

"When we were thirteen," she said, speaking in a voice that would carry to Walker, wherever he might be in the tall grass, "Honor and I sneaked out after bedtime and rode our bikes to the local make-out place."

"Keep talking."

"We watched Archer at work on Libby Tallyman, who was two years older than he was. Talk about sucking tonsils . . ."

Walker laughed out loud. He eased the flat-bottomed, leaky skiff through a shallow spot, poling against mud that was almost as liquid as water in places. For a moment he thought he was going to get stuck. Again. Then the skiff went through the narrow opening between clumps of grass.

A startled heron took off with a squawk.

"What was that?" Faith asked anxiously.

"Shitepoke. Keep talking. It's easy to lose direction in all this grass."

"Kyle followed us." She stood on her tiptoes and looked, but all she saw was the marsh grass. She hadn't known it was tall enough to hide a man. Maybe Walker was wading through the mud. "He threatened to snitch us off to Archer unless we agreed to do his dishes for a week and his laundry for a month."

"Out-and-out blackmail."

Walker's voice now came from Faith's left. She turned and stared. Nothing.

"The worst kind of blackmail," she agreed. "You know how unpleasant a brother's dirty socks are? Especially to delicate little flowers like we were. Yuck! But we agreed. Anything was better than one of Archer's endless lectures."

Walker chuckled.

She looked for him again. She could tell he was closer, but she still couldn't see him. Sound carried a long way in the marsh. "Where are you?"

"Behind a tongue of mud and marsh grass. Keep talking. I'm liking the picture of you and Honor doing your brother's laundry."

"We're smarter than that. We let Kyle herd us home, then we waited. Sure enough, he slipped out and got on his bike. We followed him back to the make-out spot. He hid where we had before and watched. You should have seen his eyes. Did I mention that Libby had the biggest boobs in the county?"

"Nope, but I'm getting the picture."

"A cow at milking time?" Faith asked innocently.

"Never seen one of them."

"She had two, actually."

Walker gave up and laughed. "There you go."

"Where? I haven't moved."

He pushed back from a blind tongue of water that ended in a mudbank. "Just full of sass and vinegar, aren't you?"

"*Moi?* You must be thinking of my twin."

Quietly he poled around a bunch of reeds. Faith stood thirty feet away, her back to him, just on the other side of a low ridge of grass. She wore jeans that were old enough to be soft and tight enough to make him remember where she was the hottest.

"What I'm thinking about," he said, "is that sweet spot I found last night."

His voice was low, husky, and seemed close. But she still couldn't find him. She made an impatient sound and peered over the grass toward the trees. No one. "Think out loud. I can't see you yet."

"I'm thinking about how I'd like to slide you out of those jeans again. I'm thinking about the way the backs of your thighs feel against my palms when I—"

She cleared her throat loudly and started talking. Fast. "And I'm thinking about the front page of that newspaper you mentioned."

"Turn around, sugar. No one's here but us."

She looked over her shoulder. Walker was screened by a clump of grass. Or standing in the mud. Or something. It was a lot wetter out where he was than where she was.

"I knew you were good, sugar," she said huskily, "but I didn't know you could walk on water."

Laughter and an odd sort of pain sliced through Walker. He found himself wishing that he could put Faith into the skiff, glide from marsh to bayou, and disappear with her.

Forever.

Take care of her any way you have to. Lawyers are cheap.

The best way he could take care of her was to get her back to Seattle and then disappear. She was a forever-and-family kind of woman. All he would let himself be was a here-and-now, solitary kind of man. The cost of failing someone else was just too high.

For the second time in his life, Walker wished all the way to his soul that things could be different.

Nothing changed except the amount of pain he carried around inside him.

He wasn't surprised. He had learned a long time ago that wishing didn't change a damned thing.

"What are you doing?" Faith asked.

He eased the skiff around the mound of grass. "I'm thinking about the best way to get you into this skiff without getting you muddy as a frog hunter."

The sexy humor in her eyes disappeared as she saw the disreputable-looking skiff. "Me? In *that*? Forget it. I'd rather be lost in the marsh."

"It's a good skiff."

"It's a piece of crap."

He gave the oars a deceptively easy pull. The prow of the little boat buried itself in the grass about six feet away from her. "Climb aboard."

"I wouldn't get in if my life depended on it," Faith said flatly.

Walker looked over his shoulder at her. She wasn't kidding. "Don't like small boats?" he drawled.

"Wrong. I loathe them."

"Any particular reason?"

"I spent the most terrifying hours of my life with Honor and my brothers in a small boat. Naturally the younger sisters were facedown in the fish and stinky water at the bottom of the boat while the boys worked like hell to get us ashore before the wind or waves dumped all of us into the strait. Where, by the way, the water temperature would have killed us in about half an hour."

"There's no wind here, no waves, and the water isn't cold."

"I'm happy for you."

"But you're not getting in the boat."

"Right."

"I'll let you sit up just like one of the guys," Walker drawled.

"No, thanks."

"I'll bail it out."

"Hang colored lights and banners if you like. I'm still staying on land."

"You're really scared, aren't you?" he said quietly.

"Give the boy a gold star for figuring it out." Faith's voice, like her mouth, was tight.

He laid the pole aside and climbed out easily over the bow, dragging the little skiff well above the reach of the slowly rising tide. When he turned toward her, she backed away as though afraid he would grab her and dump her in the skiff.

"Easy, Faith," Walker said. "I wouldn't do that to you."

She took a shaky breath and a better grip on her nerves. Walker wasn't the kind of bully who would grab her and force her to do something— for her own good, of course.

"I know," she said. "Sorry. Some people are terrified of snakes, or bats, or moths, or heights, or caves. I'm terrified of little boats."

"Sounds like you have reason. I guess it didn't take Honor that way, since she and Jake spend so much time on his boat. Or is it only open skiffs and such that bother you?"

"Both Honor and I were terrified by anything less than a ship for years. Until Kyle disappeared, Honor refused to board any craft shorter than two hundred feet. But the only way for her to help Kyle was to use a small boat." Faith shrugged jerkily. "Honor used the damn thing. After a while, she came to love it. And Jake. He had a lot to do with it."

"Well, nothing so dire as death or love is at stake, so let's see if we all can't find our way out of this little bit of tidal marsh on foot."

"What about that?" she asked, pointing toward the skiff as though it was a snake.

"I'll take care of it."

Walker checked that the skiff was secure before he led Faith over her back trail. It took several false turns before he found the point where she had turned wrong. Soon muddy clumps of grass gave way to sandy scrub. From there, the path to the beach was clear.

"If you know the way to the house from here," he said, "I'll get the skiff and meet you at the dock."

"I know the way. Just go up that dip in the sand berm and follow the path to the live oaks. But I want to go shelling some more."

Walker tried to think of a nice way to tell her to head back to Ruby Bayou where he could keep an eye on her. If he gave her an order, she would get her back up and walk the beach until hell froze solid.

Sensing his reluctance, Faith dug in her jeans pocket and pulled out the swirling fragment of whelk. "The lines of the shells here are incredible. Elegant yet powerful."

"Sounds like your jewelry."

She smiled almost shyly, pleased all over again that he truly liked her work. "With luck, some of it will be."

Walker made his decision—roundabout rather than head-on. "Watch what you pick up. The cone shells are poisonous if the snail is still alive. They won't kill you, but they sure won't help you, either."

She blinked. "Poisonous snails?"

"This is the Low Country, sugar, home of copperheads and cottonmouths and even a rattler or two. Anything that survives here likely has teeth or a stinger. Or both."

"Does that include people?"

He smiled, showing two rows of hard white teeth. "What do you think?"

She looked beyond the smile to the tension around his dark blue eyes. "I think I'll head back to the house and see if Mel is awake. She hasn't been here long enough to bite or sting."

"There you go."

"Since I'm being so nice about it, why don't you tell me the real reason you don't want me on the beach alone."

"Kyle's gut. Archer's orders."

"Oh." She blew out a breath as she shoved the shell back in her pocket. "Well, damn," she drawled as she turned toward the path to Ruby Bayou. "I sure do wish that boy would eat more antacids."

Walker laughed, then grabbed Faith and held her close. The gardenia, salt, and woman scent of her went to his head like the best bourbon.

"Thank you," he said against her hair.

"For what?"

"For not making me use the tie-and-stuff method."

She looked at him curiously. "Should I know what that means?"

"I sure do hope not. See you at the dock."

"You might as well tell me. Sooner or later, I'll find out what it means."

"Later works for me."

With a sideways look that promised retribution, Faith headed for the path that led to Ruby Bayou. Walker watched until her bright hair disappeared beyond the brown marsh grass. Then he went back to get the skiff.

It was gone.

Adrenaline slammed throught Walker. He didn't bother looking for the little boat. He knew it hadn't wandered off on its own. Heart racing, he ran back to the path to Ruby Bayou, hoping that whoever had stolen the boat wouldn't beat him back to the house. Back to Faith.

Protect her however you have to.

He had tried. But now it looked like he had screwed up.

Again.

29

Davis Montegeau drove the dirt road to Ruby Bayou with the blind stubbornness of a wounded animal dragging itself to its lair. He had to use his left foot for both accelerator and brake pedal, because his right leg was useless. The pain in his right knee was excruciating and nauseating by turns.

At least there was nothing left to throw up in his bruised stomach but the blood he had swallowed since Buddy smashed his nose. Now his entire face was so swollen that he could barely see. The rest of his body joined in the chorus of agony that stabbed through him with every breath, every beat of his heart.

Sal had watched the whole process with all the

animation of a man watching paint dry. He hadn't even spoken until Buddy began to stomp Davis, who by then was curled around himself on the floor.

That's enough, Buddy. The stuff he brought is worth a week's interest on what he owes. But if I don't have the principal, half million, in seven days, you can stomp him into tomato paste and spread him on a pizza.

Tears of pain, hopelessness, and terror streamed down Davis's face like blood from his split lip. The bumpy drive made him whimper. He kept going anyway. There were several dizzying times when he came close to passing out before he finally saw the big, decaying house. He hung on to the wheel and steered around to the rear.

After a few fumbling tries he managed to turn off the engine. Then he looked longingly at the broad gallery that circled the lower floor. Only twenty feet to the house. Maybe thirty. Six steps up to the porch. Through the kitchen, out, turn in to the library.

In his mind he could already see the clear bottle, feel bourbon's hot oblivion searing away the taste of blood.

But he couldn't even open the car door. Through eyes glazed with pain, he looked up at the old live oak that shaded one side of the house. The moss on the thick, twisted branches looked dusty, and the resurrection ferns growing on the broad limbs were shriveled. Like him. Dimly he wondered if blood would revive the ferns even better than rain did.

"Daddy Montegeau, is something wrong?"

Mel's light, sweet voice called out from the screen porch. The door slammed as she hurried down the steps to the car.

He wanted to turn toward her, but it hurt too much.

She opened the car door for him. "Oh, God! What happened?" she asked anxiously.

With an effort, he summoned the energy to speak. "Fell."

"Can you walk?" Without waiting for the answer, Mel turned and shouted toward the house. "Jeff, come quick! Your daddy's hurt!"

❧

Walker had caught Faith halfway up the path. He was still out of breath from his sprint when they both heard Mel's cry through the scrub. Faith reacted out of instinct, gathering herself to run for the house.

"No." He grabbed Faith's arm. "From now on you're staying close to me."

"Just because that skiff drifted off doesn't—"

"It didn't drift," Walker said curtly. "Somebody set it adrift. Somebody who followed you. Or me."

"But—"

"But nothing," he cut in. "Give me your word you'll stay close to me or you'll find out exactly what tie and stuff means."

His eyes told Faith she would lose the argument. "Fine," she said tightly. "Consider me your bloody shadow."

"I'm holding you to that."

He took her hand and together they broke into a run, heading for the house. Walker's leg had begun giving him a twinge somewhere during his sprint through the sand. Now it ached, but he ignored it. As he passed the battered dock, he saw both skiffs tied off to a post, but he didn't slow down. Ahead he could see Davis Montegeau's big white Caddy parked carelessly on the grass. The driver's door was open and Mel was trying to help Davis out of the car.

"Mel, let me," Walker said, pulling her aside. "You're in no shape to lift anything."

"Jeff must be in the shower. He didn't hear me when I yelled."

Walker hunkered down and took a good look at Davis. The man's face looked like he had been hit with a baseball bat. He seemed to be barely conscious.

Faith came and put her arm around Mel.

"What happened?" Walker asked.

"He fell," Mel said quickly.

Walker's dark eyebrows lifted, but he didn't say anything except, "Where?"

"He had a doctor's appointment in Savannah," Mel said.

"They got a funny way of drawing blood in Savannah," Walker said neutrally.

Mel made a nervous sound that could have been a laugh. "Daddy Montegeau? What happened?"

Slowly Davis gathered his concentration. "Happened after the doctor. Going down to the river. Tripped."

Faith thought of the steep, narrow stairways down the bluff from Water Street to the river below. The footing was tricky at best and in some spots the cobblestones were lethal. Shaking her head, she bit her lip in silent sympathy. Davis was lucky he hadn't broken his neck.

Walker looked at the older man's hands. They were trembling but unmarked.

"Waterfront stairs, huh?" Walker said easily. "No wonder you look like you tangled with a truck. Let me help you move over to the passenger side. I'll drive you to the hospital."

"No!"

The women were surprised by Davis's response. Walker wasn't. It fit the picture growing in his mind.

Archer wasn't going to be happy.

"Are you fixing to go inside soon, or do you want to sit out here awhile longer and get your breath?" Walker asked mildly.

"I want a drink."

"I'm sure you do," Walker agreed. "Doubt that you'll keep it down, though. Your stomach is going to be twitchy for a time."

Davis groaned.

"Hurt anywhere else?" Walker asked. "Your back?"

Davis shook his head.

"How about your kidneys?" Walker asked.

The older man nodded. "Knee, too."

Walker wasn't surprised. "Mel, why don't you get my cane for Mr. Montegeau. Right now he needs it more than I do."

"Where is it?"

"Last time I saw it, it was in the shorter skiff tied at the dock."

Mel hurried off down the path to the ragged little dock. A few moments later Jeff called from the house, looking for his wife.

"Out back," Walker called in a carrying voice. "Your daddy had a little accident. He'll be needing help getting into the house."

Jeff appeared about thirty seconds later. His hair was still wet, his jeans were buttoned wrong, and he was barefoot and shirtless. He took one look at his father and went pale. "Daddy? Good Lord, what happened?"

"We'll go into that later," Walker said. "Right now, help me get him to bed."

"A drink," Davis said roughly.

Jeff's eyes narrowed. "Looks like you already had more than enough."

"It wasn't booze," Davis said painfully. "Damn stairs."

"Uh-huh," Jeff muttered.

Together Jeff and Walker half carried, half supported Davis as far as the library. There they stretched him out on the couch. Faith came in from the kitchen with a pan of warm water and a wad of clean dish towels. She washed away enough blood to assess the damage to Davis's face. Walker took his knife out of its concealed sheath and carefully slit his host's ruined right pant leg up to the knee. It was swollen, bruised, ugly as a nightmare.

"Got any ice?" Walker asked.

Jeff headed for the refrigerator. With vicious jerks he broke ice cubes from their plastic trays and went back to the library.

Mel arrived with Walker's cane. She turned as pale as one of Ruby Bayou's ghosts at the sight of her father-in-law's knee.

"Sit down, darling," Jeff said as he wrapped ice in damp dish towels. "Daddy's going to be just fine."

Faith gave Jeff a sideways look and kept dabbing gently at Davis's nose and split lip. "Some ice would help here, too."

"Drink," Davis said.

"Water," Walker said calmly. "If you keep that

down, we'll go on to something with more kick."

By the time they were finished cleaning up Davis, he had kept down a cup of water and a double shot of bourbon. While Faith gently stuffed a pillow under his head and Mel covered him with a colorful afghan, Walker led Jeff out of the library, through the kitchen, and onto the back porch where the women couldn't overhear.

"I still think we should take him to the hospital for X rays," Jeff said unhappily.

Walker shrugged. "X rays won't show soft-tissue damage, and that's where he's hurting most."

"What about his knee?"

"Wrenched but not broken."

"You sure?"

"He couldn't walk. But these guys were pretty careful. They aren't through with your daddy yet."

Jeff started to talk, then stared. "What are you talking about?"

"The rubies weren't in the safe."

Jeff's eyes narrowed. "Is that supposed to mean something?"

Walker bit back a curse. He had been hoping that Jeff wouldn't play hard to get. "It means that whoever robbed your safe came away disappointed. No ruby necklace. There was enough inside to make the mob go away for a day or two. Maybe even a week. But they'll be back.''

"You're making less sense than Tiga," Jeff snapped.

"Then listen up, boy. Your daddy is in deep shit with some real nasty folks. That's why they beat him half to death.''

Jeff's eyes widened. He rubbed his face as though to prove to himself that he was indeed awake. "No.''

"If he had tumbled down cement stairs, he'd be bruised front and back. He'd have cut up his hands breaking his fall. But his hands are smooth as rose petals and the back of his head doesn't have a mark on it. He's been worked over by a professional. And he knows if he goes to a hospital, they'll have to call the cops and he'll have to answer their questions, not ours.''

Jeff closed his eyes and struggled for self-control. "All right. I'll talk to him.''

"We both will.''

"No. It's none of your—'' Jeff clamped back the hot words and said stiffly, "That's not necessary. This is a Montegeau problem.''

"Wrong. Until Montegeau insurance covers that ruby necklace, it's a Donovan problem.''

"But—''

"Shut up,'' Walker cut in coldly. "Faith's store

was robbed in Seattle. The expo safe in Savannah was robbed. She was mugged. She lost three pieces of her art jewelry when your safe was robbed. All in all, I'm slam out of patience with this home-fried southern circus. Either I get answers or I give your daddy to some folks he won't like any better than the ones who just worked him over."

For the first time Jeff looked past Walker's open, amiable exterior to the man beneath. "Who are you?"

Walker wasn't in any mood for long explanations, so he went for the one that would cause the least questions. "Faith's bodyguard."

Jeff swallowed. "I thought you were her boyfriend."

"So does she. It keeps things easier all around."

"I'll just bet it does," Faith said from the kitchen door, *"sugar."*

Shit. She was supposed to be in the library taking care of Davis. "I'll explain later," Walker said through his teeth.

"Don't bother. There's a woman at the front door who wants to see you."

"Me?" Walker said.

"You. Her clothes look like she's been sleeping in them, but she has a really shiny badge."

Walker felt like kicking something. He had

been hoping that the FBI would stay back in the swamp.

Wrong again.

"She asked for you by name," Faith continued, smiling at Walker's anger. "Said you knew her."

"At least it isn't April Joy," Walker muttered as he stalked past Faith.

"How do you know April Joy?" Faith asked. "And why would she want you?"

Walker didn't answer.

Faith had a feeling that it would be the first of many questions he ducked.

Not that she was going to be asking any. She had the only answer that mattered.

Cindy Peel thought about it for all of ten seconds before she arrived at the same conclusion Walker had: Davis Montegeau's bruises weren't a random collection gathered bouncing down a flight of cement steps. He had been worked over by a pro.

"Who did this to you, Mr. Montegeau?" she asked.

Davis gave her a sullen look. "I fell."

"They'll be back," Peel said. "Next time they'll break both knees. You'll spend the rest of your life in a wheelchair. Unless they decide to kill you."

She moved in closer, filling the old man's view. She had confronted uncooperative witnesses before, but never with her own career so clearly on the line. April Joy wanted that ruby and she wanted it a week ago. Anyone who didn't deliver it could expect a lifetime assignment in Fargo, North Dakota.

Davis closed his eyes, shutting out the FBI agent. She couldn't say anything he wanted to hear.

Peel looked up at the other people in the room. "Does he have a lawyer?"

Jeff's handsome face flushed with shame or anger or both. "Since when is it a crime to fall down stairs? Or to get pushed, if it comes to that?"

"The FBI has documented your father's dealings with two known members of the Atlantic City mob," Peel said evenly.

"What dealings?"

Peel didn't answer.

"Land scams," Walker said succinctly to Jeff. Then, to Peel, "You going to arrest anyone right away?"

"I have probable cause," she said. "It's an option."

"Well, as long as it's still just an option, why don't you and Mel go make some coffee or something while I have a little heart-to-heart with the Montegeau men."

"What's in it for me?" Peel retorted.

"More answers than you'll get when a lawyer named Samantha Butterworth gets here and advises her client to keep his bloody mouth shut."

Peel frowned, considering the offer. "Deal." She gave Faith a cool look and asked Walker, "What about her? She doesn't make coffee?"

"She's not leaving my sight until I get some answers."

Peel's dark eyes narrowed. "Interesting."

"Yeah. Downright fascinating, I'm sure," Walker said. "About that coffee . . . ?"

"I make coffee for no man," Peel said. "But I'll wait in the kitchen on one condition—Faith Donovan doesn't leave the house without checking in with me."

"What?" Faith said. Her eyes went from summer mist to ice. "Who are you to tell me where I can or can't go? I'm not the one who fell down the stairs. I don't have any business with mobsters."

"You wish to make a statement to that effect?" Peel asked. "If you do, I'll be glad to give you the opportunity . . . in more formal surroundings, like the Federal Building in Savannah, for instance."

"Is that an official request or are you just being a—" Faith began.

"Let's try cooperation first," Walker cut in,

putting a hand on Faith's arm. "It gives us a fall-back position."

She swallowed the rest of her sentence, looked at him for a long moment, and nodded curtly.

Walker looked at Peel. "You better have a reason for this. A real good one."

"I do."

"When I'm done here, you'll tell me."

Peel thought of refusing. Then she shrugged. "I'll check back with my supervisors. It's up to them."

Walker hadn't thought it could get much worse.

Wrong for the third time.

"Let's go," Peel said to Mel.

Mel looked at Jeff with a question in her beautiful eyes.

"Go ahead, darling. No need for you to be getting more upset." He smiled and kissed her cheek. "This is all just a misunderstanding."

Mel ran her hands anxiously over the mound of her pregnancy, as though reassuring herself that something was still going well. She gave her fiancé a smile that was as fleeting as the one he had given her, but like his, it was real. She kissed him, looked at him for a long moment, and said to the rest of them, "Y'all call out when you're ready for coffee."

As soon as Mel and the federal agent left, Walker put his hands on Faith's shoulders and looked at her with a combination of regret and anger and hunger.

"I want you over on the other side of the room, out of earshot," he said. "That way you can't be called to testify about anything."

"What's going on?" she demanded tightly.

"The less you know, sugar, the less chance you'll end up talking to a lot of badges."

"Forget the 'sugars' and 'darlings,' " she said in a clipped voice. Her eyes were like her tone, remote. "We both know why you've been *close* to me. I do hope you were getting overtime."

Walker's temper went to flash point. He only had himself to blame. He knew before he ever touched Faith that he shouldn't become her lover. He had been right.

He wished being right made him feel as good as being wrong made him feel bad.

"Faith—"

"If I knew what was going on," she said, talking over him, "maybe I wouldn't need a body-guard. Did any of you almighty males think of that?"

He counted to ten. To twenty. Forty. "I take it you're staying," he said neutrally.

"You take it right."

Walker turned his back on Faith and looked at both of the Montegeaus. He didn't bother to disguise his temper from them.

He smiled.

Jeff backed up a step.

"Good for you, boy," Walker said gently. "You're finally getting a handle on just what kind of trouble you and your daddy are in."

30

Walker walked over to shut the heavy library door. He came back across the room and stood a foot in front of the younger Montegeau.

"We'll start with the easy stuff," Walker said. "Which one of you boys set up the robbery of Faith's store in Seattle?"

Both Montegeaus stared at him as though he had two heads and neither one of them was speaking English.

"What robbery?" Jeff asked finally.

Walker looked at Davis.

The older Montegeau shook his head, winced at the result, and reached for the bourbon decanter. He splashed some into a glass and drank. It didn't kill nearly enough of the pain.

"Don't look at me," Davis said roughly. "Hell, if I was robbing jewelry shops, I wouldn't be broke, would I?"

Walker stared at both of the men. They could have been lying like parlor rugs, but he didn't think so.

"Well, damn," he muttered. "Archer was right. This is a real Charlie Foxtrot."

"Why would they want to rob my store?" Faith asked.

Walker looked over his shoulder. "If you're asking the Montegeaus, they don't know. If you're asking me, make a list and put it in your pocket. I'll answer every one of your questions when we're alone. That's a promise."

Faith started to ask what good his word would do her, but she bit back the angry question. Walker might not have told her he was guarding her, as well as the rubies, but he hadn't outright lied to her. If she had been too stupid to see what was in front of her face, it was her problem.

"All right," she said. "Later."

Walker saw the coldness in her eyes, heard it in her voice; but it was the hurt beneath the anger that made him feel like bayou slime. He turned back to the Montegeaus.

"We'll try something closer to home," Walker said softly. "Who planned the burglary at the B and B?"

Jeff gave him another blank look.

Davis avoided Walker's eyes and reached for the decanter. Jeff moved quickly, putting the bourbon beyond his father's reach. Davis closed his eyes and sagged back against the couch.

"Daddy?" Jeff asked.

"I don't know, boy."

Jeff pinched the bridge of his nose as though to give himself a pain that he understood. He wanted to believe his father.

He was having a hard time.

Walker had no such problem. He was certain the old man was lying.

"Was it Sal Angel?" Walker asked.

Davis didn't answer.

"The Donovans have some influence with the Feds," Walker said. "We have good lawyers, too. We can help you or we can bury you. So let's try it one more time, and if I don't believe the answer, I'll give you to the Feds and let them hang you high. *Was it Sal Angel?*"

"He'll kill me," Davis groaned.

"I'll take that as yes." Walker's voice was as grim as his eyes. "Were they after the ruby necklace?"

Davis looked at the bourbon.

"No," Jeff said in a low voice. "It's too late for that."

"Yes," Davis said hoarsely. "The necklace."

"Was it Sal who set up the expo robbery?" Walker asked.

Faith stared at Walker but didn't say a word. Anger seethed just beneath her calm. With every question Walker asked, he showed just how much he knew.

And how little he had told her.

She was used to high-handed brothers doing what they thought was best for her, but she made allowances because at least they loved her. Walker simply didn't trust her to have enough sense to come in out of the rain.

"I guess it was Sal or his partner," Davis whispered. "Sal didn't talk about that with me."

"You just told him where Faith was and when, is that it?"

Davis nodded.

"Did you know they were planning to murder her?"

The shock on Davis's face was just as real as Faith's. She made a low, strangled sound and stared at Walker as though asking for a reason why people she didn't know should want her dead.

He didn't have an explanation that would make her feel better. When she insisted on staying in the room, she bought in to the whole ugly mess. He hated that almost as much as he hated himself for not keeping her clear of it. She was too classy to be dragged through this kind of muck.

But here she was.

And here he was, doing the dragging.

"I—I—" It was all Davis could manage.

Walker glanced at Jeff. No help there. The son looked almost as broken as his father was. With a silent curse, Walker realized that nothing about the situation was going to be clean or easy. Not one damned thing.

He turned back to the elder Montegeau. "Did you set up the mugging at the shrimp shack?" Walker's voice was as calm as a man discussing the weather.

"This is ridiculous!" Jeff said. "Dad wouldn't do anything that would hurt someone."

Walker's head swung back toward Jeff. "Scared men do a lot of things they wouldn't normally do. Your dad is scared to the soles of his feet. He has reason to be."

Davis shifted, groaned, and reached for the towel-wrapped ice that was sliding off his knee. Walker caught the ice, put it back in place, and waited with the patience of a hungry hunter.

"I didn't know about any murder or mugging," Davis said shakily. "Honest to Christ." Tears leaked from the corners of his eyes. "Nobody was supposed to get hurt. If the land had just sold faster, none of this would have happened. There would have been money to put in the golf course and the marina and then the rest of the lots would have tripled in value and we'd all be rich."

"But the lots didn't sell faster," Walker said, "and you went to Sal for money. Or was he with you from the start?"

"He and Joe. Partners." Davis covered his face with his hands. "No one else would lend me money and everything else was mortgaged twice and the land was going into foreclosure unless I closed the deal. It would have worked if—"

"The lots had sold faster," Walker interrupted with little patience. So far he hadn't learned anything new. "So the development went tits up and your partners lost money. How much?"

"Quarter of a million. Plus interest. Half a million total."

Jeff shot his father a startled look. "One hundred percent interest on a one-year loan?"

"That's the thing about the mob," Walker said. "They don't report to the federal government. You borrow twenty bucks on Friday and you owe forty on payday."

"If the lots had sold—" Davis began.

"They didn't!" Jeff said savagely. "They never do and you never learn!" Then he looked at his bruised, bloody father and regretted his temper. With a sound of frustration and pain, Jeff turned away. "Never mind. We'll survive somehow. We always have."

"It won't be on insurance money from the ruby necklace," Walker said. "Because you were real careful not to be responsible for insuring it while Sal was trying to steal it.''

Davis didn't answer.

''Was Sal going to split the money from the necklace with you?'' Walker asked, then added dryly, ''Minus extra interest, of course.''

With a sigh, Davis nodded.

''Christ, Dad, why didn't you just sell the rubies and pay off Sal?''

Davis closed his eyes.

''Were you trying to avoid taxes?'' Jeff persisted.

Davis leaped for that answer as though it was a glass of bourbon. ''Yes. Taxes. Don't leave nothing for an honest man.''

''Is that why the FBI is knocking at the door?'' Jeff asked Walker. ''Back taxes?''

''There's a whole other branch of the government that takes care of taxes,'' Walker said. ''But I'm thinking your daddy had a different reason for not selling the rubies.''

''They were on consignment,'' Faith said suddenly. ''You can't sell what you don't own. But you can arrange for someone else to steal it and then split the money with them.''

Walker looked at her.

''It wasn't a question,'' she said coolly. ''Or am I supposed to be as silent as the wallpaper you think I have the IQ of?''

By the time Walker sorted out her barbed question, Jeff was talking.

"Any gems that valuable would go through the jewelry store's books," he said. "I'd have noticed inventory like that. I didn't. Dad said they were from the last of the Montegeau stones, the ones that hadn't vanished with the Blessing Chest."

Davis didn't say a word.

Walker was getting an idea he really didn't like, one that would explain how April Joy intersected with two over-the-hill boys from the Atlantic City mob.

Shit.

"We'll come back to the rubies," Walker said grimly. "Right now we're working on Sal. He came up empty in Savannah every time he tried to grab the necklace, even though you fingered Faith for him."

Wearily Davis nodded.

"Whose idea was it to cancel the Savannah wedding and get married in Ruby Bayou?" Walker asked. "Yours or Sal's?"

"Mine," Davis said tonelessly. "Sal told me to get Faith to Ruby Bayou or else."

"Figures. Did he give you the burglary tools to make it look like an outside job?"

"Yes. Oh God, my knee's killing me."

"Take more aspirin," Walker said curtly. He looked at Jeff. "When did you get in on the fun, or were you in on it from the start?"

Jeff looked at the bottle of bourbon as though considering a drink himself.

"He didn't know anything or do anything," Davis said, struggling to sit up. "It was me all the way."

"You weren't the one to talk Faith into leaving her jewelry in your safe," Walker said.

"I told Jeffy to do it and he did." Despite the bruises and split lip, Davis managed to look defiant. "He didn't know what would happen."

"So you drugged Boomer, jimmied the French doors, and opened the safe."

Jeff flinched.

"Yes," Davis said between his teeth. "So go call the Feds and tell them I robbed my own safe. *I need a drink.*"

"That your story, too?" Walker asked Jeff mildly.

Jeff poured his father a drink.

"Nice story," Walker said. "Except that Davis was too stinking drunk to crawl down the hall, much less to open a safe."

Faith looked at Jeff and remembered what he had said after she put her jewelry in the safe: *I have to keep reminding myself that even if something happens, it's the insurance company that loses, not us, and the good Lord knows they have money to spare.*

"It was you," she said distinctly to Jeff.

"It was me!" Davis insisted.

She ignored him and watched Jeff with growing anger. "You played on my sympathy for you, all embarrassed over your father the drunk, so that I'd—"

"That's enough," Jeff snarled. He slammed the decanter onto a marble-topped side table with enough force to rock it. "Why should Dad care about justifying himself to a con artist like you?"

"What does that mean?" Faith demanded.

"The safe was empty when I opened it, that's what it means," Jeff retorted. "And you damn well know it! So let's just bury the moral outrage. I'm sick of hearing it from a little scammer like you!"

"My heart bleeds for you," Walker said sardonically. "But don't jump Faith. I'm the one who held on to the necklace. So you stole a hundred thousand in glitters instead of a million. Poor baby."

Jeff looked at Walker and then laughed hard enough to make his thick blond hair shake. "She got to you, too. Those big sad eyes and long legs and pretty lying mouth. Well, listen up, fool. There wasn't anything in that safe but papers and the family Bible! Bet her insurance company would be real glad to hear it."

"That's a lie!" Faith said instantly. "I left three of my pieces in there and now they're gone."

Jeff gave her a disgusted look. "You stick with that story, sweet pea. We'll see who's buying and who's lying. I know what I found in that safe. *Nothing*. Dad had to clean out the vault at the jewelry store to buy Sal off and they still beat him half to death anyway."

Faith looked from Jeff to Walker. "I put jewelry in the safe."

"The hell—" began Jeff. A sharp motion from Walker cut off his words.

"Keep your voice down," Walker said. "If you accuse Faith again, of anything, you better have a running start. You listening?"

"So you're in on it with her," Jeff said. "I wondered."

"Wondering is a good thing," Walker said gently, "as long as you don't wonder aloud."

Jeff gave him a bitter look. "The safe was empty."

Walker was afraid that he believed him. "Who else has the combination?"

"Dad. Me. That's it."

Walker looked at the elder Montegeau.

"Forget it," Jeff said. "When I went to try and talk him out of robbing our own safe, he was passed out and snoring fit to make the house shake."

"All right. Let's go back to the interesting stuff," Walker said.

"Interesting?" Faith snarled furiously. "My missing jewelry isn't interesting?"

"The Feds wouldn't break a sweat over it,"

Walker said. "But they've been staked out around the Montegeau house like cats at a rathole. Watching you."

"Me?" Faith's eyes widened. "That's ridiculous. Why would they waste time watching me?"

Jeff snorted.

Walker shot him a look. "Where did the rubies come from that your daddy sent to Faith?"

"I told you," Jeff said through his teeth. "The rubies were taken from the last of the family jewelry, the only decent stones that didn't vanish with the Blessing Chest."

Walker looked over at Davis. "That your story, too?"

Davis didn't answer.

"Remember what I said about the Donovans and lawyers?" Walker asked.

"Bad luck," Davis whispered. "Nothing but bad luck since we lost the Blessing Chest."

"You haven't managed to dig out on your own," Walker agreed. "You sure you don't want a helping hand?" He sounded kind and understanding, unless you looked at his eyes.

Davis groaned like a man turning on a spit over a big fire. "Jeffy, I'm really sorry, boy. I tried so hard since your sweet mama died. So hard."

Jeff's eyelids flickered with pain.

Walker hooked his boot under a side chair, yanked it toward the sofa, and said to Jeff, "Sit down. I got a feeling you're not going to like what your daddy has to tell you."

Jeff sank into the chair and watched his father with eyes that didn't want to believe, but already did. The last of the child inside him died as he took his father's hand between his own and said to him what he himself had so often heard as a boy. "Whatever it is, tell me. We'll find a way."

After a shuddering breath, Davis nodded. Both men ignored the tears welling from the older man's eyes.

Faith bit her lip and fought against the sympathy that came when she thought how she would feel if she was in Jeff's place.

Walker lifted her hand, rubbed his cheek against it in silent comfort, and released her before she could object to the intimacy.

"The jewelry that I've been taking on consignment for the last several years comes from Russia," Davis said tonelessly.

Hello, April Joy, Walker thought savagely. But he didn't say it aloud. "Stolen."

"I . . . didn't ask."

Walker grunted. No surprise there. "But you got a real generous slice of any sale, right?"

Unhappily Davis nodded. "It kept us out of bankruptcy until I could develop Bayou Estates and sell them. It should have worked. It would have if the—"

"Dad," Jeff interrupted with as much gentleness as impatience. "That's over. We have to go on from here."

"Who was your contact for the jewelry?" Walker asked.

"Tarasov International Traders. They're legitimate," Davis said, but he didn't sound completely convinced. "I checked. They have licenses and Customs stamps and everything."

That was April Joy's problem, not Walker's. His problem was figuring out why the Feds were camped on Faith instead of on the folks who were laundering stolen Russian jewelry in America.

"How about the appraisals on the Customs forms?" Walker asked. "Bet they always came in kind of light."

Davis sighed. "That's where the real profit was. The stones were always a lot better than the import documents suggested. But it's much harder to appraise stones that are set, so we never had any trouble."

"Especially when the good is mixed in with a lot of routine estate junk," Walker said. It was an old scam, because it was a successful one. Customs didn't have many inspectors who were GIA-certified appraisers. A lot of civil servants wouldn't know top-quality pink amethysts from decent rubies. "So what went wrong?"

"I guess I got something I shouldn't have in a shipment. Something really valuable."

"A high-quality ruby?" Faith asked sharply. "About the size of a baby's fist? Engraved?"

Walker almost smiled despite the adrenaline flooding his veins; Susa Donovan hadn't raised any dumb ones.

"Yes," Davis whispered. "It was the most beautiful gem I've ever seen, as good as the best gems that were supposed to be in the Blessing Chest. Bigger than a walnut and surrounded by tear-shaped natural pearls. The rest of the necklace was gold with fourteen Burmese rubies, all at least two carats. They weren't well cut, but they were very fine as to color and clarity."

Jeff stared at his father in hurt and disbelief. "Why didn't you tell me?"

"I wanted to keep you out of it," Davis said.

"Did it have a name?" Walker asked.

"What?"

"The big ruby. Did it have a special name?"

Davis looked confused.

"Never mind," Walker said impatiently. "What did you do with it?"

"It was made to detach from the chain, so it could be worn as a pin as well as a necklace. I took it off and brought it here, to my own safe. I didn't want Jeff to see it at the jewelry store. He would have asked . . . questions."

"I sure as hell would have," his son said bitterly. "Was it as good as the rubies in Mel's necklace?"

"Better," Davis said simply.

"Jesus. A stone that size would be worth millions."

"When were you at the exhibit?" Faith asked.

"While you were at lunch," Jeff said.

"Getting mugged?" Walker asked coolly.

Jeff flinched. "I didn't know anything about where the rubies came from then. I just wanted to see the necklace. Anyway, I still don't believe my father knew about the mugging."

Walker switched his attention to Davis.

"Who else knew the big ruby was in your safe?" Walker asked.

"No one. I'm the only one with the combination. Except Jeff, now."

Jeff shifted uncomfortably. He still got a sick feeling when he thought about how he had forced his father to sign over power of attorney.

"When did you give your son the combination?" Walker asked.

Davis thought about ducking the question. The memory of that scene in the library was too painful. He rubbed his bristly chin, winced when his split lip protested, and dropped his hand back to his side.

"Just before you got here," Davis said unhappily. "Jeff made me agree to give him power of attorney."

"How?" Walker asked bluntly.

"It had nothing to do with the rubies," Jeff said quickly. "It was personal."

"So is being murdered." Walker fixed his cold blue eyes on Davis and waited.

"Hell," Davis mumbled. "He wrestled me to the floor and wouldn't let me have a drink until I signed."

Walker's estimation of Jeff's backbone went up. "Where is the ruby?"

"I don't know!" Davis said hoarsely. "I told him and told him, but he didn't believe me either. Goddammit, the ruby is gone!"

"No sign of forced entry or dangling earphones?" Walker's voice was matter-of-fact, but the line of his mouth was thin and flat.

"Nothing." Davis covered his face with his hands, hissed at the pain of touching his nose, and dropped his hands again. "Nothing," he said in despair.

"Who was the guy you told again and again that the ruby was gone?" Walker asked.

"I don't know his name. About a week after the consignment arrived, I got a phone call. The man spoke English but in a foreign kind of way. I assume he works for Tarasov."

Faith watched Walker. It was like watching Archer when he was all business and no compassion. Uncomfortable.

"What kind of accent?" Walker asked.

"Russian, probably," Jeff said impatiently. "That's where the shipment came from, isn't it?"

"I didn't ask you. I asked your daddy."

"Look," Jeff retorted. "If you're not going to believe his answers, why badger him?"

Walker spun with the deadly grace of a hunting animal. "I like you for standing up for your daddy. It's an admirable thing in a son. Do you know anything about rubies, Russians, and robbery that you haven't told me?"

"No."

"Then shut up."

"Who the hell are you to—"

"Faith," Walker interrupted without turning away from Jeff, "go holler up Special Agent Peel. Jeff wants to talk to folks with badges. Good thing, too. He's sure going to see a lot of them."

"No," Jeff said quickly. "I just don't like watching you after Daddy like a cat after a rat."

"Then close your eyes, sonny."

Faith flinched at the soft words.

So did Jeff.

Walker looked back at Davis. "What kind of accent did your nameless caller have?"

"It wasn't French or German or English," Davis said. "That's all I could tell."

"What did he want?"

"The big ruby. Right now."

"How long had you known it was missing?" Walker asked.

"I don't know when it was taken, honest. It could have been any time in the last week."

"Bullshit. Anybody with a stone like that takes it out and rolls it around in his hand at least twice a day and three times on Sunday," Walker cut in savagely. "The nice lady with the badge isn't going to watch Mel make coffee much longer, so cut the crap."

"Three days. Four, maybe. Hard to remember. I got so I didn't believe I ever had it in the first place."

"Yeah, too much bourbon is hell on the brain cells," Walker said without sympathy. "What did you say when this guy demanded you give the ruby back?"

"I was really scared," he whispered. "He said he would kill me slow and painfully if I didn't tell him where the ruby was, *and I didn't know!*"

"What did you tell him?" Walker asked.

Davis looked longingly at the bourbon. This was the part he didn't like, the part that made him hate to see himself in the mirror. "I said . . ." He cleared his throat and tried again. "I said I had sent it out on consignment."

Walker knew the answer to his next question, but he had to ask anyway. He had been wrong too many times already.

"Who did you nominate for dying slow and painfully in your place?" he asked coldly.

"No one! I wouldn't—"

"Bullshit," Walker said. "You knew you were a dead man if you didn't have the ruby. Who did you select as your stand-in?"

Faith knew before Davis opened his mouth.

"Me," she said. "He told the Russians I had their gem."

Walker watched the older man the way a cat watches a rat. "Davis?"

"I didn't know what else to do," Davis said, weeping slowly. "He was going to kill me."

Walker wouldn't have minded doing the job himself. "Seems like a lot of folks are trying to kill you, Mr. Montegeau," he said. "That's what comes from playing marbles on the wrong side of the schoolyard. But the bottom line is that the rubies you gave to Faith were in the same consignment as the big ruby, right?"

Davis closed his eyes. His mouth flattened as though in pain or in anticipation of pain. "Yes," he said hoarsely.

"Part of the same necklace?" Walker asked, wanting no possibility of misunderstanding.

"Yes."

Walker asked the multimillion-dollar question as casually as a man asking for a match. "Where is the big ruby now?"

"I don't know."

"Bad answer." Walker's voice was cold, as cold as the fear in his belly. He looked at Faith as though to make sure she was still safe. Then he glanced at Jeff.

"Get a lawyer," Walker said. "Your dear daddy just might live long enough to need one."

31

Two hours later, April Joy showed up on the shabby front porch of the Ruby Bayou mansion. A tight-lipped Cindy Peel briefed April over cold coffee in the parlor while Davis Montegeau's lawyer drafted a plea and protection agreement in the kitchen. The terms of the agreement were clear: In return for Davis's full cooperation, all charges would be dropped against the entire Montegeau family. As soon as arrangements could be made, the FBI would take Davis into protective custody so that he would stay alive long enough to put Sal, Joe, and Buddy in federal prison.

If the choice had been April Joy's, she would have wrung the old bastard out herself, but she knew the FBI would squawk all the way to the president if she tried to steal their witness. Turf battles irritated her, especially when she knew it was wiser to let the other side win. The best she could do for now was to send Max Barton to listen in on every interview the FBI had with Davis.

The real reason April didn't pull rank and set off a federal pissing contest was that Davis didn't appear to know anything about the only thing that mattered to her: the Heart of Midnight. The old drunk kept insisting that he'd lost it. Cindy Peel claimed to believe him.

April hoped that Faith Donovan knew more than she admitted. That hope was the only reason April had left Seattle in the first place.

"All right," she told Peel in a frosty voice, "the drunk is yours. But you send copies of every sentence he says about the Russian pipeline the moment he says them. If he so much as hints that he knows anything at all about the Heart of Midnight, you get me ASAP. Agreed?"

Peel was a realist. April Joy might be petite and damned gorgeous, but she hadn't gotten where she was on her looks. She was smarter and tougher than anyone—man or woman—Peel had ever known. If April wanted to make life hell for someone, she could.

And would.

"Of course," Peel said smoothly. "We're always glad to cooperate with other federal agencies."

April snorted and shoved her hands in the pockets of her sleek black slacks. "Sure you are, sis." She shifted her shoulders beneath her carelessly draped scarlet jacket. The clothes were off-the-rack, but on her they looked like custom designs. Her long, intensely black hair was held back in a severe knot at the nape of her neck. "Where are the rest of the civilians now?"

"Junior is upstairs. The rest are eating dinner." There was an envious edge to Cindy's voice. Camping in the swamp had been bad enough. Now they were outcasts in a house with the most incredible cooking smells wafting through every room.

"Smells good," April agreed.

"Walker brought us some leftover biscuits about dawn. I've been thinking about food ever since."

For a moment April considered the problem of Owen Walker. There were some interesting gaps in his file, gaps that she hadn't had the time to fill before she flew out. Even without hard information, she was assuming that Walker's easy, drawling style was an act. Archer Donovan didn't employ dolts, not even amiable dolts. Walker had rapidly become invaluable to the Donovans.

Which meant that Walker was the sort of man

who could get the job done, no matter what the job.

"I think I'll give dinner a try," April said. "Maybe I'll be able to steal some leftovers for you."

Peel managed not to say what a swell person April was.

❦

Faith had just taken the last, creamy spoonful of she-crab soup from her dish when Tiga marched in from the kitchen with a huge platter of barbecued ribs and another of deep-fried hush puppies. A big bowl of coleslaw followed, the real kind of slaw, where the cabbage was crisp and the dressing was light and clean.

"Cold grape pie for dessert," Tiga said, smiling at Faith, "so be sure to leave room, Ruby angel."

Faith managed to turn a grimace into a smile. She had given up trying to convince Tiga that her name was Faith.

"I'll do my best," Faith said.

"You always were a good one. Never a sound from the moment you were born." She set the platter down beside Faith, then looked at the young woman intently. "I wanted to keep you, truly I did, but Mama said you were already gone, so long, sad song, wrong wrong, he never should have, but he could, so he did and did and did . . .''

The singsong voice sent chills over Faith, yet she managed to smile at Tiga.

"I heard you crying in silence, trying, sighing, dying, precious Ruby child. So good to see you, be with you, me with you, forever in the sea with the she-crabs and the red souls. The three small gifts were pretty, but not enough, not enough. Thirteen new souls just for me, and the fourteenth to set you free, a soul as big as your sweet little fist. I wish you could see it, Ruby angel. When you give me the thirteen, we'll both be free. Take more food, precious baby. The marsh is a hungry place."

Speechless, Faith watched while Tiga stacked her plate with food. Walker waited until Tiga drifted down to her end of the table before he swapped plates with Faith and started eating. With the first bite, he made a rumbling sound of pleasure. Tiga might be nutty as a pecan farm, but she was one hell of a good Low Country cook.

For once, Mel wasn't hungry. She took a little slaw, a hush puppy, and a single rib. Then she pushed it all around on her plate as though trying to decide where the food looked best.

Jeff wasn't at the table. He couldn't bring himself to eat with Faith, the woman who had so completely fooled him. But he didn't want to upset Mel, who still refused to believe Faith was a thief. So he avoided the issue entirely by avoiding Faith.

"Eat something, Mel," Faith said quietly. "The baby needs it even if you don't."

Mel looked up, smiled despite the shadows in her brown eyes, and put a sliver of pork in her mouth. "I'm sorry Tiga keeps calling you Ruby."

Faith shrugged. "No harm done. Who was Ruby, anyway?"

"Her baby." Davis answered the question from the doorway. He had changed out of his ripped and bloody clothes, but he was still a long way from well dressed. His white shirt was almost transparent with sweat. The waistband of his brown slacks had wilted. He leaned heavily on the cane Walker had loaned him.

Mel's head came up. "Her baby? As in her *child*?"

Wearily Davis nodded. He walked slowly to the table and eased himself into his normal chair. Boomer crawled out from under the table and nudged the old man's hand. Absently he fondled the hound's long ears.

"I didn't know Tiga was married," Mel said.

"She wasn't. The baby was a bastard."

"Then the man who abandoned her was the bastard," Faith corrected. "The baby was innocent."

Davis looked at her. "Oh, the father was a righteous son of a bitch, sure enough, but that's not why he didn't marry her. He was already married. To her mother."

For a moment Faith thought she had misunderstood. Then she was afraid she hadn't. She set her fork down with a clatter. It bounced from her plate and went spinning off the table.

With a lazy motion, Walker caught the fork. "Davis, you have a purely uncivilized turn of table conversation."

Davis's laugh was as dry as his throat. He hadn't had a drink for three hours. As far as he was concerned, it wasn't an improvement. "Don't like the truth, boy? Stop up your ears with good bayou mud, then."

"Daddy Montegeau, please don't," Mel said.

He leaned his elbows on the table and gave his future daughter-in-law a look that was both sad and impatient. "Don't worry, darlin'. Jeffy ain't anything like the randy bastard his grandfather was. Neither am I, thank the good Lord. Besides, it happens in the best of families."

"Incest?" Faith asked in disbelief.

Tiga stood suddenly, shoved back from the table, and said in a clear, childish tone, "I am a naughty girl. He tells me every time how very, very naughty I am. I flaunt myself." She smiled with a terrible kind of desperation, a prayer whispered in the face of disaster. "I don't mean to, Papa. Truly I do not. Please. Don't. I won't ever.

Again." Her long, pale fingers trembled. "But I do and he does and Mama sees my ruby birthday gift and Papa goes away, away, thunder and lightning. My fault. I flaunt." She looked vaguely around the room. "It's blessing time. The crabs, you see. Dinner at eight. Don't be late."

No one spoke after Tiga left. Mel gave a shuddering kind of sigh. "Does Jeff know?"

"Probably," Davis said. "Kids always know, even when their parents don't want them to."

"Kids have a way of learning too much," Walker agreed quietly.

Faith knew he was talking about himself as much as the Montegeau children.

"You spend much time hiding behind doors when you were a kid?" Walker asked Davis.

"Doesn't everyone?" He swore tiredly. "Papa was a drunk who liked girls best before they were ready. He didn't much care whose little girl he poked. Even his own."

"Pity that burglar didn't kill him sooner," Faith said distinctly.

Davis shrugged. "There are more like him. Lots are worse."

"Lots are better," she shot back.

"Don't much matter. It was a long, long time ago."

"Not for Tiga. For her it was yesterday, today, and tomorrow."

Davis eyed the bourbon decanter. Nearly

empty. He would have to hobble into the pantry, rummage in the sacks of rice and flour and sugar, and find his stash. He wondered if he had the strength.

"Bet it wasn't a burglar," Walker said.

"Huh?" Davis asked, distracted.

"Did Tiga pull the trigger on your dear old pappy, or did his wife finally stand up on her hind legs and do it?"

For a moment Davis looked startled, then speculative. "Could have. Ma was hard as a shovel handle before she took sick that last time. But then we wouldn't have lost the Blessing Chest, would we? She was always screaming at him for paying off his little girls with rubies from the chest."

Tiga's words echoed in Faith's mind, words that almost meant something yet never added up to anything real. The unhappiness was there, always, the fixation on rubies as dead or lost souls. She wondered if Tiga had seen family jewelry on other young girls and known just how the rubies had been earned. It would explain her obsession with them, her belief that rubies were the price of a soul.

"Maybe after all those girls, the chest was empty," Mel said softly. "As empty as your father's heart."

"Sweet thing," Davis said in a weary voice, "hearts have damn all to do with wealth. I saw

the Blessing Chest not long before Pa was murdered. There was jewelry in it. The kind that sets
a boy to dreaming of being a pirate and having
his own silver chest overflowing with rubies
and gold."

"Sell treasure maps," April said sardonically as
she strolled into the room. "You'll make more
money than passing off salt marsh as a world-
class golf course."

"Who the hell are you?" Davis asked, looking
over the beautiful, confident Amerasian who
stood in the doorway as though she was queen
of Ruby Bayou.

"April Joy," Walker said before she could. "Figured you would turn up sooner or later."

"Bet you were hoping for later."

"Hope is a good thing," Walker said, smiling
slow and almost shy.

April gave him a second, narrow-eyed look,
and almost smiled herself. "Do men have to pass
a handsome test before they're allowed into the
Donovan empire?"

"No, ma'am," Walker said promptly. "This ol'
boy would have flunked, anyway. They hired me
for my skills, not for my looks."

This time April did smile. "Modest, too. I think
we'll do just fine together."

Walker was much too smart to show his response to that suggestion. "Have you eaten,
ma'am?"

"Is that an invitation?"

"For supper, yes," Faith said clearly. "Dessert is optional."

Walker gave her a smile that was very different from the one he had given April. "Dessert, huh? Is that how you think of it?"

April measured the two of them and dropped the idea of divide and conquer. Walker had found the woman he wanted, and that was that. Experience had told April that some men strayed easily and others never even looked over the fence.

Walker wasn't looking over the fence.

With a shrug, she sat down at Jeff's place, where an empty plate waited for someone to care. "Forget dessert," she said. "I'd like some of those ribs."

"Who are you?" Mel asked bluntly.

"Government."

"FBI?" Mel asked.

"No."

"Then what?"

Walker handed over the platter of ribs. "If she tells you, she'll have to kill you."

"Funny," April said. "Really funny." She piled ribs on her plate. "Ms. Buchanan, you're not cleared to take part in the discussion I'm about to have with these people. If you stay, you'll end up in protective custody along with your future father-in-law. That's assuming that the wedding is still on?"

"Valentine's Day," Mel said, standing up. "Two days from now."

"I doubt that the matter will be cleared up by then," April said, picking up a rib. "Your call."

Mel hadn't been hungry to start with. She had even less appetite now. She tossed her napkin on the table. "I'm glad you find our situation so amusing."

There was no humor in April's clear black eyes when she looked up from her plate. "Ms. Buchanan, I'm doing you a favor by letting you walk out of here. I could jail both you and your unborn child as material witnesses with criminal knowledge about an international smuggling operation."

"She doesn't know anything," Davis said roughly. He scrubbed his hands over his face, flinched at the pain, and stopped. "Damn it, she doesn't know!"

"He's right," Mel said in a tight voice. "All I know about the Montegeau finances is that Daddy Montegeau held the reins until very recently."

"So take a walk and keep your ignorance intact," April said. She bit into a succulent rib and chewed thoughtfully, as though comparing southern barbecue with the Hunan her grandmother made.

Mel stalked out of the room. She shut the door behind her. Hard.

April worked on the rib until the bone was as clean as the Cheshire cat's smile. Then she licked her fingers, scrubbed them off on her napkin, and said to Walker, "I'm giving you the same invitation I gave Ms. Buchanan."

"I'm turning you down."

"You figure you owe Archer Donovan enough to risk protective custody?"

Faith slammed her knife down on the table, drawing April's attention. "Walker doesn't know anything about the Montegeau money," Faith said flatly.

"You keeping him in the dark, is that it?" April picked up another rib, bit into the spicy, savory meat, and began cleaning the bone.

"Is that supposed to mean something?" Faith asked sardonically.

"You're a Donovan, so you can't be as stupid as you sound."

Beneath the table, Walker's hand closed over Faith's thigh. She stiffened, then relaxed. There was nothing intimate in the pressure of his fingers. He was simply warning her to be careful.

April glanced at Davis. "Nothing to say?" she invited.

"I told the FBI every—"

"Tell me," April said coolly. "Tell me how you got the Heart of Midnight."

"I thought that was just a legend," Walker said, lying easily.

"It's as real as the blood that will be spilled if we don't get that ruby back to Russia real fucking quick." April's voice was flat, like her eyes watching Davis. "How did you get your hands on the stone?"

"In a shipment with other jewelry."

"From?"

"Marat Tarasov."

"You do much business with Russian *mafiyas*?"

"Tarasov is a businessman. At least, I believed he was."

April's quick tongue flicked over her fingers while she watched Davis with eyes like slices of midnight. "So are half the businessmen in the former Soviet Union. What about Dmitry Sergeyev Solokov? You do business with him, too?" Even before Davis answered, she read the blank look on his face. *Bloody hell. There goes that possibility.* The clean bone hit her plate with a faint clinking sound.

"I've never heard of him," Davis said. "Is he another exporter?"

"What did you do with the Heart of Midnight?" April asked.

Davis looked at his plate. Grease and barbecue sauce swirled against the white bone china like an ugly nouvelle sauce. Slaw wept trails of milky tears. He picked up a hush puppy and bit into it. Tender, fragrant . . . and it tasted like sawdust.

"I lost it," he said heavily.

"That's not what you told Ivan Ivanovitch."

"Who?"

"The man with the accent," April said, reaching for another rib. "The one who likes to carve pictures into people with his knife, while he watches them bleed to death."

A choked sound was Davis's only answer.

"You listening, Faith?" April asked.

"Why?" she countered.

"Because unless you turn the Heart of Midnight over to me, you're next in line for the knife."

"I can't give you what I don't have."

April shrugged, wiped her fingers on her napkin, and reached for a glass of ice water. "You'd do better to have it. Trust me. If you can't do that, trust your brother. Archer would be the first to tell you to hand the damned stone over. Right, Walker?"

"Sure enough. There's just one little problem. Faith doesn't have the stone. She never did." He smiled ironically as he gave April's words back to her. "Trust me. If you can't do that, wire Davis to a little black box and ask him whether he ever sent the stone to Faith Donovan." Eyes the color of dark blue death focused on Davis. "So tell me, old man, did you send Faith the big ruby?"

"No," Davis said hoarsely. "I lied to the Russian who called. I was too scared to do anything else. I thought I could buy some time to find it. But it's gone. Most of the time I can't even believe I ever had it."

April leaned forward and tapped a clean rib bone against the china. She didn't want to believe Davis.

But she did.

She dropped the bone against the plate where it lay beside the other, like ivory against snow. "Well then, boys and girls, you've got yourselves one hell of a problem. Ivanovitch is after the stone and he's not going to believe you don't know where it is. If I were you, Davis, I'd cozy up to the FBI like stink on shit. They'll keep you alive."

Davis closed his eyes.

April's black glance shifted to Faith. "Too bad you can't get the same protection. If what you and Davis say is true, the Heart of Midnight is gone. Too bad Ivanovitch won't believe you. After he works on you for a while, you'll tell him whatever you think he wants to hear. That's the problem with torture. As a way to get the truth, it's overrated. But that won't be your problem. You'll be dead as a plate of barbecued ribs."

32

Walker paced in the garden until he was out of patience. Then he went inside and headed for the dining room. Faith had been avoiding being alone with him, and he was damn tired of it. She had been in the dining room for more than an hour now, with the door closed, supposedly drinking after-dinner coffee.

He opened the door. "Is this a solitary game, or can two play?"

Reluctantly Faith looked away from the lineup of Montegeau ancestors and their bloodred ruby jewelry. Something about the jewels and Tiga's odd monologues kept teasing her mind. She hadn't been able to chase it down yet, but she kept feeling there was something there, something important.

In any case Faith wasn't eager to face Walker, who was watching her with blue eyes burning darkly. She had been an idiot to be angry with him for not telling her up front that he had been assigned by Donovan International as her body-guard. The evidence had certainly been there, right in front of her eyes.

She just hadn't wanted to admit that Walker looked at her as a job. With some delightful side benefits, to be sure, but still just a job.

Yet what made her furious was that even now, even knowing that she was his job rather than his woman, her skin still heated and her stomach still quivered just at the thought of being his lover again. She knew how soft his beard was, how clever his tongue, how easily he brought her the ecstasy that she hadn't even believed existed.

Even worse, she liked being with him out of bed. She liked his slow smile and quick mind, his gentleness with those who deserved it and his impatience with those who didn't.

It was hard to stay mad at a man you loved.

And no one could wound her as fast and deep as someone she loved.

"Game," she said bitterly. "That's what it all is, isn't it? Just a damned game with rubies and souls as the markers."

"That's all life is, a game, and when you lose you're dead."

Walker came into the room and stood close

enough to Faith to inhale her gardenia and woman scent with every breath he took. He knew he was torturing himself and he didn't care.

"Right now you're thinking I checked in to your bed like it was a Holiday Inn, and that I'll check right out of it the same way when my business is done," he said roughly.

She shrugged despite the tightness of her shoulders. "As you said, just a game."

"You're wrong, sugar. And I wish to hell you weren't."

"Is that supposed to mean something to me?"

"Lot played life as a game. Pull the devil's tail and run like hell. And if he wasn't fast enough, I'll take care of the demons. It worked, up until he tried to beat some Afghani smugglers at their own game. By the time I fought free of the men who jumped me, Lot was dead. Game over."

Faith grimaced in unwilling sympathy.

"I lost the game for him," Walker said flatly. "I don't deserve to play with anyone else."

She tilted her head to one side and studied him as though he was an unusual gem. "If you keep saying that long enough, *sugar,* maybe you'll really believe it. I don't."

"Damn it, Faith. I'm no good for you."

"Well, you fooled me on that one."

"I'm not talking about sex."

"Neither am I."

"Shit."

"Same here." Her smile was all edges and no warmth. "As Hannah would say, no worries, mate. I'm finally an adult. I'm responsible for my own feelings and what I do about them. You're responsible for yours. And I'll make sure Archer doesn't fire your very talented ass for sleeping with his baby sister. If I word it right, he might even give you the raise you've been after."

For a raging instant, Walker thought he was going to lose his temper.

So did Faith. She was looking forward to it. She wanted to know, *needed* to know, that she could cut him as hard and deep as he cut her. She stood up from the table and turned to face his rage.

"Is that what you think of me?" Walker said finally, softly. "That I'm fucking my way to a raise?"

She wanted to say yes, to light the match to both their tempers and watch the explosion. She was shocked that she would deliberately goad a man to fury; the realization told her just how much she trusted Walker's steely self-control.

"No," she said tightly. "I'm sorry. Neither one of us deserved that. I could plead the pressure of circumstances, but it would be a lie. You hurt me without meaning to. I wanted to hurt you back." She almost smiled. "Guess I'm not as adult as I thought."

Walker didn't know he was going to reach for

her until he felt her in his arms. He didn't know he was going to kiss her until her taste filled his senses like thirty-year-old bourbon, hot and fine and potent.

She didn't fight him or herself. If this was all there was, she would take it.

"Damn, sugar," he groaned finally. "What am I going to do about you?"

She took a shaky breath. "What do you want to do?"

"Remember that book we talked about?"

"The *Kama Sutra?*"

"Yeah." He grinned slowly. "That's the one."

"Sounds like a good start. Except . . ."

"What?"

"Did they have Victorian claw-footed bath-tubs then?"

"We'll write a new book."

"Good idea."

Walker went to the door, closed it firmly, and jammed a side chair under the knob. Then he went to the windows and drew the drapes. "I just had a better idea than bathtubs."

She raised her elegant blond eyebrows. "So did I. Bet I can get you out of your clothes before you get me out of mine."

"You're on."

It was close, but they both won. The ruby necklace hit the floor the same time her panties did.

❧

Faith lay on the dining room floor with her head on Walker's bare, muscular shoulder. Idly she traced the line of his ribs as she studied the portraits again.

"You trying to tickle me?" he asked lazily.

"Nope."

"You're doing a damn fine job of it."

"Suffer."

He laughed silently and started to pull her over on top of him. To his surprise, she fought.

"Wait!" she said urgently.

"What's wrong?"

"Remember what Tiga said?"

Walker drew back until he could focus his eyes on Faith. "Which time?"

"In the marsh. Oh, damn, you weren't there." Faith stared at the ancestors on the wall. "She talked about a wide gold bracelet with hundreds of rubies."

Walker shifted until he could follow Faith's glance. "Like the one that hook-nosed battle-ax in the picture is wearing?"

"She's not that ugly."

"The hell she isn't."

Faith looked at the next portrait. "There was something about a crown of thorns with blood at the tips."

"Like the blond beauty on the left, the one who reminds me of you? She's wearing a spiky tiara with a ruby at the end of each needle."

"She's not that beautiful."

"The hell she isn't."

Faith laughed softly while Walker's beard stroked her throat like a silk brush. The gentle edge of his teeth made her breath catch. "Don't distract me," she said. "I'm working on something here."

"So am I," he said, but he stopped nibbling.

" 'A long ruby rope, burning hate, burning hope . . .' " she whispered, remembering Tiga's words.

Walker sensed as much as felt the uneasy shiver course through Faith. He looked at the wall and saw a portrait of a young woman with a necklace of ruby beads wrapped around her neck six times before falling almost to her hips.

"Then she talked about pecans. . . ." Faith said.

"Nuts, in more ways than one."

"No. It makes a kind of weird sense, somehow. Let me think." Faith frowned. It wasn't hard to remember her conversation with Tiga in the marsh. Eerie, spooky, like a kid tiptoeing through a Halloween cemetery. "Rope. There was something about silver rope. And souls—those are rubies in Tiga's personal language—the size of pecans, hanging by silver rope from her ears, swinging like dead men."

Walker grunted and looked around the dining room. "Behind us. The brunette with the big teeth."

Faith looked. Sure enough, the young woman was wearing a pair of earrings with spectacular rubies dangling from twisted silver.

" 'They don't cry, can't sigh, dead as only a hanged man can be,' " she murmured, remembering.

"So Tiga remembers what some of the ancestors are wearing. So what?"

Unconsciously Faith's fingers tightened on Walker's arm. "Find the king or the queen," she said, "the ruby that is 'too big for a cat or a child to swallow.' "

Walker stared around the room. "There are lots of rubies in those portraits, but none of them look quite that big."

"Nor are any of them surrounded by gems that are as white as blood is red. Angel tears. Pearls, Walker. Natural pearls."

"Sweet Jesus," he whispered. "She saw it. She saw the Heart of Midnight."

"She saw more than that. She told me, ordered me, begged me, to find the rest of the queen's court."

"The rest?"

Faith looked around the room at the Montegeau ancestors lined up in all their silks and satins and ruby glory. The detail in the portraits was precise, as though the artist had been instructed as to just what was important to show future generations: rubies, not people.

Thirteen new souls just for me, and the fourteenth to set you free, a soul as big as your sweet little fist, angel tears for my dead baby. When you give me the thirteen, we will both be free.

"Thirteen curves, thirteen rubies," Faith said simply. "Mel's necklace. Tiga knew."

"Wait. From what Davis said, there were fourteen rubies in the Heart of Midnight necklace, not counting the big one."

"And only thirteen in Mel's, because one was mine to keep for making the necklace. But Tiga didn't know that. She only saw the drawings."

"Not if Davis kept them locked in the safe the way he said he did. No. Scratch that. Tiga probably knew the combination."

"She was more than four years older than her brother," Faith said. "Maybe her mother gave her the combination before she died. Maybe Tiga knew it all along. Whatever. Tiga told me I had to bring the thirteen souls to her, that they belonged in the Blessing Chest, that I wouldn't be free until I brought them to her."

"And you're her precious baby."

Remembering Tiga's pain and urgency and hope, Faith closed her eyes in helpless empathy and whispered, " 'You must bring it to me, precious. It belongs in the Blessing Chest, not a noose around your neck. I can't bear hearing you scream, *let-me-go, let-me-go . . . .*' "

Walker grimaced and held Faith even closer. "I'll bet Ruby was her baby's name. I'll bet that little girl baby was blond with misty blue eyes. I'll bet the first time Tiga saw you, she thought her prayers had been answered, that God had given her daughter back."

"Child of incest," Faith said raggedly. "It wasn't the baby's fault. It wasn't Tiga's. But they're the ones who suffered. My God, Walker. Do you suppose that Tiga's mother actually took her granddaughter into the marsh and drowned her?"

"Maybe. And maybe the child was stillborn. Didn't Tiga say she had never heard her baby cry?"

Faith let out a long breath. "Stillborn. Yes. That has to be it."

Gently Walker's hand smoothed over her hair. Like her, he would prefer to believe that the baby had been stillborn. "Tiga's birthday was on the same day her father died."

Faith made a low sound. "What a bitter present."

"That's it," Walker said suddenly. "He was getting her present out of the Blessing Chest when he was killed."

Faith tried to regret the man's death. She

couldn't. "Maybe when he gave Tiga rubies for her birthday, his wife knew who had gotten her daughter pregnant."

Walker didn't say anything. He was remembering other rumors from his childhood, people whispering that the daughter had seen her father murdered and had never been right in the head after that. If Tiga had indeed been present, she was the last living person to see the Blessing Chest.

"Get dressed, sugar." He dropped a handful of clothes on Faith's belly.

"Any particular reason?"

"I'm fixing to take a look around Tiga's bedroom and I figured you'd want to come."

"You figured right." Faith hesitated. "I suppose you're not going to ask permission before you search."

"No point."

Faith opened her mouth, then sighed. "What about April Joy?"

"I don't care if I ever see that lady again, with or without my clothes."

Faith snickered. "I meant, are we trying—er, *fixing*—to keep this a secret?"

"I looked in a little while ago and saw the predatory Ms. Joy was debriefing the FBI and Davis. Poor ol' Davis. His lawyer's face was the color of boiled crawdads. I guess Mrs. Butterworth had never met anyone like our April, who doesn't give a damn about noble Lady Justice, much less that cold bitch Mercy.''

Walker did an interesting little jig with the smuggler's briefs and their expensive cargo, getting everything into a relatively comfortable place. "Ms. Joy knows what she wants—the Heart of Midnight—and no silver-tongued southern lawyer is going to get in her way. I'm figuring not to distract her until I have something in my fist instead of in my briefs.''

Faith tried not to think about helping Walker adjust his underwear. To distract herself, she started pulling on her own clothes. "What about Tiga?''

"I'll knock first, but she spends more time in the marsh than she does in the house.''

"That leaves Jeff and Mel. What makes you think they won't notice us sneaking around upstairs?''

"Their bedroom door was closed.'' Walker pulled his jeans into place and buttoned quickly. "I'm betting they're consoling each other same way we did.''

"Consolation?'' Faith pulled her blouse on the same way it had come off—half-unbuttoned and over her head. "Is that what you call it?''

He gave her a sideways glance. "I call it the best I've ever had. It's worrying me, sugar girl. I keep thinking about matching leg shackles.''

"Shackles, huh?'' She grimaced and buttoned

her jeans. "No wonder you're worried. Only a moron would sign up for a life in chains. Neither of us is that stupid." She looked up, pinning him with eyes that were misty blue and very, very certain. "So forget it, Walker. No strings, no promises. I mean that."

He knew she did.

He just didn't know why it made him feel worse, not better.

❦

Tiga's bedroom was at the far end of the hallway. The door was half-open.

Walker knocked softly. "Miss Montegeau? Tiga?"

No one answered.

He knocked again, less gently.

Silence.

"Let me go in first," Faith said quietly. "A man might frighten her."

Walker stepped aside.

"Tiga?" Faith said, walking through the doorway. "Is it all right if we talk?"

Walker was right behind Faith. The bedroom was empty. Several small bulbs burned dimly. Walker shut the door. When he looked for a lock, there wasn't any. This was a child's room, with night-lights but no lock.

"Stay by the door," he said. "I'll do the searching."

"You could be a long time. The Heart of Midnight might be a giant as rubies go, but there are a thousand places to hide it in here."

"The Blessing Chest is harder to hide."

Faith made a startled sound. "Do you really think you'll find it in Tiga's bedroom?"

"I'm thinking that Tiga saw her father murdered. That means there's a real good chance she saw whatever happened to the Blessing Chest afterward. Pretend you're Tiga. Pretend that feeding the Blessing Chest rubies will set you free. Now, where would you store any rubies you could get your hands on?"

"In the Blessing Chest. If I had it. Big *if.*"

"Yeah. But so far it's the best *if* we've got."

"Right. I'll search the dresser."

Walker started to argue, then shut up. The less time they spent in Tiga's bedroom, the less chance they would be caught there.

Quickly he opened the small closet and started going through its contents. There were a few faded and stained shirtwaist dresses that would fit a grown-up, but most of the clothing looked too small, even for someone as slight as Tiga. The little dresses were fussed and fretted with lace and more than a generation out of style. The closet contained one adult-size pair of muddy tennis shoes and a dozen more pairs of smaller shoes, all patent leather, and all cracked and dull with age.

None of the small clothing had ever been worn. Some of it was still tagged, as though it had just come from the local mercantile.

Faith worked almost as quickly as Walker. The chest was a dainty cherry highboy, just right for a child. The first four drawers were stubborn, their brass handles tarnished, as though they had not been touched in years. They were filled with fragile little camisoles and lace-trimmed panties, ankle socks edged with more lace, shades of pink and lavender and mint and baby blue, delicate white kid gloves that were too small for Tiga's marsh-roughened hands.

The bottom drawer worked more easily. It held four pairs of plain cotton underpants, four pairs of white cotton socks, and two well-washed white tank tops. That was it. No bras. No hose. No perfume. No jewelry. No makeup. Nothing at all to suggest that a grown woman used the chest.

Remembering her own childhood hiding places, Faith removed each drawer. There were no hidden compartments, and certainly not enough room to hide the Blessing Chest, but a lone ruby was a different matter. She checked the top and bottom and sides of each drawer. She found only the peculiar dryness of aged wood. Nothing but time and dust.

Frowning, Faith looked back toward the closet. Walker was going through hatboxes. The hats, like most everything else she had seen, looked too girlish for an adult to wear. Certainly she couldn't imagine Tiga in any of the fancy, frothy things.

The bed drew Faith next. The canopy was as delicate as the camisoles. Silk ruffles and faded pink flowers. Beautifully dressed dolls covered the lacy pillows and spilled down onto a rumpled and faded silk bedspread that matched the canopy overhead.

When Faith touched one of the dolls, dust rose in puffs. Stepping back, she wiped her hands on her jeans as though removing something foul.

She knew with chilling certainty that Tiga hadn't touched that bed since the last time her father had dragged her there.

Faith made a sound that drew Walker's attention. They looked at one another. He could see that she understood, and that her understanding turned her stomach just as it did his. They were searching the room of a girl whose life had stopped the first time her father raped her. It was an endless, consuming nightmare that Tiga escaped only in madness.

And even then, the escape was not complete. Part of her knew, always. That was why the bed was dusty and the lumpy couch beneath the window was threadbare with use.

"Don't think about it," Walker said softly.

"I can't help it." *It's my fault. I flaunt.* "She blamed herself for her father's brutal lust."

"Then think about this: the bastard was executed with his own shotgun."

"Too quick. Much too quick."

"Yeah. It's enough to make you pray for hell everlasting."

Grimly they searched the rest of the room. They found nothing but dust and the ghost of a girl who screamed in silence.

33

Faith paced the sitting room between their two bedrooms. Her fingers itched for the cell phone, but she had already outlined their plan to Archer. Now it was up to Walker to win her brother's agreement.

"You're sure you want to go along with it?" Walker asked Archer. "No guarantees, boss. You could lose a million in stones real quick."

"Or I could get that Russian killer out of Faith's picture," Archer said. "It's a bargain at twice the price."

"How is Kyle's gut feeling?"

"Don't ask."

Walker hesitated, but he couldn't think of a better way to get to the Heart of Midnight.

534   **Elizabeth Lowell**

"Okay. If I like what Davis tells me, we'll put the plan to work."

"Any sign of Ivanovitch?" Archer asked.

"No. I wish I could feel good about that."

"Don't let Faith out of your sight."

"I may have to. She's afraid of small boats and I've got a feeling I'm going to be taking one into the marsh around midnight."

Faith frowned. That part of the plan, she hated. The thought of those leaky skiffs made her stomach knot and cold sweat spring out on her spine. But she was damned if she was going to be left behind. She would just have to suck it up and do what had to be done.

"Bloody hell," Archer muttered. "I forgot about that. Leave Faith with April Joy. I'd back that little shark against any assassin I've ever met. If you can't do that, park Faith with the FBI. *Just don't leave her alone.*"

"I hear you."

❦

From the parlor in front of the house came the keening sounds of a lawyer wrangling with two separate federal agencies. From the blunt lawyerly talk, it sounded as though Davis had been sent away to await his fate while everyone else settled the small details of his life.

Faith let out a silent breath of relief. Walker

didn't need any distractions wearing badges right now. Neither did she. She was going to watch quietly while one good old boy interrogated another good old boy.

Walker and Faith found Davis in the library. He was alone, sitting in an overstuffed wing chair of faded navy brocade. Boomer was stretched out at his feet, snoring softly, his glossy coat reflecting flickers of the fire in the hearth. A piecrust table next to Davis held a Tiffany-style lamp and a tarnished silver tray. A captain's decanter filled with dark amber liquor sat on the tray. So did several empty cut-crystal highball glasses.

The sparkling glass in Davis's hand held four fingers of smooth Kentucky bourbon. He was watching the liquor warily, as though he expected it to burst into flame.

"Liquid painkiller?" Walker asked easily.

Davis looked up. Though weariness and pain lined his face, his hair was combed, his clothes were clean, and his eyes looked less haunted. "I'm thinking about it. Doesn't sound quite as good as it used to, though."

"Probably because you're not quite as afraid of getting killed anymore."

"It makes a difference," Davis admitted. "That, and knowing Jeff and I won't have to go to prison."

Walker nodded. It was what he had expected. Faith had refused to press charges for her missing jewelry and the government wanted information more than they wanted Davis behind bars. As long as Davis delivered Sal and the others with his testimony, he was a free man.

And as long as the FBI and April Joy did their jobs, Davis would be a live man.

"They said I don't have to worry about the Atlantic City crime family coming after me," Davis added. "Sal wasn't real popular. Too old-fashioned, the Peel woman said. As for Buddy, well, that boy is just plain stupid."

"That leaves the Russians," Walker said.

Davis lifted the cut-crystal glass to his lips.

"April Joy have any ideas about that?" Walker asked.

"You know, I hear Yankees talking about southern women as steel magnolias and such," Davis said, sipping instead of swigging on the potent liquor. "But for sheer balls, that little woman in the parlor beats any female raised on grits and gravy."

"She's not going to help you?"

"If I give her the Heart of Midnight, she'll make me a saint. If I don't, she'll help my killer bury me."

"Sounds like the April Joy we all know and love," Faith muttered.

Boomer twitched and yipped softly, dreaming of the chase. Davis leaned over and stroked the big dog with slow sweeps of his hand. Boomer sighed and relaxed.

Walker sat down on a short sofa that faced Davis's overstuffed chair. He touched the seat beside him, but Faith hesitated. The love seat was an antique, made in an era when people were smaller. Gingerly she sat down. It was a close fit. And oddly comforting. The solid strength of Walker's thigh along hers was reassuring. The fact that she noticed it, and needed it, told Faith that she was still shaken by her search through Tiga's tragic past.

When Walker turned his hand over in silent offering, she put her palm on his. His warmth, like his strength, reassured her on an elemental level.

"We think we might be able to help you out with the stone," Walker said.

"The Heart of Midnight?" Davis asked, startled.

Walker nodded. "I'm thinking you probably looked for the Blessing Chest from time to time."

Davis paused. "Sure."

Faith had the oddest feeling he was lying.

So did Walker. "Turned the house upside down, huh?" he asked sympathetically.

"Jeffy sure did." Davis smiled, then grimaced at the pain in his split lip. "That boy was a fool for treasure hunting."

"How about your mama? Did she search?" Walker asked.

Davis laughed dryly. "She made life in this house a living hell for a year after Pa died. Tore out walls, ripped up floors, dug holes in the garden. Purely crazy."

"Find anything?"

"What do you think?" he retorted.

"I'm thinking she was skunked."

"Amen." Davis took another sip. Crystal sparkled with light and reflected fire.

"What about Tiga?" Walker asked softly. "Did she go treasure hunting?"

"No."

"Why do you suppose that would be?"

Davis took a bigger drink of whiskey and cleared his throat. "She's not right in the head and never will be. Doctors, pills, we tried them all." He sighed. "I can't bring myself to lock her up somewhere. She's harmless, and she loves the marsh."

Knowing that a drinker often was more relaxed when others drank, too, Walker reached over to the bourbon decanter, picked a glass off the tarnished silver tray, and poured himself a shot. He tilted the glass against his mouth, inhaled the fragrance of aged bourbon, but didn't let any past his lips. "Was Tiga always the way she is now?"

"No."

"Did it start after your father died?" Walker

asked. "Or was it earlier, when he began raping her?"

Davis's hand jerked, making liquor lick up the sides of his glass like amber flames. He gave Walker a hard look.

Walker smiled gently. "I hear that Russian is a real artist with his knife. Takes a long time. A long, long time."

"It started when he raped her," Davis said hoarsely. "She was always a little fey, but after that . . ." He shook his head.

"Did you see your papa killed?"

"No."

"Did your mama?"

Davis hesitated, thought about the Russian assassin, and said roughly, "Yes."

"Did Tiga?"

Davis closed his eyes. "Yes. Dear Lord, yes. It broke her."

"Which one pulled the trigger?"

"Does it matter? He's dead!"

"Do you know which one killed him?" Walker repeated calmly.

"I—I'm not sure. Tiga was screaming about how it was her fault and the Blessing Chest caused it, all those dead little girls in the chest, and how she had to bury them so they could never cause trouble again. I was eight years old and scared like I've never been, before or since. While Mama called the sheriff, I went back to

bed and pulled the covers over my head and
didn't come out until daylight. And that's where
I told the sheriff I'd been all night, in bed with
the covers over my head. He didn't get anything
out of Tiga, either. She was drugged and rambling. Mama took care of everything. There was
gossip, but it died out after Billy McBride was
caught in bed with the preacher's wife. That gave
all those tongues something new to wag about."

Boomer shifted and snuffled. He awoke and
nudged Davis's knee, disturbed by the agitation
in his master's voice. Automatically Davis
scratched the hound's long ears in reassurance.
With a groan, Boomer flopped down again.

"So Tiga took the Blessing Chest," Walker said.

"I don't know."

"Sure you do," Walker said gently. "Your
mama tore up the place looking. Jeff tore it up.
Tiga didn't. You didn't, because you knew your
sister had taken it to the marsh."

"I don't know where the damn thing is!" Davis
took a hard hit of bourbon, coughed, and cleared
his throat. "Do you think I would have gotten in
bed with Sal if I had the Blessing Chest?"

"No. And you didn't find it years ago, either."

"How did you know?" Davis asked. "I never
told anyone."

"No one found any sign that you or your ma
started spending money that couldn't be explained. In fact, you were dirt-poor after your

mother sold a ruby brooch—Tiga's birthday present from her daddy, I suppose?"

Davis nodded and cursed wearily. "It was the only family piece that wasn't in the Blessing Chest the day Papa died."

"And you never saw another piece?" Walker asked.

"Never," Davis said grimly. "Not ever."

"Tiga never showed up with another ruby bauble?"

Davis's laugh was as brittle as the crystal glass he held. He emptied it with a toss of his head and watched Walker with pale, haunted eyes. "My dear, crazed sister with a handful of rubies? Hell, no, that would have been too sane. She was out of her head. She took the Blessing Chest somewhere out there—" he waved the empty glass toward the windows "—in that maze of marsh and bayou, buried it, and never bothered to remember where."

"I take it you asked her," Walker said.

"Asked, coaxed, scolded, threatened." Gingerly Davis put his fingers just above the bridge of his nose and massaged the headache that wouldn't go away. "None of it made a difference. She just looked through me with those sad, fractured eyes and started talking like a girl, then she would scream and hold her hands over her mouth and say, 'Mustn't scream, mustn't, good girls don't scream.' "

Faith's nails dug into her palms. She didn't even feel it.

Davis made a rough sound and closed his eyes. "I stopped asking. I couldn't bear sending her back to that time when he was alive and she was—" His voice broke. "Christ Jesus, how could a man do that to his own daughter?"

There was no answer. There never had been. There never would be.

A faint flicker of movement at the edge of Faith's vision made her turn her head toward the hall door. Walker's hand tightened in hers as a warning. He didn't want Davis distracted right now.

"On the theory that lightning doesn't strike twice," Walker drawled, "we'd like to lock Mel's necklace in your safe until the wedding."

Davis would have laughed if his lip didn't throb so much. "I can guaran-damn-tee that Jeff won't be opening it. Neither will I. Our bungling-burglar days are behind us."

"There you go." Walker stood and held out his hand. "Why don't you just open the safe and watch us put the necklace in. Boomer, move your lazy butt."

A nudge from Walker's foot got the hound to his feet. He gave Walker a hurt look and moved closer to the fire.

Painfully, with Walker's help and using Walker's cane, Davis stood and hobbled over to the safe. Walker made a point of turning his back and moving off a few feet while Davis fiddled with the dial. Both Faith and Walker were careful not to look at the doorway, where they hoped an eavesdropper hovered like a flesh-and-blood ghost.

"She's open," Davis said.

Walker reached into his jeans pocket and pulled out the chamois-wrapped necklace.

"It was in your pocket all the time?" Davis asked, shocked.

"More or less." Gently Walker took the necklace from its protective wrapping.

Gold glowed in sheltering curves, whispering of angel wings and eternal safety. Rubies shimmered as though they were alive, gathering light, transforming it into silky, incandescent red.

Thirteen curves, thirteen souls.

Davis's breath came in with a whistling sound that was close to a cry of pain. "Lordy, Lordy, would you look at that. It's as beautiful as anything my ancestors ever wore."

"More beautiful," Walker said. "Faith designed it."

Desperately Faith wanted to look over her shoulder, to see who, if anyone, was eavesdropping. Instead, she watched Walker hand over the necklace.

Davis took it reverently, placed it in the safe,

and spun the dial. "Almost hate to lock it up. I only ever saw one thing more beautiful."

"The Heart of Midnight," Walker said.

Davis nodded. He glanced toward Faith. "You did a fine piece for Mel. Shame she won't get to keep it."

"Is the FBI going to use it as evidence?" Faith asked.

"They don't give a damn about the Russian stones. It's Sal they want."

"They'll get him, thanks to you," she said.

He grimaced and shifted against the pain that throbbed through his body in time with his heartbeat. "Yeah. I sure do hope they kick that mean bastard's ass hard. Real hard. As for the necklace, well, I'm figuring Ms. Joy will have something to say about it. I guess the goods I've been getting from Tarasov came from museums and such."

Walker hoped that he would be in a position to bargain with the lovely Ms. Joy. Part of that bargain would include Mel keeping the necklace; it was too beautiful a piece to be trashed just for its rubies. But all he said aloud was, "There's a lot of housecleaning going on in the former Soviet Union. Hard currency is scarce."

"Surprising, though," Davis said. "Except for the Heart of Midnight, most of the stuff I saw was, well, ordinary, the kind of thing any wealthy woman might have owned in the eighteenth or nineteenth century."

"Museum basements are stacked full of fairly ordinary things," Faith said. "Especially state museums. Only the best goes on display."

Walker was more worried about a Russian assassin than the quality of goods in Russian museum basements. He had a lot to do tonight. The sooner they left the library, the sooner he could begin.

"You're looking like a man who would rather be in bed," Walker said to Davis. "I'll help you upstairs."

Davis glanced at the bourbon decanter, then firmly looked away. "I'd appreciate it."

As soon as the two men left the room, Faith shut off the light and swept open the drapes that covered the French doors leading to the gallery. She left the hall door open for good measure as she hurried after the two men.

Walker had been very definite about two things: First, the trap had to be baited with real rubies. No sleight-of-hand switch this time, no artificial stones.

And second, once the trap was laid, Faith had to stay in his sight.

Always.

Dressed in clothes that blended with the dense, cloud-covered night, Walker crouched in a thicket of azaleas, camellias, and feral rambling roses that once had been the far edge of the Montegeau garden. The night was alive with a warm wind that sent leaves to rubbing and whispering over each other and made grass and long-needled pines sound like dancers wearing long silk skirts. The air smelled damp, earthy, with an overlay of brine and secrecy.

But even on the darkest night, there is always some light. The night-vision goggles Walker had borrowed from Farnsworth and Peel sucked up every bit of stray illumination and turned it into a sickly green glow. The lenses gave him a surprisingly clear view of the interior of the library.

Peel's night-vision goggles were buckled around Faith's head. Like Walker, she was wearing dark clothes. Unlike him, she was wearing a dark cap as well, concealing her telltale pale hair. She was watching the back door of the house and the path that led to the bayou and salt marsh. Without the glasses, she would have been seeing ghosts every time the wind stirred trees, marsh, and water. With the glasses, she only jumped half the time.

Until the past few hours, she had never guessed how much a sapling resembled a human being.

"Bingo," he said very softly.

Faith stiffened. "The library?" she asked, her voice as low as his.

"Yes."

"Who is it?"

"Can't tell. Just a dark silhouette with two arms, two legs, one head. Not limping, so it isn't Davis. No way he could do anything but hobble."

Faith tried not to think of her hard work and beautiful design vanishing into a thief's pocket.

"Don't worry," Walker murmured, guessing her thoughts. "I'll get it back for you."

"You should have let the FBI do this."

"We've been over that twenty times. They're city cops, not bayou hunters."

She bit her lip. He was right. She just didn't like it. "No necklace is worth your life."

Walker's teeth flashed in a pale curve against his black beard. "I'm not fixing to die."

"Who ever is?"

"Hush. The French doors are moving. The thief will be in the gallery real quick. Then he could come out anywhere."

Faith readjusted the goggles and watched the back of the house. Although the lower gallery had four exits—more if you counted the possibility of simply going through one of the rotten screens—Walker was betting that the thief would head for the bayou rather than the front road.

He was right.

"Got him," Faith breathed.

"Where?"

"In back, just like you said."

"Go inside real quick and quiet," Walker said softly. "Get next to April and stay there."

"No," Faith murmured without looking away from the back of the house. "We've been over that twenty times, too. I'm staying with you."

"Even if it means going facedown in a leaky, smelly skiff?"

She hesitated "Whatever it takes."

"You'd be safer here."

"So would you."

"Damn it, Faith," he said in a soft, desperate voice, *"I can't guarantee you won't get killed."*

"Did I ask you to?"

Walker's mouth flattened. It was too late to argue anymore. He could only follow the thief and pray that Faith wouldn't regret trusting her life to him.

And that he wouldn't regret it even more.

34

The figure that hurried down the path at the back of the house would have been invisible but for the high-tech night-vision goggles Walker and Faith wore. Knowing that wind would cover most sounds, Walker eeled out of the overgrown garden and fell in a hundred feet behind the dark shape.

Faith fell in behind Walker.

He tried not to look back to make sure she was safe, but he found himself doing it so often he finally stumbled. Only the need for silence kept him from cursing savagely. He couldn't divide his attention and hope to keep up. The thief was moving fast.

Wind breathed down across the marsh, sending pale green ripples over the surface. At least, the ripples looked pale green to Faith. The trees had a dancing green nimbus of light around them that was frankly spooky. Even as she told herself she would be blind without the goggles, she shivered and wished that some tech wizard had figured out how to correct the color.

Abruptly Walker yanked her off the path and under the cover of a whispering, wind-trembling pine. Her stomach sank as she watched the dark figure get nimbly into one of the skiffs, cast off, and begin rowing down the bayou toward the marsh.

"It isn't Jeff," Walker said softly. "Too small."

"It must be Tiga. You were right."

"Even a broken clock is right twice a day." He stepped out of the tree's cover, pulling Faith behind him. "I hope you meant it about the skiff, sugar. There's no going back now without losing her, because I'm not letting you out of my sight."

Silently, biting her lip, Faith hurried after Walker to the skiff.

"Sit on the bottom with your back to the stern and stretch your legs under the rowing bench." He knelt on the dock and held the little craft as steady as he could while he watched over his shoulder to see where the other skiff was going.

This isn't a small boat, Faith told herself desperately. *It's a raft in a swimming pool. That's not stinking fish bits I'm smelling, it's chlorine.*

Teeth embedded in her lower lip, Faith scrambled into the boat before she lost her nerve. The skiff teetered wildly. She barely bit off a scream.

"Easy, sugar," Walker whispered, balancing the boat. "Slow and easy is the secret of a small boat."

She let out a breath and inched over until her weight was centered in the skiff.

"That's good," he said. "Now stay put."

With a skill she could only envy, Walker slid into the skiff as smoothly as if it were on dry land. He pushed off and bent to the oars, pulling the skiff through the water with the limber speed and silence of an aligator.

"Lean slowly to your right and look past me," he murmured. "That's far enough. Can you see her now?"

Faith nodded.

"Let me know if you lose her."

She nodded again.

Walker watched Faith with equal parts irritation and approval—irritation for her stubbornness and approval for her guts. He knew she was so scared of being in the little skiff she could spit cotton. She would probably look pale green even if he took off the goggles. Yet there she sat, her mouth a flat line of determination as she watched the boat ahead.

"She's turning right," Faith said quietly.

Walker searched through his memory. It was

high tide now, which meant there were several places up ahead where the bayou unraveled into channels that led to the larger marsh.

Tiga could have chosen any of them.

"Pick a landmark," he told Faith.

"How? It all looks the same to me."

"Then don't take your eyes off the place where she turned."

Less worried about making noise than about losing Tiga, Walker quickened his stroke. The skiff shot forward.

"Just ahead," Faith whispered.

Walker glanced over and recognized the dead pine where cormorants roosted during the day, patiently drying their wings after hours of fishing. He rowed on hard, suddenly certain that Tiga wasn't taking the arm of the bayou that headed out to sea. She was heading into the marsh.

Even with night goggles it would be too damned easy to lose her there.

He lifted one oar, pulled sharply with the other, and turned where Tiga had. He found himself in an inky little channel that was passable only at high tide. Very quickly shrubs gave way to dry, tall marsh grass whose thin blades rattled and trembled in the wind. The passage was so narrow that fronds of coarse grass reached out to rasp over the oars. There was barely enough room to row at all, but the marsh was so shallow here that he could use an oar to push off the bottom if it came to that.

He hoped it didn't. Some of that mud was deep enough to bury a man alive.

"See her?" Walker asked as he leaned forward on the oars.

"Sort of. There's more room up ahead."

"Well, there's a blessing."

Faith peered through the goggles into an eerie, luminous, green-on-green world. The shape of the skiff ahead melted into clumps of marsh grass and then solidified on open stretches of water. Tiga couldn't see them without night glasses of her own, but Faith still felt naked, vulnerable. She guided Walker with low, terse whispers.

Ahead a small night heron shrieked and flew up, its hunt ruined by Tiga's passage. Her skiff never hesitated. Obviously she was used to the marsh at night.

To Faith, Tiga's path was marked in swirls of pale green, which was the enhanced light thrown off by the water disturbed by Tiga's rowing. She was turning again.

"Left as soon as there's an opening," Faith murmered.

Walker drew on old memory and recent experience. Tiga was getting close to the edge of Ruby Bayou's holdings. Soon they would be among the high-rise dinosaurs of the twenty-first century, beachfront condos for Yankees who had grown

too old for skiing, sledding, and driving in the
Northeast's harsh winters.

"Here," Faith said.

Walker glanced over his shoulder. The opening
looked too narrow for a skiff. "You sure?"

"Either that or we've been following ghost
trails left by the wind."

Walker turned the skiff in to the small opening.
There wasn't room to row. Quietly he shipped
one of the oars, reversed his position, and used
the other oar as a pole to push the small craft
forward. The smell and sheen of the water ahead
told him that Tiga was doing the same, stirring up
pungent marsh mud with each thrust of the oar.

Faith leaned to one side and got a face full of
marsh grass. She leaned the other way. More
coarse edges scratched her arms. Straight ahead
of her, Walker was a solid column of darkness
outlined by a shifting green nimbus of light.

"I can't see," she said.

"I can."

"Well, hooray for you," she muttered.

Walker ignored her. Ahead, the little channel
opened into a wider swath of water. Abruptly he
quit poling. "She stopped."

Faith spit out a piece of grass that the wind
had slapped over her face. "What's she doing?"

"She's fixing to pull a pot."

"What?"

"She's pulling up a crab pot," he said.

The undercurrent of excitement in his voice was as clear as the gusts of wind hopscotching through the marsh.

"I want to see." Forgetting her fear of tippy little boats, Faith switched to a kneeling position.

Automatically Walker steadied the skiff. "Slow and easy, remember? Spread your knees."

She started to make a smart remark, then realized that he wasn't teasing her. Cautiously she inched her knees apart. He was right. It was easier to balance that way. When he leaned slightly to the left, she took the hint and leaned the other way. Carefully.

Both of them watched as water dripped like pale, liquid emeralds from the line in Tiga's hands. There was a soft explosion of green as she swung the pot into the boat. The metal cage hit the bottom of the skiff with a solid thump that carried over the sound of the wind.

"How much do crabs weigh?" Faith said against Walker's ear.

"Depends on the catch. From the sound of that, come suppertime tomorrow, Ruby Bayou's folks will be ass-deep in deviled crabs."

"Or something."

"Or something," he agreed.

Tiga bent over the trap. Her body screened their view.

"What's she doing?" Faith asked very quietly.

"Can't tell. Could be putting crabs in a bucket and baiting the trap again."

"Or . . ."

"I'm hoping, sugar. I'm not guaranteeing."

"I'm not asking for guarantees, remember?" Faith said.

"You should."

"Why?"

"You're worth it."

"So are you, and you're not asking."

Walker didn't know what to say, so he shut his mouth and said nothing.

A few moments later, the trap made a muffled splash as it hit the water again. It sank rapidly. Tiga straightened, rubbed her hands over her clothes, and picked up the oars again. Expertly she turned the skiff in place and rowed back toward them.

"Damn," breathed Walker. "We gotta get out of here."

He switched positions and grabbed an oar. There was no room to turn the boat around. He would have to pole stern-first. It was going to be awkward, especially with Faith in the way.

"Sit down and don't move if you can help it," he said.

For once, she didn't ask questions. She just sat as fast as she could without dumping both of them over the side. Walker poled quickly, powerfully, but Tiga was gaining.

They burst out into the main channel a few seconds before she did. Walker looked around quickly and spotted the only possible cover, a dense clump of marsh grass. He nosed the skiff into the grass as Tiga's bow appeared a dozen yards away. They froze and sat motionless.

Faith felt as naked as a heron's legs. She held her breath as the sounds of Tiga's oars grew closer. The old woman's skiff would pass a few yards from theirs. She would surely be able to see them, even without goggles. And if she did, she would be able to double-back before they could stop her, snatch the trap, and disappear again into the marsh, this time forever, with a million dollars in gems plus God only knew what else.

But if Tiga noticed anything wrong, she didn't show it. She simply rowed toward Ruby Bayou with an easy rhythm, as though she was headed home after a pleasant night on the water.

Walker waited until he was certain Tiga had gone before he backed the skiff out and looked around.

Nothing but marsh, wind, and night tinged green by the glasses.

His grin flashed, pale against the darkness. "Let's go see what's for dinner."

He made quick work of getting through the tight channel and into the opening beyond. The float that marked the crab trap's location was so covered with mud and algae that he looked for five really long minutes before he found it. He wondered how Tiga had managed without high-tech aids.

The line attached to the float was dark and overgrown with slime. It was as slippery as fish guts and just as cold. He wrapped the line around his hands and pulled. Drops of pale green water whipped off the nylon rope as he drew it in.

"Well?" Faith asked after a few seconds.

"Doesn't feel like crabs."

"How do you know?"

"Experience."

She would have danced with impatience if there had been room. She forgot to be afraid of the skiff and almost tipped them over trying to stand up.

"You fixing to dunk us?" he asked without breaking the rhythm of pulling up line.

Before Faith could answer, the crab pot broke the surface of the water. Streamers of green glowed as water sheeted off the pot and back to the marsh.

Walker grunted as he heaved the pot aboard. "Tiga's stronger than she looks."

Faith didn't say anything. She stared at the black, rectangular box that all but filled the trap. It didn't look at all like silver. "Is it . . . ?"

"The Blessing Chest," Walker said. "She's had it all along."

"It doesn't look like much."

"Wrong. It looks exactly like silver that's been in brackish water for forty years."

The hinges of the chest had long since corroded through. The lock was equally useless. With a few flashing motions of his knife, he cut the line that was wrapped around the chest. Automatically he sheathed the blade again. Gently, carefully, he sat facing Faith with the cold, heavy chest on his thighs. "Why don't you ease that lid off, sugar?"

"Sure thing." She brushed her lips over his mouth, teased the outline with her tongue. "Sugar."

His blood leaped. "You're fixing to get in trouble."

"Sure am. Later."

He grinned. "I'll hold you to it."

The chest was about fourteen inches by eight. Faith reached for the lid, then hesitated.

"What wrong?" he asked.

"I'm thinking about Pandora," she admitted.

"The lid on this box of trouble was lifted a long time ago. There's nothing but good luck left."

"I hope so." She let out a breath, grasped the lid carefully, and tugged upward.

Nothing moved.

Walker took a better grip on the bottom, which was a lot cleaner than the rope had been.

The deeply incised design on the chest gave him a good hold. "Go ahead."

Faith clamped her hands on the cold metal and lifted. With a gnashing sound the lid came off.

Wearing a halo of pearls, the Heart of Midnight lay on the top of a gleaming pile of jewelry.

Pushing aside his night glasses, Walker lifted the big stone out. Night stole color from the ruby, but couldn't fully quench its fire. It shimmered blackly, like fresh blood welling up in moonlight.

Faith watched him stare at the stone for a long, long time while wind whispered secrets to the marsh. The look on his face was one of utter fascination and a kind of reverence that made her throat tighten with emotions she couldn't name. She only knew that she would have given a thousand stones like the Heart of Midnight if Walker would look at her the way he looked at it.

"You could go a lifetime and never touch a gem half so fine," he said, his voice deep. "Damn, but she's beautiful. Every ruby hunter's dream lying in the palm of my hand . . ."

Finally he pulled the chamois pouch from his pocket and put the Heart of Midnight in it. Standing, he unbuttoned his jeans and slid the ruby into the hidden pocket of his shorts. He sat down lightly, then reached inside to shift everything into a more comfortable position. It wasn't easy.

Faith's teasing little kiss had sent blood rushing to his crotch.

"Need any help?" she asked blandly.

He shot her a look. "Later."

"I'll hold you to it."

"Sugar, I'm counting on it. This is a night worth celebrating."

She smiled despite the sadness wrapping around her throat like a ruby rope wound too tightly over soft flesh.

Walker pulled his goggles into place and picked up the oars. Fifteen minutes later, the dock at Ruby Bayou appeared in the night. The lights in the big house were still on when he brought the skiff to the rickety wharf. Boomer was inside, baying his fool head off. He had caught a hot scent and he damn well wanted to chase it.

"I'll steady the boat while you get out," Walker said.

Faith climbed out more skillfully than she had scrambled into the skiff an hour before. Her jeans were clammy and slick from sitting in the bottom of the boat, she wouldn't have paid a penny for another ride, but at least she was no longer terrified at the thought of being in a small boat.

That's worth something, she told herself. Not as much as the Heart of Midnight, nowhere near as much as Walker's love, but she wasn't going to howl at the moon over it. Tony had taught her that wishing for something didn't make it happen. You were better off enjoying what you had and leaving the yearning for people who hadn't learned just how little wishing was worth.

"You falling asleep?" Walker asked. He set the Blessing Chest on the wharf with a soft thud.

"Nope." Faith set her goggles aside and rubbed her burning eyes. "Just tired. All the excitement, I guess." She started down the narrow wood strip toward the scrub-lined trail. "I'll go tell April Joy that her ship has come in."

"Hold on, sugar. The tide is dropping. I have to loosen the line on the skiff."

Faith turned back toward Walker and waited.

Neither of them saw the shape separate itself from the scrub and glide down to the wharf. Neither of them sensed the danger until much too late. Suddenly a strong arm encircled Faith's neck. Before she could scream, a hand clamped over her mouth.

"Do not struggle, Miss Donovan," Ivanovitch said calmly. "The slightest movement and I will slit your throat."

35

Walker saw instantly that the Russian was in control. Faith was a breath away from dying. Like his brother Lot, she had made the mistake of trusting the wrong man.

An icy, lethal rage swept through Walker. "She doesn't have the ruby." He wrenched off the lid of the Blessing Chest and dropped it on the dock. "I do."

"The Heart of Midnight?" the Russian demanded. The night goggles he wore were smaller and less effective than theirs, but worked well enough. "You have this?"

Their only chance was to shift Ivanovitch's attention away from Faith. Walker dug into the cold chest and came up with a handful of gleaming jewelry. "It's right here."

He opened his fingers and let the gems fall back into the tarnished silver chest before Ivanovitch could see any more than a tumble of glittery light.

"Bring the ruby here," the Russian ordered.

That was the last thing Walker intended to do. The instant Ivanovitch got his hands on the Heart of Midnight, Faith was dead and so was he.

Faith knew it as well as Walker did. She tried to move. She couldn't. The least motion choked her. Her shoes were soft, useless as a weapon. Nor could she slam an elbow or fist into his balls. The man holding her was much more experienced than she was. He knew all the moves and had already countered them.

"No ruby until you let her go," Walker said.

"Bring it here or she dies now."

"Kill her and you're a dead man."

Like everything else pale, Ivanovitch's smile looked green. "I'm not afraid of you, little man. Bring me the ruby."

"I'm not the one who's fixing to kill you," Walker drawled. "Marat Tarasov will take care that. But I imagine he'll amuse himself first. He wouldn't want the man who lost the Heart of Midnight to die an easy death."

"Bring it now!"

Walker lifted the chest like a man ready to fling water from a bucket. "Let her go back to the house or I'll scatter this jewelry all over the bayou. You won't be able to do a damn thing about it." His voice was like his stance, matter-of-fact. "You might get lucky and find the Heart of Midnight again, but not in time to do you or your boss any good. I'm counting to three. One."

A combination of fear and fury made Ivanovitch tremble.

"Two."

Both Faith and the Russian saw Walker turn toward the dark waters, preparing to throw all the gems into the bayou.

"No!" Ivanovitch said. He turned and shoved Faith from him so hard that she staggered up the path toward the house. "See this? She is free!"

Walker didn't look away from the Russian.

One down, one to go.

But first he had to get Ivanovitch close. "Get going, sugar."

"But—"

"Now," Walker said.

As Ivanovitch started for Walker, Faith turned and sprinted toward the house. She knew just where the Montegeaus kept their infamous shotgun. A minute away, two at most. Two for running back. Four minutes.

Surely Walker could hold the Russian at bay that long.

But she was very much afraid he couldn't. Ivanovitch was strong and frighteningly precise. He

knew exactly how much pressure it took to sub-
due, to stun, or to destroy.

She took the steps to the back porch in a single leap and slammed through the screen door.
The kitchen was dark, the hall light was almost
blinding. She ripped the goggles from her eyes
and kept running. She burst into the library,
where April, Peel, and Farnsworth were taking
turns working Davis like a tag team. The lawyer
had given up and gone home.

"What the hell?" Farnsworth said, reaching
for her.

She twisted free and grabbed the gun off its
pegs. "Get out of the way!" As she spun around,
she automatically shifted the shotgun so that its
barrel pointed toward the ceiling. She may not
have been a fisherman, but she had listened while
her brothers taught her to handle guns. "Ivanovitch has Walker on the wharf!"

She ran for the door.

Farnsworth didn't ask for explanations. He just
started after Faith. But as quick as the agent was,
Faith had an edge. She knew where she was
going. She beat him through the house, out the
kitchen door, and onto the path. Farnsworth's
eyes had to adjust to darkness. Faith's didn't.
One-handed, she yanked the goggles back into
place and lengthened her stride. Running hard,
she burst out of the shrubbery at the base of the

dock just as the soul-chilling wail of Crying Girl rose like black mist ahead.

"Walker!" Faith screamed.

The wharf was empty except for a huddle of clothes.

"Walker!"

Crying Girl's scream was the only answer, rising and falling, rippling like dark water through the night.

"Walker," Faith said raggedly. "Where are you?"

When Farnsworth lifted the shotgun from her hands, she didn't fight him.

The gun was heavy, double-barreled, and fully loaded, as Farnsworth discovered after a quick check. It was far more effective than the service weapon on his hip. He cocked the twin hammers and pointed the gun toward the end of the wharf.

"What's that on the dock?" Farnsworth asked evenly.

Faith was afraid it was Walker. "I don't want to know."

"Then give me the goggles."

Faith ignored him.

The terrible cry rose for a third time.

"Christ," Farnsworth muttered. "Makes me hope they use silver bullets around here."

The bundle at the end of the dock stirred, then seemed to grow into human form. The green-tinged reality of the goggles showed a woman's pale, wild eyes and equally wild hair gleaming above darkness. Then a dark cape parted to reveal the pale clothing beneath.

"Tiga," Faith said in disbelief. "It's Jeff's aunt."

As though answering, Tiga threw back her head and wailed, Crying Girl come to life.

"You see anyone else?" Farnsworth asked, watching the path over his shoulder.

"No. Here." Faith took off the night goggles and yanked them over the agent's head. "I'll see if Tiga knows anything."

Carefully Faith inched down the dock, letting her reflexes adjust to a much darker night.

Tiga felt the old boards move and turned around. "Ruby? I thought you were gone. Your soul is."

Faith looked at Tiga's feet. The contents of the Blessing Chest were scattered around on the boards. She recognized her three missing pieces, but there was nothing that looked like the Heart of Midnight. Then she saw a pool of something thick and wet and black on the dock. It didn't look like water. She touched it and shuddered.

Blood.

"My soul and I are together," Faith said to Tiga, forcing her voice to be gentle. "Did you see Walker?"

The older woman sank down on the dock and began sorting through a fortune in ruby jewelry.

If she noticed the blood, it didn't matter to her. She was intent on putting the Blessing Chest back together. Stones made tiny, almost musical sounds as they tumbled back into the silver box's cold interior.

"Tiga? Did you see Walker?"

"They left, precious."

"Where did they go?"

Tiga flinched at the sharp demand in Faith's voice.

"Where did they go?" Faith repeated softly.

"Out there, with the other dead ones."

Faith looked beyond Tiga's pale, outflung hand to Ruby Bayou. She saw nothing but night. Then she realized that there was only one skiff tied at the dock.

"They took a skiff," she said to Farnsworth. "Can you see anything?"

"No. But don't worry. Walker is a lot tougher than he looks."

"So is Ivanovitch."

"Yeah," Farnsworth said reluctantly. "The man's a pro."

"Professional what?"

Farnsworth didn't answer. He didn't think that Faith would be comforted knowing that Walker and a professional killer had rowed off into the night together.

Tiga stepped over the Blessing Chest and went

to her skiff. "Watch these souls for me, precious baby. I'll be getting yours."

"It's safe, Tiga. It's with me. Walker kept us safe."

The old woman hesitated in the act of untying the skiff. "Walker? Is he the young man who likes my gravy?"

"Yes."

"Oh." Tiga looked at the line as though wondering what it was doing in her hand. "You sure, precious? I can't rest if you're unhappy."

"I'm sure, Tiga. Go rest. I have everything I need. Thank you."

Tiga let out a long sigh. "I'm tired. I haven't slept for a long, long time."

"Then go up to the house and sleep. No one will ever harm you again. You're safe, and so am I."

A slow, warm smile spread over Tiga's face. "Thank you for coming back, Ruby darling. Seeing you eased my mind. I know you can't stay long. God has other things for his angels to do. But you be sure to say good-bye to me before you go, so I won't be roaming the marsh and crying for you."

"I will, Tiga. Good night."

"Good night, precious."

Farnsworth watched the old woman merge with the darkness on the path back to the house. He shook his head, wondering what that had all been about. When he turned to ask Faith, she was putting the lid back on the chest. He saw the gleam and slide of tears on her face and decided not to ask any questions after all. He simply stood close by, watching the night.

Finally, slowly, a skiff separated from the marsh grasses and headed for the dock. Farnsworth watched intently for several moments, wanting to be sure. Then he was.

"Dry your tears," he said softly. "Your man is back."

"He's not mine."

"Then he's a damn fool."

"He wouldn't be the first," Faith said.

The skiff slid up to the dock. "You calling me names, Farnsworth?"

"Just the ones you earn," the agent retorted.

"There you go."

Faith knew her tears showed. She didn't care. "Where is Ivanovitch?"

Walker pulled the night goggles off and rubbed at the sweat that was stinging his eyes. "I lost him."

"He must be a hell of a swimmer," Farnsworth said neutrally.

"Like a fish," Walker said. "Just like a fish."

One look at Walker's weary, grim eyes told Farnsworth that the Russian was indeed swimming with the fish. "April Joy is going to be one irritated lady."

"Not when I show her this," Walker said, reaching into his pants.

When he pulled out his hand again, the Heart of Midnight gleamed on his palm, a baby's fist surrounded by angel tears.

April Joy came out of cover and walked onto the dock, where she could hear what was being said. The lethal-looking pistol in her hand was a gleaming piece of night. "Where's Ivanovitch?"

"He got away," Walker said.

"Bloody hell. Farnsworth, go help Peel guard the Montegeaus. They're in the library."

Farnsworth gave her a long look before he headed for the library, taking the shotgun with him.

Walker pulled Faith closer to his side with one hand. The other was clenched around the Heart of Midnight. Faith put her arm around his waist and held him as hard as he was holding her. On either side of the dock, the bayou shifted in response to hidden tidal rhythms.

"Don't think you need to be worrying about Ivanovitch," he drawled softly. "He'll have his hands full just swimming out of the marsh. Doubt he'll make it, if you're wanting the truth. That mud covers better marsh rats than him."

"Does he have the Heart of Midnight?"

Walker shook his head. "I do."

April measured him for a few seconds, then accepted the inevitable. Whatever really had hap-

pened tonight in the marsh, Walker had taken
Ivanovitch out of the game. Permanently. Too
bad from her point of view; he could have given
her a lot of information about Tarasov. But given
the choice between the ruby and Ivanovitch, she
would have killed him and fed him to the bayou
crabs herself.

April put the pistol on safe and stashed the
gun beneath her jacket at the small of her back.
She had never found a shoulder harness in size
four. She looked at her watch, calculated the time
in St. Petersburg, and smiled. They would make
it with a few hours to spare.

"Hand it over, slick," she said. "There's a
Gulfstream G-5 on standby at Savannah Interna-
tional, flight plan in place for dear old Mother
Russia."

"Slick, huh?" Walker said. "Thought that was
Archer's nickname, or Kyle's."

"Any man who can go for a boat ride with
Ivanovitch and come back smiling is slick in my
book. The ruby," she said, holding out her hand.
"We're on a short clock."

"Why?" Faith asked.

April narrowed her beautiful black eyes,
weighed Faith thoughtfully, and shrugged. The
Donovans had their faults, but talking out of
school wasn't one of them. Besides, it was hardly
a state secret. "The Hermitage is opening a new

wing of its museum dedicated to the czars' possessions. Specifically jewelry."

"Always a crowd pleaser," Faith said.

"That's the whole point. Getting crowds in, pleasing them, having them walk away proud of being Russian."

"There's a lot to be proud of," Walker said.

"Slick, they could be descended from angels or mud balls and it wouldn't make a damn bit of difference in the here and now, where all that matters is that I get the ruby back in time for the opening."

"So that Tarasov doesn't get his tit in a wringer?" Walker drawled.

"More like his cock."

"Is Solokov really that much worse than Tarasov?" Walker asked.

"Tarasov is ours. Solokov isn't. Do I have to connect the dots for you?"

Walker shrugged, then feinted as though to toss the stone in her direction and to hell with the chance of losing it in the bayou.

For what was perhaps the first time in her life, April Joy flinched.

Walker smiled almost gently, then held out his hand.

April looked at him like he was a copperhead. Slowly she reached out, still expecting a trick.

Walker passed the gem over. "That's one you owe the Donovans. A big one. Consider letting

Mel keep the necklace as kind of a down payment."

"I've already made a down payment," April said dryly. "All of Tarasov's future jewelry sales will go to Donovan Gems and Minerals on a first refusal basis."

"Sales?" Faith asked. "As in stolen goods?"

"Marat Borisovitch Tarasov is a high government official with responsibilities that include overseeing the 'deacquisition' of museum goods," April said neutrally. "Russia needs hard cash. Culling museum basements is one way to get it. If he takes a cut for himself, nobody's shocked."

"It ain't stealing if the government does it," Walker said. "That what you're saying?"

"I didn't make the rules, slick. I'd rather live in a world where a revolution yielded more than starvation, torture, executions, and a new herd of swine sucking at the public trough. But this is the only world I've got. I take care of it the best way I can."

"Do you really need to take Faith's design apart?" Walker asked.

April thought about it, then thought about how little she liked dancing to the tune of a Russian *mafiya* lordling. "All the bastard asked for was the big ruby. That's all I'm taking back to him."

April Joy turned and walked into the night.

A minute later the sound of a powerful engine drowned out the wind. Wheels spat gravel and a car headed swiftly down the long drive leading out of Ruby Bayou.

When Walker could no longer hear the engine, he turned to Faith. She was watching the night where April had disappeared.

"What are you thinking, sugar?"

"I'm designing spoons with really, really long handles."

He took her face between his hands and tipped it, as though to see it better in the light. "I'd rather you design matching leg shackles—"

"I told you how I feel about—"

"—but seeing as you don't like them, I'll settle for rings. How would you feel about getting a ruby instead of a diamond engagement ring?"

She went very still. "Depends on who's giving it to me."

"I am."

She tried to make out his expression. She couldn't. "You said you didn't want that kind of burden."

"I thought about that a lot tonight on my way back to you. I decided it isn't a burden if you choose the right partner to share it."

Her arms tightened around him. "Then, partner, I don't care if it's diamonds, rubies, or dirt."

Walker laughed. "I'm thinking a ruby. A very, very special one. Like you."

"No fair. Where will I find one like you?"

"We'll go looking for them."

"When?"

"Right after you design those spoons."